the detachment

Printed in the United States of America.
No part of this book may be reproduced, or stored in a retrieval system, or transmitted in any form or by any means, electronic, mechanical, photocopying, recording, or otherwise, without express written permission of the publisher.
Published by Thomas & Mercer
P.O. Box 400818
Las Vegas, NV 89140
ISBN-13: 9781612181554
ISBN-10: 1612181554

the detachment
barry eisler

Published by

Thomas & Mercer

To novelists J.A. Konrath and M.J. Rose,
for seeing the way and blazing the trail.

Behind the ostensible government sits enthroned an invisible government owing no allegiance and acknowledging no responsibility to the people.
—Theodore Roosevelt

We're entering an era of the educated establishment, in which government acts to create a stable—and often oligarchic—framework for capitalist endeavor.
—David Brooks

My view is that Washington and the regulators are there to serve the banks.
—Chairman of the House Banking Committee Spencer Bachus

All governments lie.
—I.F. Stone

part one

...of course, we can always get lucky. Stunning events from outside can providentially awaken the enterprise from its growing torpor, and demonstrate the need for reversal, as the devastating Japanese attack on Pearl Harbor in 1941 so effectively aroused the U.S. from its soothing dreams of permanent neutrality.

—Michael Ledeen

The only chance we have as a country right now is for Osama bin Laden to deploy and detonate a major weapon in the United States.

—Michael Scheurer, former head of the CIA's Bin Laden Unit

The government in a revolution is the despotism of liberty against tyranny.

—Robespierre

chapter one

I hadn't killed anyone in almost four years. But all good things come to an end, eventually.

It was good to be living in Tokyo again. The face of the city had changed, as it continuously does, and the great Touhoku quake and tsunami continued to make their presence known in the form of dimmed lights and weakened summer air conditioning, along with an atmosphere newly balanced between anxiety and determination, but in its eternal, essential energy, Tokyo is immutable. Yes, during my sojourn in safer climes, there had occurred an unfortunate profusion of Starbucks and Dean & Delucas, along with their innumerable imitators, but the havens that mattered remained impervious to this latest infestation. There was still jazz at Body & Soul in Minami Aoyama, where no seat is too far from the stage for a quiet word of thanks to the band members at the end of the evening; coffee at Café de l'Ambre in Ginza, where even as he nears his hundredth birthday, proprietor Sekiguchi-sensei arrives daily to roast his own beans, as he has for the last six decades; a tipple at Campbelltoun Loch in Yurakucho, where, if you can secure one of the eight seats in his hidden basement establishment, owner and bartender Nakamura-san will recommend one of his rare bottlings to help melt away, however briefly, the world you came to him to forget.

My sleep was sometimes restless, though I told myself no one was looking for me anymore. But I knew if they were, they'd start with a place I'd been known to frequent. Unless you had unlimited manpower, you couldn't use the bars or coffee houses or jazz clubs I liked. There were too many of them in Tokyo, for one thing, and my visits would be too hard to predict. You might wait for months, maybe forever, and though there are harder surveillance duty stations than the oases haunted by Tokyo's roving night denizens, eventually you'd start to stand out, especially if you were a foreigner. Meanwhile, whoever was paying would be getting impatient for results.

Which made the Kodokan a unique vulnerability. I'd trained there for nearly twenty-five years before powerful enemies forced me to flee the city, enemies I had, by one means or another, managed to outlast. Judo at the Kodokan had been my only indulgence of anything like a routine, a pattern that could be used to fix me in time and place. Going back to it might have been my way of reassuring myself that my enemies really were all dead. Or it could have been a way of saying *come out, come out, wherever you are.*

Randori, or free training, was held in the *daidojo*, a modern, two-storied space of four connected competition zones open to bleachers ringing the area a floor above. On any given night, as many as two hundred *judoka* wearing the traditional white *judogi*, male and female, Japanese and foreign, buzz-cut college stars and grizzled veterans, take to the training hall, and the vast space is filled with cries of commitment and grunts of defense; earnest discussions of tactics and techniques in mutually incomprehensible tongues; the drum beat of bodies colliding with the *tatami* and the cymbal slaps of palms offsetting the impact with *ukemi* landings. I've always loved the cacophony of the *daidojo*. I've stood in it when it's empty, too, and its solemn daytime stillness, its enormous sense of patience and potential, has its own magic, but it's the sound of evening training that imbues the space with purpose, that brings the dormant hall to life.

On training nights the bleachers are usually empty, though nor is it unusual to see a few people sitting here and there and watching the *judoka* practicing below: a student, waiting for a friend; a parent, wondering whether to enroll a child; a martial arts enthusiast, making a pilgrimage to the birthplace of modern judo. So I wasn't unduly concerned one night at the sight of two extra large Caucasians sitting together in the stands, thickly muscled arms crossed over the railing, leaning forward like carrion birds on a telephone line. I logged them the way I reflexively log anything out of place in my environment, giving no sign that I had particularly noticed them or particularly cared, and continued *randori* with the partner I happened to be training with, a stocky kid with a visiting college team who I hadn't yet let score against me.

My play had reached a level at which for the most part I was able to anticipate an opponent's attack in the instant before he launched it, subtly adjust my position accordingly, and frustrate his plan without his knowing exactly why he'd been unable to execute. After a while of this invisible interference, often an opponent would try to force an opening, or muscle a throw, or would otherwise over-commit himself, at which point, depending on my mood, I might throw him. Other times, I was content merely to flow from counter to counter, preventing battles rather than fighting them. A different approach than had characterized my younger days at the Kodokan, when my style had more to do with aggression and bravado than it did with elegance and efficiency. As the offspring of a Japanese father and Caucasian American mother, I once wore a heavy chip on my shoulder. My appearance was always Japanese enough, but appearances have almost nothing to do with prejudice in Japan. In fact, the society's worst animus is reserved for ethnic Koreans, and *burakumin*—descendents of leather workers—and those others guilty of hiding their impurities behind seemingly Japanese faces. Of course, my formative years are long behind me now. These days, with my dark hair increasingly shot through with gray, I no longer pine for a country that might welcome me as its own. It took time, but I've learned not to engage in those conflicts I've always lost before.

From their size, close-cropped hair, and Oakley wraparound shades, favored these days by Special Forces and their private sector counterparts, I made the visitors as military, maybe serving, maybe ex. That in itself was unremarkable: the Kodokan is hardly unknown among the American soldiers, Marines, and airmen stationed in Japan. Plenty of them come to visit, and even to train. Still, I prefer to assume the worst, especially when the assumption costs me little. I let the college kid throw me with *tai-otoshi*, the throw he'd been trying for all night and obviously his money move. In my former line of work, being underestimated was something to cultivate. I might have been out of the life, but I wasn't out of the habit.

I was careful when I left that night, my alertness at a higher than usual pitch. I checked the places I would set up if I'd been trying to get to me: behind the concrete pillars flanking the building's entrance on Hakusan-dori; the parked cars along the busy, eight-lane street; the entrance to the Mita-sen subway line to my left. I saw only oblivious *sarariman* commuters, their interchangeable dark suits limp and rumpled from the diesel-laced humidity, their brows beaded with sweat but their expressions relieved at the prospect of a few undemanding hours at home before the next day's corporate exertions. Several riders on motor scooters went by, the two-stroke engines of their machines whining in and then fading out as they passed, but they weren't wearing the full-face helmets favored by motorcycle drive-by gunners, and they never even slowed or looked at me. A woman rode a bicycle past me on the sidewalk, a chubby-cheeked toddler secured in a basket attached to the handlebars, his arms outstretched and his tiny hands balled into fists at what I didn't know. No one felt out of place, and I saw no sign of the soldiers. If they didn't show up again, I'd classify their one-night presence as a nonevent.

But they did show up again, the following night. And this time, they stayed only briefly, probably just long enough to scan through the scores of *judoka* and confirm the presence of their target. If I hadn't been doing my own frequent, unobtrusive scans of the spectator seats, I would have missed their appearance entirely.

I continued training until eight and then showered as usual, not wanting to do anything out of the ordinary, anything that might suggest I'd spotted something and was preparing for it. But I was preparing, and as a plan unspooled in my mind and adrenaline snaked out through my body, and as the presence of danger and the certainty of how I would deal with it settled into place with an awful, familiar clarity, I had to acknowledge to myself that I'd been preparing my whole life, and that whatever intervals of quiet I had ever briefly indulged were as meaningful and relevant as dreams. Only the preparation was real—the preparation, and the purpose it always enabled.

chapter
two

Ben Treven and Daniel Larison sat on stools at the window counter of a Douter Coffee shop fifty yards south of the Kodokan on Hakusan-dori, sipping black coffee and waiting for the two contractors to return. Treven had wanted to join them, to get a firsthand look at the man whom up until the week before he'd thought to be a myth, but Larison had insisted there was no upside to sending in more than two of them, and Treven knew he was right. It bothered him how easily and naturally Larison had established himself as the alpha of the team, but he also had to admit that Larison, in his mid-forties, ten years Treven's senior, had seen more of the shit even than Treven had, and had survived heavier opposition. He told himself if he kept his mouth shut he might learn something, and he supposed it was true. But after ten years in the Intelligence Support Activity, the deliberately blandly named covert arm of the military's Joint Special Operations Command, he wasn't used to running into people who acted like his tactical superiors, and even fewer he thought might be right about it.

Treven was facing the window in the direction of the Kodokan, and saw the contractors, whom he knew only as Beckley and Krichman, approaching before Larison did. He nodded his head slightly. "Here they come."

Larison had instructed all of them to use their mobile phones as little as possible and to keep them shut off, with the batteries removed, except at previously agreed-upon intervals. The units were all rented, of course, and all under false identities, but good security involved multiple layers. The CIA's careless use of cell phones in the Abu Omar rendition from Milan had led to the issuance of arrest warrants from an Italian judge for a bunch of CIA officials, including the Milan station chief, and Treven figured Larison was applying the lessons of that op to this one. Still, the current precautions struck him as excessive—they weren't here to kill or kidnap Rain, after all, only to contact him. On the other hand, just as with sending only the two contractors into the Kodokan for the initial recon, he supposed there was no real downside to the extra care.

The contractors came in and stood so they were facing Treven and Larison and had a view of the street. Treven had seen plenty of foreigners in this section of the city, but even so he knew they were all conspicuous. Treven's blond hair and green eyes had always been somewhat of a surveillance liability, of course, but he figured that to the average Japanese, such features wouldn't much distinguish him from Larison, with his dark hair and olive skin, or from any other Caucasian foreigner, for that matter. What the natives would notice, and remember, was the collective size of the four of them. Treven, a heavyweight wrestler in high school and linebacker for Stanford before dropping out, was actually the smallest of the group. Larison was obviously into weights, and, if Hort could be believed, maybe steroids, too. And the contractors could almost have been pro wrestlers. Treven wondered if Hort had selected them in the hope their size might intimidate Rain when they made contact. He doubted it would make a difference. Size only mattered in a fair fight, and from what he'd heard of Rain, the man was too smart to ever allow a fight to be fair.

"He's there," the man called Beckley said. "Training, just like last night."

Larison nodded. "Maybe we should switch off now," he said in his low, raspy voice. "Two nights in a row, he's probably spotted you. Treven and I can take the point."

"He didn't spot us," Krichman said. "We were in the stands, he barely even glanced our way."

Beckley grunted in agreement. "Look, if the guy were that surveillance conscious, he wouldn't be showing up at the same location at the same time every night in the first place. He didn't see us."

Larison took a sip of coffee. "He any good? The judo, I mean."

Krichman shrugged. "I don't know. Seemed like he had his hands full with the kid he was training with."

Larison took another sip of coffee and paused as though thinking. "You know, it probably doesn't really matter that much whether he saw you or not. We know he's here, we can just brace him on his way out."

"Yeah, we could," Krichman said, his tone indicating the man found the idea hopelessly unambitious. "But what kind of leverage do we have then? We found him at the Kodokan. Tomorrow he could just go and train somewhere else. Or give up training, period. We want him to feel pressured, isn't that what Hort said? So let's show him we know where he lives. Brace him there, make him feel we're into his life in a big way. That's how you get people to play ball—by getting them *by* the balls."

Treven couldn't disagree with the man's assessment overall. He was surprised Larison didn't see it that way, too. But Larison must have realized his oversight, because he said, "That makes sense. But come on, he must have seen you. Treven and I should take the point."

"Look," Beckley said, his tone indicating the tail end of patience, "he didn't see us. Krichman and I will take the point." He gestured to one of the buttons on his damp navy shirt. "You'll see everything we see, through this. If he spots us, and I doubt he will, we'll switch off like we planned. Okay?"

The button was actually the lens of a high definition pocket video camera that shot color in daylight and infrared-enhanced black-and-white at night. Each of them was similarly outfitted, and each unit transmitted wirelessly to the others on the network. A separate unit, about the size of a pack of playing cards, could be held in the hand to display what the other units were transmitting. It was nothing fancy, just a stripped-down and slightly modified version of the Eagle Eyes monitoring system that was increasingly popular with various government agencies, but it enabled a small surveillance team to spread out beyond what traditional line-of-sight would allow, and also enabled each team member to know the position of all the others without excessive reliance on cell phones or other verbal communication.

Larison raised his hands in a *you win* gesture. "All right. You two cover the entrance of the Kodokan. Treven and I will wait here and fall in behind you when you start following him."

Beckley smiled—a little snidely, Treven thought. And it did seem like

Larison, maybe in a weak attempt to save face, was pretending to issue
orders that had in fact just been issued to him.

Beckley and Krichman went out. Larison turned and watched
through the window as they walked away.

Treven said, "You think he's going to come out again at the same
time? Hort said he was so surveillance conscious."

Larison took a sip of coffee. "Why do you think Hort sent those
assholes along with us?"

It was a little annoying that Larison hadn't just answered the question. Treven paused, then said, "He doesn't trust us, obviously."

"That's right. They're working for him, not with us. Remember that."

Colonel Scott "Hort" Horton was Treven's commander in the ISA,
and had once been Larison's, too, before Larison had gone rogue, faked
his own death, and tried to blackmail Uncle Sam for a hundred million
dollars worth of uncut diamonds in exchange for videos of American
operatives torturing Muslim prisoners. He'd almost gotten away with it,
too, but Hort had played him and kept the diamonds for himself. Treven
wasn't entirely sure why. On the one hand, Hort's patriotism and integrity
were unquestionable. A black man who might have been denied advance-
ment in other areas but who was not only promoted, but held in awe by
the army meritocracy, he loved the military and he loved the men who
served under him. Yet none of that had prevented him from fucking
Larison when he'd needed to, as he'd once tried to fuck Treven. He'd told
Treven why: America was being run by a kind of oligarchy, which didn't
seem to trouble Hort much except that the oligarchy had become greedy
and incompetent—grievous sins, apparently, in Hort's strange moral uni-
verse. The country needed better management, he'd said. He was starting
something big, and the diamonds were a part of it. So, he hoped, would
be Treven and Larison, and this guy Rain they'd been sent to find, too, if
he could be persuaded.

So of course Hort didn't trust them. They weren't under duress,
exactly, but it wasn't all a positive inducement, win-win dynamic, either.
Larison had to be looking for payback, as well as a chance to recover the
diamonds. And Treven had wised up enough to recognize the strings
Hort had been using to manipulate him, and to know he needed to find
a way to cut them, too. There was the little matter of some unfortunate

security videos, for example, that could implicate Treven in the murder of a prominent former administration official. It didn't matter that it had been a CIA op and that Treven had nothing to do with the man's death. What mattered was that Hort and the CIA had the tapes, and might use them if Treven got out of line. So for the moment, the whole arrangement felt like an unstable alliance of convenience, all shifting allegiances and conflicting motives. Hort would never have sent them off without a means of monitoring them, and under the circumstances, Larison's injunction that he remember who Beckley and Krichman were really working for felt gratuitous, even a little insulting. Maybe the man was just chafing at the fact that the contractors didn't seem to give a shit about what Larison assumed was his own authority. Treven decided to let it go.

But what he wouldn't let go was that Larison had ignored his question. "Same place, same time, same way out, two nights in a row?" he said. "That sound like our guy?"

Larison glanced at him, and Treven could have sworn the man was almost smiling.

"Depends," Larison said.

"What do you mean?"

"Rain spotted them last night for sure, when they were there for longer. Very likely, he spotted them again tonight, too."

"How do you know?"

"Because I would have spotted them. Because if this guy is who Hort says he is, he would have spotted them. Because if he's not good enough to have spotted them, Hort wouldn't even be bothering with him."

Treven considered. "So what does that mean, if he spotted them but comes out the same way at the same time anyway?"

This time, Larison did smile. "It means I'm glad it's not us walking point."

chapter
three

When I left the Kodokan, I knew someone would be waiting for me. Most likely it would be the pair of giants I'd seen twice inside. Possibly they were just recon, and someone else would be set up outside, but if whoever it was had more manpower, the sensible thing would have been to rotate different members of the team to deny me the chance to get multiple IDs. Of course, it wasn't impossible that I was supposed to see the two I'd already spotted—after all, their bulk was hard to miss—so that I'd keep searching for them when I went outside and consequently overlook the real threat. But if that had been the game, they would have stayed longer that evening, to be sure I had a chance to see them again. My gut told me it was just the two of them, handling both recon and action.

I kept to the left side of the exit corridor as I left the building, using the book and souvenir kiosk as concealment until the last moment to deny them additional seconds to prepare for my appearance. I doubted they had guns—firearms are tightly restricted in Japan, and anyone with the connections to acquire them would likely have fielded a larger and less conspicuous team. A sniper rifle would have been even harder to get than a pistol, and even if they'd managed to procure one, what were they going to do, rent an apartment overlooking the entrance of the Kodokan? Too much trouble, too much paper trail. There were better ways.

As I hit the glass doors, I kept my head steady but let my eyes sweep the sidewalk and street within my field of vision. Nothing yet. The night before, I'd gone left and taken the subway, and though I hadn't seen them at the time, I now assumed they'd been lurking somewhere and had logged my movements. So if they were hoping to follow me tonight and introduce themselves on terrain they found more favorable, they'd set up to the right. If the plan was for me to walk into them, they'd be to the left. No way to be sure, but other things being equal, I prefer to see what's coming. And why not let them see me repeating the pattern I'd established the night before? It would give them a little more data to rely on in underestimating me. I turned left onto the sidewalk, my eyes still moving, checking hot spots, my ears trained for footfalls behind me.

I spotted the first instantly, leaning against one of the pillars fronting the building. He was bigger even than I'd estimated from seeing him in the stands. His hands were visible and one of them held a cigarette. Not the best cover for action in Tokyo. The country is a little behind the times on the nonsmoking front, and with the exception of smokers visiting Starbucks and hospital intensive care units, no one goes outside for a tobacco break, especially in the wet summer heat.

I passed him and hit the stairs of Kasuga station, keeping my head down to conceal my face from the security camera staring down from the ceiling, my footsteps echoing along the concrete walls. Ordinarily, I found the cameras a hindrance if not an outright threat, but for the moment, their presence was cause for comfort. No one wants to do a hit in the Tokyo metropolitan subway system, where the number of closed circuit video cameras could make a Las Vegas casino blush. In the past, the cameras had never been a particular concern, but then again my specialty had always been the appearance of natural causes—one of the advantages of which is that no one examines security tapes afterward, trying to find out what happened. The Mossad team that did the Hamas official in Dubai, for example, had likely been planning on the appearance of a heart attack, and so wasn't worried about the hotel and airport cameras that filmed them. But they'd blown the job, and what was obviously an assassination led to an investigation. I wondered at the time why they hadn't called me. Maybe Delilah had told them I was out of the life. I smiled bitterly at the notion, and the memory, and kept moving down the stairs.

I turned the corner into the station proper and there was the second guy, standing under the florescent lights in front of the ticket vending machines, looking at the wall map above like an extra-large, extra-confused tourist. Kasuga isn't a main thoroughfare, and the area was mostly deserted—just a glassy-eyed ticket puncher in a booth, looking about as sentient as a potted plant, and a couple of high school kids who were testing their English trying to help my new friend find whatever it was he was looking for. I heard him grumble that he was fine as I moved past and could almost have sympathized—having a civilian address you when you're trying to be invisible is always a bitch. I slid a prepaid pass into the ticket machine and went through to the platform.

I strolled slowly along, the grimy tracks below me and to my right, the white tiled wall gleaming to my left. I passed a few Tokyoites standing here and there—a girl with tea-colored hair and garish makeup texting on a mobile, a *sarariman* absently practicing his golf swing, a couple of people I recognized from the Kodokan—but no one who tickled my radar. About two thirds of the way to the end I stopped and stood with my back close to the wall. But for the hum of an air conditioning unit, the platform was silent. From somewhere inside the tunnel to my left, I could just hear dripping water.

I might have glanced back, but doing so would only confirm what I already knew: they had fallen in behind me. They'd keep well down the platform, and when a train arrived they'd get on it, two or three cars away. At each stop, they'd check through the sliding doors to see if I was getting off, and follow me when I did. When they'd tailed me to a venue they found sufficiently dark, or isolated, or otherwise suitable for the business at hand, they'd do what they came for and depart.

But that's the problem with dark, isolated, and otherwise suitable venues. Like tracer rounds, they work in both directions.

I felt a rumble approaching from far down in the tunnel to my right, and a voice over a public address system announced the arrival of a Meguro-bound train. The rumble grew louder. I glanced to my right and glimpsed the two giants, pressed against the wall about halfway down the platform—the spot I'd most likely overlook if I glanced in the direction of an approaching train. Not too close to alarm me; not so far that they'd get picked up in the natural angle of my vision. I didn't know who I was dealing with, but the positioning showed some experience.

It wouldn't have been hard to lose them. I doubted they knew the city well at all and they couldn't possibly have known it the way I do. But

I didn't see the point. A long time ago, in another context, a man I considered dangerous told me the next time he saw me, he would kill me. I took him at his word, and prevented him from carrying out his promise. It was the same now. If these guys wanted to meet me, we'd get the meeting over with tonight. I wasn't going to spend the rest of my days looking over my shoulder, wondering when they'd show up next. And I wasn't going to look for an opportunity to politely ask them about the nature of their interest, either. When you've spent a lifetime in my former line of work, and when two guys this big show up at your only possible known locale and start following you, it's time to assume the worst, and to act accordingly.

The train hurtled out of the tunnel and began to slow, its brakes hissing, its wheels screeching against the metal tracks. It shuddered to a stop and the doors slid open. A few passengers stepped out. I walked into a mostly empty compartment and stood facing the doors, just in case. No one else got on. After a moment, a loudspeaker voice warned passengers the train was leaving, and then the doors hissed closed and the train jerked into motion.

I thought I'd take them to Jinbocho, two stops away on the Mita line and best known for its numerous antiquarian book shops. I liked the area, too, for a coffee shop not far from the station, appropriately enough called Saboru, the Japanese word for lounging, loafing, playing hooky, or otherwise taking a timeout from the world. Though I would only take the giants past the coffee shop, not inside. And the timeout I had in mind for them was going to be longer than what *saboru* ordinarily implied.

When the train stopped at Jinbocho station, I got unhurriedly off and headed for the A7 exit. I didn't look behind me. I didn't need to. They might have been sufficiently familiar with Tokyo to know how quickly you can lose the subject of surveillance in the shifting nighttime crowds, the unmarked, narrow alleys, of a section of the city as old and labyrinthine as Jinbocho. Or they might not have been even that familiar, in which case they'd lack the confidence to let anything more than a short gap open up between us. Either way, they would stay close now until their first opportunity.

When I was a kid, I had to learn to deal with bullies. First in Japan, where small half-breeds like me attracted the righteous attentions of larger children for whom cruelty and joy were indistinguishable; later, after my father died, in small town America, where I was an exotic half-Asian kid with limited English and a funny accent. During my first week at the American public school in which my newly-widowed mother had enrolled me, I'd noticed a much larger kid eyeing me, a meaty, crew-cut blond boy the other kids called the Bear. The Bear had acquired his nickname, apparently, because his favorite thing to do was to grab his victims in a frontal bear hug, squeeze them senseless, then throw them to the ground, where he could hurt and humiliate them at will. I saw one hapless kid get the treatment—the Bear sucked him in; the kid tried to push away but then his arms crumbled; the Bear threw him down and beat the crap out of him. I figured everyone he'd ever grabbed must have reacted the same way: if someone is trying to draw you in to squeeze you to death, you'd naturally resist. So it stood to reason that the Bear might not be prepared for someone who failed to resist his embrace. Who, instead, embraced him back.

It didn't take long for my turn to come. Though I lacked the frame of reference at the time, I recognized the behaviors—the looks, the comments, the accidental-on-purpose hallway shoulder slams—that for bullies on both sides of the Pacific constituted a kind of foreplay. And I instinctively understood that the little signs were all a tactical weakness, too, because they informed the intended victim of what was coming, and when. I resolved never to display such warnings myself, and I never have.

It was on a grass berm behind the school's weedy baseball field that the Bear decided to consummate our incipient relationship. I'd studied him enough, and was experienced enough, to recognize even before he did that this would be the place and time. So when he nudged his friends and pointed at me, it was almost comforting, like watching an actor dutifully playing his part in a drama the conclusion of which I already knew. He swaggered over to where I was standing and demanded, *What are you looking at?* It was so much what I'd expected, I think I might have smiled a little, because although I didn't respond, for an instant I thought I saw doubt pass across his features like the shadow of a fast-moving cloud. But then it was gone, and he was again accusing me of looking at him, the one line of inquiry apparently having exhausted his creative capacity, and he threw out his arms and lunged at me, just as I'd hoped he would.

As his arms circled my back and he started to pull me in, I shot my hands forward and dug my fingers into the back of his neck, my elbows braced against his chest. I felt him jerk in surprise but he only knew the one move and it had always worked before, so he didn't stop—he locked his hands and started to squeeze, but now I was squeezing, too, my biceps tightening with the effort, my forearms corded, bringing his head alongside mine, and as our left cheeks connected I dug my face in, bit into his earlobe, and ripped it free with a jerk of my head. He screamed, suddenly trying to push me away, but I was clamped onto him like pliers and I bit him again, this time on the back of the ear. Cartilage crunched and tore loose and my mouth was filled with hot, coppery blood, and a primal frenzy swept through me as I realized how I'd made him bleed. He screamed again, lost his balance, and fell onto his back with me on top of him. I spat out what I'd chewed off, reared up, and started raining punches down on his face. He covered up blindly, in a panic. Someone tried to grab me but I slipped free and darted in for another go at his ear. This time I couldn't find it—there was too much blood, and not enough ear—but just the feeling of the renewed attack made the Bear shriek in terror and scramble from beneath me as the other kids pulled me loose.

We both stood, the Bear crying now, his eyes wide in disbelief, his left hand groping shakily at the mutilated stump on the side of his head. The two kids who were holding my arms let me go and stepped warily to the sides, as though realizing they'd been standing too close to a wild animal. I looked at the Bear, my fists balled, my nostrils flaring, and felt a bloody smile spread across my face. I took a step toward him, and with a hitching, anguished squeak, the Bear turned and fled for the safety of the school.

The Bear's parents made a fuss, threatening a lawsuit and excoriating my mother for raising such a wanton, savage child. The school held disciplinary proceedings, and for a while it looked like I might be expelled. But the hearings turned to a discussion of previous incidents in which the Bear had been involved, and of how he was so much bigger than I was, and I sensed in the official expressions of disapproval something pro forma, something with the aroma of a whitewash. Eventually, I realized that some cabal of frustrated teachers and outraged parents had been secretly pleased at the Bear's comeuppance, and had used the hearings as the means by which they could achieve an outcome that had already been decided. It was the first time I'd seen such a thing, but later, I came to understand the dynamic is common, occurring, for example, every time some government appoints a blue ribbon commission to investigate the latest scandal. In the end, my run-in with the Bear blew over. Surgeons were able to save what was left of his ear. He grew his hair long to cover his deformity, and he never came near me again.

I learned two things from my encounter with the Bear. First, the importance of surprise. It didn't matter what size, skills, or other advantages your enemy had if you didn't give him a chance to deploy any of it.

Second, that there's always an aftermath. Following the fight, I was lucky not to have gotten in more trouble with the authorities. Meaning it was better to take care of such matters in a way that couldn't be attributed to you. Winning the fight itself wouldn't mean much if you lost more afterward, legally or otherwise.

At the top of the stairs, I turned left onto the nameless narrow street fronting Saboru, with its eccentric mountain hut façade and profusion of potted plants around the door and under the windows. The light hadn't yet entirely leached from the sky, but the area was already thick with shadows. A few knots of pedestrians passed me, probably heading home from work, or perhaps for a beer and *yakitori* in nearby Kanda. I knew my pursuers were close behind me, but they wouldn't be comfortable yet—the pedestrian density wasn't quite right. They'd be waiting for an especially congested area, where there would be so many people and so much tumult that no one would notice what had happened until several seconds after the fact. Or for an especially empty area, where there would be no witnesses at all.

I had a knife, a Benchmade folder, clipped inside my front pants pocket. But I would use it only for contingencies. Knives make a lot of mess, all of it laced with DNA. Guns, too, create an evidence trail. For sheer walk-awayedness, there's really nothing like bare hands.

Past Saboru, the neighborhood grew more residential; the yellow streetlights, fewer and farther between. Within a block, the sparse clusters of pedestrians had evaporated entirely. Over the incessant background screech of cicadas I could just hear a set of footfalls from ten meters back. Coming, no doubt, from whichever of them was keeping me in visual contact. The secondary guy would be about the same distance behind the first, needing only to maintain visual contact with him. If they narrowed the gap between them, it would mean action was at hand. I wasn't going to give them that chance.

There was a small parking lot on the left side of the intersection ahead. I had noted it on one of my periodic tactical explorations of the city's terrain, and liked it because among a cluster of dim vending machines to its rear was the entrance to a series of alleys, more like crevices, really, leading back to the street we were walking on now. In fact, I'd just passed a gate that led from one of the alleys, though I doubted my pursuers would notice it, or, even if they did, would understand its current significance. From the sound of the lead guy's distance behind me, I estimated that I could make it through the alley to the inside of the gate at about the same time the first guy would be pausing at the parking lot's corner, trying to figure out where I'd gone, and the second guy would be passing the gate.

I made a left into the parking lot, and then, the instant I'd turned the corner, accelerated and turned left into the entrance to the alleys. Another left, past a row of garbage cans, and I was at the inside of the gate I'd just passed. I paused, my back to the wall, enveloped in darkness, and watched as the secondary guy passed my position. I waited several seconds before gripping the metal rail at the top of the gate and moving it back and forth to confirm solidity and soundlessness. Then I hopped up, eased my belly over, put a hand on each side, and rotated my legs around, landing catlike on the street side. There was the second guy, just a few meters ahead, approaching the edge of the parking lot. He was moving so slowly, it seemed he was aware his partner would have stopped just around the corner to look for me, and was trying to give him time. I wondered for an instant how he could have known his partner had paused—maybe just a sensible precaution when turning a corner?—but it didn't matter. What mattered was that I was closing in on him, and that for the moment I had his back.

I traded stealth for speed, knowing I had only an instant before he might check behind him, and in fact as I reached him, he was just beginning to turn. But too late. I leaped into him, planting my left foot in the small of his back as though trying to climb a steep set of stairs. His body bowed violently forward and his head and arms flew back, and a startled grunt, loud enough, I was aware, for his partner to hear from around the corner, forced itself from his lungs. As he plunged to his knees, I wrapped my left arm around his neck, trapping his upturned face against my abdomen, secured my left wrist with my right hand, and arched savagely up and back. His neck snapped as easily as if it had been made of kindling, and with a similar sound. I let him go and he crumbled to the ground.

His partner appeared instantly from around the corner. He cried out, "Oh, fuck," the vernacular, and the accent, I was distantly aware, both American, and lunged at me. I had no time to get out of the way, but neither the inclination. Instead, I held my position, extending my torso away from him so he was forced to reach for me, and twisted slightly counterclockwise as we came to grips. I extended my left leg, planted the sole of my foot against his right knee, grabbed both his biceps, and used his momentum to spin him counterclockwise in *hiza-guruma*. He was overbalanced and couldn't get his legs out to correct because of the way I was blocking his knee. There was an instant of resistance, and then he was sailing past me, perpendicular to the ground, trying to twist away from me and turn his body toward the coming impact. But he was moving too fast for that now, and I was assisting his rapid descent, applying pressure to his shoulders to make them fall faster than his feet, wanting his cranium to bear the brunt. He hit the pavement with a thud I could feel as well as hear, his shoulders connecting first, then the back of his skull as his head snapped back. I dropped to my knees next to him but he wasn't out, and even shocked and dazed as he must have been, he managed to turn into me and go for my eyes with his left hand. I grabbed his wrist with my left hand, slamming my elbow into his face on the way, snaked my right arm under his shoulder, secured my own left wrist, extended my body across his chest, and broke his elbow with *ude-garami*. He shrieked and tried to buck me loose. I scrambled back, reared up, and blasted a palm heel into his nose. The back of his head bounced into the pavement and I hit him again the same way. He rolled away from me, trying to get up, and I launched myself onto his back, throwing my left arm around his neck, catching my right bicep, planting my right hand against the back of his head, and strangling him with classic *hadaka-jime*. He struggled and thrashed and I kept an eye on his remaining good arm, in case he tried to access a concealed weapon. The choke was deep, though, and his brain was getting no oxygen. In a few seconds he was still and, a few more after that, gone.

I released my grip and came shakily to my feet, my heart hammering. I wiped sweat from my eyes with my sleeve and looked around. There had been that single scream, but I saw no one, at least not yet. Not likely either of them was carrying identification, but I felt I could afford a moment to check.

I knelt and pulled the guy I'd strangled onto his back. He rolled over with liquid ease, his broken arm flopping unnaturally to the pavement next to him. I patted his front pants pockets. A folding knife in the right. Something hard and rectangular in the left—a cell phone? I pulled it out and saw that it was a phone, as I'd hoped. But there was something else in the pocket. I reached back in and felt something metallic. I pulled whatever it was out and stared at it. It took me a moment to realize what I was holding: a small video camera.

Oh, shit.

A wire extended from the unit, disappearing beneath his clothes. I slipped my fingers between the buttons of his shirt and tore it open. The wire ran to one of the buttons. I leaned in—it wasn't easy to see in the dim light—and looked more closely. Shit, it was no button at all, but a lens. And I was staring right into it.

I tore the wire free and stuffed the camera and phone into my pockets, then scrambled over to where the other guy lay. He was similarly equipped. I pocketed the second phone and camera, too, then walked off, keeping to the quiet streets paralleling Yasukuni-dori. I would take the batteries out of the phones to make sure they were untraceable and examine the cameras when I was safely away from the bodies. If the two giants had been using the equipment only to monitor each other, I would be okay.

But I had a feeling they weren't just monitoring each other. And if I was right, I was in for another visit, and soon.

chapter
four

L arison stood just beyond the ambit of a streetlight, watching the silent images on the handheld video feed. One second, an empty street; the next, a crazy montage of kaleidoscopic images: limbs/grimaces/a car/a building/the sky flashing past. Darkness. Then the sky again, and glimpses of Rain, apparently going through Beckley's pockets. Rain's face in close-up, peering with dawning recognition directly into the button lens on Beckley's cooling torso. A flash of static, then, finally, darkness.

He heard rapid footfalls from the direction of the Jinbocho subway station and looked up to see Treven come tearing around the corner. Larison pocketed the video monitor and stepped into the street with his arms forward, palms out.

"Stop," he said. "It's already over."

Treven slowed, his face registering confusion. Probably he'd been expecting Larison to be riding to the rescue, too, no matter how futile a rescue attempt would be at this point. Meaning he hadn't absorbed what Larison had told him about the contractors not being part of the team.

"Go!" Treven said, moving to go around. "Didn't you see the video? Rain ambushed them!"

Larison moved with him and shoved him back. Treven's face darkened and he dropped his weight like a bull about to charge.

Larison held up his hands again. "Don't make a scene," he said. "There's nothing we can do. They're already dead."

"We don't know that. Rain's gone, okay, but—"

"They. Are. Dead."

Treven straightened and some of the tension went out of his body.

"What about the cell phones?" he said. "The equipment. We need to retrieve it."

"Rain took it all."

"How the hell do you—"

"Wouldn't you have? But it doesn't matter. I watched him, over the video feed. He took the equipment and he's gone."

Treven watched him silently for a moment. Then he said, "You were close enough. You could have done something, if you'd wanted to."

Larison glanced at the street behind him, then back at Treven. In some ways, he sympathized with Treven, who Larison understood was grappling with his recent first contact with the real world in the same way Larison once had. On the other hand, he didn't care for Treven's stubborn patriotism, which he found sanctimonious and naïve. And he hated that Treven knew his secret, having discovered Nico, Larison's other life, when he'd tracked Larison to Costa Rica, looking for the torture tapes Larison had stolen.

"You manipulated them," Treven said. "All that talk about taking the point... you goaded them. Because you knew what would happen."

Larison shrugged. "What did I owe them? They were sent over here to spy on me. On both of us."

Treven's expression was incredulous bordering on disgusted. "They were Americans."

Larison blew out a long breath. The contractors had been a hindrance, and he had gotten rid of them. It was no more complicated than that. He tried to remember a time when such a thing would have been a problem, when he might have paused beforehand and maybe even felt a pang of conscience after. He couldn't. It had been too long ago, and too much had happened since.

"What does that have to do with anything?" he said.

Treven shook his head. "You're a burnout."

Larison didn't respond. He didn't know what to do. Kill Treven? But he needed him to get to Hort, and anyway Hort knew about Nico, too.

But once Hort was dead...

Once Hort was dead, the only person who would even know Larison was alive, let alone about his other life, would be Treven. Plus Rain, soon enough, and this other guy they were supposed to find. Larison needed them for now, he knew that. But once Hort was dead, all they'd represent would be downside.

Use the others to finish Hort, then finish them, too. Walk away with the diamonds, and silence everyone who posed a threat.

It was perfect. It could be done. All he had to do was bait the hook. The rest would take care of itself.

He tried not to smile. "Let's just call Rain," he said.

chapter
five

I had nearly reached Ogawamachi subway station, where I would catch a train and examine the items I'd taken from the two dead men, when one of their phones vibrated. I stopped and checked the readout—just a number, no name.

I looked around at the bustling street scene, cars crawling, pedestrians hurrying past me, the sky dark now, the area lit only by streetlights and headlights and storefronts. I pressed the "receive call" key, held the unit to my ear, and listened.

A low voice, almost a whisper, said in American-accented English, "I know who you are. Don't worry, I won't say your name on an open line. You took the phones you're carrying from the two men I was with. It's okay. I know they don't need phones anymore."

The natural question was, *Who is this?* I ignored it because of its likely futility, in favor of something more relevant.

"What do you want?"

"To meet you. I have a message from a fan."

"Tell me over the phone."

"No. If this is going to work, we'll need to establish our bona fides."

"Who's 'we'?"

"My partner and me."

"Two messengers?"

"There were four originally, but yes."

I paused, thinking about the video camera, trying to get my mind around what the hell this could be about. The evening was still sultry and I realized my shirt was soaked with sweat.

"Look," the voice said, "I wasn't any more enamored of the two guys you just met than you were. If I had been, I wouldn't have encouraged them to get so close. I sent them inside twice. I knew you'd see them."

I wondered whether that was bullshit. But the timing of the call and the calm confidence of the voice suggested I was talking to someone who'd foreseen this, even planned it.

"It's up to you," the voice said. "But I have something you'll want. A unit that was receiving from the two you're carrying now. Take your time examining them, you'll see I'm telling the truth. Then, if you want the one I'm holding, we can meet."

I considered proposing a creative rectal use for the unit he claimed to be carrying, but decided against it. The calculus was the same as for the two giants. I could face this now, tonight, or I could spend the rest of my days wondering who was after me, what they wanted, how far they were willing to go. And let whoever it was answer my questions at a time and in a manner of their choosing, not mine.

"Where are you right now?" I asked.

"If you're still on foot, we can't be more than a half mile apart."

"There's a coffee shop near the subway station I came out of. I'm assuming you were somewhere behind the two who followed me out?"

"That's right."

"You passed it ten seconds after you hit the street. Big yellow sign, distinctive frontage. On the right coming around from the station."

I clicked off and pulled the batteries from the phones and the video cameras. The timing wasn't great—if they'd been behind me the whole time, they were closer to Saboru than I was. I would have preferred to get there first and watch from the street. But there would have been disadvantages in proposing someplace farther away, too. First, I would have had to give explicit rather than oblique instructions over the phone. Second, they would have had more to time to set something up, if that's what this was about. Overall, I judged my chances best if I could keep them on a short clock.

It took me less than ten minutes to get back to Saboru. I made two circuits, the first wide, the second passing directly in front. Sepia lights glowed in the windows but the bamboo plantings made it impossible to see inside. I stood at the dim corner of the street for a moment, looking left and right, considering. The cicadas had gone temporarily quiet, and the only sound was of the *suzumushi*—bell crickets—Saboru's centenarian proprietor keeps in a cage by the entrance because he finds their evening music pleasing. I saw no Caucasians and nothing seemed out of place. My guess was, whoever had called me was already inside.

I walked over and went in, my gaze sweeping the softly lit interior. A young hostess offered to seat me and I told her as I continued to check tables no thank you, I expected my friends were already here. The ground floor was about half-filled with an ordinary assortment of after-work *sarariman* types and loafing college students. There was a quiet background murmur of conversation mixed with J-pop music emanating from speakers affixed to the corners of the low ceiling. No foreigners, nothing out of place. I took the wooden stairs to the second floor. Again, nothing. Then to the basement, squatting as I descended the stairs to get a view of what I was up against before I'd gone all the way down.

I spotted them immediately, in a corner booth, their backs to the brick wall, both big and fit-looking. One, in his thirties, with blond hair and a strong jaw, quintessentially American; the other, about a decade older, with shorter, dark hair and darker skin, harder to place. I wondered which had spoken to me and for some reason sensed it was the darker one. There was something dangerous-looking about him, an explosive quality I could feel from across the room even though he was sitting perfectly still. Their hands were open, resting on the pitted wooden table. A good sign, or at least the absence of a bad one. They kept still and watched me, their steady gaze the only indication there was any connection between us.

I kept moving, sweeping the cave-like room with my eyes, confirming there was no one else here who looked like he didn't belong. There was another table open in the opposite corner. I inclined my head toward it to indicate they should follow, walked over, and stood by the bench with my back to the wall. I didn't want to sit in the spot they had chosen, or to offer them a view of the stairs while I was denied it. And I wanted to have a chance to see them head to toe, to watch how they moved, as they had just done me.

They got up and walked slowly over, no sudden movements, keeping their hands clearly visible. We all sat down wordlessly and watched each other for a moment. A waitress came by and handed us menus, which were in Japanese. The darker guy glanced at his, then looked at me with the trace of a smile. "What do you recommend?"

I'd been right: the same quiet, raspy voice I'd heard on the phone. "I hear the house coffee is good," I said.

He glanced at the blond guy, who shrugged. Their demeanors intrigued me. The blond guy seemed on edge, as he ought to have been, as indeed I was. The dark guy, on the other hand, was incongruously relaxed, and seemed almost to be enjoying himself.

I ordered three coffees and three waters and the waitress moved off. I nodded at the dark guy. "What do I call you?"

"Larison."

I turned my head to the other guy, who said, "Treven."

"All right, Larison and Treven. What do you want?" The more on-point question, of course, would have been, *Who do you want me to kill?* But it didn't matter which route we took. We'd arrive at the same destination.

"We were sent just to find you," Larison said. "The one who wants something from you is Colonel Horton. Scott Horton."

The name was familiar, but for a moment, I couldn't place it. Then I remembered something from Reagan-era Afghanistan, a time that felt to me now, when I considered it at all, so remote it could have been someone else's life. The CIA had recruited former soldiers like me to train and equip the Mujahadeen who were fighting the Soviets, and though deniability had been imperative, there were a few active-duty military in theater, too, to liaise with the irregulars. There had been a young Special Forces noncom everyone called Hort, whom we'd teased because, despite his obvious capability and courage, he was black, and so an absurd choice for a covert role in Afghanistan. He assured us, though, that this was the point: if he was captured, Uncle Sam wanted to be able to say to the Russians, *You think we'd be stupid enough to send a black soldier to blend in Afghanistan? Must have been a freelancer, a black Muslim answering the call of jihad. See how your wars are radicalizing people? What a shame.*

I said, "This guy cut his teeth in Afghanistan?"

Larison nodded. "Training the Muj, yeah."

"White guy?"

"No. Black."

"Does he go by a nickname?"

"Hort."

Sounded like a match. He must have received a commission somewhere along the way and then never left the military. I estimated that today he'd be about fifty. "And he's a colonel now," I said, more musing than asking a question.

"Head of the ISA," Treven said.

I nodded, impressed. It was a long way from deniable cannon fodder to the head of the Intelligence Support Activity, the U.S. military's most formidable unit of covert killers.

"And you?" I asked, looking at Larison, then Treven. "ISA?"

Treven nodded. He didn't seem entirely happy about the fact, or maybe he was just uncomfortable acknowledging an affiliation he would ordinarily reflexively deny.

Larison said, "Once upon a time. These days, I just consult."

"Pay's better?"

Larison smiled. "You tell me."

"The pay's okay," I said. "Healthcare's not so great."

Treven glanced at Larison—a little impatiently, I thought. Maybe the kind of guy who liked to get right down to business. He didn't understand this *was* business. Larison and I were trying to feel each other out.

"And the other two?" I said.

"Contractors," Larison said. "One of the Blackwater-type successors. I can't keep track."

I glanced at Treven, then back to Larison. "So, ISA, a consultant, contractors... That's a fairly eclectic gang you've got there."

"We didn't ask for the contractors," Larison said, turning his palms up slightly from the table in a *what can you do* gesture. "That was Hort. I guess you could say he... overstaffed this thing."

"And you downsized it."

He dipped his head slightly as though in respect or appreciation. "You and I both."

He seemed determined to let me know there were no hard feelings about the two dead giants—indeed, to acknowledge he'd deliberately sacrificed them. And now he was implying some distance between himself and Horton, too, and implying some commonality between himself and me. I wasn't sure why.

"What's Horton's interest?" I asked.

"We don't know the particulars," Treven said. "All he told us was, he's rebuilding, and he wants to make you an offer."

"Rebuilding what?"

"I don't know. Something about an operation you took down, run by a guy named Jim Hilger."

Hilger. I didn't show it, but I was surprised to hear the name. In all the times we'd crossed paths, first in Hong Kong, where he was brokering the sale of radiologically-tipped missiles and nuclear materiel, and then in Holland, where he'd been running an op to blow up the port in Rotterdam and drive up the price of oil, his affiliations had never been entirely clear to me. The last time I'd run into him was in Amsterdam, which was the last time he ran into anyone. If Horton had been involved with the late Jim Hilger, whatever he wanted was apt to be hazardous.

"What do you know about Hilger?" I asked.

Treven shook his head. "No more than I just told you."

Larison said, "I've heard of him."

"Who did he work for? Was he government? Corporate?"

Larison laughed. "You really think there's a difference?"

Treven frowned just the tiniest amount, and I sensed Larison's comment made him uncomfortable. I wasn't sure why. Well, neither was going to tell me more. And, given Hilger's current condition, I supposed it didn't matter anyway.

"Anything else?" I said.

Treven said, "Yeah. This thing Hort's trying to rebuild is going to include a former Marine sniper named Dox, who you're supposed to know."

I didn't respond. I hadn't seen Dox in a while, but we were in touch and I knew he was still living in Bali. He didn't need work, but this would probably interest him anyway. It wasn't a question of money with Dox. He just liked to be in the thick of it.

A part of my mind whispered, *And you?* I ignored it.

Larison said, "You might want to contact Dox yourself. If you don't, we have to, and what's the point of getting more contractors killed?"

Again, I was intrigued by his hint that he didn't mind what happened to the contractor elements of his team.

The waitress returned with our order and left. Larison took a sip of coffee and nodded appreciatively. Treven didn't touch his.

I drained my water glass and looked at them. "What does Horton have on you two?"

Neither of them responded. Well, he had something. And now they had something on me.

But then Larison surprised me. He said, "The video recorder is in my pocket. Mind if I reach for it?"

The question was appropriate. In a situation like this one, with someone like me, you want to keep your hands visible. Especially once you've established that you're too smart to reach for something suddenly. The only reasonable inference would be that you're going for a weapon, and the inference would lead to an unfriendly response.

I gestured that he should feel free. He stood and slowly extracted from his front pocket a unit like the two I'd taken from the giants. He placed it in the center of the table and sat back down. Then he glanced at Treven, who repeated the move, producing an identical unit.

I made no move to pick up the recorders. I'd expected the intent of the initial offer was only to get me to meet them, but now they seemed actually to be following through on it. Give up leverage for free? If they'd been clumsy civilians, maybe I could have read it as a naïve attempt to beget goodwill with goodwill. But neither of these guys was naïve. On the contrary, both of them had the quiet, weighty aura of men who've repeatedly killed and survived, an experience that tends to extinguish belief in the power of goodwill, along with most other such happy indulgences.

"There are no copies," Larison said. "We don't have anything on you. You want us to get lost, we'll walk out of here right now. But the next team Hort sends, they won't give you the video. They'll use it."

Probably he was lying about the copies, but I would never know for sure until someone tried to use them against me, and that would happen only if friendlier tactics proved useless. So Larison could be expected to try something relatively subtle to begin with. And so far he'd handled it deftly, I had to admit. You never want to present extortion as a threat: doing so just needlessly engages the subject's ego and creates unhelpful

resistance. Instead, you want to present the threat as though it has nothing to do with you, as though in fact you're on the subject's side. Maybe
that explained the hints about a gap between Horton and them. It would
have been a good way to help me persuade myself that my problem
wasn't with these two, but with someone else. If he was ruthless enough,
and I sensed he was, he might even have sacrificed the two giants for the
same end.

"Look," Larison said, "no one can just disappear anymore. Everyone
is findable. It's a condition of modern life. You want total security? You
have to disconnect. Live off the grid, remotely, no contact with the outside world. But if you like cities, and judo, and jazz, and coffee houses,
and culture, all of which is part of your file, you don't have a chance if
someone like Hort is determined to find you. The only way is to make it
so the people who are looking for you, stop looking for you."

"How do you do that?" I asked, my tone casual.

He took another sip of coffee. "You wait for the right opportunity."

"Or you make one," I suggested.

He nodded. "Or you make one. And I'll tell you one other thing.
If you decide to accept Hort's offer, whatever it is? Charge him for it.
Charge him a lot. He can afford it."

He sounded unhappy as he said the words, even acrimonious, and
if I hadn't picked up earlier on some kind of rift, I couldn't miss it now.
Whatever Horton was up to, I decided it must be important to him,
if it was generating animosity in someone as seemingly formidable as
Larison.

No one said anything after that. Larison obviously knew when it
was time to shut up and let the prospect close the deal with himself, and
Treven was smart enough to follow the older man's lead.

We sipped our coffee in silence. Either this was an impressive piece
of theater that included two dead extras, or what they were telling me,
and what they were hinting at, was largely true. Horton wanted to make
Dox and me an offer, most likely one we couldn't refuse. He'd made
similar offers already to Treven and Larison, who were unhappy about it
and looking for an alliance or some other way out, but were also smart
enough to keep those particular cards concealed for now. As for copies
of the evening's home video, for now there was no way to know. And for

the moment, it didn't really matter.

For the third time that night, I saw no advantage in waiting. I finished my coffee and took the video units from the table.

"How do I contact Horton?" I said.

chapter
six

Later that night, in the endless, twisting depths of the Shinjuku sub-way complex, where the multiple levels and concentrated crowds make tracking and locating someone from a signal nearly impossible, I checked the video on the cameras. The footage was grainy and helter-skelter, but properly enhanced it might provide damaging evidence for the prosecution, if it ever came to that. I destroyed the drives on all the units and disposed of them. The phones were useless—the only num-bers dialed were to each other. I disposed of them, too. Then I found an Internet café and Googled Larison, Treven, and Horton. Larison and Treven drew precisely nothing. Horton was mentioned in passing in a few news articles, and had a Wikipedia entry consisting only of a brief outline of a distinguished military career and a note that he was divorced and had no children. Finally, I made three calls, all from separate pay-phones.

First, the number Larison had given me. A deep, Mississippi Delta baritone I remembered from Afghanistan, but with more age behind it, more gravity, answered, "Is this who I hope it is?"

I said, "I don't know. Is there someone else you were hoping to hear from?"

He laughed. "There are people I hope to hear from, and people I hope to never hear from again. Glad to say you're in the first camp. How've you been?"

"I've been fine. I heard you want to propose something."

"You heard right."

"I'm listening."

"With all the water under the bridge here, it'd be better if we did this face to face."

"All right, come out here. Your guys can tell you where to find me."

"They already did. Thing is, I'm too tied up right now for overseas travel. But I'll tell you what. I'll meet you halfway. How about Los Angeles? Anywhere in the city you'd like."

Los Angeles was easy enough to get to from Tokyo, and a destination with so many indirect routes I didn't think I'd have trouble concealing my movements. Reflexively, I started considering how I would approach the situation if I were trying to get to me, and was surprised, and a little unsettled, at how familiar and natural it felt to slip back into the mindset. Almost as though I'd missed it.

"If you want me to come to you," I said, testing what Larison had told me, "you'll need to cover my travel expenses. And I travel first class."

"I wouldn't expect anything less. Tell you what. However our conversation turns out, you'll get twenty-five thousand dollars just for showing up. That ought to cover your travel expenses, and then some."

"Fifty," I said. "You've already created problems just by the way you contacted me."

There was a pause, and I wondered if I'd asked for too much, if only because my boldness might suggest someone had encouraged me to press. But so what? If there was some kind of ill will with Larison, Horton would have to be a fool not to know it already. And the man I remembered from Afghanistan wasn't a fool.

"I understand you've created some problems yourself," he said, and I realized Larison and Treven had likely already checked in and briefed him about the dead contractors. I wondered again about copies of the video. "But okay, we'll make it fifty. If you can be there tomorrow."

I wondered what this was about. If he was willing to pay fifty thousand U.S. just to get me to show up, it was something special. Meaning, almost certainly, something dangerous.

"Tomorrow's impossible," I said. "The day after I can do. For the fifty." The truth was, it didn't matter that much to me one way or the other. I just don't like to be rushed. Time pressure is what you do to someone when you're trying to get him to react without pausing to think.

"All right," he said, "the day after. You can reach me at this number.

I'll be in the center of the city, but we can meet anywhere you want."

I paused before responding. Why did I want to do this? The money? The advantages of dealing with whatever it was head-on rather than waiting? Some dark, subversive part of me, sick of my civilian pretensions, grabbing on to a way back in—the killer inside me, the Iceman, demanding his due?

"I'll call you," I said, and clicked off.

No doubt his emphasis on flexibility was intended to mollify my security concerns. He'd already chosen the city and had tried to choose the day; if his demands got much more specific than that, he knew it would make me jumpy.

The next call was to Tomohisa "Tom" Kanezaki, an ethnic Japanese American I'd first encountered when he was a green case officer with the CIA's Tokyo Station. I didn't trust him, exactly, but we'd traded enough favors for me not to view him as an active threat, and to know he could be counted on to do what he said he would. We'd lost touch about a year earlier, when I was living in Paris with Delilah, thinking I was happy. The last time we'd spoken, he was on a rotation at Langley and hating it.

He picked up with a characteristically noncommittal *Yes*. In Japan it had usually been *Hai*. Either way, it felt oddly good to hear his voice.

"Still living the good life at company headquarters?" I said.

There was a pause, and I could picture him smiling. I wondered if he was still wearing the wire-rimmed spectacles. Probably. They made him look bookish, as he once genuinely had been. These days, they'd conceal the street smarts he'd developed, and he was astute enough to know the value in that. *No aru taka wa, tsume o kakusu*, as the Japanese saying goes. The hawk with talent hides its talons.

"I wouldn't call it particularly good," he said. "What are you… is everything okay?"

"I have a small favor to ask—very small."

Kanezaki could always be counted on to ask for a favor in return. Some of his return favors were pretty damn big, so it paid to establish that what I was asking for was trivial.

"You want to do this with Skype?" he said. "If you don't think my mobile is secure enough."

This was both a concession to my security paranoia and a way to build the favor up with some indices of importance. "No," I said. "It's not that kind of thing. I just want the skinny on a JSOC colonel named Scott Horton. People call him Hort. You know of him?"

There was a pause, and I wondered if Kanezaki was considering whether I was going to kill Horton. It was the way he was used to thinking of me. But he'd know if that were the case I wouldn't have asked him.

"Yeah, I know of him. But his position is—"

"Classified, I know. I know what his position is. I want to know about the man. Any reason he wouldn't have my best interests at heart?"

"That's hard to say. The kind of thing you do tends to create enemies."

"Used to do."

He laughed. "And yet, here you are."

I ignored it. "He wants to meet me."

"You think it's a setup?"

"I always think it's a setup. Sometimes it even is."

"Well, all I can tell you is, he's got a lot of weight behind him. In the last administration, JSOC was reporting directly to the vice president and doing some extremely off-the-books stuff. Seymour Hersh called it a hit squad."

"Any truth to that?"

He laughed. "You're not really asking me to verify a Sy Hersh story, are you?"

It was true, then. "What else?"

"Let's just say the new administration hasn't changed JSOC's mission. I don't know all the details, but I do know that a lot of traditional Agency responsibilities have been taken from us and transferred to the military."

"Why?"

"We've been in Afghanistan for over a decade now. Iraq for nearly that long. Plus other places that don't make it into the news quite so much. A decade of global war means a lot of prominence for the military. They get what they want, and they want a lot."

"What about a former ISA operator, last name Larison? And a current ISA guy, last name Treven?"

"The names don't mean anything to me, but I can look. And I'll keep my ear to the ground for anything on what Horton might want with you."

Coming from Kanezaki, that might actually mean something. "I appreciate it."

"Do the same for me. I'd like to know what he's up to. You're not easy to find, so he must be motivated."

I sensed a hint of professional jealousy in the comment. I couldn't blame him for not wanting to share his assets. Or his former assets. And as a return favor, it wasn't much. I told him I'd keep him posted and clicked off.

The third call was to Dox. "It's me," I said, when he'd picked up.

"'Me'? Who's 'me'?" he said in his thick southern drawl.

We'd been through this before. "You know who 'me' is."

He laughed, obviously pleased. "I know, I know, just trying to see—"

"If you can get me to say my name on the phone, I know. You're going to have to try harder than that."

"Oh, I don't know. You're getting older. I'll get you sooner or later. How've you been, man? Goddamn if it's not good to hear your voice, even with no name behind it."

I briefed him on what was going on, and I could imagine him grinning on the other end.

"Sounds like someone's going to get a mighty special going-away party," he said.

"Yeah, and they want us to cater."

"Well, I'm usually amenable to preparing some tasty victuals, if the per diem's right. But what about you? I thought you were out of the catering business."

"I'm just going to listen to a proposal."

He laughed. "Whatever you say, partner."

Dox was perfectly comfortable employing his deadly talents and could never understand my ambivalence. I said, "I'll let you know what I learn."

"Let me know? You're fixing to go out there alone?"

"Look, there's no sense—"

"I'll tell you about sense. There's no sense in leaving your dick flapping in the breeze while you walk into God knows what. I'll meet you there and cover your back. And don't tell me you don't need it. You say that every time, and plenty of times you've been wrong."

He was right, of course. He was as reliable a man as I'd ever known, and had once even walked away from a five-million-dollar payday to save my life. I just don't like to have to rely on anyone.

But under the circumstances, the reflex felt like stupidity, like denial. "All right," I said. "They're paying me just for the face-to-face. I'll split it with you."

"Fair enough. What about your particulars? Secure site?"

Where possible, and especially with travel or other details that could be used to fix me in time or place, I prefer to communicate via an encrypted Internet site. Lately I'd begun carrying a Fire Vault and Tor equipped iPad—small, convenient, and a lot more secure than dedicated machines in Internet cafes, which are often compromised. "You know me," I said.

"Yeah, I do, and I've learned to see some of the wisdom behind what lesser men would call your paranoia."

I told him I'd post something within eighteen hours, then clicked off and strolled over to an Internet kiosk. There were plenty of seats available on all four daily JAL flights to Honolulu. Not the most direct route possible, but no sense in being obvious. I'd buy the ticket at Narita the next day, and likewise would take care of the L.A. leg once I landed. And I'd fly business, not first. Creating a larger data set for them to sift through wouldn't indefinitely prevent them from zeroing in on the legend I'd be traveling under, but it would delay them, and under the circumstances a delay would be good enough.

Probably I was being overcautious. Parsimony suggested this was no more than what it looked like: JSOC wanting to contract out a particularly sensitive job, and probably one that involved natural causes. But as an organizing principle, parsimony has its limitations. Like most of what exists in nature, it can be manipulated by men.

chapter
seven

Two days later, I sat alone at a corner table of the Beverly Wilshire's The Blvd, enjoying a bowl of oatmeal and an Economic Energizer smoothie and slowly working my way through a pot of coffee, surrounded by a mixture of hotel guests in tourist garb and studio factotums preening about deal points over power breakfasts. I liked the hotel and would have spent the night there, but didn't want to be a guest at the same place where, if things didn't go well, I might have to leave Horton's body behind. Instead, I'd stayed at the nearby Four Seasons, then strolled over to take advantage of the Beverly Wilshire's low-key but pervasive security, which would make things more challenging for Horton's forces if the meeting were a setup. Multiple entrances and exits on three separate streets would also complicate things for anyone planning something untoward. And on top of all the sound tactical reasons, it didn't hurt that I liked their food.

Kanezaki had come through with information on Larison and Treven. Daniel Larison was indeed a former ISA operator, but was now deceased, blown up in the bombing attack on Pakistani Prime Minister Bhutto in Karachi on October 18, 2007. Either the death was staged, or this guy was someone else who had stepped into the dead Larison's shoes. And Treven was apparently Ben Treven, ISA, though this wasn't a sure thing either because Kanezaki couldn't get photographs that I might use to match against the men I'd met. But I supposed it didn't matter all that much what their names were. What mattered was they were working for Horton.

I'd called Horton earlier that morning to let him know where he could find me, then headed straight over to ensure I could get a table with a view of the restaurant's hotel and street entrances. Dox was a few tables away, facing me, concealed from the entrances by one of the giant, wood-paneled pillars.

We'd spent the previous evening catching up over dinner at XIV, a restaurant on Sunset Boulevard. Over the chef's tasting menu of heirloom tomato & peach salad and Dungeness crab ravioli and other such delectables, Dox told me he'd grown bored with the little patch of paradise he'd built in Bali.

"It's beautiful and all, you've been there," he said, stroking his sandy-colored goatee. "I always thought it would be exactly what I wanted, my own place on the other side of the world. You know, far from the madding crowd, and all that, but… I don't know, maybe it's not Bali, maybe it's the life."

"How so?"

"Well, shit. I can get work pretty much anytime I want it… there's so much from the CIA and the Pentagon I'm not even taking anything from foreign clients anymore. I'm just tired of playing whack-a-mole with Achmed, I guess. I mean, what's the point of being in the fire brigade, if the people you're working for keep tossing matches on the underbrush? I should be glad, I realize—the big bad Global War on Terror means a nice annuity for people like you and me. What the hell, maybe it's a midlife crisis. Maybe I should just buy a fancy car." He took a healthy swallow of the Bombay Sapphire he was drinking, then said, "What about you and Delilah? How's that going?"

I was drinking a 2007 Emilio's Terrace from Napa Valley I'd discovered, strangely enough, in Bangkok. It was a cabernet and still young, but the fruit was delicious anyway. I felt vaguely sad for a moment to imagine how it might taste when it was really ready, in another decade or so. I looked at the dark liquid in the glass and said, "It's not."

"What does that mean?"

"It means I left her in Paris. I'm back in Tokyo."

"Back in Tokyo?" he said, rubbing the back of his neck. "I thought you loved Paris. Hell, I thought you loved Delilah."

I sighed. "She wouldn't leave the Mossad. I don't know how many times I told her that one of us in the life and the other trying to leave it was making me insane. I finally just... I gave her an ultimatum."

"I think I can tell by where you're living these days how that worked out."

I drummed my fingers on the table. "Probably for the best."

"I don't know. Thought you two had something special, tell you the truth."

I nodded. The three of us had been through a lot together: first, as opposing players on hair triggers; then, when the Mossad had brought me in to take out a rogue Israeli bomb maker named Manheim Lavi, on the same team; and then, most improbably, watching each other's backs for reasons that had nothing to do with national interests and everything to do with personal allegiances. What had bloomed between Delilah and me, I knew, was as improbable as it was precious.

"You think about her?" he asked.

I looked away. "What do you think?"

"Well, what was it about her being in the life you didn't like, exactly? I'm in the life, and you seem to tolerate me."

"I don't live with you."

"Is that really the critical difference?"

"Yeah, it is. I was trying to learn... how to relax over there. You know? New city, nobody knows me, nobody's looking for me. I just want to take it down a notch, not always feel like I need to be looking over my shoulder. Well, how am I ever going to manage that when I'm around someone whose job could bring a shitstorm onto us at any minute, and once actually did?"

He frowned. "Someone made a run at y'all in Paris?"

I nodded, remembering. "Paris is a bitch."

He dipped his head gravely and looked at me. "You'll have to tell me about that sometime. But partner, you, relaxing? That I'd like to see. Go ahead, do it for me, just for a minute. But let's bet on it first. I could use the money."

I didn't answer. I hated when he pulled the psychoanalysis shit with me. I hated it more when there was substance to his observations.

"Anyway," he went on, "here you are, back in the life but without Delilah. Even with me as a dinner companion, it doesn't seem like such a great bargain, if you want my opinion. Which I know you don't, but there it is."

"I'm not 'back in the life.' Someone tracked me down. I'm trying to straighten it out. It's not like I have much choice."

I expected him to laugh at my protestations, which would have been classic Dox. That he didn't irritated me even more.

"What?" I said.

He raised his eyebrows in mock innocence. "I didn't say anything."

"I know. It's not like you. What are you thinking?"

He leaned back and scratched his belly. "Just that… maybe you were more bothered by what Delilah does in the life than you were by the life itself."

I didn't answer. Delilah did a lot of things for the Mossad. But chief among them were long-term honey trap operations with high-value targets. She was a gorgeous natural blonde, intelligent, confident, and sophisticated, and she knew how to work all of it. I doubted they'd ever had anyone on the payroll as effective as she was, not that they ever appreciated her for it. In fact, she'd told me the missions they sent her on—to literally sleep with the enemy—made her continually suspect, even stained in the eyes of management. Which was part of the reason I found it maddening she wouldn't quit. What did she owe them? Why was she loyal? They didn't deserve her.

"You going to tell me it never bothered you, her going off for a month at a time without being able to tell you where or who with? You going to tell me you never woke up alone in your big bed in the middle of the night, wondering if right then, at that very moment, she might be straining the gravy with—"

"'Straining the gravy'?"

"Yeah, it means—"

"Forget it, I can imagine."

"It's all right, it means—"

"You made your point."

He grinned. "I wasn't being too oblique?"

"No, you weren't being too oblique."

The grin widened, for the most part his usual shit-eater but with some sympathy in it, too. I might have argued further, but what would have been the point? Like Kanezaki, he could think what he wanted.

What mattered at the moment was, he was armed—a Wilson Combat Supergrade Compact. I'd asked him how he'd managed to procure it so soon after arriving from Bali, and he'd smiled and told me only, "The old underground redneck railroad." It was comforting to know he had my back in the Beverly Wilshire now, amid the ambient music piped in from the high ceiling, the oblivious background chatter, the incongruous tinkling of quality silverware cutting fine food on high-end china.

Forty minutes after I'd been seated, I saw a black man come in through the restaurant entrance. Older than I remembered, of course, his head hairless now, the body thicker with age but obviously still powerful. He spoke briefly with a hostess, who gestured to where I was sitting and then led him over. I watched as they approached, noting that he was carrying what looked like a ballistic nylon computer case but that otherwise his hands were empty, and that the red, short-sleeved, collared shirt he wore, tucked into a pair of khaki trousers, would offer relatively poor opportunities for concealed carry. He was dressed to reassure me, but I'd still check his ankles and for any telltale irregularities in the fit of his clothes, and watch the entrances to see who came in behind him.

I stood as they came near and shook his hand when he offered it. When the hostess had moved off, he said, "John Rain. Goddamn, but I don't think you've changed a bit. What's your secret?"

"Avoiding trouble, mostly."

He laughed. "You're keeping busy, is what I hear."

"Not recently, no."

"Well, I hope we can change all that. Shame for a man like you to be idle."

We sat down and he placed the computer case on the table between us. He glanced around the restaurant, his gaze settling momentarily on Dox. He might have pretended not to recognize him, but because I assumed he had access to military photos, that would have put me on edge. So it was smart of him instead to say, "I imagine he's supposed to shoot me if things here go sideways."

I was glad he acknowledged it. If he'd invited Dox over, I would have had to spell things out. "Something like that."

"An understandable precaution. But I don't think it'll come to that. I left my men outside, and I myself am unarmed." He slid his seat back from the table and eased up his pants legs. Nothing but socks, from ankle to bulging calf. "Okay? I'm just here to talk."

It was bold of him to show up without protection, especially after losing two men in Tokyo. But I supposed he'd put himself in my position, and knew I wouldn't take a chance on killing him before at least learning more.

I was carrying a full spectrum portable bug detector in my pocket— all transmitter frequencies and mobile phone frequencies within five feet. It had been vibrating silently since his arrival.

"I need you to turn off your phone," I said. "And take out the battery." He could have called someone before arriving, someone who could be recording our conversation now. Or he could have the phone itself set to a dictation function. And if it wasn't a phone setting off the detector, it must have been a transmitter.

"Of course," he said. Because he didn't ask me to do the same, and because my phone was turned off, I assumed the detector he must have been carrying, which would have been set to ignore his own phone, was quiet. He took out his phone, powered it down, removed the battery, and placed the empty unit on the table. The vibrating in my pocket stopped.

He leaned forward and put his elbows on the table, his fingers laced together. "Well, you'll be unsurprised to learn it's about a job. One requiring your unique set of skills."

"I don't know what you mean."

"I think you do, but all right, I'll spell it out. That's why we're here, after all."

He ordered a full breakfast—a Blvd Omelet, with mushrooms and black truffles; orange juice; a pot of coffee. I wondered how much of it had to do with appetite, and how much to demonstrate how relaxed he was.

When the waiter had moved off, he said, "Does the name Tim Shorrock mean anything to you?"

The name was familiar, but for the moment, I couldn't place it. "Should it?"

He shrugged. "It depends on how closely you follow these things. He's not the most prominent player in the Beltway establishment, but he is the Director of the National Counterterrorism Center."

The information clicked with the name's familiarity, and I felt a small adrenaline surge as I realized what Horton wanted. Without even thinking, I shook my head and said, "No."

There was a pause. He said, "No, you don't want the job?"

"No one would want it. It's too difficult and it's too dangerous."

A detached part of my mind registered that I was objecting on practical grounds, not on principle. If I hadn't known better, I might have thought my response wasn't so much a refusal as it was a negotiating gambit.

"Look, we've both come all this way. If you're not in too much of a hurry, why don't you just hear me out?"

His point was completely reasonable. And yet I sensed danger within it. Why?

Because you're interested. Admit it. If you weren't, you wouldn't even have come.

No. I came to find out what this is about. Because forewarned is forearmed. Sound tactics, that's all.

The rejoinder felt weak. Kanezaki and Dox, always chuckling at me when I said I wanted out. Were they right? Did they know me better than I knew myself?

The waiter brought over Horton's beverages and departed. Horton stirred some cream into his coffee and said, "The National Counterterrorism Center focuses primarily on analysis and coordination, but Shorrock has been developing an ops capability. You see, prior to nine-eleven, al Qaeda wasn't able to recruit Muslim Americans, but that's changed."

"You're talking about the Fort Hood shootings?"

"And the attempted Northwest Air bombing, the attempted Times Square bombing, the planned D.C. Metro bombing, the planned Portland bombing... all the work of American Muslims."

I laughed. "You mean after a decade of two open wars, a dozen covert ones, predator strikes, torture, bomb, bomb, bomb Iran, hysteria about mosques... American Muslims are getting susceptible to calls for revenge? It's shocking."

He took a sip of coffee, then set the cup down. "I wish I could share your levity. But the problem is getting worse."

"What does this have to do with Shorrock?"

"His men are involved with several domestic cells. Theoretically,

Shorrock is supposed to penetrate a cell just deeply enough to gather evidence sufficient for criminal prosecution. In fact, he is now running these cells for real. You follow?"

"Shorrock's a secret radical?"

"Shorrock is planning a series of false flag attacks on America."

I didn't like where this was going. "Why?"

He looked at me. "To provide an emotional and political pretext for the suspension of the Constitution."

"You're talking about a coup," I said, my tone doubtful. "In America."

"A coup against the Constitution, yes. You don't think it can happen here? Do yourself a favor. Even if you don't want the job. Google COINTELPRO, or Operation Mockingbird, oh, and especially Operation Northwoods. You might also look into Operation Ajax, Operation Gladio, Operation Mongoose, and the so-called Strategy of Tension. And those are just the ones that have leaked. There are others. Unless you think the Reichstag Fire and the Gleiwitz incident and the Russian apartment bombings were unique to their respective times and places and could never happen elsewhere, least of all in America. But you don't strike me as that naïve."

"Was nine-eleven an inside job, too?"

"It wasn't, though the way it's been exploited, it might as well have been. But are you arguing that because not all cataclysms occur behind a false flag, that none of them do?"

The waiter brought over the omelet and Horton started in on it. I wondered how much of what he was telling me was true. And why, if it were true, I would even consider getting involved.

"You want some?" he said, chewing and gesturing to the omelet. "It's delicious."

"Why are you coming to me for this?"

He swallowed and nodded as though expecting the question. "The plotters are prominent individuals in politics, the military, corporations, and the media. They can't just be killed or otherwise obviously removed, or the factions they represent would sense a threat and retaliate. I need their misfortunes to look natural for as long as possible, so we can do maximum damage to the plot before opposition can coalesce."

I didn't care for his premature use of *we*. But natural would explain why he was interested in me. "What else?"

"Some of the targets have significant security details, meaning you'll need a team. That's where your man Dox comes in, along with my men, Larison and Treven. This job could actually stand for a larger detachment, but size entails risks, too. I think the four of you can manage."

"I don't buy it. You don't have the manpower in the ISA?"

"The manpower? Sure. The expertise? My friend, you're being too modest. There are people who say you pushed a man in front of a moving Tokyo train in such a manner that a dozen bystanders didn't see it, that even the security cameras didn't pick it up."

I didn't see any advantage to correcting him, but the target in question had actually committed suicide with no assistance from me, and I was as surprised as everyone else standing on the platform when it happened. But my employer at the time believed it had been my doing and was awed. Funny, how legends get started.

"What do you have on Treven and Larison?"

"That's between them and me."

"Are they even part of the ISA?"

"They're status is…"

"Deniable?"

"I suppose you could put it that way."

"I hear 'deniable' and think, 'hung out to dry if it comes to that.'"

He nodded. "Then don't let it come to that."

"And you want me to run this," I said. "Not one of your guys."

"That's right."

"Why?"

"You've got the most experience with this kind of thing. You know what you're doing, and the other men will respect you. Plus they're accustomed to following orders. You're not. No disrespect."

I looked at him, considering. He really thought I was going to do this.

"Plus," he said, "Larison, while a capable soldier, needs guidance."

I sensed beneath the simple sentence a great deal of meaning. "What kind of guidance?"

"Discipline, for one. He's like a gun—you want to make sure he's always pointed in the right direction."

"I don't follow you."

"Let's just say… he's a man who has too much to keep hidden. A man in turmoil."

First Larison, trying to show me there was distance between him and Horton. And now Horton, doing the same. I might have said something, but didn't want to give away to one the possible maneuvering of the other.

"Why are you telling me so much?" I asked.

"You wouldn't take the job if I didn't."

"I'm not taking the job either way."

I expected him to say, *Then why are you listening?* But he didn't. He'd know I'd be asking that question of myself, and answering it more convincingly than he could.

"Let me ask you something," he said. "What's been relentlessly drilled into the heads of the American citizenry since nine-eleven, and following every attack and attempted attack since then?"

I glanced over at the restaurant entrance. "I don't know. That they hate your freedoms, I guess."

"Close. That we have to give up our freedoms. Every time there's an attack or attempted attack, the government claims that to keep America safe, it needs more power and that the citizenry has to give up more freedom. Hell, by now, if the terrorists ever did hate us for our freedoms, they'd hate us a lot less. But they don't. They hate us more. Meanwhile, Americans are being taught that if their country is attacked, it's because they haven't given up enough freedom, and all they have to do is give up a little more. Some determined individuals have recognized the situation is ripe for exploitation, and they're on the verge of doing something about it."

We sat in silence for a few minutes while he worked on his omelet. Dox kept a watchful eye on us, his left hand resting on the table, his right out of view.

When the plates had been cleared and we were down to just coffee, I said, "Here's the problem. Let's say everything you've told me is true. You still couldn't pay me enough to take out the director of the National Counterterrorism Center."

I wondered why I was still acting as though we were negotiating, rather than just telling him outright I had no interest under any circumstances. Was I really considering this? I wondered again whether Dox and Kanezaki were right about me, whether all my protestations about wanting out of the life were bullshit. But then why would I have pushed Delilah so hard to leave?

Horton was looking at me—a little critically, I thought. "You don't care?" he said.

I shrugged. "It has nothing to do with me."

"Nothing to do with you? What's your country?"

"Are you talking about my passports?"

"I'm talking about your allegiances."

"I don't pledge allegiance to anyone who doesn't pledge it back."

"Let me ask you this, then. How many people have you killed?"

"More than I'll ever remember."

"Then what's one more?"

I looked at him. "If he's a threat? Nothing."

He nodded. "I understand. It's the same for me. I've taken a lot of lives, directly and indirectly, and some of them were under fairly questionable circumstances, I have to admit. One day, I believe I will have to face my maker and account for what I've done. Do you believe the same?"

I didn't answer. Somewhere in my mind, an image slipped past the guards. A boy in Manila, clinging to his mother's dress, crying for the father I'd taken from him. I remembered his voice, regressed, childlike. *Mama, Mama.* A voice I sometimes hear in my dreams.

"Occasionally I wonder," Horton said, "when that day comes, if it could help my case to be able to say, 'Yes, I've taken many lives. But look how many lives I've saved.' You ever wonder anything like that? You ever wonder if there's anything that could redeem men like us?"

Again, I said nothing. That single prison break from memory was emboldening others. Another boy, about my age at the time, supine on the steaming, pre-dawn river grass, whispering in a tongue I couldn't understand, tears rolling from his eyes as his life ebbed through a chest wound into the sodden ground beneath him. A wound I had delivered.

Enough. Enough.

"Here's the thing," Horton said. "If we don't stop this, in a few weeks' time you're going to turn on CNN and see video of the most horrific civilian carnage you can imagine. Rolling mass casualty attacks on the homeland calculated to cause maximum suffering and to achieve maximum media impact. You will watch those videos, and see the anguish of the survivors and listen to the bereavement of the families of the dead and you will know that it happened because you stood down. Because you could have done something about it but just didn't care to. And on the day you stand before your maker, as one day you will, you'll have to explain all that to him, explain to him and to the spirits of the slaughtered thousands how none of it was really your fault. You want that on your conscience? You want that on your soul?"

His delivery was strong, even impassioned, and I wondered what was feeding his fervor. His own sleepless nights, I decided. The wrong decisions he'd made, where he had pulled the trigger too quickly and shot an innocent, or held back too long and lost a friend. A mission he had missed. A wrong order he had issued. The deaths he had caused in trying to save lives.

A detached part of me was impressed at how effectively he'd made his case. He had at least three selling points he was prepared to use, and when each of the first two—loosely speaking, patriotism and "It's just one more"—failed to elicit a response, he smoothly abandoned it and continued his reconnaissance by fire. My determined silence in response to his third line of inquiry would have told him all he needed to know. Not the specifics—the fallout of having been raised a Catholic, the increasing weight of the life I've lived and the lives I've taken, my nebulous hopes for some means of atonement, maybe even redemption—but the general, and accurate sense that he'd hit a nerve.

I sighed and glanced at the computer case. "What's in there?"

"Particulars for Shorrock. Oh, and the fifty thousand we discussed. Yours, whatever you decide."

Smart. I've rarely been shorted on a financial arrangement. No one wants to needlessly antagonize someone like me.

"What are you offering for this suicide mission?"

"There's no reason it should involve suicide. Still, I'm offering one million dollars."

I didn't say anything. I had to admit, it was an attention-getting number.

"Divide it with your team any way you see fit," he said. "And don't tell me it's not enough. I know that game, and I respect you for playing it, but we both know that even if you decide to keep only a quarter for yourself, that's more than you've ever been paid for a single job in your life. The next one will pay even better, too, but this one is one million, no more."

I considered milking him for expenses, but decided there was no point. It was true, a quarter million for a hit was a huge premium, even factoring in the difficulty of the target.

"How are we supposed to get to someone like Shorrock?"

"I'd recommend this coming weekend, at the GovSec Expo in Las Vegas."

"GovSec?"

"Government Security Expo and Conference. Every homeland security, defense, law enforcement, and intelligence contractor in America, all under the roof of the Wynn convention center, jostling for a more favorable position at the government teat."

"What's Shorrock doing there?"

"Nominally, he's there to give the Saturday morning keynote. In fact, he's there to be wooed by the boards of a half dozen contractors who are trying to lure him away from government service into a seven-figure advisory position. Access like Shorrock's is worth more than a dozen lobbyists to these people. He'll be getting the royal treatment all weekend."

"You know how hard it would be to be to get close enough and alone enough to make something like this look natural, in a casino?"

"You'll have some special tools. Go ahead, take a look in the case."

I opened it. Inside were two Primatene asthma inhalers, held in place with Velcro straps.

"What are they?" I asked.

"The one with the red top is aerosolized hydrogen cyanide, three thousand parts per million."

I whistled softly. Three thousand ppm is about what's delivered in a gas chamber.

"That's right. You spray it in a man's mouth, or even just in his face, and he will be dead in under thirty seconds. But it dissipates extremely rapidly, and is—"

"Hard to detect, I know."

"Especially if you're not specifically looking for it. You'll want to hold your breath when you administer it and I'd advise that you not linger in the vicinity, either."

"Even so, three thousand ppm…"

"Yeah, it's dangerous stuff, true. But you see the vial with the blue top? That's the antidote, in case you accidentally inhale some yourself."

"Hydroxocobalamin? Sodium thiosulfate?"

"You know your compounds. It's both—they work best together. There are also hydroxocobalamin ampules in there, labeled adrenaline for bee stings in case anyone goes looking, and syringes. If you decide to go the cyanide route, and obviously it's up to you, I recommend you all dose yourselves beforehand, just in case."

"What else is in there?" I said, feeling myself getting sucked in, wondering why I wasn't trying harder not to.

"Everything you could reasonably need. Encrypted phones, miniature wireless audio and video, everything. You work with me, you don't need to spend time in a military surplus store. This is state of the art."

Maybe so. It would still all need to be examined for tracking devices.

I looked around the dining room. Waiters moved briskly from table to table, carrying trays of pastries and fresh-squeezed juice and omelets to order. The tourists munched on forkfuls of eggs Benedict, excited at how soon the Rodeo Drive boutiques would be opening for them. The movie industry types smiled vacuously as they did their deals, bleached teeth radiant against salon tans. Dox sat watchfully, still as a statue of Buddha.

I'd need to test the spray before we went live. I might have tried it on Horton then and there and let him take his chances with the antidote, but it would have caused too much of a commotion. Well, I'd think of something. As for injecting myself with the contents of a syringe Horton or anyone else provided me, the chances of that were about zero. Anyway, I wouldn't need to. There were commercial kits available.

I realized that, even with myself, I was raising only practical concerns. And neatly addressing them.

I asked myself what I was doing. I'd left Delilah because she wouldn't get out of the life. But it seemed that, if anything, the problem wasn't that I didn't want to be in the life. The problem was, I wanted it too much. I was like a recovering alcoholic, and being with Delilah was making me want to drink.

So what was the first thing I'd done after leaving her? It looked like I'd found myself a bar.

I looked over at Dox. Just a prearranged signal, and he'd put a bullet in Horton's head, then follow me out through the side entrance.

The problem was, I didn't know if that would be the end of trouble for me, or the beginning.

Or maybe that was a rationalization. I didn't know. Maybe Dox and Kanezaki were right about me.

I took a deep breath and slowly let it out. "I've only ever had two clients I found out were lying to me," I said. "You know what happened to them?"

"I can imagine," he said dryly.

"When I do a deal, the client's life is his collateral. You comfortable with that?"

"It's what I expected."

"No women or children. No non-principals. No B-teams."

"Understood."

"Have you told Treven and Larison how much you're paying?"

"No, I have not."

He probably thought I wanted to hold out on them. "Make sure you do," I said. "We're going to split this four ways even, and I don't want any confusion about the size of the pie."

He sipped his coffee. "I admire an honest man."

"Where are they now?"

He smiled just slightly. "Waiting for you. In Las Vegas."

chapter eight

I sat on one of the twin beds in a room at an off-strip Embassy Suites, Dox to my left, Larison and Treven facing us on the opposite bed. We would all check into the Wynn later that day, but once we were there, it would be better if we were seen together as little as possible. This would be our only chance to discuss Shorrock face-to-face.

It was strange to be in charge of the op. I prefer to be in charge of nothing larger than myself, and though I supposed that several years and multiple close calls of teaming with Dox and sometimes Delilah constituted a kind of practice, managing Larison and Treven was going to be a challenge. Neither struck me as a natural team player, and I imagined each was accustomed to long stretches alone in the field and to doing things his own way. Also, because I knew Horton had something on each of them, though I didn't know what, it meant that in addition to whatever innate alpha male stubbornness I might encounter in taking charge of things, I also had to remember that their agendas might range considerably beyond the money the op represented.

But Horton was right—I needed four at least, and even so it wasn't going to be easy. We knew Shorrock would be staying at the Wynn, but that was about all. We didn't know what room he'd be in, and, outside the keynote, we had no details about his schedule. Given the size of the resort, without more it would take a lot of luck to find and fix him, let alone make him expire of "natural causes." Nonetheless, I had an idea for how we might close to him, and I might have proposed it directly. But I decided it would be better to solicit opinions. I had no command authority over these people, and I sensed things would go more smoothly if I helped them reach their own conclusions, rather than presenting them with mine. So I asked Treven and Larison what they thought.

"The keynote," Treven said immediately. "Cover the exits, follow him when he's done, rotate the point, wait for the opportunity."

It was the response I was expecting from Treven, who struck me as a little more eager and a little less devious than Larison, and I didn't like it. "The keynote's tempting because it's our only real fixed point," I said. "But that's also the problem. Most likely he'll be surrounded by hangers-on before and after. And worse, because it's on his public schedule and therefore an obvious vulnerability, his security detail will be alert and keeping very close. It couldn't hurt to try, especially if we find we can't pick him up any other way, but I don't think it's our first choice."

"Then what?" Treven said.

I rubbed my chin as though thinking. "The file says he's a fitness fanatic," I said. "I wonder if there's something we could do with that."

"You think the gym?" Treven said.

I nodded slowly as though favorably considering his idea. "Maybe. Yeah, maybe." I turned to Dox. "What do you think?"

A dog was barking outside, the sound high-pitched and screechy, probably a small breed and apparently an exceptionally neurotic one. It had been going off intermittently since we'd checked in and its fingers-on-a-blackboard pitch made it hard to tune out. Dox got up, opened the drapes a crack, and looked down. "Wish that mutt would simmer down," he said. "Looks like somebody tied it up by the pool. Nobody's even there, what the hell's it yapping at? Lucky for it I don't have my rifle."

When Dox was engaged—on what he was watching through his sniper scope, for example—his focus was supernatural. But when he wasn't all the way on, he tended to be all the way off. "What do you think?" I said again, drawing on the patience our partnership required.

Dox let the drapes fall closed and sat back down on the bed. "Shoot, partner, you know I do my best work outdoors. I defer to you on this kind of situation. Main thing, it seems to me, is that we get him alone and away from all the cameras for a minute. Could be that means something with the gym. Or maybe a lavatory. Figure he'll be drinking a lot of coffee, or green tea if he's a health nut, he'll have to hit the head at some point. Follow him in, spray him in the face, head back to L.A. for a beer."

"We'll need to test the cyanide first," Larison said. "And assuming it works as advertised, pick up a commercial antagonist. No telling what Hort has in that 'antidote.'"

At some point, when the moment was right, I'd press him on what was up between Horton and him. But not now. "How do you see it?" I said, looking at him. "The keynote, or the gym?"

Larison smiled, and I wondered if he knew what I was doing. "I think we can exploit the gym," he said.

"I'm not saying we can't," Treven said quickly. "But it'll take some luck. The file says he's into CrossFit. Well, I do some CrossFit WODs myself, and you'd have a hard time predicting on any given day whether you'll find me in the gym or out on the road. So for all we know, Shorrock could decide the hell with the gym, I'll go for a run and see the sights."

"Wads?" I asked, not revealing that I was pleased by his objections.

"Workout Of the Day," Dox and Larison answered simultaneously.

I mentally corrected to WOD. "Am I the only guy who's not doing this CrossFit stuff?"

"You do it already," Dox said. "You just don't know the name."

"Well," I said, "whatever Shorrock does, let's take the potential obstacles one-by-one and see if the workout intel could be useful. First, how likely is it he'll go for a run?"

Dox tugged on his goatee. "Hundred degree heat, hordes of tourists to dodge? Plus I guarantee the gym at the Wynn is fancy, and there'll be ladies in spandex. Who'd want to miss that? So I'd bet against a run."

As was often the case, I wouldn't have put it the way Dox did, but I couldn't disagree with his logic.

"All right," Treven said, holding up a hand in a *maybe so, but...* gesture. "Let's assume he'll be at the gym at some point. It's still a huge window. A real CrossFit guy would get up extra early if necessary to squeeze in a WOD before a full day of meetings. Or he might skip lunch to get one in, or maybe right before bedtime."

The dog barked again. Dox said, "Christ almighty. That is the worst bark I've ever had to endure. Sounds like someone's giving the damn thing an electrified enema."

I tried not to picture it. Which of course just made it worse.

"You're right," I said, looking at Treven. "Still, if there were a way we could catch him at the gym, it could really put us in business. It's not on his schedule, so not a hot spot from the perspective of his security detail. In fact, if one of us could be in there when he arrived, we'd likely be overlooked. He's supposed to have two Secret Service bodyguards, right? That's not a full detail. If it were the president, they'd have a full team to clear every room ahead of time, whether he was announced or not. But with just two, they'll be focused more on anyone trying to follow Shorrock than they will be on people who are already in a place he randomly decides to visit."

There was quiet for a moment. Treven said, "Well, we could try rotating through the gym. We're all in shape, so to anyone else in the gym, the staff or whoever, a ninety-minute workout wouldn't seem unusual, and probably each of us could kill a good amount of time showering or using the sauna or whatever in the locker room before and after. If we rotate through one at a time, two hours each, that's an eight-hour window we'd have covered. Still fifty-fifty in a sixteen-hour day, but not bad, either."

I nodded, pleased. I had the same idea, of course, but by expressing it as a vague wish, I'd let Treven turn it into a plan he could now feel was his own.

"It's an interesting suggestion," I said. "And now that you mention it, I think we might do even better. We don't need wall-to-wall coverage, do we? Figure Shorrock will work out for at least an hour. If he's not there when the first of us is ready to leave, the next person could show up, say, thirty minutes later and still easily overlap with Shorrock. That means we're up to almost ten hours of coverage. And I'm betting he's more likely to show up early than late. The part of his day that'll be easiest to manage is the part before the meetings. Plus, the main reason he's out here is to be wined and dined. That would all happen at night. So if we play it right, we're actually doing significantly better than fifty-fifty."

Dox drummed his hands on his belly. "Not bad odds, for Vegas. And there's one other possibility, though I'd call it a long shot given the Sin City venue and all that. The file says he's a church-going man. Every Sunday."

"What are you thinking?" I asked.

He shrugged. "Well, he's scheduled to leave on Sunday. Maybe a pious man would stop at a local house of worship on his way out of town. By the time his flight gets to the East Coast, with the three-hour time difference, he'd be too late for anything back home."

I nodded. "Agreed, a long shot, and hard to know where he'd be going ahead of time, assuming he goes at all."

"Yeah, you're probably right. Though how many churches could there be in Las Vegas?"

"Hundreds," I said. "If you want to make money in hospitals, you build where people are sick."

Larison said, "I like the gym. We can rotate like Treven said, with thirty-minute intervals in between to extend our coverage. Whichever one of us sees him in there can alert the others. They have extensive spa facilities, and if he uses any of it—toilet, shower, steam room, hot tub, sauna—we'll only need him alone for a second. Sauna or toilet would be perfect, in fact. Easily explained as a heart attack with the first, embolism with the second."

I nodded thoughtfully, again trying to convey that these were persuasive points I hadn't fully considered myself.

"Doing a man in the steam room," Dox said. "When you say it like that, it sounds dirty."

I didn't bother pointing out that no one else *had* said it like that.

Treven said, "The gym makes sense."

The dog barked again. Dox winced and said, "Car alarms, people who yell on cell phones in public, and people who don't bring their yapping dogs inside. And people who put their seats all the way back in coach, while we're on the subject. I swear, there's no more civility in the world. Listen, I'm gonna grab a soda from the machine. Anyone want anything?"

The others shook their heads. Dox stepped out.

We talked more about how to approach Shorrock, what we'd do if he showed up in the gym, what we'd do if he didn't. I noted Dox had been gone a little longer than a trip to the vending machine would have warranted, and wondered if maybe he'd felt an uncharacteristic need for some privacy and had actually gone out to use a restroom in the lobby.

"What about reconnaissance?" Treven asked. "We need to walk the resort to get the layout and nail down details. We can't do it together, obviously, but we'll be conspicuous as singletons wandering the casino. It's strange behavior, and staff monitoring the cameras might pick up on it."

No one responded right away, and in the silence, I realized the dog had finally stopped yapping. It was a relief.

"That's a good point," I said. "What I usually do in a situation like this is get an escort. They don't care what you do or what you talk about as long as they're being paid, and if they notice you watching your back or doing anything tactical, they usually attribute it to the fact that you're married and afraid of being seen."

"Works for me," Treven said. "I've done it myself."

Larison nodded. "It's a good idea."

There was the sound of a keycard sliding into the door lock, and a moment later Dox walked in. He was grinning.

"Well, the cyanide works," he said, holding up the canister.

For an instant, I couldn't figure out what he was talking about. Then it hit me. I said, "You didn't."

Dox nodded. "I did. If I had to listen to that thing for one more minute, I was going postal, I swear. This way, it was two birds with one stone. The cyanide works, and we get to enjoy the sounds of silence."

I shook my head and sighed, thinking I should have seen it coming.

"Oh, come on," Dox said. "Tell me you didn't think of it yourself."

Treven said, "I wish I had."

We all laughed at that, and maybe the laughter was good. Nothing brought a team together better than shared laughter—well, shared fighting, maybe, but bar fights were a younger man's game, and anyway we couldn't afford the attention. But the momentary sense of camaraderie struck me as likely to be just that: momentary. Nothing more than a lull, a veneer temporarily obscuring differences that might soon impel each of us to very different sides of a board, the contours of which I sensed but couldn't yet discern.

chapter
nine

Treven benchpressed a hundred eighty pounds at a dead weight station in the spacious Wynn fitness center, taking his time, going easy. He could have put another hundred on the bar, but that kind of weight would have been conspicuous, and besides, he was only here in case Shorrock showed up, not for a real workout. Shorrock was scheduled to check in that day, with the keynote tomorrow, and though check-in was at three, it wasn't inconceivable he'd arrive earlier. So Treven had started in at the gym at noon, doing nothing other than the length of his workout to distinguish himself from the other guests who'd been coming and going. It had been nearly two hours already, and no sign of Shorrock. It was about time for him to move on and let Dox, who was on deck, take over. It was silly, but he'd been hoping he'd be the one to make the initial contact. He wasn't used to feeling like the junior member of a team, and although it embarrassed him to admit it, he wanted a chance to prove himself.

They'd been here for three days now, and knew the public layout of the hotel well enough to be employees. They'd been over every inch of the property—every bar, every restaurant, every club, every store, every men's room. The parking garages, the pools, the perimeter. Everything. They were as ready as they could be on short notice and given the other constraints they were operating under. All they needed now was a little break, something they could leverage into something bigger.

He set the bar back on the rack and walked over to the mats to stretch. He hoped he was doing the right thing, taking out Shorrock. He'd always been fine knowing the military would disown him if he ever blew an op, but at least he'd always been able to comfortably assume his actions had been sanctioned by the proper chain of command. This one was different. The president had an assassination list, true—in fact, its existence had recently leaked, along with the fact that among its targets were American citizens. None of which was news to anyone in the ISA, but it wasn't like the president had called him personally. Treven didn't know where Hort's orders had come from, or whether there had been orders at all. But what was he supposed to do? The kind of shit the military used him for was so deniable he hadn't received written orders in longer than he could remember. If he'd asked Hort for something in writing now, Hort probably would have referred him for a psych evaluation.

He rotated his neck, cracking the joints, and started doing some yoga stretches. It was a tricky situation. On the one hand, Hort had repeatedly proven himself manipulative and worse. On the other hand, if what he claimed about Shorrock was true, that he was planning domestic mass casualty attacks, taking the man out could save thousands of American lives.

But was that really the reason he was here? He'd never been so confused about his own motivations… hell, he'd never been confused at all. The deal had always been simple: a photograph; a file; intelligence on who, what, and where. How was always up to him. Why was never even a consideration. Now, everything was different. Maybe it was all a natural transition. Maybe before he'd been nothing but a tool, albeit a sharp one, and now he was waking up to the way real hitters played the game. Yeah, maybe. That's what Hort had told him, anyway—that he was beginning to understand the way the world really worked, that he was on his way to being a player in his own right.

He was afraid of those security tapes, he had to admit. The way Hort had presented it, it was the CIA that had the tapes—the deputy director, a guy named Stephen Clements, specifically—and Hort was leaning on Clements to keep the tapes under wraps. But Treven wondered. Isn't that exactly how an operator like Hort would position this kind of leverage? *Someone else is trying to extort you, and I'm your best friend who's stopping him.* How could he ever really know? If he stepped out of line, he could easily find himself arrested and charged with murder. Regardless of the truth of it all, Hort would just tell him he was sorry, he'd done all he could to prevent it from happening.

He knew he couldn't live this way forever. At some point, he would have to go after Clements, and probably Hort, too. That, or just tell them all to fuck off and take his chances. He wondered if the real reason he'd accepted Hort's orders this time was just to defer that day of reckoning.

Or was it something else? Having learned through multiple near-death experiences just how much of the noble-sounding king and country rhetoric was bullshit designed to fool the impressionable and empower the corrupt, was it possible he still craved being on the inside so much he was pretending not to know better? When he put it that way, it felt pathetic, but the notion of abandoning the military—abandoning the ISA—was horrible. Just imagining it made him feel anxious to the point of panic. What would he do? Who would he be?

He blew out a long breath and popped up on his palms in upward facing dog, his pelvis on the floor, his back arched. He liked the yoga. He found he didn't bounce back quite as quickly as he had in his football and wrestling days, and that the esoteric stretches seemed to help.

One of the attendants walked over, an attractive brunette wearing a spa uniform with a nametag reading *Alisa*. Treven had noticed her watching him earlier and wondered if she was interested. Apparently that would be a yes.

"I didn't figure you for a yoga aficionado," she said.

"I don't know about aficionado," Treven said, coming to his feet. "But I like the stretches."

"It's smart. A lot of guys who are into weights don't stretch enough."

"Do you teach this stuff?"

"Personal trainer. I don't think you need it, though. I was watching you, you know what you're doing."

She was certainly easy on the eyes, and any other time, he would have been happy to follow wherever this led. But not today.

"Well, I better wrap it up," he said. "You can only do so much yoga in a day."

She smiled, just a hint of *Oh, well* in the way her eyes lingered on his. "Can I bring you anything? A towel, water…?"

"No, I'm good. Thanks for asking."

"Okay, then." She held his gaze for another instant, then turned to head back to the front of the room. Treven was about to follow her when a muscular, crew-cut guy in a dark suit came in. Treven made him instantly as a bodyguard—the build, the watchful presence, and no way was the guy here for a workout wearing a suit.

"Oh, one thing," Treven said to Alisa, who turned back to face him. "The spa. There's a steam room in there, right?"

He was stalling for time, wanting to see what the bodyguard did and who might come in behind him. It wasn't necessarily going to be Shorrock. The Wynn did a lot of business with VIPs. Whoever it might be, he knew he'd look less noteworthy chatting up one of the attendants than he would on his own.

"There is," Alisa said. "The steam is infused with Eucalyptus, so it'll really clear out your pores and open up your sinuses."

"I'll have to give it a try. I don't think I've ever had a Eucalyptus steam bath before."

She smiled. "You'll like it. I use the women's every day I'm here."

Treven tracked the bodyguard in his peripheral vision. The man scoped the room, but not carefully. Treven had the sense he was only confirming there was no other way in or out. And why be more thorough than that? Shorrock was important, true, but it wasn't as though he was the president. And like Rain had said, if Shorrock was doing something unscheduled, the security detail would be more focused on someone following him than they would be on people who were already there.

"Every day?" Treven said. "You must have the cleanest pores in Vegas."

Alisa laughed. "I don't know about that, but it's definitely good for your skin."

The bodyguard walked back to the glass doors and held one open, and *bam*, in walked Shorrock. Treven felt his heart rate kick up a notch. Son of a bitch, they had him.

"I'll tell you," Treven said, keeping Shorrock in his peripheral vision, "I've always been jealous of people who get to work out for a living."

"You look like you're doing okay," Alisa said, glancing down at his torso. "What are you in town for?"

The guard, he noted, hadn't come back in. Shorrock was heading for the back of the room, where the free weights were.

"Just a reunion with some friends," Treven said. She'd pinged him with that glance and the question about his plans. If he pinged back, she'd escalate. "Play some poker, maybe see that Cirque de Soleil show."

She nodded, noting, no doubt, that this was the second time he'd failed to return a volley. "Enjoy," she said. But then, keeping the door open: "And let me know how that steam bath goes."

He smiled. "I will."

He knew it would look odd if he stuck around much longer, but he thought he could afford to take just a few minutes more and see if he could pick up anything operational.

He walked to the water cooler and filled a cup, then strolled over to the front of the room to grab a towel. Through the glass he could see the bodyguard, pacing slowly in front of the salon, which put him between the elevators and the entrances to the gym and the spa. Yeah, the guy wasn't worried about people who were in the gym already, but he might key on new arrivals. Treven thought Dox should hold off, that it was time to send in Rain. Rain was the only one of them whose size wasn't itself conspicuous, plus he was Asian, or Asian-looking, anyway, which likely put him generally outside the kind of profiling Shorrock's bodyguards would be doing. And beyond that, there was something about Rain's demeanor that made him easy to overlook. There was a stillness about him when he was in public that might initially be mistaken for blandness, or even timidity. It was the mistake the contractors had made, and Treven would never forget the way the average-sized, meek-seeming Japanese guy he had assumed Rain to be had suddenly decloaked and dropped the two much larger men with his bare hands before anybody could even get there to stop it.

Besides, they'd agreed Rain would do the actual hit. He had the most esoteric experience—the rest of them were strictly firearms guys. In fact, of all the men Treven had killed, more than he could remember in combat, assassinations, and self-defense, he couldn't think of a time he'd used anything other than a gun. Not that it would be so terribly complicated to spray someone in the face with cyanide, but on the other hand aerosolized cyanide was dangerous shit, and in an op anything could go wrong. The surest, and safest, way to deliver the dose would be directly into the target's open mouth, and if there was anyone who could get close enough to make that happen, he guessed it was Rain.

He walked back to the free weights area. Shorrock, a wiry guy of about fifty wearing Under Armour shorts and a tee shirt, was doing pushups, his movements crisp and efficient. He had an iPod Shuffle strapped to his arm. Treven noticed he'd set down an aluminum water bottle at the base of the dumbbell rack, probably filled with some sports drink. The guy looked at home in the gym. Treven started to turn away, then noticed something on the carpet next to the water bottle. Son of a bitch, it was a keycard, in the hotel's signature flaming red.

His mind raced through the implications. They'd expected Shorrock to take a locker in the spa. Obviously he hadn't—maybe because he didn't have time, maybe because Eucalyptus steam baths weren't his thing. He'd come straight to the fitness center, after which, presumably, he'd be heading straight back to his room.

Was there a way to get the room number? There was a sign-in sheet at the desk outside. To use the gym, Treven had needed to write down his name and room number. The people at the desk then checked the computer to confirm he was a registered guest. Presumably, Shorrock had filled out the form, too. Maybe the bodyguards had told him not to, but Treven doubted it. Their security posture seemed pretty relaxed. It was a Las Vegas casino, after all—what could possibly happen?

He stood behind the massive pillar in the center of the room so the bodyguard outside couldn't see him if he looked in, and glanced around to confirm no one was within earshot. The place was huge and the closest people were on the treadmills and exercise bikes, a good fifteen feet away. The whirring of the machines was audible from where he stood.

He pulled his cell phone from his shorts pocket and called Rain. "He's here," he said quietly.

There was a brief pause. Rain said, "Okay. I know you can't plausibly stick around much longer. We'll rotate my partner in and I'll head to the spa to wait."

"No, the spa's no good. I'm pretty sure he's not using it. He set his keycard down on the floor right here, so I'm guessing he never got a locker."

"His keycard?"

Treven moved from one side of the pillar to the other to ensure no one had approached. "Yeah, we're thinking the same thing. I'll check the sign-in sheet at the desk and see if I can learn his room number. You send your partner down to the spa—have him tell the desk he's just checking it out to see if he wants to spend the forty bucks. There's a bodyguard outside but I don't think he'll care about your partner if he's heading into the spa instead of the gym. I'll swap our friend's card for mine—"

"Don't forget, the Wynn stamps guest names on the cards. They're not just keys, they're like credit cards for the resort."

"He'd have to look awfully closely to notice that—he's just going to see his red plastic keycard where he left it, not the little gold lettering on the bottom."

"You're right. Keep going."

"I'll head to the spa like I need to hit the head, and hand off the key to your partner. He lets you into our friend's room, then heads back to the spa on some pretext, gives me back the key, and I swap it back. You take care of business in the room, perfect privacy, and we're done."

"The room's too risky. Security detail might routinely check it just before our friend goes in."

"Fuck, that's true."

"Plus these keys are smart cards. They can be programmed to log the times they're used. No way to know whether the Wynn does that, but if they do, and someone were to check, it would look strange for the key to have been used to access his room while he was signed in at the gym."

"Then why not take the key off him when the job's done and disappear it? Keys get lost all the time, who knows where it's gone. Anyway, no key, no evidence."

Silence for a moment. Then Rain said, "That's true. Still, if I let myself in and a bodyguard shows up for a sweep, the whole op is blown. But now that you've got me thinking, the key's still useful. Do what you said. Call me if you can get the room number. If you can, I'll call it from a hotel phone. If no one answers, I'll take a chance on going in, plant one of the wireless cameras, and get out."

"So we can know when he's coming and going and then pick him up by the elevators."

"Exactly. And maybe overhear something about his schedule, too. Better to anticipate him than follow him. I'll let the others know what's going on."

"Understood. Okay, let me see what I can do here. I'll call you back."

He clicked off and put the phone back in his pocket. Shorrock had switched to sit-ups, twisting alternately left and right at the apex of each rep. Looked like a warm-up routine of bodyweight calisthenics. Treven took out his room card and undid the Traser watch he was wearing. He walked over to the dumbbell rack, squatted as though to select the one he wanted, and dropped the watch next to the base of the rack. As Shorrock came up, twisting to his left and away from Treven's position, Treven hefted a dumbbell with his right hand and smoothly swapped the keycards with his left. He moved a few paces away, used the dumbbell to do a tricep stretch for a few moments, then set the weight back in its place and headed out.

The bodyguard was still pacing by the salon and paid Treven no particular notice. Why would he? Treven had come from the gym. The guard had already classified him as harmless. Mistake.

He stopped at the sign-in desk. There was another pretty woman stationed there, a new one whose nametag read Victoria, not the woman who'd signed him in two hours earlier. "Hi," he said. "I'm going to use the spa now, but if I want to come back later, am I still covered?"

"Absolutely, sir," Victoria said. "Spa privileges are always applicable for the whole day you've paid for them, or else they're already included in your resort package. But you're good either way."

"Terrific," Treven said. He glanced down at the sign-in sheet. The last entry read, *Shorrock*. And under room number, *5818*. "Do I have to sign in again?"

"No, sir, you're fine. Enjoy the facilities. Joshua inside will give you a tour, if you like."

Treven thanked her and went in. The place was huge and absurdly deluxe—half locker room, half gentleman's club, all leather and granite and inlaid mosaic tile—and he couldn't imagine what it must have cost. An attendant—Joshua, from the nametag—came over and asked him if he needed anything, a tour, instructions, recommendations. Treven told him he was fine and the man moved discreetly off.

Treven took out the phone, sat in one of the overstuffed leather chairs, and called Rain. "Got the key," he said quietly. "Room 5818. Repeat: 5818. I'm in the spa."

"Good. My partner's on the way."

Treven clicked off and tried to look like he was relaxing. Three minutes later, Dox walked in. "Hot damn," he exclaimed, the hick accent especially thick. "Have you ever seen anything like this? I swear, I love Las Vegas!"

Treven winced inside. There was something to be said for hiding in plain sight, but Dox was pushing it.

Joshua walked over. "Would you like a tour of the facilities, sir?"

"It's good of you to offer, son," Dox said, "but I'm already a believer. Wondered whether a glorified locker room would be worth forty dollars, but you've set my mind at ease. Just going to take a little look around so I can see what I'll be coming back to."

"Very good," Joshua said. "If you need anything at all, please just ask."

"Well," Dox said, "now that you ask, you got anything to drink?"

"Cucumber infused water? Or citrus infused?"

"Oooh, a cucumber infusion. That sounds nice. I'd like to try one, if you don't mind."

Joshua walked over to a crystal cooler filled with water, ice, and cucumber slices, and began filling a glass. Treven got up and walked past Dox, palming him the keycard without looking at him as he went by. He went inside one of the toilet stalls, from which he heard Dox say with theatrical satisfaction, "I swear, that is refreshing and delicious. You're a good man, Mister Joshua, and I'll be back in a little while for sure. Going to be the best forty dollars I've ever spent."

Treven used the toilet, then got himself a cucumber infusion and returned to the leather chair, where he leafed through a hotel magazine. A soft-looking guy in a plush hotel robe, his face red and dripping with sweat, presumably from the eucalyptus steam room, came from around the corner and sat nearby. Too bad. Well, they couldn't expect to have the area to themselves. They'd been pretty lucky already.

Less than ten minutes later, Dox was back. He started to head toward Treven, then saw the guy in the robe. He stopped and called out,

"Mister Joshua, I forgot to ask you. Will I need bathing attire to enjoy the hot tub? Or is a more natural state of affairs permissible at this facility?"

Joshua appeared from around the corner. "Uh, it's, whatever you're comfortable with, sir," he stammered.

"Well, I'm comfortable with just about anything myself. It's anyone else I don't want to make uncomfortable. Some people, you know, they don't like the sight of the naughty bits." He smiled at the guy in the robe as though he might be a prime example.

In spite of the tension, or actually because of it, Treven had to suppress a laugh. Joshua said, "Really, sir, it's entirely up to you."

Dox beamed. "Thank you again, Mister Joshua. I'll just help myself to another cucumber infusion and be on my way. Sorry for distracting you from your duties."

"No distraction at all, sir," Joshua said. "If you need anything else, please just let me know."

Joshua disappeared around the corner again. Dox picked up one of the hotel magazines. "The Robb Report," he said, flipping through it. "Lifestyles of the rich and famous. Look at this, a new Veyron Super Sport for two point four million dollars. Yeah, the old model just wasn't doing it for me anymore. Maybe I'll order one, if things go well at blackjack tonight." He set the magazine down and walked off.

The guy in the robe started to get up. "There's a new Veyron?" he said.

Treven was out of his seat so fast he might have been a Veyron himself. "Wow, I need to see that," he said, snatching up the magazine. He held it in one palm and it opened naturally to the page where Dox had wedged Shorrock's room key.

"Jeez," the guy in the robe said. "You going to buy one right now?"

Treven palmed the key and made an expression of chagrin. "You're right," he said, "that was rude." He held out the magazine.

"No, that's okay," the guy said. "I can wait."

Treven glanced at his wrist. "Oh, shit, I left my watch in the gym. No, take it, I shouldn't have grabbed it like that and anyway, I need to get my watch." He handed it over and headed back to the gym, wondering if Dox was as dumb as he seemed. He was starting to think maybe not.

He walked past the bodyguard, who glanced at him without interest, and into the gym. Alisa saw him and said, "Did you forget something?"

"I did, actually. My watch. Did anyone turn one in?"

"Uh, no, I don't think so. Where did you leave it?"

"Back by the dumbbells. I'll take a look."

He started to head back. Shorrock was gone. So was the water bottle. So was the keycard.

Shit, shit, shit...

He glanced around wildly, momentarily forgetting himself. Shorrock was on an elliptical machine. He'd been obscured by one of the pillars. Okay, okay. The water bottle and keycard were on the floor next to him—he must have been in the habit of taking his things with him as he moved from station to station. And he obviously hadn't noticed the card wasn't his. The problem was, the card was now on the floor right next to him, and the glass wall he was facing was reflecting like a mirror because the corridor outside it was lit less brightly than the gym itself. And unlike before, when he was twisting from side to side as he did sit-ups, the elliptical machine had him facing unwaveringly ahead into the mirrored glass.

He had to swap the keys back. If Shorrock made it back to his room with the wrong key, he'd know somebody had switched them. The security detail seemed relatively relaxed, but this would be a giant red flag. They wouldn't leave Shorrock alone for a minute, not to mention all the attention that would be focused on the guy whose key Shorrock had wound up with.

He remembered why he was ostensibly in here, and walked over to the dumbbell rack. Alisa came up alongside him. "Left side or the right side?" she said.

Shit, this was getting more complicated. "Left side," he said.

She knelt down. An idea came to him. He squatted down next to her and pulled the laces loose on one of his sneakers.

"There it is," she said. "You're in luck." She reached back and retrieved it, then stood and handed it to Treven.

He smiled. "Nothing like a little luck in Vegas."

They started heading back to the front, passing the elliptical machines. Alisa said, "So, are you going to try the—"

Treven tripped. He let the watch go flying and arrested his fall by placing his hand on the floor right next to Shorrock's key. Alisa lunged for the watch. She missed it, but her attention had been drawn long enough for Treven to make the switch. He was betting Shorrock's gaze had followed her lateral movement rather than his downward one, but even if not, he'd look down and see his card and water bottle exactly as he'd left them.

"Shit," Treven said, straightening up. "That's embarrassing."

Alisa picked up the watch, glanced at it, and gave it back to him. "Looks like it's okay."

Treven looked at it and nodded. "These are good watches."

She looked down at his feet and smiled. "You better tie that lace."

He bent and took care of it and they headed back to the front. "Okay," he said, "this time I'm trying the steam room. I'll be safer in my bare feet."

"Let me know how it goes," she said, giving him another smile.

He headed back into the spa and called Rain. "We're good. Cards are switched back. Our friend is still at it. He'll probably be an hour or so. You should head down here to the spa in case he pops in to use a toilet. Other than that, though, I don't think he's coming."

"It's okay," Rain said. "The camera's in place. That'll be a huge help. If we can't get to him in the spa, we'll get another chance."

Treven hoped he was right. But two near things in a row—the magazine, then Shorrock moving the key—had him on edge. Both had been saved by luck. It was hard to imagine they'd be that lucky a third time.

chapter
ten

Getting a camera into Shorrock's room was a lucky break, but we still had to exploit it. Overall, though, the signs were good. We had him on audio, discussing his plans for the evening: dinner at the Michelin-starred French restaurant Alex at seven; drinks at the nightclub Tryst at ten; the casino floor for gambling, or "gaming," as the industry marketeers insist on prettifying it, before and after. I thought there was a decent chance we could wrap the whole thing up that night.

Larison and I, each accompanied by an interchangeable platinum blonde Las Vegas escort, managed to get tables at Alex, and even better, Larison had line-of-sight to the private dining room where Shorrock was being entertained. Halfway through the long meal, I felt my mobile phone vibrate in my pocket—the signal from Larison that Shorrock was heading toward the restroom. I excused myself quickly and got there ahead of him, just as we'd planned. It was empty, even the stall doors all slightly ajar. My heart kicked up a notch. This was it.

I stood at the urinal on the far right as though taking a leisurely piss and waited. A moment later, I heard the door open behind me. I concentrated on listening and resisted the urge to glance back. Footsteps, coming closer. And suddenly there he was, walking up to the urinal on the far left, obeying the unspoken men's room etiquette that you leave as much space between you and the other guy as the arrangement of urinals will allow.

Larison would have signaled Dox by now, who would be waiting just outside the restaurant so I could duck out and hand off the cyanide canister when it was done. There was only a remote chance that anyone in the restaurant might immediately fall under suspicion, but I didn't want to be holding the murder weapon if it happened.

I glanced over and saw Shorrock was swaying slightly, his face flushed from alcohol. My phone buzzed in my pocket—Larison again, the signal for someone else on the way. But damn it, I only needed a second. I dropped my hand into my pants pocket, gripped the canister, and started to pull it out. Just as it started to clear my pocket and in the instant before I turned and advanced on Shorrock, I heard the door open again. I froze and let the canister drop back. Footsteps, and then another patron was standing between Shorrock and me, unzipping his pants.

"Hey, Tim," the guy said. "How are you enjoying the meal?"

"Unreal," Shorrock said. "I can't believe there are still three more courses. I'm stuffed."

"Trust me, you have to save room for the poached apple cream puff. You'll die."

I ignored the irony and kept my eyes fixed on the marble wall in front of me, hoping unrealistically that Shorrock would be so overloaded with wine that he'd piss long enough for the other guy to depart first. But it wasn't to be. Shorrock shook off, zipped up, and headed over to the sink. I heard water running for a moment, then heard him say, "See you in a minute." And then he was gone, the opportunity gone with him.

I didn't give up hope. It was a safe bet the industry executives who were wooing Shorrock had bought him not just the chef's tasting menu, but also the accompanying wine course—a wine course that would result in frequent additional trips to the rest room. And it did—once more at Alex, and twice afterward, at the nightclub, Tryst. But every time, the restroom was occupied afterward: by another diner at Alex; by a washroom attendant at Tryst.

After Tryst we improvised, trailing Shorrock and his party onto the casino floor, keeping Dox at a slot machine where he could watch Shorrock play blackjack and signal me the moment Shorrock excused himself for what looked like a bathroom break. Everything went smoothly, better than I would have reasonably expected, in fact—other than that I couldn't get him alone.

What was doubly frustrating was that even though we knew the room he was staying in, we couldn't get to him there. The two Secret

Service guys had been keeping a fairly low profile, maybe because Shorrock wasn't in the same league as, say, the secretary of defense, maybe because they were relying in part on the hotel's own extensive security systems, maybe because Shorrock preferred his security detail to give him room to breathe. Whatever it was, one of them always stood guard outside Shorrock's room when Shorrock was in it, as I'd confirmed via a discreet trip to the 58th floor, aided by a dental mirror, the day before. We could fix him in the room, but we couldn't finish him there. It would have to be somewhere else.

The next day was the same. Shorrock used the gym in the morning, but not the spa, not even for a toilet break. The lunchtime keynote was a no-go because of the likely security posture. Then there was Shanghai cuisine at Wing Lei restaurant for dinner; a head-splitting mix from a DJ called Pizzo at XS nightclub; and more blackjack, this time with Treven watching from a slot machine. Five restroom visits overall, not one of them offering a moment alone.

At just before one in the morning, Treven called and told me Shorrock's party was breaking up. He was heading toward his room, flanked by the bodyguards, and there was nothing more to be done that night, his last at the convention. Dox would monitor him until he was asleep via the camera I'd emplaced, and barring anything new, we would try for one more shot at him in the gym in the morning. But if that didn't pan out, in the absence of some fresh intel regarding his subsequent movements, a stop at a church, for example, as Dox had been hoping, we were done.

I headed back to my room and opened the drapes, then sat silently in the reflected lights of the Strip outside and below.

It was dispiriting. I've never failed to complete a job, and I was disturbed at the sudden prospect of blowing this one. It was, I had to admit, nothing high-minded. Just the old and simple obsession with finishing what I'd started and doing it exceptionally well. Not a pretty motivation, no doubt, but at that moment, at least an honest one.

I ran through an increasingly wild set of scenarios, feeling the temptation to try something higher-risk. But that was Vegas talking, encouraging me to redeem my losses with increasingly reckless spins of the wheel. I've lasted a long time by not being stupid. It wasn't a good time to start.

I sat for a long time in the disconsolate glow, waiting for the feel of being on the hunt, the sharp adrenaline edge, to subside. I was tired but I knew I couldn't sleep. I had just decided to boil the tension out of myself in the room's generous bathtub when my mobile buzzed—Dox. I snatched it up and said, "Tell me he's going to church in the morning and I'll buy you a bottle of Bombay Sapphire."

"Oh, he's going to need to go to church, but I don't know if he will."

"What are you talking about?"

"Well, partner, I am watching our friend, whose daily workouts have obviously gifted him with a level of stamina to which you can only aspire, banging the hell out of a call girl even as we speak."

"You're shitting me."

"No, sir. She arrived ten minutes ago, but I didn't call you because I heard a knock but couldn't see what was happening—they must have started in the corridor or in the extra bathroom, and the camera feed's only of the main room of the suite. But he's got her on the couch now, and oh yeah, oh, look at that, he's turning her over, a little doggy-style, I like this man's proclivities! Tell me, partner, why is it so hilarious to watch other people fucking?"

I didn't answer. My mind was racing. There had to be a way we could use this. There had to be.

"Hot damn, look at him go! I am proud, proud to know that our great nation is being steered by men of such exceptional energy and passion. Not to mention rectitude."

Rectitude. That was it.

"We've got him," I said. "This is our chance."

"I don't see what you mean. Right now, the man couldn't be more un-alone."

"No, but he'll be alone soon. I want you to keep watching—"

"Yes, sir, I love my work."

"—and the second she leaves, buzz me, then meet me on the casino floor. There's a phone bank, just to the right of Blush nightclub when you're facing the entrance. The second she leaves, understand?"

"Understood," he said, his tone suddenly all business.

I clicked off and took three slow, deep breaths, forcing myself to pause, to think it through from every angle. If I missed even just one variable, we would blow the whole thing. But there was a chance. Dox had been joking about rectitude, but rectitude, or more accurately, the threatened loss of its façade, was what we suddenly stood to exploit. I thought about the shame this married, church-going, top-secret-SCI-cleared intelligence official would fear if word—if a damn celebrity porn video, from what Dox was describing—got out. And I thought about how, of all the emotions, it's shame that most craves solitude, the very solitude we now required.

I imagined an approach, and quickly realized that with just a little luck, I wouldn't even need the cyanide. I decided to do it the old-fashioned way—more difficult, but also more certain. I closed my eyes and began to picture every step, every variable, every when/then possibility.

When I was done visualizing all of it, I took a roll of sports tape from my toiletry kit and wrapped my forearms and wrists, all the way down to the first joint on my thumbs. Then I pulled on a long-sleeved white tee shirt, buttoned a blue oxford cloth shirt over it, and slipped on a navy blazer whose sleeves were a touch too long. Taped wrists and long sleeves might attract some attention at one of the card tables, but I wasn't going to be gambling, or at least not in the Vegas sense of the word.

My mobile vibrated forty minutes later—Shorrock must have had the girl for an hour, and I supposed there were few professionals as punctual as a Vegas call girl. I stuffed a pair of deerskin gloves into one of the blazer jacket pockets and the sports tape into the other, then headed down.

Dox was waiting when I arrived, and I was pleased to note the continued density of the crowds on the casino floor, which would offer plenty of concealment. "Let's walk," I said, and while we circumnavigated the resort, I explained the plan, and his role in it.

When we were done, we walked back to the phone bank next to Blush. I stood close while he dialed Shorrock's room, and he held the phone away from his ear so I could hear. Two rings, then a "Yes?" in a slightly nervous tone. I wondered whether Shorrock was concerned the girl, or her company, was calling, whether he was suffering from an afterglow comprised mostly of guilt and fear.

"Mister Shorrock," Dox said, in his deepest hick drawl.

"Yes?"

"I'll get right to the point. My associate just left your room. While she was there, she placed a camera under the television in the main room. We used that camera to record a video of your escapades on the couch."

"What?"

"May I recommend that you just walk over to the television in question and feel along its bottom edge? You'll find the camera, and then I can tell you how we can settle this so no one else ever sees the video we made."

"This… this is ridiculous. I don't know what you're talking about."

"Sir, just go retrieve the camera if you would. Oh, and by the way, doggy-style is one of my favorite positions, too. Well done, sir, well done."

That was a nice touch, I thought, and not one I'd scripted. The trick was to feed the subject critical bits of information that would cause him to believe you had more. That, and his growing panic, would prevent him from thinking clearly, and from asking potentially show-stopping questions like, *Oh yeah? What was the girl's name, then?* Which, if Dox really were her associate, he could be expected to know.

There was silence for a moment, presumably while Shorrock examined the television and located the camera. Then he said, "What… what is this about?"

"Sir, it's about you compensating me for giving you the thumb drive on which your steamy encounter with a Las Vegas prostitute is now clearly recorded."

"This is a hoax. Who are you?"

There was no conviction in his voice, and I decided he was just trying to be careful about what he said. At the moment, fear of being recorded would naturally be prominent in his mind.

"Right now, sir, I'm the only person who can save you from personal and professional humiliation and destruction. Which I would sincerely like you to help me do."

"Help you how?"

"Just by paying me a thousand dollars in cash. Which, I think you'll agree under the circumstances, is a hell of a bargain."

In the business he was in, Shorrock would know something about blackmail, and his next question demonstrated experience. "Just for the sake of argument, if it were true that you had some sort of tape, which you don't, because nothing untoward happened, but if you did, you'd keep a copy and turn your blackmail demands into an annuity. Why would anyone want to play your game?"

"Sir, that is a reasonable concern and I can only assure you that I've been playing this game, as you call it, for a long time, and my discretion is the reason I've been able to continue without undue fuss. Have you ever heard about anyone being caught out at the Wynn? Of course not, and I'll tell you why. It's because every time this happens, I'm paid promptly for delivering the incriminating recording and that's the end of the matter. But if you want to be the first person to get huffy and take a stand, that's up to you. Personally, I'd recommend you do what everyone else does, which is fork over the thousand, chalk it up to experience, and live to fight another day."

There was a pause, during which Shorrock must have been mentally running the odds. His voice was tight, but he managed to say, "Okay, just because I can't sleep and this amuses me. Even if I wanted to pay you, I don't have a thousand in cash with me."

An objection about price, not principle. That, and the fact that he hadn't hung up, made me confident this was going to work.

"Of course you don't, sir, that's not unusual after a night of gambling. Which is why I'm standing right next to an ATM. So here's the deal. You come down and withdraw the money. I'll be watching from somewhere on the casino floor. When you have the money, I'll stroll on by. I'll give you a thumb drive and you'll give me the cash. A very discreet exchange and considering the damage it'll prevent, I'd say it'll be the best money you'll ever spend in your life. But if you're not here in five minutes, I'll assume you're not interested—in which case, you can watch the trailer of the video on select Internet sites. And who knows? Maybe on the evening news, too."

I knew we had him even before he said, "Where are you?"

"Not far from Blush nightclub. There's an ATM to the club's right as you're facing the entrance. That's the one to use. Oh, and I almost hate to ask this under the circumstances, but could I trouble you to return the camera to me? They're expensive."

"I don't believe this."

"I understand, sir, and I know this is unpleasant, but if you just follow the plan, in five minutes the whole thing will be behind you. And if
it makes you feel better, again you're hardly the first. Vegas, you know
what I mean?"

Dox hung up and we moved off to separate slot machines with a
view of the ATM. I imagined what Shorrock would be doing now: trying
to control his panic, weighing the odds of his thousand dollars buying
him what it was supposed to buy, coming up with a story for why the
bodyguard outside his room had to stay put and not trail him despite
security protocol to the contrary. He only had a few minutes to figure
it all out, and again the time pressure would be key to preventing him
from coming up with anything we hadn't foreseen. His most obvious
move, aside from compliance, would be to have the bodyguard, or both
of them, tail him and move in on Dox when he revealed himself from
the casino floor. I didn't think he'd do it—there wasn't much upside to a
move like that, only a lot of risk—but if he did, we'd stay put and repeat
when he returned to his room.

It turned out there was no need to worry: Shorrock came alone. I
watched him scanning the casino floor, but there were too many patrons
communing with slot machines for him to pick out Dox or me. When
he'd passed my position, I got up and made my way to the men's room.
I felt a small adrenaline rush spreading through my trunk and limbs and
deliberately breathed slowly and deeply to manage it.

The bathroom was shaped like an L, with sinks along the horizontal
axis and urinals and stalls along the vertical. It appeared to be empty. I
pulled on the deerskin gloves and quickly checked each stall door to confirm no one was inside. Outside, Dox would be taking Shorrock's money
and explaining that he didn't have the thumb drive on him—that he'd
taped it to the back of the folding diaper-changing table in the farthest
stall, the large one designed for handicapped use. The one I now quietly
entered, latching the door behind me.

The stall was exceptionally private: high, white marble walls resting
on casters just an inch above the tiled floor; close-fitting wood-paneled
doors; no cracks or gaps anywhere through which someone might catch
a glimpse from without. I closed my eyes and took a deep breath, held it
for a beat, then slowly released it. I only needed a few seconds alone with

him. It was ridiculous I hadn't found those seconds yet, but I felt like the time was finally at hand.

I kept my eyes closed and concentrated on listening. A moment passed, and I heard a single set of footsteps around the corner of the L. If it was someone else, he might stop at the urinals or the sinks. But the footsteps were moving quickly, deliberately. And they kept coming, past the unoccupied stalls, closer and closer to my position.

Three seconds, I thought. *It won't matter if someone walks in after that. Just three seconds.*

The footsteps stopped outside the stall door. Someone pulled on the handle. The latch rattled.

"Hey," a voice called. "Is someone in there?"

Shorrock was an intelligence professional. Even frightened and confused, he might be alerted by an incongruity. I had to keep it natural for as long as I could.

"Yeah, someone's in here," I said. "Is this the only stall?"

"Just hurry, okay? It's an emergency."

If he'd been thinking clearly, he would have claimed to be handicapped, which would have been calculated to make the current, likely un-handicapped occupant feel guilty and accordingly move more quickly. Apparently, he was under stress sufficient to make that kind of calculation impossible. Which meant he would miss other things, too, or catch on only when it was too late.

I pressed the button on the wall control and the toilet flushed. I wasn't worried about him recognizing me from one of the restaurants or other venues in which I'd gotten close to him—people don't usually notice me unless I want them to. But even if he did notice, and wonder, the momentary puzzlement and distraction would work to my advantage.

I unlatched and opened the door, keeping my left hand to my side and slightly behind me and keeping my body close to my other hand as it pushed the door outward and to the right. Gloves would seem weird enough to possibly induce a rapid response, and I didn't want him to see them until it no longer mattered.

"All right," I said, "it's all yours."

"Thanks," Shorrock said, shouldering past me. As he did so, I pivoted counterclockwise and popped a palm heel strike into the base of his cranium. Not hard enough to injure his neck or drive him into the marble wall on the other side of the stall, where he could break his nose or lose a tooth. But enough to scramble his circuits for a second at least, which is how long it took me to step inside behind him and latch the door.

He had stumbled from the palm heel but he didn't fall, and as he started to turn and try to face me, I threw my left arm around his neck, catching his trachea in the crook of my elbow, caught my right bicep, and planted my right hand firmly on the back of his skull. *Hadaka-jime* again, as versatile as it is effective. I tightened everything up, clamping his carotids in the walnut-cracker vice formed by my bicep and forearm, burying my face in his back and turtling it between my shoulders. I felt panic course through his body and he tried to twist away, one way, then the other, neither to any avail. I let him shove me into one of the marble walls and hung on, concentrating on maintaining the correct pressure. Unlike the choke I had put on that giant contractor in Tokyo, which was deliberately deep and cutting, this one was calibrated. It was firm enough to occlude the carotid arteries, but not so deep that it would result in bruising. As any judoka can attest, a proper choke isn't necessarily painful, and doesn't even have to interfere with breathing. Strangled on the mat by an expert, you might pass out with almost no distress at all.

I felt him raise a foot to try to stomp my instep, which showed some training, but I easily shifted to avoid the shot. He scrabbled back for my eyes but couldn't reach them. His twisting and flailing became more frantic. He scratched madly at my hands and arms, but his nails scraped harmlessly against the tape and multiple layers of material. Then, all at once, I felt the tension drain from his torso. His arms dropped limply to his sides and his body sagged against me. I leaned against the wall, breathing evenly, concentrating on the steady pressure. I heard a set of footsteps enter the room, but they stopped at the bend in the L, probably at one of the urinals. It didn't matter anymore—time was finally on my side. Moments passed, then I heard a toilet flush, the sounds of water running in a sink, paper towels being used and discarded, then footsteps again, this time departing.

When I was sure Shorrock was beyond recovery, I laid him flat on the floor and quickly went through his pockets. All he was carrying was his room key and the camera I'd placed in his room. He must have refused to turn the latter over when Dox told him he'd have to retrieve the thumb drive from the bathroom. Probably he thought he was maintaining some leverage. It didn't matter. The main thing was, we had it back now, and wouldn't have to worry about anyone finding it in his room and raising suspicions. And having his key was useful, too, in case the times of his coming and going might be stored on it. I didn't expect that anyone would be investigating, but the less evidence, the better. I took a thousand dollars from one of my pockets and put it in one of Shorrock's. Probably no one would look into his immediate pre-death ATM withdrawal, but if anyone did, it would look strange if the money weren't on him.

I examined his fingertips to ensure he hadn't managed to scrape any skin or hair off me while he was struggling—I hadn't felt anything, but adrenaline masks pain and it wasn't impossible that he'd managed to scratch my scalp or pull some hair. I found nothing. I took the sports tape from the blazer pocket and wrapped it sticky side-out around both hands, then methodically patted down the floor under and around Shorrock. The Wynn's cleaning people must have been pros, because I came up with only a bit of lint and a few strands of pubic and head hair. I had no way of knowing whether any of it came from me, but now it wouldn't matter. I turned Shorrock over and patted down his back, too, where my face had touched him. A few new hairs, probably his. But again, now a moot point regardless. I unwound the tape carefully over the toilet, balled it up, and pocketed it again. Then I flushed the toilet, eliminating any matter that had fallen into it unseen.

I was almost done. I paused, taking a moment to think, to double check my progress against a mental checklist. Everything was in order. Just one last thing.

I undid Shorrock's belt, pulled his pants and briefs down to his ankles, and wrestled him into a sitting position on the toilet. Then I stepped back, extending an arm to keep him upright as long as possible. When I withdrew my arm, Shorrock slumped forward and to the right, landing face down on the floor next to the toilet. I knew I hadn't left a mark on his face or otherwise, but even if I had, the minor damage caused by a fall from the toilet would be adequate explanation. As for the death itself, it would look like some sort of cardiac event—a problem in the plumbing, possibly, or perhaps something electrical. There might be an autopsy: he was prominent enough for that, and there was the anomaly and irony of someone so fitness-obsessed perishing from an apparent heart attack. But when they found nothing, a body devoid of evidence of what had happened or why, wise physicians would stroke their chins and opine about the Brugada syndrome and the long QT syndrome, and potential abnormalities in sodium and potassium channels, and lethal arrhythmias hitting with the destructiveness and unpredictability of rogue waves, all in the same solemn tones that were once the exclusive province of monks invoking the mysteries of the will of God.

I gripped the top of the marble stall divider and listened intently for a moment. Nothing. I pulled myself up, rotated over the edge, and lowered myself to the stall on the other side. I heard someone else come in, so I latched the door and waited, using the extra moment to run through my mental checklist again and ensure I was overlooking nothing. When I heard the latest patron leave, I moved out, pocketing the gloves en route.

I saw Dox sitting at a slot machine outside, watching the entrance, and dipped my head once to let him know it was done. We would call Larison and Treven from the road, giving ourselves a head start, then reconvene later, far from the Wynn. But I wouldn't tell either of them I'd eschewed the cyanide. Or Horton, for that matter. I prefer people not to know what I can do with my hands. It makes it easier for me to do it to them, if it comes to that.

We'd had some bad luck along the way. A few near misses, or rather, near hits. But it had worked out fine in the end. A perfectly natural-looking death for Shorrock, a clean getaway, an exceptional payday. And maybe, for once, some larger good that would come from all of it. On balance, not a single thing to complain about.

That in itself should have told me something was seriously wrong.

chapter
eleven

Larison and Treven drove through the desert on Interstate 15, the sun rising behind them. Larison had heard from Rain and Dox two hours earlier that the job was done, and they were on their way back to Los Angeles to meet and debrief.

Rain had been vague about how and when he'd finished Shorrock, and Larison had a feeling that while some of this reticence was due to sensible communications security, Rain also didn't want to let on that he'd waited to inform Larison and Treven so that he and Dox could get a head start leaving town. Larison understood. He would have done the same. As far as Rain knew, Larison and Treven could be under orders to tie up loose ends by eliminating Rain and Dox once Shorrock was done. They weren't, though Larison's actual plans weren't so far off from what Rain probably suspected. Regardless, it was natural that Rain would be careful. Assassinating the assassins was practically SOP for a job as high-profile as this one.

Larison had called Hort from a sterile phone while on the road and briefed him. Hort told him to check in when he knew more, but hadn't asked where he and Treven would be meeting Rain and Dox. Hort would understand that Larison had the same concerns about Hort that Rain had about Larison.

The car was a gray Ford Taurus rented at LAX, with no navigation system or automated toll payer that someone might use to track them. Treven was driving, nice and easy, not a mile over the speed limit, just a couple of white guys heading back to California after a few days of gambling. Larison looked out the window at the passing brown hills and dusty chaparral and considered how much he ought to tell him. A lot, he decided. There was no other way to properly motivate him. But he had to do it cleverly, and with certain key omissions. Treven's instincts might be blunted by an excess of infantile patriotism, but he was far from stupid.

He turned and looked at Treven. "So what has he got on you?"

Treven glanced at him, then back to the road. "Who?"

"You know who. Hort."

There was a pause. "Why do you think he's got something on me?"

"Because Hort has something on everyone. It's how he works."

Treven didn't answer. Larison said, "You know what he has on me."

Treven nodded.

Larison said, "You know what he told me will happen if I ever release those torture videos?"

Treven nodded again. "Your friend will be killed."

Larison was weirdly grateful that Treven would be so oblique. The man knew perfectly well what Nico was to Larison. For an instant, Larison imagined what it would be like to be able to trust someone with his secret, and then, with a scary, giddy rush, what it would be like not to have to keep it a secret at all.

He shook off the feeling and said, "He told me they would send contractors to rape Nico's nieces and nephews and mutilate his parents and sisters and brothers-in-law. Bring down the wrath of God on his entire extended family, every last one of them. And then tell Nico why it had happened, how it had been my fault."

There was another pause. Treven said, "Then don't release the tapes."

"Yeah? And what is it you're not supposed to do? Who's getting fucked on your side to keep you in line?"

Treven didn't answer.

Thinking he needed to push a little harder, Larison said, "Do I really need to point out that we have similar problems? Which might have similar solutions, if we try to solve them together?"

"Meaning?"

"How can I answer that if you won't tell me what he's got on you?"

They drove in silence. A revelation of Larison's own to build trust, the possibility of working together to create hope, silence to draw Treven out. If the man was going to open up, this would be the time.

Come on, Larison thought. *Talk. Once you start, you'll keep going.*

He had just begun to think he'd miscalulated when Treven said, "You know that former vice presidential chief of staff you told me about? The one who was tortured to death in his office?"

Larison smiled. "Ulrich."

"Yeah, David Ulrich."

Larison's smile lingered. "I thought you might have been the one who did him."

"I wasn't. But I was in his office shortly before it happened, and I tuned him up pretty hard. Hort says the CIA has security tapes that place me there at the time of his death."

"You believe him?"

"There was no other way for him to know I was there."

"Well, then, I'd say you have a real problem on your hands. Unless you don't mind being Hort's fuckboy for the rest of your life."

"It's the CIA that has the tapes."

"Hort told you that?"

Treven didn't answer.

"Because that's what he would tell you. You know that, right?"

Again, no answer.

"Look," Larison said. "I'd lay good odds Hort has those tapes himself. He's not going to tell you that, otherwise you know he's the one squeezing your nuts. Instead, he positions himself as the guy who's trying to help you relieve the pressure. It's the way it's done."

"Yeah. I get it."

"And even if it were true the CIA did have the tapes, they don't give a shit about you, not as long as you don't get in their business. Get rid of Hort and you don't have to worry about anyone using those tapes against you, regardless of who's holding them."

"Get rid of him?"

"Come on. You're telling me you've never considered it? How stupid do you think I am?"

Treven shook his head. "You don't need me for that. You can make Hort dead on your own."

"But there's something else I want."

There was a pause. Treven said, "The diamonds."

"Correct. And that's not a one-man job. It'll take two, minimum."

"But you're thinking four would be more like it."

Larison smiled. No, Treven wasn't stupid at all.

"We're talking about a hundred million dollars," Larison said. "Rain and Dox could have a quarter each. So could you. Once we have the diamonds, I'll take care of Hort gratis."

Treven didn't answer, and Larison couldn't tell what he was thinking. But he could guess. Twenty-five million and the removal of the man who was blackmailing him? Who wouldn't jump at the chance?

"Well?" Larison said. "Are you in?"

There was a long pause. Larison waited, letting the silence do its work.

Finally, Treven said, "You'd have to tell me the plan first."

Larison smiled. Treven was in. Now all he had to do was dangle the diamonds in front of Rain and Dox, too.

chapter
twelve

I called Horton as Dox drove us past Pasadena. There are those who would suggest I'm paranoid, or they would if they were still alive, anyway, but I didn't want anyone triangulating on the position of our rental car while we were on some deserted stretch of Route 15, with no alternate routes possible and nowhere to run or hide.

"It's done," I told him.

"I heard," he said, pleasure in his rich baritone.

That was pretty fast—Dox and I had left Las Vegas less than four hours earlier. Ordinarily, a body can sit for a long time in a closed restroom stall without anyone noticing anything amiss. Usually it'll be discovered by a cleaning person, trying to clear and close the bathroom before getting to work. Maybe an early morning crew had found Shorrock. More likely, the bodyguards went looking for him when he didn't come back from his mysterious solo errand. I realized I should have foreseen they'd find him sooner than normal. But it didn't really matter.

"You hear about any problems?" I asked.

"None at all. Glad to see your reputation is well deserved."

"We were lucky."

"I doubt it. You used what I gave you?"

"Yes."

"Good. Now, to save you from asking the obvious question, your remuneration has already been distributed per your instructions. You can each confirm receipt."

The conversation was so familiar I might have been having déjà vu. It was appalling, how natural it felt to be doing this again. How... normal. As though I'd been forced to use only my weak hand for the last few years, and was at last again able to use my strong one.

"I'll tell the others."

"Good. And if you're heading back to the area where we previously met, I'd like to see you again."

Alarm bells went off in my head. "Why?"

"To brief you on the next one."

"Why do we have to meet for that?"

"Because I'm not going to put the details in writing or say them over the phone. Look, under the circumstances, I completely understand your hesitation. So, needless to say, we can meet anywhere or anyway that's comfortable for you."

I didn't like it. Ordinarily, the probable quality and quantity of the opposition were such that I could implement satisfactory countermeasures. But Horton could bring some exceptionally heavy firepower into play if he wanted to. I imagined a SWAT team, briefed about the presence of Shorrock's armed-and-dangerous killer, surrounding a restaurant with me inside it.

"The guy who just left the project isn't enough?" I said, stalling for time.

"Not quite. I need two more personnel changes to make sure the project doesn't get off the ground. If it does, it's going to cost the company a lot of money. You've proven you're the man for this. Finish the job and there's a hell of a bonus."

I didn't know if I wanted this. But what did I want?

"Where are you now?" I said, improvising.

"In the city."

"Close to where we met before?"

"I could be there in twenty minutes."

"Go to the same hotel. I'll call in less than an hour."

"Good."

I clicked off.

"He's got some more work for us?" Dox said.

"Two more. And a big completion bonus, apparently. How's that sound to you?"

He smiled. "Sounds like money, partner."

"Maybe. How do you feel about a face-to-face?"

"You worried he's gonna be Jack Ruby to our Lee Harvey Oswald?"

"Something like that."

He reached under the seat and produced the Wilson Combat. "Old Oswald should have carried one of these."

I thought about it for a moment, and decided there was a way. "Head to West Hollywood," I said.

When we were off the highway and had driven a couple of miles west on Santa Monica Boulevard, I called Horton again. At this point, anyone listening in wouldn't have time to scramble a team after us, so the momentary breach of communication security I was about to commit would be harmless. "Urth Caffé," I told him. I knew the place from previous visits to L.A., and though I liked their coffee, we wouldn't be enjoying it today. "Corner of Melrose Avenue and Westmount Drive."

"I'll be there in under ten minutes."

I clicked off. Horton was a precise man, and it occurred to me that he must know the city reasonably well to be able to instantly offer such an estimate. I wasn't sure what that meant, if it meant anything, but I filed the information away for subsequent consideration.

We parked on Westmount, just south of Melrose, and got out. The air felt cool compared to the blast furnace heat of Las Vegas, and the late morning sky above the mixed palm and deciduous trees was a clear, hard blue. We both headed to the restroom in Urth, squeezing past tables of chattering, oblivious Angelenos clustered around metal tables under the shadows of green umbrellas on the sidewalk and patio. The coffee smelled like heaven, but we didn't have time and I was already amped for the meeting with Horton. Maybe later.

We went back to the car, Dox in the backseat this time while I took the wheel. I drove around the block, right turn following right turn, single family bungalows, walk-up apartment houses, low slung commercial establishments like Bodhi Tree Bookstore and Peace Gallery, repeat. Knots of pedestrian shoppers shifted and glided along the sun-drenched sidewalks, but no sign of Horton. And no sign of anything untoward, either—black Chevy Suburbans with darked-out windows; sedans with hard-looking men inside idling at the curb; a formation in sunglasses and unseasonable jackets taking up positions around the perimeter of the restaurant and beginning to move in.

My phone buzzed—Horton. I clicked on and said, "Yeah."

"I'm here, but I don't see you."

"Walk out of the restaurant left on Melrose and immediately turn left onto Westmount. We'll be there in a minute."

"Still being cautious, I see."

"I'm sure it's unnecessary."

He chuckled. "I fully understand."

I clicked off and handed my phone back to Dox. "Phones off," I said. "And take out the batteries." Horton knew the number, and someone could triangulate on it while we drove. Probably unnecessary, as Horton put it, along with my other precautions, but if you're serious about having something life-saving in place the one percent of the time you really need it, you'll have to have it in place the other ninety-nine percent, too.

Dox laughed. "This about automobile cell phone use being illegal in the great state of California?"

"No," I said, glancing in the rearview and trying to hide my exasperation. Dox's cell phone habits had once nearly gotten us killed in Bangkok. "It's about—"

He laughed. "I know, I know, we don't want anyone triangulating on us. Just pulling your leg, partner. Though I don't know why I bother, it's so easy."

I sighed. Probably I would never get used to it. I always go quiet in the moments before a mission, but Dox needed to crack jokes, most of them at my expense.

I turned on the bug detector and circled the block again, right on Westbourne, right on Sherwood, right on Westmount. I spotted Horton halfway up the street, on the sidewalk to our right, heading toward us. He was dressed the way he had been the other day—short-sleeved shirt, tucked in, nowhere good to conceal a gun except in an ankle holster. Or maybe, for the moment, in the back of his waistband, which we couldn't see from our current position, but Dox had the window down now, the Wilson Combat just below it, and if Horton's hands went anywhere we couldn't see them, he'd have to be able to draw faster than Dox could shoot, which was another way of saying he'd be dead right there.

We pulled up next to him and I indicated he should get in the front passenger seat. He nodded, but first courteously hiked up his pants to expose his ankles, then turned around so we could confirm he wasn't carrying in the small of his back, either. He got in and I did a quick K-turn that would be the first of the maneuvers I would make to ensure we weren't being followed. The bug detector was still.

"I appreciate the two of you taking the time," Horton said. "And let me say, nice work in Las Vegas. We'll never know how many lives you saved and how many grievous injuries you prevented, but from what Shorrock was planning, probably it was thousands."

"Don't thank me," Dox said. "I'm just here to shoot you if something goes wrong."

Horton was smart enough not to mistake Dox's genial tone for a lack of serious purpose. He said, "Well, then, let's make sure nothing goes wrong."

I headed south on La Cienega, then kept us on neighborhood streets to weed out traffic. I judged it unlikely Horton would risk having us followed—he would have known that as our passenger he would literally have a gun to his head. Still, I stopped several times to make sure no one was behind us and did a few strategic U-turns, too. With Horton's reach, of course, I couldn't rule out satellite surveillance in addition to the more common vehicular variety, but that wasn't an immediate threat and Dox and I could deal with the possibility later. I knew Horton might have seen and memorized the plates as we approached to pick him up, too, but I'd rented the car under an identity that wouldn't lead back to me. As long as we were careful, we'd be all right.

When I was satisfied no one was trying to tail us, I said, "If we've already saved all these lives, why do you need the other two plotters taken out, too?"

Horton nodded as though expecting the question. "Shorrock was the tip of the spear, so he was the most important immediate target. But while the spear still exists, its tip can be relatively easily replaced. There are two more key players, the loss of whom will completely end anybody's hopes of using false flag attacks as the basis for a power grab."

"Who?"

"Are you interested?"

"I can't answer that if I don't know who."

He paused, then said, "Have you heard of Jack Finch?"

"No."

"He keeps a low profile for a man in a powerful position."

"Which is?"

"The president's counterterrorism advisor."

Dox laughed. "You sure do pick some hard targets. I'm afraid to ask who the third one might be."

Horton said, "Let's just keep talking about them one at a time for now."

"What's Finch's role in the plot?" I asked.

"Finch," Horton said, "is what you might think of as an information broker."

"Meaning?"

"Meaning he is the modern incarnation of the illustrious J. Edgar Hoover, who as you might know maintained his position as head of the FBI for nearly half a century by amassing incriminating files on all the important players in Washington, including every president he served under."

Dox laughed again. "Sounds like old Murdoch and Fox News."

"In a sense," Horton said, "it is. But more focused. And more extensive."

"What does any of that have to do with the coup?" I said.

"The first step is the provocation, which was Shorrock's department. After the provocation, though, the plotters need to ensure that certain key players in the government—the president, highly placed military and law enforcement personnel, and the judiciary, if there's a challenge—support the president's assumption of emergency powers in response to the crisis. You can see why this is critical. America is a big, fractious place. There are a number of people who want things to be run more efficiently, as they might put it. But not enough of them to guarantee success in the face of opposition."

"He's got dirt on the president?" Dox said.

Horton chuckled. "He has dirt on everybody. I told you, like Hoover. But Hoover didn't have much more than phone taps and surveillance photos. Finch has intercepted email, Internet browsing histories, copies of security video feeds, records of hacked offshore bank accounts—everything you can imagine in an interconnected digital age. We're talking about dossiers documenting financial corruption and sexual depravity, in such detail they'd make Hoover weep with envy."

"I'm not buying it," I said. "I don't care how many people Finch controls. The president can't just suspend the Constitution and get away with it."

"Ah," Horton said, "but he won't call it a suspension. He'll simply ask for certain emergency powers to deal with the crisis, and he'll ask Congress for these powers for only ninety days, the powers to expire unless Congress agrees to renew them. Very serious and sober people will talk about the unprecedented nature of the threat, and how the Constitution isn't a suicide pact, and other such things, and they'll show how independent and level-headed they are by telling the president he can have only thirty days, renewable, they'll be damned if they agree to ninety."

"All right," I said. "Let's say you're right. Let's say it could be done. Still, what's the point?"

"What do you mean?"

"The point of all of it. These people… don't they already have enough? Power, money… they're already running things. Why upset the apple cart if they've got all the apples?"

"The people behind this don't care about apples. They're doing this because, in their misguided way, they care about their country."

"They're going to destroy it to save it?"

"They don't think of it as destruction. In their minds, America's democracy is suffering from a fatal disease. Legislative gridlock, capture of the government by special interests, a war machine that's become like an out-of-control parasite on the economy."

"Are they wrong?"

"They're not wrong, but their means of redress are. Their plan is to take the reins of power, set things right, and then return power to the people."

Dox laughed. "Yeah, that always works out well."

"They don't think the chances are good. They just think they're better than the chances of the current course, which they judge to be nil. Like an emergency procedure for a patient who, if heroic measures aren't undertaken, is going to die regardless."

"Sounds pretty insane," I said.

"It is insane. In no small part because they're not factoring in the cost of the thousands of people who will have to be terrorized, burned, maimed, crippled, traumatized, and killed in order to create the groundwork for their plan. And this is why we need to stop it."

I told myself I should just walk away. We'd done Shorrock. That was enough.

But then I thought of something. Something I should have spotted sooner.

"How do you know so much about this?" I said.

There was a pause, then he said, "Because I'm part of it."

I glanced over at him, then back to the road. "Part of it how?"

"Never mind how. I was brought in, I played along, I want to stop it."

"Without leaving a return address."

"By the time the third and final critical player succumbs to 'natural causes,' they might catch on to me, in which case I'm prepared to face the music, which I expect will be a funeral dirge. But yes, in the meantime, I have a chance to destroy this thing root and branch. For that, I need an untraceable outside detachment, and speed, and no signs of foul play."

We drove in silence for a few moments. Horton turned to Dox.

"Can you take that gun off my back long enough to tell me what you think about all this?"

I glanced in the rearview and saw Dox grin. He said, "I've just been waiting to hear about the per diem."

chapter
thirteen

Treven listened to Rain's briefing over the sounds of the speeding
L.A. Metro subway car, both impressed and concerned. Impressed
that Rain had spotted a weakness in Shorrock's defenses, had immediately improvised to exploit it, and had finished Shorrock with the cyanide
as planned. Concerned that Rain and Dox had since met Hort and now
seemed to be controlling the flow of information in both directions. He
wasn't used to having a buffer between himself and Hort, and even aside
from what he recognized was an unworthy, petulant reaction to being
placed on the periphery, he also understood that having to rely on Rain
and Dox as intermediaries put him at an operational disadvantage.

The late morning train was mostly empty, a few bored-looking passengers dispersed among the seats. The four of them stood facing each
other in the center of the car, swaying slightly as it hurtled along, Rain's
voice just audible although their faces were only inches apart. Rain had
called them with instructions for the meeting, and Treven assumed he'd
chosen the subway to frustrate any satellite surveillance Hort might be
employing to track him. There were video cameras in the stations, of
course, but even if Hort had access to a local feed, he'd have to know
where to look and there would be layers of local bureaucracy to wade
through. By the time anyone had a fix on their position, they'd all be long
gone.

Larison said, "You think this Finch thing is for real?"

Rain took a moment before answering. "I didn't know if Shorrock
was for real, either. But the money's been deposited."

"He's offering three hundred apiece for Finch," Dox said. "And he says it'll be five hundred apiece for the third one, whoever that turns out to be. That's over a million for each of us when this is all done. I don't know about you, but where I come from that's a lot of green."

"Where do you think Hort's getting all this money to throw around?" Larison said, and Treven wondered where he was going with this, how much he was going to tell them.

"I don't know," Rain said. "Do you?"

Larison glanced casually around the swaying train car, then said, "What if I told you that instead of exposing ourselves for one million, we could protect ourselves, and walk away with twenty-five million?"

"Twenty-five million... dollars?" Dox said.

Larison nodded. "Apiece."

Dox laughed. "You're bullshitting us. Protect ourselves how, kill the president?"

Larison shook his head. "Kill Hort."

Dox laughed again, but Treven could tell from his expression the number had gotten his attention.

Rain said, "What does he have on you?"

Larison smiled coldly. "That's not what matters. What matters is, Hort is holding one hundred million in uncut diamonds. Well, make that ninety-nine million, after paying us. Portable, convertible, completely un-traceable."

Rain said nothing. Treven wondered whether he believed it.

"It's a lot of upside," Larison said. "But you want to know something? The diamonds are really just a bonus. They're not even the point."

"You know," Dox said, "I've always wanted to be involved in a conversation where someone would say, 'the hundred million dollars isn't even the point.' Between that and the twins in the bathtub at the Suko-thai in Bangkok, I can now retire a contented man."

Larison flashed his cold smile again. "What I mean is, focusing on the money makes it sound like we have a choice. We don't."

"What do you mean?" Rain said.

"I mean, you don't understand Hort. So let me explain a few things about him. One, he always protects himself from blowback. Therefore two, when he's done using us for whatever Shorrock and the rest of this is really about, he'll move to silence us. Therefore three, one of these hits, maybe the next one, maybe the third, will be nothing but a setup to fix us in time and place."

"But he just paid us a million even," Dox said.

Larison nodded. "To establish his bona fides. And to make us believe the rest of what he's promising is real. You see why he's structuring it this way? To get our greed to override our judgment."

Dox glanced at Rain. Treven read the glance as *I'm deferring to you on this, partner.*

Rain said nothing. The man's expression and tone never seemed to vary. It made him hard to read. That was bad enough, but after seeing what Rain had done to the contractors, and knowing that he'd efficiently taken Shorrock off the board, too, Treven was starting to find Rain's mildly flat-lined demeanor outright unnerving.

"Do you get it now?" Larison said. "After what we just did in Las Vegas, as long as Hort is alive, he's a threat to all of us."

"You knew this going in," Rain said.

"I wanted us all to be in the same boat, facing the same set of options, if that's what you mean. But I didn't con you. I didn't mislead you. You made your own decision for your own reasons. Anyway, even if I'd told you what I thought, you wouldn't have listened. I'm not sure you're listening even now."

No one said anything.

"All right," Larison said. "Go ahead and let him jerk your strings. Chase after his promises, if you want. Eventually, you'll die trying. Or, you can recognize what's going on here, preempt the threat, and walk away clean with twenty-five million apiece in the process."

Treven had the sick sense that he had been turned into a bystander on all of this. Kill Finch? Turn on Hort? No one was asking him what he thought. And the truth was, he wasn't sure himself.

He couldn't disagree with Larison's analysis of the current state of play—after all, he knew firsthand how manipulative and ruthless Hort could be. And the points Larison had made about the security video placing Treven at a murder scene were persuasive, too. If Larison was right, the choice was pretty straightforward: kill or be killed.

Still, the thought of taking out Hort made him anxious, almost dizzy. Could he really do this? To his own commander? He tried to think of it as a fragging, like what enlisted men had sometimes done to incompetent lieutenants in Vietnam. But when he imagined himself putting a round into Hort's forehead, the neat hole, the momentary pressure bulge of the eyes from cavitation in the cranium, the instantaneous loss of expression from the face and rigidity from the body… something inside him rebelled.

What would he do afterward? Hort would be replaced, naturally, but it was hard to imagine things ever going back to the way they were. He was afraid he would have committed a kind of patricide, that he'd be tormented by conscience, that his fellow elite soldiers would sense he'd committed some primordial sin, maybe even suspect precisely what it was. He'd bear the mark of Cain, always suspect, forever an outsider.

No. He wasn't like Larison and Rain, and he didn't want to be. He'd done his share of killing, most of it at close quarters, but except when it had been self-defense, it had always been under orders. He was part of something, why would he fuck that up? And who was Larison, anyway? A skilled operator, no doubt, but still, a loose cannon, a rogue. And Rain was beginning to strike him as a borderline sociopath. Dox was a buffoon, too dumb to know better. They did what they did for money, which meant they could always be bought. Had he really been considering turning on Hort, turning on the unit, to throw in his lot forever with this group of burnouts?

And then suddenly, he saw a way through this. A way to protect himself, stay on the inside, and get clear of Rain, Larison, and Dox. All at the same time.

"You might be right," Rain said, over the sounds of the train. "But still, I want to finish Finch. That's what I was hired to do, and I'm not in the habit of turning on a client just for a better payday, even a much better one. If you and Treven want in, we'll split the fee three hundred apiece. Otherwise Dox and I can handle it alone, and we walk away with no hard feelings."

Larison said, "You're making a mistake."

"Do you want in on Finch?" Rain said.

Larison looked away for a moment as though considering. Then he said, "What would you do if you found out Hort is lying to us about Shorrock and Finch? About what all this is about?"

Rain said nothing.

"Yeah," Larison said. "I thought so. All right, I'm in on Finch. Because soon enough, you'll be in on Hort."

Later, after they'd split up, Treven did a long surveillance detection run. When he was sure he was alone, he used a payphone at a gas station to call Hort. Hort picked up with a typically noncommittal, "Yes?"

"It's me," Treven said.

There was a pause, then, "It's good to hear your voice, son. Nice work in Las Vegas."

"That wasn't me so much."

"Could you have done it with fewer players?"

"Probably not, no."

"Then it couldn't have been done without you. Which is why I wanted you to be a part of it in the first place."

Treven didn't answer. He felt like he'd arrived at a fork in the road. Whichever way he went, there'd be no turning back. Ever.

"What's on your mind, son?" Hort said.

Treven took a deep breath. "There's something you need to know," he said.

part
two

Faced with intractable national problems on one hand, and an energetic and capable military on the other, it can be all too seductive to start viewing the military as a cost-effective solution.

—The Origins of the American Military Coup of 2012,
Charles J. Dunlap

I am beginning to think the only way the national government can do anything worth-while is to invent a security threat and turn the job over to the military.

—James Fallows

The environment most hospitable to coups d'etat is one is which political apathy pre-vails as the dominant style.

—Andrew Janos

chapter fourteen

Vienna seemed an unlikely locale for killing the president's counter-terrorism advisor.

When Horton had briefed Dox and me in Los Angeles, I'd initially pictured Washington, where Finch worked, or maybe some beachside place, where he might enjoy a summer vacation with his family. But as it turned out, Finch wasn't in Washington just then, and nor did he have a family. What he did have was a single sibling—a sister, who taught at the Universität für Angewandte Kunst Wien, the University of Applied Arts in Vienna, and whom Finch tended to visit whenever he was in Europe on official business. At the moment, as it happened, he was in London, tasked, no doubt, with reassuring the British that the Special Relationship was still special, along with the other important activities presidential counterterrorism advisors are expected to carry out. The problem with London was that the people he was meeting would have their own security details, meaning getting close to him would involve penetrating veritable Venn diagrams of overlapping protection. But Vienna was neither an announced part of Finch's itinerary, nor an official one. Unless art professors in the former seat of the Hapsburg Empire had their own bodyguards, Finch's security would be all we had to worry about, and with luck, even that would be light, perhaps even nonexistent.

I had called Kanezaki from a payphone after going through security at LAX. My fellow passengers and I went through the new security machines with our arms raised over our heads as though we were criminals. A few chose to get patted down instead, like prisoners. No one seemed to mind the new normal.

Kanezaki hadn't learned anything about Horton, but he did mention that a certain Tim Shorrock, the director of the National Counterterrorism Center, had died of an apparent heart attack in Las Vegas. "You wouldn't know anything about that, would you?" he asked.

"Why would I know anything about it?"

"Just seems like a lot of coincidences. Horton is obviously a key member of the counterterrorism community—"

"It's nice you guys have a community now, with members. It makes it sound so friendly."

"—and a heart attack for Shorrock, at the same time Horton is reaching out to you, makes me wonder. Especially because apparently Shorrock was some kind of fitness fanatic."

"You ever hear of an earthquake causing a church to collapse on its parishioners?" I asked. "It happens. Same as a fitness fanatic with a faulty valve or whatever. I tend to think of it as God indulging his sense of irony. Or maybe his sense of humor."

"Maybe. Did you ever meet with Horton?"

"Maybe."

"You were going to keep me posted, remember?"

I might have reminded him that keeping him posted was in exchange for his finding out about what Horton was planning, which he hadn't done. But if I told him that, he would just respond that he had tried but hadn't managed, and anyway that he had come through with information about Treven and Larison. It would be a circle jerk at best; more likely, it would erode some of the trust and goodwill Kanezaki and I had spent years building.

Still, I hesitated to tell him, even in broad strokes, what Horton was up to. Need-to-know and other aspects of operational security are a long-honed reflex in me. But if Larison was right, it was in my interest to learn everything I could about Horton, who might be as much opposition as he was client. Offering some information of mine in exchange for data that might give me a clearer view of the movement of pieces on the board, and of the players behind them, would be a smart trade.

"It'll sound a little crazy," I said.

He chuckled. "It's a crazy business. My own COS tried to have me taken out, remember?"

Back when he'd been a green CIA recruit in Tokyo, Kanezaki had run dangerously afoul of his chief of station, a certain James Biddle, who tried to hire me to kill him. I warned Kanezaki, instead, and that warning had fostered a relationship that had since become highly useful to me.

"All right. Horton says there's a coup afoot in America." When I was done giving him the 30,000-foot view of the landscape, I asked, "You think that's possible?"

There was a long pause, then he said, "I think the public's been... prepped for this, yes. Even before nine-eleven, but especially since then. There's a ratchet effect, and nothing, not even killing bin Laden, seems to change it. I can see where some people could realize they could take advantage, whether out of greed or rationalized patriotism or whatever. What does Horton want you to do?"

"I think you can imagine."

"The plotters?"

I didn't answer.

"Shorrock?"

Again, I didn't answer.

"It might be true," he said, after a moment. "In which case, you're doing something pretty heroic. But... if the people behind this thing get wind of your involvement, I think you're going face opposition like you've never seen."

"I've been thinking about that," I said, remembering, again, Larison's admonitions about Horton.

"You trust Horton?"

"No," I said.

"Then why are you doing this? The money?"

There was a time when Kanezaki's inquiries were obvious and callow. He'd come a long way.

"Not just the money. I wouldn't call it heroic, the way you did, but... look, maybe it wouldn't hurt for me to do something good for a change."

"If it is good. You only have Horton's word to go on, is that right?"

"That's why I called you. I was hoping for some kind of corroborating evidence, one way or the other."

"I wish I'd been able to find something. So far not."

"Let me ask you something. Horton… does he have any vulnerabilities?" I was thinking of what Larison had said about hostages to fortune. I wondered whether Horton had one of his own.

"My friend, that's a line I can't cross. I'm not going to help you take out an American army colonel."

"I'm not asking you to. But… if this thing turns out to be other than what it's been billed as, heroism might require a different course. Just keep it in mind."

"The two operators you asked me to follow up on—Larison and Treven. Are they involved?"

But I'd said enough. I told him let's just stay in touch—after all, he wanted to know if Horton was right and what was being done about it, and I wanted an early warning system in case I was being set up. He told me he'd keep trying to find out more, and I headed off to Vienna.

Horton's intel had been spotty. He had Finch's roundtrip Washington to London flights, and he knew his schedule of meetings in London. The meetings ended two days before the return flight, and Horton claimed to be ninety percent sure Finch would spend those two days in Vienna, taking a roundtrip flight from London on his own dime before heading back to Washington on his government-sanctioned ticket. What we didn't know, though, was on what flight Finch would arrive, or where he would be staying. We might have called various airlines and Viennese hotels to "confirm" the reservation of a Mr. Jack Finch, but doing so would have created too many possibilities of an airline or hotel employee learning from the evening news about the selfsame Jack Finch's demise, finding the previous call to be too weird under the circumstances to be merely a coincidence, and contacting the authorities, who might then want to check on whether other airlines and hotels had received similar calls. If Finch had been conducting his business like a good, oblivious civilian, Horton would have been able to nail down his travel details easily enough. The fact that he couldn't indicated some security consciousness on the part of Finch, and suggested too that Horton felt circumscribed in his ability to look, lest his inquiries tip Finch off. Regardless, the upshot was that the locus of our attention had to be the sister. If we could get a fix on her, we would also be fixing Finch. After that, we would have to improvise.

On the one hand, Emma Capps, widowed but retaining her married name, was fairly easy to track. For starters, we had both her home and work addresses, courtesy of standard IRS paperwork. We also had plenty of photographs, scraped from the university's website, from Capps's Facebook page, and from Capps's own website, where she blogged about trends in the art world and advertised her paintings—impressive oil works that were at once recognizably realistic but also bathed in an otherworldly, melting luminescence. On the other hand, none of us was particularly familiar with Vienna, we knew nothing of Capps's daily habits, and we had only four days before Finch was expected to arrive in the city.

Still, an experienced four-man team, operating within urban conceal-ment, can typically nail down the details of a civilian's routine within a matter of days, and so it was for us with Capps. The fourth-floor flat in the déclassé 15th District, near Westbanhof, the main train station; morning yoga at Bikram Yoga College, a few blocks away; breakfast at Café Westend, also in her neighborhood; the university in the afternoon, where, given the paucity of students because of the summer break, we assumed she was painting rather than teaching. She was an attractive woman of about fifty with wavy brown hair, an erect posture, and a pur-poseful stride—easy to watch in both senses of the phrase. She seemed to live alone, and I wondered what had happened to her deceased hus-band, and how old she'd been when she'd lost him, and whether there had been any children beforehand. If there had been, presumably they were now grown and living on their own. Horton hadn't included such details in her file, either because he didn't have them, or, more likely, be-cause he understood that no one other than a sociopath wants to become overly familiar with the humanity of someone targeted, even peripheral-ly, in an op. And, indeed, as we watched Capps and learned her routines, I felt an inchoate hope that there were children somewhere, or a lover, or someone else in her life besides the brother we were about to take away.

On the fourth day we were watching her, the day we expected Finch to arrive, she stayed at the university later than usual. The four of us had shadowed her from her neighborhood that morning and were now tak-ing turns circling the university, and at first I was concerned when she failed to emerge around five as she had previously. I would have expected her to meet Finch at the airport, or at least at Westbanhof Station. Could he have been coming in on a late flight? Had he canceled, or had Horton been wrong about him coming in the first place? But then I realized there was another possibility—simply that Finch, who had been visiting his sister here for many years, would know his way around and require no escort. So maybe the deviation in routine was a good sign.

Turned out it was. Capps left the university at close to six. There were plenty of pedestrians about, all enjoying the late summer daylight, and there were also lots of bicyclists and motor scooters and cars, so following Capps without being observed was easy. I stayed on her from a discreet distance, then watched her enter Café Prückel, a classic Viennese coffee shop in one of the glorious nineteenth-century buildings that characterized the area—where, with the kind of serendipity that occasionally smiles down upon an op, Dox was presently taking a load off while Treven, Larison and I worked the street. I called him on the mobile he was carrying.

"Our girl is coming to see you," I said when he picked up. "Did you—"

"Saw her already, amigo. I'm at one of the sidewalk tables, enjoying a tasty espresso and apple strudel *mit Schlag*."

"'*Mit Schlag*'?"

"Means with whipped cream."

"I know what it means."

"Oh. Well, when in Rome and all that, you know, I just like to blend."

For a moment, I pictured enormous, goateed Dox amidst the effete students and artistes of the area. What I pictured couldn't fairly be characterized as blending.

"That's... admirable," I said.

"*Danke*, buddy, I appreciate it. Anyway, what's the plan?"

"Stay put for now. One of us will get a table on the other side of the building or inside so we have a view of both entrances. She might be meeting her friend there."

The oblique references were probably unnecessary—the phones Horton had supplied were encrypted, and at this distance we were connected by their radio function rather than through a cell tower. But no sense taking chances.

"Roger that. Tell you what, get here soon so I can get up and drain the dragon. I've got three espressos inside me at this point and I think at least two are trying to get out."

"Hold it in for five more minutes. I'll buzz you as soon as we have someone else inside."

"Can we make it four? I swear, I am currently engaged in mortal bladiatorial combat, and—"

"Look, I'll try," I said, exasperated. I clicked off and called Larison and Treven. Larison headed into the café; Treven, who was on a rented motor scooter, stayed outside.

Once Larison had confirmed he was inside and could see Capps, I told Dox to pull out. If Capps was indeed meeting Finch here, I didn't want to give him the chance to log more of us than was strictly necessary.

I waited on a bench under the shade of some trees in the nearby Stadtpark, just a harmless-looking Japanese tourist taking in the sights and sounds and smells, savoring the sense of loneliness and freedom that comes only from solitary sojourns in strange lands, where all the everyday things seem subtly wondrous and different and new, where there's no one to please or disappoint or explain to, where the traveler finds himself suspended between the beguilement of the comforts he left behind, and the allure of an imaginary future he senses but knows he can never really have.

I passed nearly an hour that way, the day's heat slowly loosening, the trees' shadows lengthening, pensioners and lovers and dog walkers drifting past me, occasionally enjoying an adjacent park bench. Maybe Horton's intel had been faulty. Maybe Finch wouldn't show. Maybe I'd get credit in the next life, or the afterlife, for trying, for a good faith effort that had ultimately failed to produce results.

My mobile buzzed. Larison's number. I clicked answer. "Yeah."

"Gang's all here," he said in his gravelly whisper.

I could hear the sounds of the café around him—music, conversation, laughter. "Good. Sound quality okay?"

The phones we were carrying were equipped with the latest listening gear—integrated electronic amplifiers. State of the art, as Horton had promised. Not as powerful as a parabolic mic, but a hell of a lot smaller and less obtrusive. Depending on overall acoustics, the user could eavesdrop on a quiet conversation as much as thirty feet away through a pair of ordinary wire-line earbuds, the kind Larison would be wearing right now.

"Excellent," he said.

"Good. Let me know if you find out where we'll be dining and staying."

"I will."

"Does it look like just us? Or should we expect extra company?"

"Unless the extra company is cooling its heels outside, it looks like just us."

So Finch was traveling without security. Unexpected, given his position, and even more so given the quality of enemy he must have developed through his information-brokering hobbies. Maybe he felt the dirt he had banked made him untouchable. Maybe he felt his side trip to Vienna had been planned discreetly enough to offer adequate protection. It didn't matter. I'd have Treven make a pass on the motor scooter and Dox on foot to confirm, but for now it seemed like good news for us.

"All right," I said. "If you learn anything or need anything, we're nearby."

"Copacetic for now."

I clicked off and considered. For the moment, I didn't want to say anything to Larison, but in my mind his cover was already blown. Even if Finch was relaxed enough to travel without a bodyguard, the way he had planned this trip suggested a degree of security sensitivity—certainly enough for him to log Larison and his danger vibe. Dox had commented on it, too, on our drive west from Las Vegas. "That hombre could make Satan's neck hairs stand on end," was how he'd put it. "He's a reloader for sure."

"A reloader?" I'd asked.

"Yeah, I'd empty the whole magazine into him, then reload and do it again, just to be sure."

I agreed with his assessment. If Larison had a weakness, it was that danger aura he put out. Most men who have it just can't cloak it. And if Finch picked up on it, he'd sure as hell take note if he spotted Larison again later that evening.

Ten minutes later, Larison buzzed me again. "Good news," he said.

"We're eating at a place called Expidit. That's how it sounds, anyway, I don't know how it's spelled. Like 'expedite' but with 'it' at the end, not 'ite.'"

"I'll see what I can find online. What about lodging?"

"A hotel called the Hollman Bell something. Again, I couldn't make it out exactly. But that should be enough to work with."

"Arrival time?"

"They're done with their drinks and waved the waiter off when he asked if they wanted another, so I'd guess soon."

"Okay, let me know if they head out. I'm going to try to find the restaurant and hotel."

It took me only a minute to locate the Xpedit restaurant and Hollman Beletage Design and Boutique Hotel, both within a half mile of the university. Finch must have chosen the hotel for its proximity, and probably Capps had proposed the restaurant for the same reason.

I thought for a moment, then called Larison again. "Does our friend have a bag with him?" I asked.

"No."

That meant he'd already checked in at the hotel. It also made it more likely that he and Capps would be on foot the rest of the evening. With no bag to carry, it would be a shame to waste the glorious weather by taking a cab.

"Okay," I said, "here's how I want us to play it. I'll let the other guys know we're going to stay nice and loose for the duration. No sense following too closely if we know where things are going to wind up. You stay put when they leave. I don't want our friend seeing you get up at the same time he does, or to spot you later tonight."

I expected some pushback, because no professional likes someone suggesting he's been made. But Larison surprised me, saying only, "Agreed. Where do you want me?"

"Give them ten minutes, then head to the hotel. It's the Hollman Beletage, on Köllnerhofgasse less than a half mile northwest of here. Find it on a map, but don't look it up directly."

"You don't want a record of multiple Google searches of the restaurant and hotel."

"I didn't use Google, but yes. No sense leaving an electronic paper trail. Not that anyone's going to be looking."

Again he said, "Agreed."

"Spend an hour getting to know the area, then let's talk again. I'll be doing the same."

I clicked off, then called Dox and Treven to pass on the information Larison had given me. I told them to keep a loose eye on the restaurant, and to let me know when Finch and Capps showed up and when they were leaving. For the moment, the restaurant was of secondary interest: a possibility, but probably less promising than the hotel, where he was more likely to be alone. I might change that assessment after reconnoitering both, along with the route in between. The Xpedit restroom might be a possibility. Or, assuming Capps and Finch said their goodnights at the restaurant and she didn't walk him to the hotel, some dark stretch of sidewalk, or an alley, on the way from one to the other. Whatever I decided, I wanted to avoid, if possible, using the cyanide, which Horton had deposited and we had retrieved at a dead drop at the base of the Mozart statue in the Burggarten, like something straight out of a John le Carré spy novel. I wasn't entirely sure why I was reluctant. Maybe it was the inherent danger of such a powerful compound. Maybe it was some vestigial security discomfort in doing things the way Horton wanted, the way he expected. Maybe it was a perverse pride in doing the work up close, without tools, in a way almost no one else ever could.

I checked the restaurant first, and could immediately see it was unlikely to work. It was a large, open, L-shaped room, with enormous windows fronting the sidewalks outside. There was a hostess standing by the door, which meant I couldn't slip in undetected for an on-site examination now without being remembered later. A hostess also suggested the need for reservations, and while presumably they would take walk-ins on an as-available basis, the place was pretty full. If a table were open, I could put Dox or Treven inside, hopefully somewhere that offered a view of Finch and Capps. Or I could lurk outside, keeping an eye on Capps and Finch through the large windows, then moving quickly inside if Finch got up to use the restroom. But that would almost certainly involve a "Would you mind if I used your restroom?" exchange with the hostess, at exactly the time one of the diners would subsequently turn up dead in said restroom. And if I couldn't get to Finch, say because another patron was in the restroom at the same time he was, he'd see me, making it harder for me to get close later on.

I moved on to the hotel, noting with disappointment that there were no good venues on the way, even assuming I could be sure of Finch's exact route and anticipate him accordingly. But as soon as I reached the hotel, I felt reassured. Call it assassination feng shui: the vibe was just more favorable. The entrance was in the center of an antique, balustraded building that occupied an entire short block. There was no doorman, no bellboy, and no driveway, just a dark, wooden door under an orange awning, flanked on the left by a clothes shop and on the right by a tobacco vendor and a hardware store, all currently closed. Parked cars lined the narrow street alongside the building, creating concealment possibilities around the hotel entrance. I saw not a single pedestrian, and compared to the revelry of the Ringstrasse, this part of the city was practically sepulchral.

I walked around the block, my footfalls against the stone sidewalk the only sound of any note. There was a restaurant around the corner, and two cafés down the street, but they were small affairs, presumably catering to people in the neighborhood and not attracting crowds from farther away. Everything else was either residential, or closed. I saw no security cameras anywhere, and was grateful that, for the moment, at least, Vienna wasn't as blanketed with the devices as Tokyo, London, and, increasingly, major American cities.

I stepped inside the entranceway, ready to provide a story in Japanese-accented broken English about needing a restroom, and was surprised to see that I wasn't yet in the hotel. The front entrance was shared, it seemed, with an apartment complex. To my right was another dark wooden door, marked with the hotel's signature orange; ahead of me was a long flight of wide stone stairs leading to a landing and then continuing on around and above it. Between the hotel and the apartment complex, how much foot traffic could be expected here at night? Not a great deal, I suspected, and the later Finch stayed out for dinner, the greater the likelihood that when he arrived at the hotel, we would have the moment alone I needed.

On the mosaic tiled floor alongside the staircase, I noticed some painting equipment—a tarp, several cans, a ladder, coveralls—and indeed, the corridor smelled of freshly applied oil paint. Nothing worth stealing, so the workmen probably just left it when they quit for the day. I walked over for a closer look, and saw a roll of translucent plastic sheeting the workers must have been using to keep splatter off the tiled floor. I pulled on the deerskin gloves I was carrying, knelt, and unrolled about a foot worth of plastic. It was strong and heavy—about ten mils, I guessed, maybe more—but still flexible. I gripped a corner and tried, unsuccessfully, to drive my thumb through it. I drummed my fingers along the roll and looked around, an idea forming in my mind.

There was a box cutter on the tarp next to the paint cans. I used it to cut off about a three-foot length of the plastic sheeting, which I laid out on the floor alongside the equipment, and then replaced the roll and the box cutter as I'd found them. I stepped outside, called Larison, and told him what I wanted him to do. Then I called Dox, who confirmed that he and Treven were close by the restaurant and that Finch and Capps were inside.

"Good," I told him. "I want you to give them plenty of space. All I need to know is when they leave, whether they're heading toward the hotel together or whether they say goodnight before, and when our friend is a minute away from the hotel."

"You sure he's going back to the hotel? It's a nice city and the weather's good, he might want to go to a club or something."

I thought of Finch, whose file photos had revealed a balding, colorless bureaucrat of about fifty—not so different in appearance, in fact, from J. Edgar Hoover, to whom Horton had compared him. "You think our guy is going clubbing?" I asked.

There was a pause. "Well, not clubbing, maybe. But there are areas of the city where a gentleman who's so inclined can find women of a certain professional disposition. If we get done in time tonight, I'm fixing to visit one of those areas myself."

"I think you might be confusing your own proclivities with those of our friend."

"I'm not sure 'proclivities' is the word I'd use, but okay, I suppose I see your point."

"Look, if he stays out for whatever reason, you just keep watching him. The later he gets back to the hotel, in fact, the better. I just need that one-minute heads-up regardless."

I clicked off, then called Treven and told him to coordinate with Dox to watch the restaurant and the route to the hotel. I hoped we could finish this thing tonight. If we couldn't, our next chance would be in the morning, which would mean watching the hotel entrance all night and trying to do the job in daylight. And every minute you spend in that kind of proximity to a target, you have to remember someone might be targeting you.

chapter fifteen

An hour later, Larison and I were strolling the cramped streets of a neighborhood near the hotel, each of us having separately examined the area as thoroughly as we could in the short time available. We compared notes on points of ingress and egress; noted the locations of ATMs, which would be equipped with cameras; and agreed on the overall approach we would employ. All we had to do now was wait.

"Why go to Washington?" he said at one point. "Forget it. Go after Hort before he comes after you."

Horton had told me the third job would be in D.C. The plan was for the four of us to meet up there after Vienna and receive instructions after we'd arrived.

"How?" I said. "A JSOC colonel? Who knows you'd like nothing more than to take him down and get those diamonds back? What's your plan?"

He looked at me. "I know how to get to him. How to get to him where he lives."

"How?" I said, intrigued.

He shook his head. "Not now. When you're ready. When you look me in the eye and tell me you understand there's no other way."

"Then we'll have to wait."

I watched him. I could see he was frustrated and trying to suppress it.

"What does your friend Dox think?" he said, after a moment.

I saw no advantage to confirming a personal attachment. "I don't know that I'd call him my friend."

"Don't bullshit me. He acts like he doesn't care about anything other than getting paid and laid, but I can see that's an act. You know how he looks when we're all together?"

"How?"

"Like a Rottweiler watching out for his master. I wish I had someone like that guarding my back."

"I'm not his master."

"You know what I mean. Behind the good ol' boy façade, he just looks loyal. Fiercely loyal. And you don't show much, but I have a feeling you must have done something to earn that. I can tell you've been through the shit together. I just don't know what kind of shit."

I wound up telling him about Hong Kong, and Hilger, and how Dox had walked away from a five-million-dollar payday to save my life, and how I'd killed two innocent people just to buy time to save Dox's life. I wondered if I was being stupid. But something made me want to tell him. I wasn't sure what, but I've learned to trust my gut.

When I was done, he said, "So they used Dox to get to you."

The question made me uneasy. I wondered if I'd told him too much. But something still told me it would be useful for him to know. I didn't know why.

"That's right," I said.

"Is there anyone else like that? Someone you care about? But who couldn't protect themselves? Who would be... what's the expression? A hostage to fortune?"

My mind instantly flashed on my small son, Koichiro, whom I'd seen only twice, as an infant in New York, whose mother would have told him by now his father was dead. Whose mother, indeed, had tried to make it so.

I didn't answer. I'd told him enough already. Maybe too much.

He nodded and said, "Well, whoever that person is, he or she is now a hostage to Hort."

I stopped and looked at him, trying to read his expression in the dim light. "Is that what he has on you?"

He answered the same way I had, by saying nothing.

It was hard to imagine this stone killer being that attached to anyone else. But I supposed people might say the same about me.

"Who?" I asked.

His mouth twisted into something midway between a smile and a grimace. "The particulars don't really matter, do they?"

I thought of Koichiro again, then said, "Probably not."

We might have moved on at that point, but instead we lingered, caught in that frustrating space between the desire for understanding and the futility of words for achieving it.

"How do you even know Horton has these diamonds?" I said. I knew he would read the small expression of interest as a weakening, and that it might therefore draw him out.

It did. He said, "Because he took them from me."

He went on to tell me an astonishing story about CIA videos of terror suspects being gruesomely tortured by American interrogators, how the videos were made, who was in them, who stood to be sacrificed as fall guys if the videos ever got out.

"I read about this a few years ago," I said. "I wondered why the Agency was admitting to making those tapes, and to destroying them."

"Well, now you know. They were missing, not destroyed."

"Missing because you took them."

He nodded. "The diamonds were a ransom for the tapes' return. But Hort stole them from me."

I almost asked why he hadn't retaliated by releasing the tapes, but then realized: the hostage. Horton, it seemed, had collected the necessary cards, and then called Larison's bluff.

"When I checked up on you?" I said. "My source told me you were dead."

He smiled coldly. "Greatly exaggerated."

"You staged that?"

A young couple was heading toward us, walking hand-in-hand, the hard consonants of their German echoing off the close-set buildings and the stone sidewalk. Larison paused. They might not have understood English, but at a minimum they would have recognized it, and why give them a recollection of having passed two American men near where a body would soon be found?

When they were safely beyond us, Larison said, "As a way of throwing off the animosity I knew I was going to stir up. Hort saw through it."

"Still, that's a hell of a feat that you managed to stay ahead of them at all. You must have had the whole U.S. government hunting for you."

"It was... interesting. I had to keep moving. A lot of buses, some hitchhiking. Rarely more than one night in the same town."

"Yeah, I've done some of that myself. You see any good parts of the country?"

For a moment, he didn't answer. His eyes drifted away, and his mouth loosened slightly as though in mild wonderment, or even reverence.

"I liked The Lost Coast," he said. "Maybe I'll get back, someday."

Something had happened there, though I doubted he'd tell me what. Knowing Larison, it was probably something dark. I decided not to press.

"The tapes," I said. "Are you in them?"

We started walking again, in silence. Finally he said, "I'm not proud of everything I've done. Are you?"

I found myself considering the question. Considering it carefully.

"There are... things," I said. "Things that weigh on me. What a friend of mine calls 'the cost of it.' You know what I'm talking about?"

He nodded. "Of course."

"I don't know about you, but when I look back, and I'm being honest with myself, which mostly I try to do, it occurs to me that I've done more bad in the world than I've ever done good."

I wondered why I'd said that to him. I'd never thought it before. At least not in those words. Was it what Horton had said to me over breakfast that morning?

I thought he was going to blow it off. Instead, he said, "I have... dreams. Really bad ones. Related to some of the shit I've done, the shit that's on those tapes. I couldn't tell you the last time I lay down at night without dreading what I would face in my sleep. Or the last time I slept through the night without waking up covered in sweat and going for the weapon on the bedstand next to me. The truth is..."

In the dark, I saw his teeth gleam in a smile that faltered into a grimace.

"The truth is," he went on, "I'm pretty fucked up. But what can you do? A shark has to keep swimming, or it dies."

I thought of Midori, the mother of my son. "You know, I once said the same thing to a woman I was trying to explain myself to."

"Yeah? Did she understand?"

I remembered the last time I'd seen her, in New York, and what she'd tried to do just beforehand.

"That would be a no," I said, and we both laughed.

My phone buzzed. Dox. I picked up and said, "What's the status?"

"Our diners have just left the restaurant. A nice familial hug good-night, and our guy is currently on his way to your position alone and on foot, ETA ten minutes. Guess you were right about the clubbing."

"Good. Have—"

"Already done. Our friend on the scooter is zigzagging the street near you. He'll see the diner when he's one minute out. When you get a buzz from scooter man, it's a one-minute ETA. And I'll move in close but not too close in case you need me. Good luck."

"Okay, good." I clicked off and said to Larison, "Less than ten minutes. Let's get in position."

We headed toward the hotel. As we neared the end of Sonnenfels-gasse, just two blocks away, a uniformed cop turned the corner, heading toward us. I wasn't unduly alarmed—there was no reason for him to pay any particular attention to us, and Larison and I had already established that "inebriated drinking companions" would be our cover for action in case we were stopped. I retracted into my harmless Japanese persona and prepared to just walk on by in the shadows.

But a few meters away, he called out, *"Hey."* Larison, I realized, and that damn danger aura he put out. The cop must have keyed on it, con-sciously or unconsciously.

I gave him a small, unsteady wave and moved to go around, but he stopped and put up his hand to indicate we should do the same. *Shit.*

The cop said, *"Wo gehen Sie so Spät noch hin?"* I shook my head. Even if I'd understood his words, and I didn't, I would have pretended not to. The less basis we had for engagement, the more likely he would be to give up in frustration, or otherwise to lose interest and move on.

"Sprechen Sie Deutsch?" he said, and this I did understand. Do you speak German?

Larison answered in slurred Spanish: *"Solamente espanol, y un poco de ingles."* Only Spanish, and a little English—close enough to the Portu-guese I spoke from my time in Brazil to be easily comprehensible.

The cop looked at me. I said, *"Mit Schlag?"*

I was hoping he would smile at that and move on, but he didn't. He said, in English now, "You are at hotel? Here?"

This was going south fast. Our cover was solid and we hadn't committed any crimes, but I didn't want a cop taking a close look at any of us. And if he detained us much longer, we wouldn't be in position in time to intercept Finch at the hotel.

"Hotel?" he said again. "Here?"

I shook my head and said in Japanese-accented English, "The Sacher Vien." It was a famous hotel in the center of the city, though not, of course, one where any of us was actually staying.

Larison said, *"Voy a vomitar."* I'm going to vomit.

I glanced over at him to see where he was going with this. He clamped a hand over his mouth as though trying to dam a rising tide of puke.

No, I thought. *Don't take out the cop. If we do, we can't do Finch...*

Larison groaned through his fingers. The cop said, *"Was zum Teufel?"*

Larison's body convulsed, his head shooting forward, his ass jerking back. Vomit spewed from his mouth all over his shoes.

The cop jumped back and cried out, *"Verdammt nochmal!"*

Larison straightened, gasping, his cheeks puffing, his hands massaging his stomach. A perfect pantomime of a drunken man about to blow for the second time in as many seconds.

"Hotel!" the cop said, pointing in the direction we'd been walking. "Go to hotel. *Jetzt!* Now!"

"Yes," I said, thinking, *thank God.* "Hotel."

Larison groaned again. The cop stepped to the side and again gestured angrily in the direction we'd been walking. I took Larison's arm and led him past. From behind us, I heard the cop muttering something disgustedly. I imagined it was along the lines of *asshole was lucky he didn't puke on my shoes.*

"Nice going," I said, when we had turned the corner. "What did you do, finger in your throat?"

"Yeah. While I was clutching my face." He coughed and spat.

"For a minute there, I thought you were gearing up to drop him. Which would have been a mistake."

"No, I just wanted to dare him to pull me into his cruiser with puke all over my shoes. I had a feeling he'd realize he had more important things to do."

"Where did you learn your Spanish?"

"Ops. Latin America." It was a sufficiently vague description to make clear he didn't want to talk about it more. Not that we had time.

"We still have a few minutes," I said. "Quick, knock the puke off your shoes. We don't want to track anything into the hotel."

He whacked his feet against the side of a building a few times, then stamped and scraped his soles along the ground. Between that and the two hundred meters we still had to walk, we'd be fine.

Treven buzzed my mobile just as we arrived at the hotel entrance. ETA one minute. Cutting it a little close, but still manageable. Larison stayed outside, hunkering down between two parked cars just a few meters from the doorway, as I pulled on my gloves and went in. The corridor was still satisfyingly quiet. I quickly slipped into one of the coveralls that had been left on the tarp. They were a little large, but not excessively so. I grabbed a can of paint and a paintbrush and the length of plastic sheeting I'd cut, put the paint can on the floor next to the interior hotel entranceway, and started running the brush up and down the wall like a painter on the midnight shift. The whole thing was sufficiently incongruous to give Finch pause while he tried to sort it through, but by the time he had figured out what was wrong with this picture, it would already be too late.

A moment later, I heard the exterior door open. I glanced right and saw Finch on his way in, then looked back to the work I was ostensibly engaged in, not wanting to alarm him by paying him undue attention. In my peripheral vision, I watched him come closer. Five meters. Four. Three.

He slowed, perhaps in concern at what the hell a workman was doing here, alone and this late at night. But then the exterior door opened behind him. I glanced right again and saw Larison coming in, looking formidable, purposeful, and deadly. Finch turned and I knew that for the next half second, his mind would be fully occupied with trying to place Larison's face; realizing he'd seen it earlier, in Café Prückel; weighing whether this could be happenstance or whether he should be concerned; deciding that the man he'd just made twice was too dangerous-looking to be merely a coincidence; combining that datapoint with the incongruous presence of a "workman" who was now behind him...

I set down the brush and headed in, taking hold of both ends of the length of plastic sheeting, palms up and thumbs out, turning my hands over and crossing my arms as I moved to create an isosceles triangle with my forearms as the long lines and the plastic as the base. Finch must have heard me coming because he started to turn, but too late. I dropped the plastic over his head and levered my forearms against the back of his skull, molding the plastic across his face, dragging him backward to ruin his balance. He clawed at what was covering his eyes and nose and mouth, but his fingers couldn't penetrate the thick plastic. He got off a single, muffled cry, but then couldn't draw breath for another. He tried to turn and I let him, staying with him, steering him toward the dark of the stairs, keeping him disoriented and off balance. He groped behind for me and I put a knee in his lower back, bending him over it, keeping my face well clear of his flailing arms. He tried scratching at my hands and forearms, but was stymied by the gloves and the same kind of wrist tape I had used in Las Vegas.

I knew his oxygen was getting used up rapidly and it was only a matter of seconds before his brain started to shut down. I glanced up and saw Larison, wearing his own gloves, his head turned to watch us, holding closed the exterior door against the small possibility of a late arriving hotel guest or apartment dweller. In a moment, Finch would be still, and at that point, even if someone came through the interior door, they would likely turn left toward the exterior door and key on Larison, remaining oblivious to the silent tableau in the dark behind them. And if anyone happened to come down the stairs, I would switch to Samaritan mode, talking to Finch's body as though trying to rouse a drunken acquaintance. Not a great detail for someone to remember, especially after our earlier encounter with the cop, but not necessarily fatal, either.

Finch's legs sagged and he went to his knees, his chest bucking and jerking as his lungs desperately tried to suck air, his hands again clawing, feebly now, against the plastic sealed across his face. And then, in extremis, some lingering, rational part of his brain must have asserted itself, because his right hand stopped clawing at his face and dropped to his front pants pocket. My mind flashed *knife!* and I shot my knee into his elbow to disrupt him—a second time, again. But the angle was awkward and the blow attenuated and he managed to get his hand into his pocket. I was about to change my grip to cover the plastic over his nose and mouth with my left hand while I grabbed the wrist of his knife hand with my right, but Larison had seen what was happening and came charging back from the exterior door, seizing Finch's hand just as it came free, a gravity-assisted folding knife popping open en route. Larison started to twist Finch's hand to make him drop the knife, and I whispered urgently, "No! No damage!" Finch's arm shook and he tried to turn the knife to cut Larison's hands, but Larison had too secure a grip, and whatever reserves Finch had drawn upon to access the weapon had been his last. His body went limp, the knife clattered to the floor, and he collapsed back into me.

"Get back to the door," I said. "Fast." Only a small chance anyone would come in at exactly that moment, but Murphy's Law had a way of turning small chances into inevitable events, and this was the one moment there would be nothing we could do to conceal what was happening. Larison dashed back to the door while I dragged Finch to the stairs. "Two minutes," I said, to let Larison know that's how long I wanted to keep the plastic in place, to be certain Finch was done.

I counted off the time and, when I was satisfied, eased the plastic away and laid Finch out at the foot of the stairs. I examined his face for damage and noted none. I took the paint can and brush and replaced them as I had found them. Then I scanned the tile floor, looking for any scuff marks Finch's heels might have left. Yes, there they were, two sets of about a meter each from when I had dragged him. I grabbed a cloth from where the painting equipment was placed, and rubbed them away. Larison glanced back but he must have understood what I was doing because he said nothing.

I recovered the knife and placed it back in Finch's pocket. Hard to imagine anyone would be in a position to note its absence if we took it, but it's best to doctor a crime scene as little as possible. The coveralls, though, I would keep. If they were missed at all, anything could explain their absence, and I didn't want to chance leaving behind something that might be contaminated with my hair or clothing fibers. For the same reason, I kept the cloth I'd just used, which might be examined and found to contain some of the material from Finch's heels.

I took a quick look around the hallway and saw nothing out of place. Well, Finch's body on the stairs, of course, but that looked like what it was supposed to be: a man in sudden distress, perhaps respiratory, perhaps cardiac, staggers over to the stairs to sit, stumbles, and collapses. The manner of his death might have left some minor petechiae—ruptured capillaries—in his face and eyes, but I expected this would be minimal and of little forensic note under the circumstances. The truly suspicious might wonder at the coincidence of his being stricken in the very hotel where he had a reservation and where he might therefore be anticipated, but like car accidents, which happen mostly in a driver's own neighborhood simply because that's where he most often drives, the coincidence of the location of Finch's collapse was also easily explained, and therefore, also, easily dismissed.

I nodded to Larison and we headed out, splitting up immediately. Larison went right; I went straight, crossing the street and cutting through a small shopping arcade, currently closed and dark. I would have gone left and therefore more directly away from Larison, but that was the direction in which we'd encountered the cop, and I didn't want to risk bumping into him again.

I wondered about the knife. It had been a near thing and I realized I'd been complacent because Finch didn't look the type. Plus, how the hell had he gotten it through security on his flights? Maybe he had a checked bag. Or maybe there was some sort of special dispensation for government officials. There usually is.

Twenty minutes later, after discarding in various refuse containers the coveralls and the plastic sheeting I had used to kill Finch, I called Dox. Larison would be doing the same with Treven. "It's done," I told him.

"No trouble?"

"A little," I said, thinking about the cop. "But we handled it."

"Good to hear. You're okay?"

"Fine."

"You want to meet and brief?"

"Better to do it on the other side of the pond. No sense being seen together here unless there's a good reason."

"Other than my fine company. But don't worry, it's okay."

I wondered for a moment whether I'd hurt his feelings. Did he really want to just… get together? Celebrate, or something?

But he quickly disabused me with a laugh. "Just kidding. Actually, since there are no more trains at this hour, I was thinking I might find a companion more closely suited to my proclivities, as you like to call them."

"Sure, knock yourself out. Just check for the Adam's Apple, okay?"

Once, in Bangkok, Dox was all set to go off with a gorgeous lady boy when at the last moment I had taken pity and warned him. But saving him from an embarrassing mistake and letting him live it down were two different things.

He laughed. "Yes, sir, I have learned my lesson. Anyway, I'm looking forward to an evening on the town. Don't forget, this was a nice payday. Though I feel like you've done most of the heavy lifting."

"I wouldn't feel comfortable doing it under the circumstances if you didn't have my back."

There was a pause, then he said, "I appreciate that, man. Thank you."

I thought of the way he'd carried me, as I was bleeding out, over a giant shoulder in Hong Kong, of the transfusion he'd saved me with afterward. "It's just the truth."

"You're not going to get all sentimental on me, though, are you?"

I smiled. "Never."

"Well, it's a good thing we're not getting together tonight. I'd probably give you a big hug, and you might embarrass yourself by hugging me back."

"Yeah, thanks for that. I appreciate it."

He laughed. "Okay, then. Gonna party like a rock star and I'll see you soon."

I clicked off and walked alone through Vienna.

I thought about everything Larison had said earlier. I told myself, *just one more*.

The mantra of many an alcoholic.

•   •   •

Larison walked slowly back to the hotel, trying to avoid civilians, keeping to the shadows. His mind was racing and his emotions were roiling and he knew when he was feeling like this the people around him could sense it, like some weird disturbance in an urban force field. A prostitute trolling at the edge of a park he passed started to smile at him with practiced professionalism, and then the smile faltered. A cloud passed across her face and she took a step away, half turning as though preparing to run. In a more superstitious culture, he knew, she might have crossed herself.

He walked on, his head tracking left and right, checking hot spots, logging his surroundings. How could Rain be so stupid about what he was up against with Hort? With Treven, he understood the psychology—the attachment to the unit, the command structure, the blessing of higher authority. But Rain, obviously, didn't need that kind of support network, and had long lived outside it. Then what was making the man hesitate? If his motives were purely mercenary, the diamonds were the obvious play. Was this really about doing something good in the world? The notion was vaguely seductive, but come on. All Larison wanted, the best he could hope for, was to eliminate the threat, get back the diamonds, and live out the rest of his days somewhere quiet with Nico, someplace with a beach and the sound of the ocean and no memories, a place where the dreams might eventually slacken and abate. Beyond that didn't matter. If death were really the end, then everything Larison had done, and all the torments it caused him, would die with him. If there were a hell, it would be his new address. Whatever he might do in whatever time he might have left would have no impact on any of it, one way or the other, and to imagine otherwise was nothing but a childish fantasy.

It was a little sad, actually. He respected Rain. Felt in some ways the man was even a kindred spirit—another self-contained, lethal loner, professionally paranoid, personally aloof.

But what difference did any of that make? In his position, sentiment was a weakness, and in his line of work, weaknesses got you killed.

Still, he was surprised to feel an uncharacteristic sense of regret at the thought of taking out Rain and the others. He wondered if it was a sign of aging, or whether it might be some last, twitching vestige of a conscience he'd long since left for dead. What if it was? He'd read his Thoreau in high school. How did it go again? Something like, *What's the point of having a conscience, if you don't listen to it?*

But Thoreau had never been a soldier. And if there was one thing he'd learned from Hort, it was that the mission came before the man. The mission. And the current mission couldn't be more clear: eliminate Hort and recover the diamonds. Protect Nico. Protect himself.

As for the rest… well, it was a rare mission that didn't involve collateral damage. You didn't welcome it, but you couldn't shrink from it, either. In the end, he supposed, all men do what they have to.

The trick was living with it afterward. But he'd had plenty of practice with that.

chapter sixteen

I arrived in D.C. on an Amtrak train from New York, having flown to JFK from Munich. I preferred not to use obvious routes to or from the places I might be expected. Dox, Larison, and Treven had traveled somewhat less circuitously, and had therefore arrived ahead of me, but that was their risk, not mine.

The meeting was at the downtown Capital Hilton, a large and appropriately anonymous conference hotel Dox had recommended and where he'd made a room reservation. I had the cab drop me off at the Hay Adams, across from the White House, instead, thinking I'd walk the few blocks to the Hilton rather than give the driver a chance to note my actual destination. But instead of heading straight to the meeting, I succumbed to a strange urge to join the throng of tourists milling along the tall iron security fence at the edge of the expansive front lawn.

I strolled over, my pores opening immediately in the afternoon humidity. It was a cloudy day, but somehow the absence of sun exacerbated the heat, which felt like it was radiating from everything rather than from some single, identifiable source. Even the squirrels in Lafayette Square seemed listless, lethargic, as motionless as the nearby humans slouching on park benches and sweating under the useless foliage in rolled shirt-sleeves and loosened ties.

As I exited the park, I was immediately struck by how fortified the area was. Pennsylvania Avenue had been shut down to automobile traffic, presumably out of fear of truck bombs. There were steel vehicle traps through which delivery trucks had to pass for inspection; multiple guard posts; swarms of uniformed cops and military personnel patrolling on foot, on bicycles, and in cars. The windows of the far-off building itself stared insensate through the thick iron bars separating the grounds from the citizenry, as blank and impenetrable as the tactical shades of the scores of men guarding them. What had once been a residence and office was now, in essence, a bunker.

I moved on, heading southwest in the beginning of a long loop that would give me ample opportunities to confirm I wasn't being followed before arriving at the Hilton. Outside the garrisoned grounds of the White House, the city was unremarkable, even bland. The streets were wide and straight; the architecture unimaginative; the ambiance, non-existent. I noted that, along with London and New York, Washington seemed one of the few remaining cities where men were determined to wear jackets and ties even in the summer. The difference being that in London and New York, the men knew how to dress. But what they lacked in sartorial sense, Washington's office workers made up for with a certain bounce in their gait. I wondered what might account for their perkiness, and decided it was proximity to power. After all, a dog wags its tail even when it's begging for a scrap, not only when it receives one.

I had called Horton from the airport and briefed him on what happened in Vienna. As with Shorrock, he'd already heard. He told me the money had been deposited and proposed that we meet to discuss the next assignment. But I saw no upside to a face-to-face. We still had the communications gear he'd given me in L.A. I'd ditched the cyanide, and didn't think I'd need a replacement. So I declined, telling him to use a secure site I'd set up, instead.

I paused in another park, fished the iPad out of my shoulder bag, and found a public Wi-Fi network. I checked the bank account and confirmed deposit of the three hundred thousand. Then I checked the secure site to see if Horton had uploaded the target file.

He had. I opened it and saw the name. I would have recognized it even if it hadn't been immediately followed by her title:

Diane Schmalz. U.S. Supreme Court Justice.

No, I thought, shaking my head at the screen. *Not a chance.*

He was ignoring my rules about women and children. Maybe he thought I wasn't serious, that the money would matter more. If so, he was wrong. I'd lived by my rules for a long time, and even the one deviation hadn't really been an exception, because I did it for personal reasons, not as part of a job. I wasn't going to change now.

But what if killing her saves thousands?

No. I didn't care. If there's one thing I know as well as I know killing, it's how subornment works. One baby step at a time. The art of getting someone to cross a line he doesn't even see until he looks back and realizes it's already impossibly far behind him.

I glanced through the file. Photographs. Home addresses, both in D.C. and a weekend place in western Maryland. Schedule. No observed security consciousness and no protection, because no Supreme Court Justice had ever been assassinated.

But it didn't make sense. I'd never had much interest in what passes for justice in America, but I knew Schmalz's name, and I knew she had a reputation as one of the court's last guardians of civil liberties. It was hard to imagine her being part of a plot to end those liberties. If anything, I would have expected her to be on the other side.

I scanned down and saw that Horton must have anticipated my concern. He had written:

When the president declares his assumption of emergency powers, he'll be sued. There are four authoritarian Justices who will back him. The other four might or might not. Schmalz would absolutely oppose him, leading to a possible five-four defeat. Not necessarily fatal to their plans, but certainly it would be a major public relations setback not to secure the Supreme Court's blessing along with that of Congress.

Schmalz's son is a lawyer, married with three small children. He is a closeted homosexual and the plotters have graphic photographic and video evidence of his infidelities. He has also twice threatened suicide, and received therapy and other treatment afterward. Schmalz understands that were her son's homosexuality revealed, it would destroy his family and career, devastate her grandchildren, and likely cause this unstable man to take his own life. She will do what's she's told to prevent all this.

But not if she passes away beforehand.

I reread the relevant paragraphs and felt an uncharacteristic anger taking hold of me. One of my rules has always been no acts against non-principals. Meaning no deaths of non-principals primarily, but still, I've never liked the idea of solving a problem with Person A by going after Person B. Kill Schmalz? If I really wanted to do something good in the world, I thought, I ought to go after the people who were threatening to ruin her son and grandchildren just to secure a favorable vote.

I wondered why Horton didn't do something arguably less extreme. Find some way to out the son in advance and defuse the blackmail bomb by preempting it? Maybe he thought that would tip his hand to the plotters in a way that a kindly-looking grandmother's peaceful demise in her sleep wouldn't.

But I didn't care. I didn't like the smell of this thing anymore, or where it seemed to be taking me. The others could do what they wanted. I was out.

I exited the site and purged the browser, then found a payphone, called the Hilton, and asked for James Hendricks, the name Dox had told me he would check in under. "We on?" I said.

"Gang's all here, partner. Twelve-thirty-four."

That meant they were in room 901. My habit with Dox was to use a simple code when mentioning exact dates, times, room numbers and the like. We just added three to each digit. It wasn't much and wouldn't be all that difficult to crack, but one more layer of defense never hurt anyone.

"I'll be there in ten minutes," I said, then hung up and unobtrusively wiped down the handset with a handkerchief. Being in the belly of the beast was making me twitchy.

I headed over to the Hilton. The lobby was crowded, apparently due to the annual convention of something called The American Constitution Society. I couldn't help smiling a little. *If you only knew.*

I took the elevator to the tenth floor, then the stairs down to nine. I emerged into the middle of a narrow corridor about a hundred meters long. I looked left, and at the far end saw two men in suits and shades who looked like bodyguards waiting outside a VIP's room. Not so unusual, and easily explained by the convention downstairs or by one of the nearby embassies. Still, I wasn't sorry to see from a sign that 901 was to the right. I walked to the end of the corridor, made a left, and found the room. I knocked once and the door opened instantly—Treven. He must have been watching through the peephole. I nodded in acknowledgement and walked in. Dox and Larison were sitting across from each other on the room's twin beds, eating sandwiches. I heard Treven latching the door behind me.

"You hungry?" Dox said, holding up an Au Bon Pain bag. "We got tuna, turkey, and roast beef."

On the beds alongside them were a couple of pistols. A Wilson Combat, which must have been Dox's; a Glock that I assumed was Larison's. I wondered if Treven was carrying, too. Seeing the guns gave me mixed feelings. In general, better to be armed, yes, but I didn't know Larison or Treven well enough to like the feeling of their carrying firearms around me.

"Where'd you get the hardware?" I said. "The underground redneck railroad again?"

Dox grinned. "This time, just a gun show in Chantilly. You know, better to have it and not need it than to need it and not have it. Picked out a Wilson for you, too. These hombres here like their Glocks, but you know me."

He handed me a Tactical Supergrade Compact and two spare magazines. I put the magazines in my front pockets, then checked the load and secured the gun in my waistband. It felt good. If Larison and Treven were going to be carrying, I was glad I was, too.

"Sandwich?" Dox asked.

"No, I'm good," I said. "You eat, I'll talk."

I sat down next to Dox. Treven hesitated, then did the same next to Larison, across from me. I briefed them all on what had happened in Vienna. Then I told them who the next target was. And told them I was out, and why.

"I don't get it," Dox said, when I was done. "I mean, who cares if her son is gay? I thought we were living in the twenty-first century. Hell, I love gay men. If they stick to loving each other, it just means more ladies for me."

"It's not that he's gay," I said. "It's that he's closeted. That's the exploitable aspect. Although I agree it's a shame."

Larison and Treven hadn't said anything yet. I was surprised they were being so quiet.

"Anyway," Dox said, "I'm not exactly okay with euthanizing a little old lady. But even more than that… damn, a Supreme Court Justice? I mean, we're already practically making history here with some of the targets we just took down. But being the first to rack up a Supreme? I'm starting to feel like we might be growing bullseyes on our backs, and I don't think I like it."

"I don't care one way or the other," Larison said. "You know why I'm in this. But if you feel like we're growing targets on our backs, congratulations, it means you're starting to wake up."

I looked at Treven. "You want this?" I said. "Do it yourself and it's a two-million dollar payday."

"Don't be an idiot," Larison said, looking at Treven. "It's a setup. This whole fucking thing is a setup. Go out on your own and you'll be the first one to get picked off."

A long moment went by. Treven said, "Whether you're in this for the money, or whether it's because you want to save a lot of lives, the calculus is the same. A false flag terror attack is still a terror attack. Innocent people die either way. If removing one more player makes the difference, I'll do it, with or without the rest of you."

"A player?" Dox said. "Have you ever seen a picture of this woman? She looks like my grandma. I'm not holding a damn pillow over her face, no sir. Give me nightmares for the rest of my life."

I didn't like Treven's response. It struck me as the product of bluster, not of thought. I wondered why he'd be so touchy. Had he been feeling left out? Jealous that he hadn't been at the center of things with Shorrock and Finch? It seemed silly that someone so capable and experienced could also be so adolescent. If I could have been paid either way and stayed at the periphery, I would have been glad to.

But it was all the same to me. "Here," I said, firing up the iPad and accessing the secure site. I input my pass code, then saw a message from Kanezaki: *Call me ASAP.*

I deleted the message and handed the iPad to Treven. "Hold on," I said. "Looks like we might have some new information about Horton." I popped the batteries in my phone, turned it on, and called Kanezaki.

He picked up instantly. "Did you do Jack Finch?" he said.

I was taken aback but didn't show it. "What are you talking about?" I saw the others glance over.

"Stop playing with me. The president is about to announce his replacement. Colonel Horton."

My stomach lurched. "Finch's replacement is… Horton?" I said. Larison was nodding as though he already knew.

"That's not all. Shorrock, the guy you say died in Las Vegas because of an ironic act of God? He was giving secret testimony to Congress about abuses within the National Counterterrorism Center. He was just a civilian manager, he wouldn't know an op if one snuck up and bit him on the ass, the last guy in the world to want to run, or to be able to run, a false flag attack. But you know who's replacing him?"

I felt sick. "No."

"The number two guy there, Dan Gillmor. And Gillmor's no civilian appointee. He's former JSOC, one of Horton's guys. Been part of the military/intelligence/corporate/security complex his entire life. And he's a fanatic. Knights of Malta like James Jesus Angleton and William Casey, crusader challenge coins—"

"Crusader challenge coins?"

"Some of these guys, like Erik Prince, think what we're doing in the Middle East is a holy war, a new Crusades. It's a network of zealots. And this one is now perfectly positioned to run the groups Horton told you were being used for these impending false flag attacks. Now his interfering boss is out of the way, and he's number one. He can do anything he wants without having to explain himself to some meddling civilian."

I didn't say anything. There was so much to process, I couldn't sort it all through.

Dox, Larison, and Treven were all watching me, their sandwiches forgotten. I'd said little, but my expression and posture must have told them everything.

"Did you do it?" Kanezaki said. "Shorrock? Finch? Was it you?"

I didn't answer.

"Jesus Christ, John. You're not preventing a coup. You just cleared the way to one."

Still I didn't answer. I was struggling to connect the dots. Larison was right. I'd been an idiot. An idiot.

"Do you get it?" Kanezaki said. "Horton isn't trying to stop this thing. He's one of the plotters. He mixed a lot of truth into his lies just to—"

"Stop," I said. "Let me think."

Dox said, "What's going on?"

I held up a hand, palm out, and said to Kanezaki, "This announcement about Horton's new position. When is it scheduled to happen?"

"I don't know. But the word is, soon."

"What about Gillmor? When will that be announced?"

"The same."

I put my thumb over the phone's microphone and looked over at the others. My mind was racing but I kept my voice calm. "Schmalz is a setup. We need to get out of here. Get ready. Just trying to learn a little more, then I'll fill you in and we'll talk about how to bug out."

The three of them stood. There was an electric feeling building in the room that I didn't like.

I moved my thumb and said to Kanezaki, "Anything else?"

"Yes. Why are you asking about the timing? Of the announcement about Horton and Gillmor."

"If the announcements are any time soon, Horton didn't care that I could hear of them before doing the third target. That means the third target was a setup."

"Third target... there's another? Who?"

"Diane Schmalz."

"The Supreme Court Justice? Are you fucking insane?"

"Relax. I was already going to turn it down. But he never expected me to do it in the first place. It was just a ploy to get me to Washington."

"Shit. You're in Washington now?"

"Yes."

"You need to get out of the city. D.C. is the last place you want Horton hunting for you. Especially now, he has local resources that can lock down that place like he's closing the door on a closet."

"Thanks for the information," I said, preparing to click off. "I'll call you when I'm somewhere safe."

"Wait," he said. "Hold on. Just got something on my screen. It's... oh, fuck."

"What?"

"Terror alert. Goes out to everyone in the intelligence and law enforcement communities. CIA, FBI, local and state police, everyone. It says... hang on, okay, Shorrock and Finch didn't die, they were murdered. According to toxicology tests, with cyanide. And that you were involved. You, the two ISA operators you asked me about, and Dox.

And that you're all armed, special-ops trained, and believed to be in the Washington metro area right now, planning another terror attack."

It had to be Horton. No one else knew about the cyanide. And Horton didn't know that I hadn't even used it.

"You can't get out of there now," Kanezaki said. "Every airport, every train station, every bus station, they'll be crawling with personnel. Every surveillance camera in the city will be looking for you."

"Do they have photographs?"

"Grainy in the alert. Like blow-ups from surveillance cameras."

Las Vegas, I guessed. Our best bet would be cabs, at least to start with. The farther we got from the city center, the less concentrated the opposition would be. But we had to move fast.

"All right, at least they're grainy," I said. "I doubt the average cop—"

"You don't get it. You're not going to be arrested. The president has an assassination list, don't you know that? There's a NOFORN addendum to this alert that says you're on it. All four of you. They'll shoot you on sight. And if you do wind up captured, there's Guantanamo, Bagram, Camp No, the Salt Pit… and those are just the ones that have been disclosed. There are others they can put you in the Red Cross has never heard of, let alone visited, you understand? You'll have a number, that's it. No one will know your name. John, some of these places, you might as well be on another planet, or in another dimension. You get there, you're just—"

"I need to go. I'll call you."

"Wait. Let me help you."

"Why would you do that?"

"Because you're the only ones who can stop this thing now."

"Bullshit. Spill it to the media. Don't you have contacts at the New York Times?"

He laughed. "You think the Times would do anything with this, even if I had proof? They sat on Bush's illegal domestic surveillance program until after he was safely reelected. Their editor-in-chief asks the White House for permission to publish, for God's sake, and is proud of it, too."

"Then one of the networks. ABC, CNN, whatever."

He laughed again. "Did you catch Jeremy Scahill's report about the Agency's secret prison in Somalia? The seventh floor had apoplexy, it was so dead-on accurate. They used Barbara Starr and Luis Martinez to discredit it. ABC and CNN, the watchdog media."

"Then call Scahill."

"The people we're up against will just instruct the networks to ignore or discredit him. The networks work for us, John. Which I admit is mostly useful and I've taken advantage of it many times myself. But it's working against us right now."

"Wikileaks, then."

"Now you're making sense. But I don't have any proof. Get me some."

"No. I don't want to get further into this. I want to get out."

"You're telling me you're not going to make Horton pay for setting you up?"

I didn't answer.

"You think he's going to stop coming after you? You know as well as I do that he'll be more motivated now than ever."

Again I said nothing.

"Damn it, John, let me help you."

I was in a box and I couldn't see a way out of it. "Goddamn it. How?"

"I'll come to you. Put you in the trunk of my car and drive you out of the city."

"The trunk? There are four of us. What kind of car do you have?"

"Honda."

"What model?"

There was a pause. "Civic."

I looked over at the collective mass of Larison, Treven, and Dox. "No way," I said.

"You'd be amazed what you can fit into a tight space with a little Crisco," Dox offered, apparently having intuited what we were talking about.

"You have a better idea?" Kanezaki said.

"We're talking about eight hundred, maybe nine hundred pounds. You couldn't get us all in there with a chainsaw and a blender. And even if you could, the back of the car would be riding suspiciously low."

"I'll borrow my sister's minivan. You can all hunker down. As long as no one stops me, no one will see you. It's built to hold seven, the shocks won't even be noticeably compressed."

That sounded more promising. "When can you be here?"

"Where are you?"

If it had been anyone but Kanezaki, I would have been suspicious of a setup. But I trusted him as much as I did anyone other than Dox. Plus, I had no choice.

"Capital Hilton," I said.

"She lives in Chevy Chase. It's not that far, but we're getting into rush hour now."

"Can you have her meet you someplace in between and swap cars there?"

"That's a good idea. I'll be there in an hour. Maybe less. If there's a problem, I can't reach her or she's out with her kids somewhere, or whatever, I'll call you."

"Leave a message on the secure site. My phone will be out of commission."

"Right, okay."

"We'll meet you in the lowest level of the parking garage. Away from the elevators."

"Got it. See you soon."

I clicked off and disabled and pocketed the phone. Larison, Treven, and Dox had moved out from between the beds and away from each other. Everyone's arms were loose and their hands open. They looked liked gunslingers in a western a half-second away from drawing.

"What the fuck is going on?" Treven said.

I didn't like the accusatory tone I heard in the question, and reminded myself to be extra calm in my response. Four armed, dangerous, and suddenly distrustful men in a small room… if things got out of hand, it was going to be very bad.

"You were right," I said, looking at Larison. "Horton set us up. Shorrock has been replaced by one of Horton's guys, and Finch is about to be replaced by Horton himself. The government just issued some kind of all-points terror alert saying the four of us killed both of them with cyanide. We were just put on the presidents' kill list. And they know we're in D.C."

"Horton and that damn cyanide," Dox said. "So that was just sup-posed to incriminate us and sound scary to the public, too?"

I nodded. "Yeah. And the hell of it is, I never even used it. And no one else…"

I stopped, realizing I'd missed something obvious. Dangerously ob-vious.

Treven's eyes narrowed. "What?"

I didn't answer. I realized there were three people who thought I'd used cyanide on Shorrock: not just Horton, but also Larison and Treven. Either one of them, or both, could have mistakenly told Horton that I'd used the cyanide. That would have given him additional confidence to order the faked toxicology reports. He would have believed there re-ally would be evidence of cyanide if anyone examined the corpses more thoroughly.

"Then how did you do Shorrock?" Larison said. "The way you did Finch?"

I was struck that despite the tension in the room, he could remain so detached and professionally curious.

"Doesn't matter," I said. But if Larison and Treven were working for Horton, they wouldn't be on that terror alert, right? Unless the idea were to make it look like we were all in the same boat, when in fact…

Treven tensed. In my peripheral vision, I saw Dox spot it, too.

There was a blur of movement, and an instant later all four of us had our guns out. Treven and I were pointing at each other. Dox was aiming at Treven. Larison had the muzzle of his angled toward the floor, but his head and eyes tracked from Treven to Dox to me and back again.

"You think I had something to do with this?" Treven said. "I'm as fucked as you are."

I saw his hands were as steady as mine. "Put your gun down if you want to get unfucked," I said.

Treven said nothing.

Larison's head kept tracking. He looked like a rattlesnake trying to make up his mind about in which direction to strike.

I thought we had maybe two more seconds before the tension boiled over. I couldn't figure out a way to stop it.

Suddenly, Dox brought the muzzle of his Wilson Combat up to his own neck. "Hold it," he said. "The next man makes a move, the nigger gets it."

I blinked and thought, *What the fuck?*

"Drop it," he said. "Or I swear, I'll blow this nigger's head all over this town!"

He looked from one of us to the other, his eyes wide in faux lunacy.

Larison started to grin, then guffawed. "All right," he said. "You win. You win." He eased his pistol into the back of his waistband and held up his hands.

Treven glanced at Larison, then his eyes went back to Dox. His pistol stayed on me. "What the hell are you talking about?" he said.

"Good Lordy-Lord," Dox said, his voice a falsetto now. "He's desperate. Do what he say! Do what he say!"

"You're crazy," Treven said, but he lowered his gun a few inches. I did the same.

"What," Dox said, "y'all never saw Blazing Saddles? Cleavon Little? I always wondered if it'd work for real."

Treven's gun dropped a little more. "You're crazy," he said again.

Dox kept his own gun in position at his neck. "Well, it's a film, you see. A very fine film, in which—"

"I know the movie," Treven said.

Dox took the gun from his neck and slid it into the back of his waistband. "Well, maybe the part you're missing, and this could be due to the subtlety of my delivery, is that two seconds ago we were on the verge of committing a big old group suicide here. Besides hoping to get y'all to come to your senses, that's what I was trying to demonstrate. You see, placing my weapon to my own neck was a metaphor—"

"We get it," I said, slowly lowering my gun. Treven did the same.

"I'm waiting for someone to thank me for not doing the campfire scene," Dox said.

Larison was still grinning, and I imagined this was the first time he appreciated just how cool Dox could be when the shit was hitting the fan. And how much method there was to his hillbilly madness. "Oh baby, you are so talented," he said, and it was incongruous enough to make me realize it must have been another line from the movie.

"And they are so dumb," Dox said, confirming my suspicion. They both laughed, and I thought maybe they would be okay now. He wasn't a man you'd want to fuck with, but laugh at Dox's jokes and chances were good you'd have a friend for life.

Treven, though, was still an open question. I slid the gun back into my waistband. Treven hesitated, but then followed suit.

"Let's try to stay chilly," I said. "We have enough people trying to kill us just now without doing the job for them." Dox and Larison were still laughing, so the message was mostly for Treven. And, I supposed, for myself.

I briefed them on my conversation with Kanezaki. We all agreed that, overall, our safest move was to stay put until we met him in the garage.

"I should have known these targets and this thing were too big for them to leave us alone afterward," Dox said. "I let the damn money cloud my reason."

No one spoke. Dox looked at Larison. "I believe you've earned the right to say 'I told you so.'"

Larison shook his head. "The question is, what do we do now?"

"Exactly," Treven said. "Wherever your guy takes us, all right, we're out of the crosshairs, at least for the moment, but what do we do then?"

I turned to Larison. "You said you had a way of getting to Horton."

He nodded. "If you're really ready to hear it."

I looked at him. "I am."

"Okay, then. We're going to need your friend's car. Not just to get out of the area. To get back to Los Angeles."

chapter
seventeen

Larison briefed us on the vulnerability he had discovered. It was Horton's daughter.

"She's a film school grad student at UCLA," he explained. "Name is Mimi Kei. Parents are divorced and she uses her mother's maiden name. The mother's Japanese."

"But I checked him out on Wikipedia," I said. "When you first mentioned his name, in Tokyo. There wasn't much outside a few highlights of his military career, but it said he's divorced with no children."

"He doesn't want people to know about her," Larison said. "He has a lot of enemies. That's probably why she uses her mother's name. Makes it that much harder for anyone to make the connection."

"Well, how did you make it?" Dox asked.

Larison smiled. "I always knew if I ever got exposed and someone came after me, it would be Hort, and I wanted an insurance policy against that possibility. So after I pulled my little disappearing act, but before I made my move with the torture tapes, I tracked him. Caught a lucky break, observed him having lunch one day with a pretty young woman in downtown D.C. Followed her back to Georgetown University. Spent some time on Facebook and found her. Her page was privacy protected, but it was easy enough to use the name to confirm she was an undergrad at Georgetown, to track the name Kei to Hort's failed marriage, and then to do some judicious social engineering to get her to accept a friend request from a Facebook profile I created. I can tell you from her photo page that she's close with both her parents. And more importantly, that Hort dotes on her. You should see his face in the photos of them together. I guarantee you, take her as collateral, and Hort will do anything we tell him."

I realized that an hour earlier, I had reacted with anger and disgust that the plotters were threatening someone's family. And yet here I was, contemplating the same. I had two routes of rationalization available: first, that unlike Schmalz, Horton had brought this on himself. Second, that unlike those of the plotters, our threats against Mimi Kei would be bluffs.

I looked at Larison's expression, and realized we weren't going to see eye to eye on that last point. I would have to watch him. Closely.

"And she's at UCLA now?" I asked.

Larison nodded. "Second-year this fall. Taking summer classes even as we speak. I've been keeping tabs."

"That's why he knows L.A. so well," I said. "I wondered about that the two times I met him there. In fact, he suggested L.A. to me. I first thought he was just proposing it as a convenient point between Washington and Tokyo, but no. He was looking for an excuse to visit his daughter."

Larison smiled again. "His little girl."

"All right," Treven said, "but what's the play? We don't know where she lives, we don't know her habits, I don't think we know much about UCLA. Where do we grab her? Where do we hold her? Without the right tools, I don't see how we're going to ensure she's quiet and cooperative without being brutal. And look, we'll do what we have to do, but if we fuck her up too much, it's hard to say which way it'll cut with Hort. We want to threaten her, absolutely, but if we have to start actually doing it, we lose leverage."

"I don't know about that," Larison said. "I'd even argue that hurting her, with the promise of much worse, would be the ideal way to ensure Hort is as compliant and cooperative as possible. But I'm confident he'll do what we want either way."

"Okay," Treven said. "Assume we grab her. Hold her somewhere, threaten to hurt her if Hort doesn't cooperate. But cooperate how? Even if he calls off the dogs, the second his daughter is safe, they'll be on us again. You planning on holding her forever?"

"Not forever," Larison said. "Just long enough to recover the diamonds."

"You're still thinking about the diamonds?" Dox said. "Shit, I'm just looking for a way to get the president to take my ass off his personal assassination list, and not put me in one of his secret prisons for the rest of my life."

"It's the same thing," Larison said. "You ever thought about how much security you can buy with twenty-five million dollars?"

"I know you want those diamonds back," I said. "But I don't think the diamonds alone are going to solve the problems we have now. We need to be clear about our new situation, and how we address it."

Larison rubbed his hands together. "What do we do?"

"I don't know exactly. But I agree it's going to involve the daughter one way or the other. Find something that'll act as... well, if not a guarantee of our safety, then at least an inhibition on Horton's ability to direct forces against us. Anyway, we don't have to figure it all out now. We'll have plenty of time while we're driving."

Dox said, "Road trip!"

I checked the secure site. Kanezaki, confirming the pickup was on schedule.

"My contact should be here in just a few minutes," I said. "Let's get moving."

We wiped down the surfaces we might have touched and policed up all sandwich wrappers and other visible evidence that anyone had been in here. Not that anyone would be looking, and there would likely be some hair and other DNA evidence regardless of our other efforts, but better to leave less of a trail to follow than more.

We moved to the door. I looked through the peephole—all clear. I was about to turn the handle when I remembered the two bodyguards I'd seen at the other end of the hallway. I hesitated.

Larison said, "What is it?"

I turned to them. "When you all arrived, was there a security detail at the other end of the hallway on this floor?"

They all shook their heads.

Well, that was odd. These weren't the kind of men who would overlook something like that.

"Why are you asking?" Larison said.

"Because there was one when I got here. Two bodyguards, who must have taken up their position after you all arrived but before I did."

No one said anything, so I went on. "Could be a coincidence, of course. Just a high-profile guest who happened to check in after you arrived but before I did. But still."

I paused and considered. As always, I assumed the worst, the worst in this instance meaning that Horton had somehow anticipated us, or followed the others, and had people in place in the hotel even now.

Put yourself in their shoes. They'd be expecting you to take the stairs, not the elevator. Which, from their perspective, would be perfect. Suppressed weapons, no witnesses, all loose ends disposed of quickly, quietly, cleanly.

"Here's how we're going to play it," I said. "Treven and I are going to head out into the main corridor first. If those two guys I saw are just someone's diplomatic security detail, fine, we'll hold the elevator for Dox and Larison and we'll all go down together. But if they're not just security, and we have a problem…"

I thought for a moment. I wanted Treven alongside, not behind me, so that was good. But…

I looked at Dox and Larison. "If we have a problem, Treven and I will drop and create a clear field of fire for the two of you. Whatever happens, we're going to use the elevator. I don't like the idea of the stairs right now. Everyone okay with this?"

They all nodded. I checked the peephole again, turned the handle with my jacket sleeve, and opened the door. The three of them moved out past me and I closed the door behind us as softly as I could. Then I moved ahead again.

I looked at Treven. "You're too tight," I said softly.

He frowned. "What do you mean?"

"I mean you look tense. Even if those guys are legitimate, they're watching for trouble. I don't want to do anything that makes them remember us. And if they're not legitimate, let's not do anything to make them feel like we're clued in. Not until we're clearing leather and putting rounds in their heads. Okay?"

He frowned more deeply.

"Goddamn it," I said, "it's not a criticism. Just relax and follow my lead, okay? Relax."

We turned the corner into the main corridor. I saw the two body-guards, same position as before. My heart kicked up a notch.

"I told him," I said, remembering a banal sports conversation I'd once overheard. "I told him, 'What the hell were they thinking, trying to play a zone defense against Kentucky?' I mean, you don't play a zone against Kentucky." I actually had no idea what this even meant, but it must have meant something.

To his credit, Treven picked up the vibe immediately and ran with it. He laughed and said, "I was saying the same thing. Told them, 'not unless you want to get your ass kicked, you don't.'"

The two bodyguards peeled off from the wall and started moving toward us. Rather, the two not-bodyguards. My heart started hammering harder.

"Best part?" I said. "Those dipshits were betting. Against someone trying to play a zone against Kentucky! Kentucky, can you believe that?"

The two not-bodyguards' hands were empty. But they were wearing suits. There were a lot of possibilities for concealed carry.

"You know what?" Treven said. "I love people like that. People who bet without thinking. Think they know the odds when they don't. Means more money for me."

We reached the elevator bank. The not-bodyguards were ten meters away. "Excuse me," the one on the left said, his eyes invisible behind his shades. "We'll need to see some identification."

"Identification?" I said, my tone indicating this was the most absurd sentence anyone had ever uttered. I reached out and pressed the down button with a knuckle.

I saw movement at the far end of the corridor. Two more guys in suits and shades, rounding the corner. These two holding guns.

"No problem," Treven said. He reached down as though for a wal-let, instead coming out with a Glock and shooting both of them in their foreheads so instantly that the first guy hadn't even begun to drop by the time the second had been drilled clean, too. The *bam! bam!* of the two shots was thunderous in the long corridor. I pulled the Supergrade and dropped to the floor so fast I actually reached it before the two dead guys. Treven was right there next to me, already firing at the two new guys, as was I. There were more shots from behind us, and the two new guys were suddenly jerking like puppets on strings, convulsed from multiple hits.

The shooting stopped and the corridor was suddenly silent again, the air pungent with the smell of gun smoke. I glanced back and saw Larison and Dox moving smoothly forward, each with his weapon out at eye level and in a two-handed grip. I looked at the two guys farther down the corridor. They were splayed face-up on the carpet, their legs twisted beneath them. I kept the Supergrade on them and came to my feet, staying close to the wall. Treven changed to a kneeling position just below me. The second two downed men were too far away for us to be sure they were dead, and we weren't taking any chances.

"Was that relaxed enough?" Treven said mildly, keeping his eyes and the muzzle of the Glock pointed downrange.

"That was very relaxed," I said.

The elevator chimes sounded—the doors on the far left. "Shit," I said, fighting the urge to approach it tactically with the Supergrade out. If there were more opposition inside, I wanted to be ready. But if it were a bunch of civilians, we'd have major witness problems.

But they hadn't known when we'd be leaving the room. And elevators are too unreliable to use tactically. If there were more opposition, they'd be pouring in from the stairwells. Assuming they weren't deliberately waiting there.

I walked over, getting the Supergrade back into my waistband and under my jacket just as the doors opened. I glanced inside. Two young Indian men, fresh-faced, navy slacks and starched white shirts. Wearing American Constitution Society badges on lanyards. They were close to the back wall, from which they wouldn't be able to see the carnage outside.

"Hi there," I said, with a friendly wave. I was trying to indicate to Treven, Dox, and Larison that there were civilians in the elevator, and that they should put away the hardware so we could get the hell out of there.

"Going down?" one of them said to me, in the characteristically sunny accent.

"Yes," I said, putting my arm out to block the doors. "Could you just hold the elevator for a second?" I turned toward Dox and Larison and called, "Someone's being kind enough to hold the elevator for us. Let's hurry."

We were lucky no one had poked a head out into the corridor so far. I supposed most of the rooms were empty at this time of day, but still, we had to beat feet.

The second Indian guy sniffed. "Do you smell something strange? Smoke, I think. Like something is burning."

"Yeah," I said, "a maintenance man just came through here. He said it was a problem with the ventilation system, nothing to worry about."

Dox, Larison, and Treven all collapsed into the elevator and I followed them in. The Indian guys suddenly looked very small. They backed up against the wall but it was still a tight squeeze. I pressed the garage floor button with a knuckle and the doors closed.

"Thank you," Dox said, smiling a smile that to my mind looked completely maniacal. "Would have hated to have to wait for the next one."

For a moment, no one said anything. There was nothing but the absurd sound of Muzak being pumped through unseen speakers.

"Are you gentlemen... with the convention?" the first Indian guy said. He was looking at Larison. Obviously, some deep portion of his midbrain was screaming, *Danger!* But he was a thoroughly modern man, and trapped in an elevator, too, and so rather than running for the hills the way our far more sensible ancestors might have, he was trying to make conversation with an obvious predator, instead.

"Not exactly," Larison said.

The elevator stopped on the fourth floor. The tension inside as we waited for the doors to open was explosive. The Indian guys must have been picking up on it, and I wondered what the hell they thought.

The doors opened. Two pretty young women in skirts and heels, and both with American Constitution Society badges around their necks, surveyed the crowd inside. "It's okay," one of them said. "We'll wait for the next one."

I knew I had maybe a second before Dox shoved the Indian guys against the wall to make room for the ladies. "Thanks," I said, and hit the close button. The doors slid shut and mercifully, we were moving again.

"We are supporters of the Constitution, of course," Dox said. "And we revere that august document. But tragically, we're not in town long enough to be part of the convention itself. How about you? Sounds like you've come some distance to be here."

I wanted to throttle him. Was he *trying* to get these two to remember us?

"Indeed, all the way from New Delhi," the second guy said. "We are studying sensible ways to amend our own constitution in India. And we often joke that perhaps you Americans could lend us yours, because you seem no longer to be using it yourselves."

The elevator chimed and came to a stop at the lobby level. Treven and I got out and Larison and Dox flattened against one of the walls to make room for the Indian guys.

"Well, goodbye," the first one said, as they got out.

"And have a good day," the second one added.

"And you, too," Dox said. "And thanks for appreciating our Constitution. It's nice that somebody does."

The doors closed. "Jesus," I said. "Why didn't you just give them a business card? Or your phone number?"

He looked hurt. "Just being a good ambassador, man. They came a long way, and for a worthy purpose."

"Yeah, and in about a half hour, when they're being questioned by hotel security and the D.C. Metro Police and JSOC fucking assassins, they'll remember very clearly the four men who got on their elevator on the ninth floor, the floor where four bodies were discovered riddled with bullet holes, the floor that reeked of gun smoke."

A long moment went by. Dox said, "Well, when you put it like that, I guess I can see your point."

The elevator chimed again. Garage level. We all reached around to the back of our waistbands and hugged the side walls.

The doors opened. We looked left, then right. All quiet, and all clear. We headed out toward the far end of the garage, keeping plenty of space between ourselves to make it harder for possible ambushers. We were all hyper alert. My mind was screaming, *How the hell did they track you here?* But I shoved the thought away. The problem now was how to get out. We could worry about the rest later.

The garage was full, probably from the convention, and we could have been attacked from any direction as we crossed it. Every parked car, the far side of every load-bearing pillar… everything felt like a potential threat. By the time we had reached the far end, the feeling of a concrete wall at my back was as sweet as a cold glass of water after a trek across the desert.

Larison looked around. "Your man's not here."

I checked my watch. "Give him a few minutes. Could be traffic, could be anything."

"I don't like it," Treven said. "If this is another setup, we're going to be pinned down. Let's find our own car, hotwire it, and get the hell out of here."

"If we have to," I said. "But unless we're ready to ram the gate, we'll need a vehicle with the ticket left inside. That, plus one old enough to hot wire, probably isn't a huge cross section. And I know we could explain that we lost the ticket, but I'd rather not have that conversation if we can avoid it. Let's just give him a few minutes."

On cue, I heard tires squealing against concrete on the other end of the garage. A silver minivan. Darkened outside windows. *Come on,* I thought. *Kanezaki.*

The van came closer. Kanezaki? I couldn't tell with the florescent lights against the windshield.

I could feel the tension building as the van approached. The rest of them were imagining the same thing I was: the side door opening and the four of us getting raked with automatic gunfire.

The van swung around and pulled up right alongside us. We couldn't see anything through the darkened windows. None of us had drawn a weapon yet, but if that side door slid open…

The passenger-side window came down, and an attractive young Asian woman in a halter top, shorts, and a ponytail leaned across. "I'm Tom's sister," she said. "How's the weather?"

I was so stunned I almost didn't answer. She'd presented her bona fides, and was now asking me for mine. Was she a spook, too? Did Kanezaki train her? And why was she here anyway, instead of him?

"It's… rainy," I said, guessing this was the right response.

She nodded. "Get in."

The side door slid open. Two little girls in booster seats, their faces and hair an appealing Asian/Caucasian mix, were in the middle row.

They looked at the four of us curiously.

"Are you… where's Tom?" I said.

"He got held up. Look, I'm in a little bit of a hurry, okay? Gotta get these guys to play practice by six, and I wasn't expecting a trip into the city first."

"Right." I looked at the others. From their expressions, I gathered they were finding this as surreal as I was.

Larison broke the tension. "Come on," he said to Treven. "Let's get in back."

Somehow, the two of them managed to squeeze into the third row. Dox took the second row middle seat, between the two girls. I got in front.

She drove around to the booth. There was an automated kiosk where she could have used a credit card, but either she was too savvy for that, or too briefed by Kanezaki. Or too lucky. Whatever it was, she pulled into the lane with an attendant, a bored-looking Latina.

"I can't believe this," she said to the attendant, rolling down the window, "but I pulled into the wrong garage."

I kept my eyes straight ahead, and in my peripheral vision saw her hand the attendant a ticket. There was a pause.

"Okay, no problem," the attendant said. The gate went up.

"Thanks," Tom's sister said, and we drove out into the hothouse sun.

"What do I call you?" I said.

She slipped on a pair of shades and made a right onto L Street. "My name's Yukie. Most people call me Yuki."

I noticed a tattoo on the back of her right shoulder. Two kanji: one for love, the other for war. Love of war? Militancy? It was a neologism, not a real word, the kind of thing favored by *otaku*—computer geeks— and *bosozoku*—motorcycle gangs, so I wasn't sure what it signified.

"Okay, Yuki. Thank you."

"Don't mention it."

"Where's your brother?"

"Hopefully on his way to White Flint Mall in Maryland. That's where he told me to take you, and if he's not there, I'll drop you off and you'll have to wait for him. I'm sorry, but I'm running late as it is."

She made another right, this one onto 15th Street. She used the turning signal well in advance. Either a conscientious driver, or someone who didn't want to give a cop even the tiniest excuse for stopping the van. Or both.

"You seemed… very competent back there," I said. "If you don't mind my saying."

She glanced over at me, then back to the road. "Look, I'm not stupid, okay? If Tom works at the State Department, you guys are the Swedish figure skating team. He's my brother and I owe him a lot. Let's just leave it at that."

She signaled again and we made a right onto K Street.

The little girl on the passenger side said, "What's your name, mister?"

I glanced back, but she was looking at Dox.

"Well, my friends call me Dox, little darling. Which is short for unorthodox. You can call me that, too, but only if we're going to be friends."

"We can be friends," she said, and giggled.

"All right then," he said. He reached out and shook her tiny hand with mock formality. "And what shall I call you?"

"I'm Rina."

"Rina. Well, that is a lovely name. It's very fine to meet you, Rina."

The girl on the other side said, "And I'm Rika."

Dox turned and shook her hand, too. "I don't believe I've ever seen two such pretty girls. Are you twins?"

Rika said, "Yes!"

Rina said, "Are not! I'm six and she's four."

Rika said, "Why can't we be twins?"

Rina said, "Tell her, Dox. It's because twins have to be born at the same time."

And it went on from there.

They were ridiculously cute. I thought of my own son, Koichiro. He'd be about their age now. What had they ever done to anyone? I couldn't imagine anyone more innocent. And I'd put them in danger.

"Tom's a good man," I said to Yuki, as we made a right onto Connecticut Avenue, heading northwest toward the Maryland border.

She nodded. "He's a good brother."

"But I don't think… I don't think he understood what he might be

getting you into. There was a… problem back at the hotel. You'll probably be seeing it on the news tonight."

"Seriously. I don't want to hear it."

"What I mean is, if that garage had any kind of surveillance cameras
in position to record license plates, it's going to be a problem for you.
The people who are looking for us are going to want to know what you
were doing in that garage."

"Then it's a good thing I changed the plates."

"You what?"

"Look, I wasn't always the inveterate suburban soccer mom who
appears before you today, okay? I told you, I'm not stupid. I borrowed
a set of plates from someone on a nice, leafy, non-surveillance camera
neighborhood street. And with a little luck, I'll get to return them before
they're even missed. So after I drop you all off, it'll be like we never even
met."

I couldn't help smiling. "Well, I'll still be glad we did."

She looked at me, sidelong, with a little smile of her own. "Don't flirt
with me, okay? Remember, I am a suburban soccer mom."

A phone buzzed. I looked down and saw a unit in the beverage
holder, flashing. She picked it up and glanced at it, then handed it to me.
"Go ahead," she said. "It's Tom."

I flipped it open. "Hey."

"You must be with my sister."

"Yes."

"Good. I'm on my way to where she's taking you. Traffic's going to
be hell, but I shouldn't be more than thirty minutes. I'll tell you more
then."

"We're going to need a vehicle. And a Civic won't do it."

"It's taken care of. I'll see you soon."

He clicked off. I put the phone back in the beverage holder. "Sounds
like we're on schedule," I said.

"Good."

The ride to the mall took about forty minutes. Dox entertained the
kids by telling them stories of parachuting out of airplanes and what
happens if a chute doesn't open, and insisting they had to be patient and
wait until they were older before doing it themselves, and advising them

they'd have to get permission from their mother before they could go with him. I envied his touch. I've never been good with children. I think because they sense things adults have learned to suppress.

Yuki made a right into the parking lot and circled counterclockwise over to a satellite parking area. It was far from the mall and mostly empty, the few vehicles belonging to employees, I guessed, not to mall patrons who would have had to trek across the baking pavement to reach the stores. One of the vehicles was a large U-Haul truck—twelve feet, I estimated, maybe fourteen. It struck me as a little odd that it would be parked in a shopping mall, and so far from the building itself, and I wondered if this might be what Kanezaki meant when he said the vehicle was "taken care of."

It was indeed. As we pulled closer, the driver-side door opened and Kanezaki stepped out. He looked like pretty much any other D.C. area drone on his way home from the office—suit jacket gone, tie loosened, skin a little oily from repeated trips between air-conditioned buildings and the blast furnace outside. He still had the wireframe spectacles, but he was a little thinner than I remembered, a new maturity in his eyes and his features. Still the same guy I'd first run into in Tokyo so many years earlier, yes, but no longer a fresh-faced, idealistic kid. He'd been grappling with the real world since then, and its weight had left marks.

Yuki pulled in alongside the truck. I got out and shook Kanezaki's hand. "Keys are in it," he said, characteristically dispensing with small talk. "You should go."

"You have anything new for me?"

He waved to Yuki. "The truck's not enough?"

"You know what I mean."

"No. No new intel. But when I do, I'll upload it to the secure site."

"What do we do with the truck? When does it need to be back?"

"I got it for a month. Hopefully by then the pressure will be off and we'll figure something out. The rental agreement is in the glove compartment."

The side door slid open and Rina and Rika both exclaimed, "Uncle Tomo!"

Kanezaki waved to them.

I said, "Uncle Tomo?"

He shrugged. "You know, for Tomohisa. Uncle Tom sounds odd, anyway."

Dox squeezed out and shook Kanezaki's hand. "Good to see you, man," he said. "Seems like you're always helping us out of a jam."

"And always in exchange for something," I said.

Larison and Treven got out. Rina called out, "Uncle Tomo, what are you doing here?"

"Your mom's picking me up, hon! It's a long story. I'll tell you on the way."

He turned to the four of us. "I don't know where you're going, and it's better if I don't. Just make it far away. They're going to be looking for you in the capital, and they can look hard there."

Larison eyeballed the truck. "I like your choice of ride."

Kanezaki nodded. "Nobody's going to notice a moving truck. This one's got Wyoming plates and no one looks twice even here in Maryland. Plus, two or even three of you can stay concealed in back while one drives. They're looking for four, so best if you're not seen together. Speaking of which. You should go."

"My lord," Dox said. "It's going to be a goddamn sauna back there. Anybody mind if I drive?"

No one said anything. Dox got in the truck. Treven and Larison went around to the back.

"I didn't have time to pick up water or anything else," Kanezaki said. "It's got a full tank of gas and I bought a bunch of boxes and rolls of bubble wrap so you'll at least have something to sit on in back, but that's about it. When it's dark and you're well clear of the city, you can stop and pick up whatever you need. I'll be in touch as soon as I learn more."

"There was a problem at the hotel," I said.

He looked at me, his expression strained. "What do you mean?"

"Four guys. They must have been Horton's. Somehow they followed us, or anticipated us. They came up short. I'm sure you'll be hearing about it."

He didn't say anything. He just looked over at the van. At his nieces.

"Sounds like your sister's pretty smart," I said. "She told me she borrowed the plates on the van from some random car in a suburban neighborhood. There must be tens of thousands of vans like hers in the

D.C. area. She's safe. No one can track her."

He wiped the sweat off his forehead and ran his fingers back through his hair. "Jesus. I didn't… Jesus."

He went to the van and slid the side door closed, then got into the passenger seat. I walked over and he rolled the window down.

"Thanks," I said. "To both of you."

Yuki looked at me and I could have sworn she was almost smiling.

"I don't want to know," she said, shaking her head. Then she pointed at Kanezaki and said, "We're even, Mister State Department."

He nodded grimly. "You could say that."

I wondered what the hell he'd done for her. Whatever it was, he'd called in his marker, and she'd paid it off.

Hopefully not at higher interest than she'd been expecting.

chapter
eighteen

We stayed off the interstates on our way out of Maryland, heading northwest and crossing the Potomac at the Point of Rocks
Bridge, far from the Beltway and Route 95, Dox driving while I rode
shotgun. The sun was getting low in the sky, but there was still plenty of
daylight left. I wanted it to get dark. I kept half-expecting a phalanx of
police cars to swing into position behind us, lights on and sirens screaming. It didn't make sense, of course, but then neither did those four guys
at the Hilton. The only thing I was sure of was that the farther we got
from the city, the better I'd feel.

We kept the radio on to see if there was any news about the hotel
shooting. There was plenty, but it was confused and incomplete. Witnesses claiming to have heard gunshots; police cordoning off the hotel;
the cops saying little other than that they were investigating a possible
shooting. It might have been routine; it might have been Horton behind
the scenes, leaning on the locals in the name of "national security," and
concealing the identities, and affiliations, of the dead men.

We talked about what had happened at the hotel, about what could
have been the flaw in our security. If we couldn't identify it, we had to assume it was still a problem, and the feeling of some hidden vulnerability
that could undermine us at any time was maddening.

"You're sure you weren't followed," I said as we drove.

"Hell, yes," Dox said. "We did a solid detection run from the airport.
Multiple cab changes, a subway ride, you know the drill. No one could
have been on us without our knowing."

I fought the urge to remind him that he shouldn't have been using the airport itself. But I recognized the impulse as driven by an urge to lash out, not by anything possibly productive. Besides, even if they should have steered clear of the airport to start with, if they weren't followed, they weren't followed.

"You said you went to a gun show," I said. "What about that?"

"We did a run after that, too. One hundred percent clean."

"What about—"

"The hotel, right? Made the reservation from a gas station payphone in Merrifield, Virginia. After I was already for damn sure we were clean."

"All right, what about—"

"Our cell phones were off the whole time. Larison double checked us. That boy's as paranoid as you."

I considered. "You think he or Treven could have tipped Horton off?"

"Hard to say. Maybe the hotel shooters were supposed to drop just us, not the two of them. If so, though, somebody didn't get the memo, 'cause Larison and Treven shot the shit out of all four of them. You saw it, too."

I nodded, frustrated and angry. Being tracked when you think you're untrackable is one of the worst, most vulnerable feelings there are.

"Know what I think?" Dox said.

"Tell me."

"I think we're entering an age where freelancers like you and me are going to have to consider the attractions of retirement. I mean, there are just too many ways the opposition can get a handle on us now. Video cameras everywhere, surveillance drones being deployed over American cities, the NSA spying domestically, the government and all the Internet and telecom companies working together, satellites and supercomputers crunching all that data... I just think we're in a world now where, if the man wants to find you, you're going to get found. Which means you either work for the man, or you don't work at all."

I didn't answer. Maybe he was right. Maybe things had reached a point where there was no room for men like us anymore. Maybe we'd become vestiges, anachronisms, cogs on one last circuit within a machine that no longer had any use for us, a machine that was preparing to snap us off and spit us out so it could grind along even more senselessly and relentlessly than it ever had before.

Outside Culpeper, as it was finally beginning to get dark, we pulled over at a gas station to fuel up and use the bathroom. Treven and Larison were soaked with sweat but they volunteered to spend a little more time in back because they were already used to it. I briefed them about the radio reports, but there wasn't much to tell. There was a brief discussion about who should pick up provisions. Treven had green eyes, Larison had that danger aura, and I was Asian. And Treven and Larison both looked like they'd just emerged from a steam room. That left Dox as the least noticeable, and least memorable, of the four of us. He bought a road atlas, a lot of bottled water, and some granola bars, and we headed back out into the slowly cooling night.

We kept moving south, the radio nothing but anodyne local news and traffic reports. Then the announcer's voice became suddenly alive and urgent.

"We have a developing situation," he said. "Reports of an attack on the White House. A suicide bombing."

"Jesus Christ almighty," Dox said, reaching for the volume.

The announcer said, "Police and paramedics are arriving at the scene. We have reports of horrific injuries. As far as we know, no one has yet claimed responsibility for the attack. It's not clear whether the president is even in the White House at this time."

"What the hell are they talking about?" I said. "That place is a fortress. A suicide bombing? It doesn't make sense."

"Maybe another airplane?"

"They would have said as much."

He glanced at me, his face grim, then back to the road. "Whatever it is, it looks like we cleared the way for it. Damn. Goddamn. Should we stop and let Larison and Treven know?"

"No, keep driving. This was supposed to happen while we were in the city, you get that? It's sealed off now. I'll bet they've got National Guard units stopping traffic on the Beltway, everything. I want to put as much distance as possible between us and whatever's going on back in Washington."

I told myself it wasn't our fault. But Dox's words kept echoing in my mind.

Whatever it is, it looks like we cleared the way for it.

We drove on, listening. There was nothing new, mostly repeats of what had already been said, in tones alternating between hysteria and ecstasy. Gradually, a little clarity emerged. It wasn't an attack on the White House itself, but on one of the guard posts outside. Still, it was a huge explosion. There were scores of civilian casualties, and a section of the iron-barred fence that protected the property had been destroyed. Apparently the president was all right. He was in the White House, and was going to address the nation at nine o'clock.

"Prime time," Dox observed, his tone disgusted. "Likely a coincidence."

At Buckingham, Virginia, we left Route 15 and started tracking west. When we were just outside Appomattox, the president went live.

"We all know what happened tonight," he said. "A cowardly individual blew himself up outside the White House, murdering and injuring many scores of innocent civilians. No one in the White House itself was injured, and, other than some damage to a fence, the building's security was not compromised.

"What we don't yet know precisely is who committed this atrocity, or why. But rest assured, our nation's military, law enforcement, and intelligence services are assembling answers to those questions now. And when they have completed their task, justice will be done to the perpetrators."

"That's what they're calling military action these days," Dox said. "Justice. I guess it has a better ring to it than invasion, bombardment, and slaughter."

"Shh."

"Now, I want to address a rumor," the president went on. "First, that before blowing himself up, the terrorist shouted, *'Allahu Akbar,'* which means 'God is great' in Arabic, and is a common Islamic invocation and sometimes a war cry. We don't have confirmation of this, and it is irresponsible of the media to report it as though it has in fact been confirmed."

"Rumor?" Dox said. "Who started the rumor? Sounds like the president is starting it himself!"

"That's exactly what he's doing, either deliberately, or because it's being fed to him."

"Well, how the hell—"

"Shh. He's talking again."

"Our task tonight," the president went on, "is to pray for the victims and their families. And to thank the men and women of our armed forces and intelligence services, who, even as I speak, are risking their lives to protect our homeland and our liberties. Let us pray for them, as well."

There was the clamor of reporters trying to ask questions, and then the announcer was back on, explaining that the president had left the briefing room.

Dox glanced over at me, then back to the road. "What the hell are we going to do?"

"I don't know."

"I mean it, John. I mean… this is some top level shit we're mixed up in here."

"Yeah."

"I mean, false flag terror attacks? And we've been fingered for it? Forgive me if I sound gloomy, but I don't see a clear way out of this."

"You do sound gloomy."

He laughed softly. "Well, cheer me up then."

"I'm working on it."

"Not to mention—"

"I know. We cleared the way for it."

We didn't stop again until Roanoke. It was nearly midnight and we'd been driving for over eight hours. Dox and I briefed Treven and Larison about the incident outside the White House. No one said anything, but I knew we were all thinking the same thing: we were fucked.

We picked up fast food, gassed up again, and agreed to change positions. "It's not that bad," Treven said. "A lot cooler than before, and your friend was smart to pick up that bubble wrap. It's actually pretty comfortable, if you're lying down on it."

Dox and I had discussed our discomfort at the prospect of being closed up in the cargo area, helpless and blind, while Treven and Larison drove. If someone put a lock on the exterior, the truck would be turned into a prison. Not that anyone was carrying a lock or had time to buy one, but still. But in the end, it didn't matter, because what choice did we have? None of us could risk public transportation. Dox had been right about our odds of hiding from the modern surveillance state. And Larison had been right when he'd told Treven that going off alone meant being the first one picked off. If we were going to resolve this, our best chance was to stick together, and to find a way to attack back.

Treven and Larison were indifferent about what we ate, so I was glad when, on the morning of the second day, Dox insisted we stop at a Whole Foods outside Nashville. We loaded up with enough chow to see us comfortably all the way to the Pacific, then found a Wal-Mart and threw a couple futons and sleeping bags in the back. The futons were something, but Dox had been right, it was a damn sauna back there when the sun was high, and there wasn't any good way to cool it down. We considered buying bags of ice but then decided against it. We didn't want to take a chance on the melting runoff attracting the attention of some highway patrol.

We also stopped at a Starbucks so I could access their free Wi-Fi, and I checked the secure site. I half-expected a message from Horton, trying to explain away the unexplainable. But he must have known how useless that would be under the circumstances. He'd used us, then tried to clip us like the loose end we now represented. We knew he would try again, just as he knew we'd be gunning to get to him first. The state of play was so clear that anything anyone might have said would have been useless, even absurd.

There was a message from Kanezaki, though. He described the attack at the White House, which the media had gotten more or less right after the initial, confused reports. And he said the NSA was picking up chatter about more attacks coming. There were rumors about the president considering a major response. Kanezaki wanted me to call him, and I wrote that I couldn't, not for another day or two. After the ambush at the hotel, my paranoia was at a full simmer. Maybe Horton had managed to stitch together enough data from airport surveillance cameras and satellite imagery to track us to the Hilton. He'd been expecting us in the city, after all. If so, and if he'd lost track of us after the hotel, then even with all the technology in the world, for the time being we'd be the proverbial needle in a haystack. I didn't want to take any chance at all about a call being traced to a location this far west, from which the opposition might predict our further trajectory. From which Horton might even guess where we were ultimately heading, and why.

On the afternoon of the second day, Treven was driving while I rode shotgun. Mostly the roads were eerily quiet, but periodically, the quiet would be shattered by a passing military convoy, after which, the absence of traffic would be more spooky still.

I asked Treven the same security questions I had put to Dox, but got no additional insights. If he was hiding something, he was hiding it well. He told me a little about himself. Cut his teeth in Mogadishu. Climbed the ops ladder from Airborne to SF to ISA. A very competent man, no doubt, both from the resume and from what I'd seen at the hotel. But I didn't feel the kind of connection with him that I'd started to feel with Larison. In Larison, I sensed turmoil, but also purpose. In Treven, what I sensed felt more like… confusion. And compensation. For what, I didn't know.

We were listening to a country music station when, just as a day before, the deejay's typically smooth and soothing voice cut in high-pitched and earnest after a song.

"Following on yesterday's attack on the White House," he said, "we have another horrifying report. A suicide bombing in the Mall of America in Minneapolis. Reports of a truck driven into the building, and a partial structural collapse. I know you can't see it, this is radio, but I'm watching the video now and I have to tell you, my God, my God, it's unspeakable. It's like the twin towers again… Folks, I'm sorry to tell you, but yesterday was not a one-off. These have got to be coordinated. Let's pray the government is doing something to protect us."

"Holy fucking shit," Treven said, and that was all, there was nothing else to say. We drove grimly on, listening for more, dreading that we'd hear it.

Outside of Memphis, we did. Two more suicide bombings: one at a Giants game at AT&T Park in San Francisco; the other at a church in Lubbock, Texas. More mass casualties. Lurid descriptions of victims, the burned and buried and blinded. Reporters interviewing dazed survivors, hysterical people trying to find their family members, wailing parents clutching the mangled bodies of their daughters and sons.

"Country's going to go mad from this," Treven said grimly.

I nodded. "That's exactly the idea. If nine-eleven, plus a little an-thrax afterward, could make the country mad, imagine what you could get away with if you could increase that kind of fear. And sustain it."

We drove on. The radio was nothing but special reports now. The at-tacks had driven everything else off the air. When the shows got tired of recycling the same news, they took to interviewing people in the streets. It was hardly a random sampling, and maybe there were some hardcore pacifists out there who were getting overlooked, or who were afraid to speak up, but the impression I was left with after hours of nonstop radio was that the country was in the grip of atavistic rage. There were calls to intern male Muslims, to close the borders, to nuke Mecca and Medina.

"I'd feel the same way," Treven said. "If I didn't know what was re-ally going on."

"Doesn't matter who's behind it. Either the response is tactically sound, or it's not."

"I'm not talking about tactics. I'm talking about how I'd feel."

"I get it. And that's the beauty of what they're doing. Think about it. Four attacks so far. The White House—a key symbol of the nation. The biggest mall in the country—a key symbol of consumer shopping and the economy. A church—to make people feel their religion is under attack. And an attack on sports—the country's secular religion. Every-thing the culture identifies with and holds sacred, and distributed all over the land. There's only one thing missing so far to make the country lose what's left of its reason, and give in entirely to the kind of feelings you're talking about."

"What?" Treven said.

"A school. One, maybe more."

He glanced over at me. "Christ."

"Yeah. My guess is, if they can't get what they want based on what they've done so far, they'll ratchet it up. Schools would do it. Think Beslan. Or that camp in Norway."

"You think they'd go that far?"

"You see any indications otherwise?"

We drove on to the hysterical cadences of the incessant recycled news stories. I watched the country going past, green hills and forests and terraced farmland, towns with names like McCrory and Bald Knob and Judsonia. The sky was an absurd, bright blue. The road was gray in the shimmering heat and looked like it might stretch on forever.

Most of the airtime was filled with speculation. Al Qaeda in Iraq. Al Qaeda in Yemen. Al Qaeda in the Arabian Peninsula. Iran. Libya. The Muslim Brotherhood. Sleeper cells in America, and how many more there could be. Why they hated us, why they loved death more than life. The topography outside the windows was indifferent and unaltered, but I felt the country we were driving through had changed irrevocably since we'd begun this journey, a time that itself already felt improbable, distant, surreal. I imagined the four of us in the truck as some sort of germ, silently delivered into America's arterial system, hunted by rogue T cells even as the unseen body politic around us convulsed in fever and delirium.

I hated that we'd been part of the horror we listened to over the radio. But what could we do, except try to protect ourselves?

Periodically, we stopped for bathroom breaks and provisions. There was panic buying everywhere: duct tape, plastic, canned food, bottled water. Iodine tablets were impossible to find, and apparently there was a thriving black market for Mexican knockoff Cipro, the anthrax treatment. We saw Wal-Marts being emptied of water purification and camping supplies. Gun sales had gone through the roof, and ammunition was sold out.

We kept driving in shifts: two in the front to make sure no one fell asleep at the wheel; two in the cargo area getting some rest, at least theoretically; our only breaks at highway rest stops, where we parked far from other vehicles so that whichever two of us were riding in back could get in and out without being noticed.

I was dozing in the back with Treven when I was awakened by the feel of the truck coming to a stop. There was no light leaking into the cargo area. It must have been night.

There were three knocks on the door outside—the all-clear signal we'd been using to prevent misunderstandings. I had already accessed the Supergrade, and kept it in my hand anyway.

The door opened, and I saw Larison and Dox. It was twilight outside, not yet dark. I could hear crickets in the grass, but, other than that, the evening was silent. The air on my skin felt wonderfully fresh and cool. The air on my skin felt wonderfully fresh and cool.

"Where are we?" I said, getting out and sliding the Supergrade into my waistband. My legs were stiff and I did a few squats to loosen up.

"Lavaca, Arkansas," Larison said. "Just south of the Ozark National Forest."

Dox stuck his head inside the cargo area. "My lord, is that what it smells like back there? I guess I got numb to it when it was my turn. Think we all might want to find a place to shower when we get to L.A."

I swung my arms around and shook them out to get the blood moving. "We're not even out of Arkansas yet? Jesus, this country is big."

Larison started stretching, too. "We're just a few miles from the Oklahoma border. Almost halfway there."

I looked around. We were on a dirt road. An old barn stood to our left, looking deserted, a small reservoir beside it. The sky, indigo overhead and behind us and deep blue fading to pink in the west, was clear. A crescent moon was already up, and the first stars were out.

"Why are we stopping?" I said. "You ready to change up?"

"I'm good either way," Larison said. "But the president's doing another prime time speech. Thought you might want to hear it."

I looked around again. It was a deserted enough place that I thought we could risk a break. I checked my watch. It was a few minutes before eight—almost nine o'clock in Washington.

We all pissed at the edge of the nearby woods, then rolled down the truck windows and stood outside the cabin, Dox and Larison on the driver's side, Treven and I opposite, listening to the announcer uselessly reminding us about the day's events, and speculating on how the president might address them. Once again, I was struck by the feeling of being part of what was happening, and yet also distinct, isolated, remote from it.

At nine o'clock sharp, the president spoke. His tone was measured and grave.

"Today our nation suffered an unprecedented string of horrific and cowardly attacks on civilian targets. We have evidence that some of these attacks have been carried out by sleeper cells of Islamic fanatics. Others have been committed by individuals who we believe to be self-radicalized."

"'Self-radicalized'?" Dox said. "What the hell does that even mean? Some guy's sitting there minding his own business, and he just radicalizes himself?"

"Today I met with leaders of Congress," the president went on. "We discussed new legislation that will ensure I have the appropriate tools to fulfill my obligation to keep the nation safe in the face of this unprecedented threat. I was very pleased at the impressively bipartisan nature of our discussions. No one is playing politics with the safety of the American people. We will announce new measures based on these discussions very soon. I will also announce a reshuffling of certain key positions in my administration intended to ensure that we have the most flexible, streamlined, and effective team possible to keep the American people safe.

"At a time like this, it is impossible for us as Americans not to recall that terrible day when fanatics flew airplanes into the World Trade Center and the Pentagon and, thwarted by brave passengers, into a field in Pennsylvania. Impossible not to recall the horror of those atrocities. But let us recall, too, the courage, and resolve, and unity of purpose of that day, and of the days that followed. Even as we bury our dead and mourn with their families, let us commit ourselves to acting, and being, no less firm today.

"Make no mistake: our homeland is under attack. And make no mistake: we will defend ourselves. Thank you, and God bless America."

A reporter shouted, "Mister President, do we have intelligence on further attacks?"

The president said, "I can't comment on that at this time."

"'At this time,'" Dox said. "Sure sign that a politician is pissing down your back and telling you it's raining. Same for 'make no mistake,' now that I mention it."

Another reporter shouted, "Mister President, can you tell us anything about the new measures you've been discussing with Congressional leaders? And why, if we're under attack, you still haven't implemented them?"

The president said, "Our laws must be not only necessary, but also appropriate. It's critical that in the course of combating the terrorist threat, we take care not to subvert our own values."

"You slick bastard," Dox said.

Another reporter shouted, "Mister President, can you comment on rumors that the deaths of Tim Shorrock and Jack Finch were related to these attacks? That they were intended to weaken your ability to respond?"

The president said, "Tim and Jack were American heroes who dedicated their lives to serving their country. I have no comment on rumors, other than to say that the work of the staffs they so ably led has continued unhampered, and that I will announce their replacements shortly."

The president left to a cacophony of shouted questions, and the announcer started repeating what we had already just heard. Larison reached in and shut off the radio.

"Well," he said. "Sounds like it's all going more or less according to plan."

"Other than the fact that we're not supposed to still be alive," Dox said. "We're the goddamned fly in their ointment, and I wouldn't have it any other way."

Then I saw it. What I'd been missing before.

"If it gets out that Finch was assassinated," I said, "isn't Horton worried people will wonder about the man who inherited Finch's position?"

The others looked at me.

"Horton's game is already high risk, but as this thing goes on, there's bound to be talk about whether it was an inside job. And who's the talk going to focus on? On the people who most obviously benefited. I mean, how big a leap is it from asking whether Finch was assassinated to wondering about the guy who replaced him?"

Larison said, "That's probably why Hort wanted it to look like natural causes."

"I thought the same thing," I said. "But then Horton put out the story about the cyanide. Sure, it's a great way of getting the whole U.S. national security state to try to hunt us down and permanently disappear us, but it also tends to implicate him, if only by highlighting the fact that he didn't benefit from an accident, but from a political assassination, instead."

Larison said, "I see your point. What do you think it means?"

It was frustrating. It felt like I was asking the right question, but I didn't know how to answer it.

"I don't know," I said. "Other than… whatever Horton is really up to, I don't think we understand it yet."

A few miles down the road, we found a Starbucks, where I checked the secure site again. Another message from Kanezaki:

Intel and chatter permeating the community are all about Islamist sleeper cells and more attacks on the way. I don't know how it's getting introduced because it's all bullshit, but it seems to be coming from multiple sources and a consensus is taking hold that it's accurate. Plus, nobody wants to be the one to err on the side of underestimating what's on the way in case the shit really does hit the fan. They're all talking about that August 6, 2001 President's Daily Brief about how al Qaeda was determined to strike the United States. How it made Bush look bad.

I have a friend with the National Security Council. He says the president's key advisors are steering him to announce what will be called a state of emergency, whatever the hell that really means. They're recommending a choice from among three possible courses of action: 1) Ride it out and let the FBI and local law enforcement handle it; 2) Declare martial law and a suspension of the Constitution; and 3) Declare a "state of emergency" and deploy the National Guard to protect key governmental and civilian targets. Obviously, compared to the political softness of the first and the demonstrable insanity of the second, the third looks like the sensible choice. Plus it gives the president flexibility to ramp things up or dial them down, depending on the course of events.

There's also chatter about attacks on schools. I think administration insiders will leak this. Reporters will then ask the president if it's true, he'll say no comment, and the establishment media will all support the Guard deployment and state of emergency, because if schools get attacked, parents will keep their kids home, they won't be able to go to work, the economy will crater.

By the time they're done, suspending the Constitution is going to seem like the only sane, centrist, responsible thing to do. This is fucked. We have to stop it.

Horton is the key. But I don't know where he is or how to get to him. Call me as soon as you can.

I overheard some of the locals talking. One guy was typical, saying, "If we find out for sure the people behind these attacks are Muslims, I say we turn their goddamned countries into glass parking lots. That's it, no more mister nice guy, no more talk, no more trying to understand each other. This is how you want it, this is what you get. But first, I say we ship every goddamned traitorous fifth columnist American Muslim back to their country of origin so they can be there, right at the center of the mushroom cloud, yes sir. And I'll press the goddamned button myself, too. I guarantee you I won't even be the first in line, either, there'll be a whole lot of other Americans lined up to do the same."

No one disagreed with him. I realized the hysteria was something we could hide in, at least among the populace, because we didn't fit the profile of what had been ginned up in the public imagination.

We kept on, up and across the Oklahoma Panhandle, steering well clear of Oklahoma City and even of Amarillo, the grief and rage in Lubbock feeling uncomfortably close. Then the dusty, flat roads of New Mexico, through the Sitgreaves and Tonto national forests of Arizona, bypassing Phoenix by way of Prescott, and finally across the Colorado River and into California. We stayed on Interstate 10 the rest of the way in, skirting Joshua Tree National Park rather than using the quieter roads farther north, which would have taken us uncomfortably close to the Marine base at Twentynine Palms. Finally, with the sun coming up behind us, we reached the Pacific in Santa Monica. The whole thing had taken us three nights, on back roads and going not one mile above the applicable speed limit, most of it in a forced march blur, some of it in the cabin of the truck, other times in the stifling heat and dark of the cargo area, all of it while government forces hunted for us wherever they could. But we'd made it. We were here.

Now we just had to get to Mimi Kei. And through her, to Horton.

part three

You can't tell anymore the difference between what's propaganda and what's news.
—FCC Commissioner Jonathan Adelstein

But what if elites believe reform is impossible because the problems are too big, the sacrifices too great, the public too distractible? What if cognitive dissonance has been insufficiently accounted for in our theories of how great journalism works... and often fails to work?
—Jay Rosen, NYU School of Journalism

We Americans are the ultimate innocents. We are forever desperate to believe that this time the government is telling us the truth.
—Sydney Schanberg

chapter
nineteen

We found a suitable-looking place called the Rest Haven Motel. It was a little ways off the Pier on a mixed commercial and residential street, a small, one-story building bleached by the Santa Monica sun, with a private parking lot in back and a second, detached unit of rooms with its own entrance. Quiet, but also close enough to the traffic and bustle of the intersection of Pico Boulevard and Lincoln Boulevard for us not to have to worry about standing out. Dox backed the truck in so Larison and Treven could slip out of the cargo area unnoticed, and paid cash for a room in the separate unit. Then we drifted in one-by-one. We all looked like hell—unshowered, unshaven, unkempt. Like people in trouble. Like men on the run.

We pulled the two twin mattresses onto the floor, then spent a few luxurious hours alternating in the tiny bathroom showering and shaving, and cat-napping on the mattresses and the box springs. Next, we examined the room for anything Kei might later use to identify where she'd been held. We policed up some matches and a motel pen; various placards advertising motel services and area attractions; and pulled a plastic insert with an address and phone number off the room phone. We would discard it all later, far from the motel. Finally, we got down to business.

The first thing we needed was commo. I'd examined the mobile phones Horton had given us and had found no tracking devices, but something had enabled him to fix us at the Capital Hilton, and we'd dumped his phones all the way back in Culpeper just to be sure. We needed new ones, and I tasked Dox, who had a forged ID he claimed was ice cold, with procuring us four prepaids from multiple vendors. Larison and Treven's job was to fix Mimi Kei. We didn't know where she lived, so the starting point would be the UCLA Film School website and the school itself. I gave myself the glory job of finding a coin-operated laundry and washing our clothes. We were all wearing our last clean ones.

Before we set out, Larison used the motel's free Wi-Fi and the iPad to access Mimi Kei's Facebook page. She was beautiful—a half-black, half-Asian mix, early twenties, dark hair in ringlets down to her shoulders. Full lips and a vivacious smile. Larison had been right about the photos with Horton: the hard, professional countenance was completely absent, replaced by that of a beaming father.

"Interesting that she doesn't identify him in the captions," I said. "Just 'my dad.'"

Larison nodded. "I'm sure he's explained to her that she needs to be discreet about who her father is. It's not like he's the president, but he has some capable enemies. I'm guessing that's why her page is so privacy protected, too. Unusual for a grad student doing her best to network in the movie world."

Treven said, "We shouldn't assume she's just a clueless civilian. If Hort taught her some things about watching her back, he would have taught her others. It's not impossible he's even told her to be extra careful right now."

I looked at him. "That's a good point. And now you've got me wondering…"

I thought for a minute, then said, "We know Horton's concerned about Kei's safety. So what does he have in place to protect her?"

"No one knows about her," Larison said.

"I don't know about 'no one,'" I said, "but yes. Horton's protecting her, essentially, by making her an unknown. There's a name for that, isn't there?"

Treven nodded. "Security through obscurity."

"Exactly," I said. "Security through obscurity. Which can be a useful supplement to other forms of security, but would a man like Horton rely on it entirely? Rely on it to protect his daughter?"

"I see what you're saying," Dox said. "Maybe he'd rely on it in ordinary times, but now isn't ordinary. He's involved in false flag attacks and a planned coup, which is crazy enough, but on top of it all, he showed his hand when he made a run at us in D.C. He's got to be worried about his daughter now."

"Good," I said. "Now, put yourself in his head. He tells himself it's probably fine, no one has a way of even knowing about Kei, but still. What does he do?"

"He calls her," Treven said. "Tells her to be careful."

"Does she listen?"

Treven shook his head. "Film school student, far from his world? No. Not in a meaningful way. And even if she listened, he'd know she wouldn't have the skills to really act on the warning."

"Agreed. So now what does he do?"

Larison said, "He sends men. To watch her."

I nodded. "Does he tell her he sent men?"

Treven said, "No. He doesn't want to scare her."

"Right," I said. "Meaning they're not functioning as bodyguards protecting a witting client. They need to hang back. So what are they doing right now?"

Larison said, "They're figuring out what we would be doing. Where we would approach her. How. And they're watching for that."

I nodded. "And now we're watching for them."

There was nothing more to be said. Maybe we were giving Horton too much credit. Or maybe he deserved the credit but, after D.C., lacked the resources. Either way, we would assume the presence of opposition. And approach Kei accordingly.

Treven and Larison headed out. They took one room key; I kept the other. My job would likely take the least time, so I'd get back to the room first and could let the others in after.

I found a coin-operated laundry place on Lincoln less than a quarter mile from the motel. A woman in a headscarf was folding her clothes next to one of the driers. The other patrons kept glancing at her and away. They barely noticed me.

I threw the clothes in a couple of machines and, while I waited for them to cycle through, used the place's Wi-Fi to check the secure site. There was a message from Kanezaki:

The D.C. area is on lock-down. All the spokespeople are giving the "Every-

thing's under control, don't panic folks" routine, but behind the scenes, it's a five-alarm freak-out. And they're looking for you. The assumption is that you're somewhere in the city, so that's good. I hope you're very far away.

The president is scheduled to give a big speech and announcement any day now. I don't know what it's going to be. I do know that a couple more attacks, and the country's going to go completely insane. It feels like we're at a tipping point.

We need a way to get to Horton. Call me.

I wrote him back: *We're working on something. Should know in a day or so. Will call then.*

When the laundry was done, I carried it back to the motel and waited in the room. Dox was the first to arrive. Grinning as usual, he dropped two large paper grocery bags on one of the beds, reached inside one of them, and extracted four mobile phones and four wire-line earpieces.

"Mission accomplished," he said. "Bought 'em from three different vendors with two different sets of ID, so they should be untraceable for as long as we're likely to need 'em. No word from Larison and Treven?"

I shook my head. "Not yet. What else have you got in the bags?"

He reached inside and started removing the contents. "Exotic fruit salads, greens salads, various tasty wraps, some protein smoothies, the usual. Plus a six-pack of Red Bulls because, I don't know about you, but I'm a bit peaked from our recent sojourn."

I picked up one of the fruit salads. "Very thoughtful of you."

"Well, with you on laundry detail, figured it was the least I could do. Did you bleach my whites and get my colors extra bright?"

I chuckled. "I think you're going to have to settle for, it all at least smells clean."

"Let me ask you something," he said. "A little off topic. So, we snatch Mimi Kei. And tell old Horton we're fixing to do harm to his daughter's personage if he doesn't play ball with the diamonds and otherwise. But what if we're wrong about him? What if he doesn't back down? How far are we willing to go? I mean, do we mail him a finger? An ear? What do we do?"

I nodded. "I know. I've been thinking the same thing."

"I don't mean to sound like I'm going soft on you, but I have some acquaintance with what it's like to be held hostage, 'hostage' in this case meaning waterboarding, shocks to my legendary genitals, and threats to

remove said legendary genitals with sharp instruments if a certain someone didn't comply with my captors' demands. Any of that ring a bell
with you?"

He was talking about Hilger, who'd held Dox hoping to get to me. It
hadn't gone as Hilger had planned, but Dox suffered anyway.

"Yeah," I said. "I know what you mean."

"I'm just telling you, between the two of us, that I'm not comfortable hurting some girl who has nothing to do with any of this. I mean,
my daddy taught me that gentlemen can kill each other, preferably with
firearms, and that's fine, but that we respect womenfolk. I'm sure that
sounds fucked up to most of your more modern, egalitarian, self-actual-
ized killers, but it's how I was raised."

"I hear you."

"And I know you have a thing about no women and children, too."

"Yes."

"So... we're just bluffing then."

I nodded. "But I think when Horton understands Larison is involved
in this, he won't take the chance."

"Well, that right there is the problem. See, I don't think Larison is
bluffing. I think that man—and no disrespect, 'cause he is obviously one
capable sumbitch—I think he's a little bit... Well, how do I put this. You
know, some dogs, big dogs, they could kill you, but they don't, because
they're good dogs. You can trust them. Other dogs, they're looking at
you, and you don't know what the hell they're thinking. Or which way it
could go. That's how Larison is to me. Any given moment, I don't know
what he's going to do. I'm not sure even he knows."

It interested me that each of them understood the other in canine
terms. But I kept the thought to myself.

"Horton said something about Larison keeping too much hidden,"
I said. "Being in turmoil."

"Well, shit, everybody has something to keep hidden."

"You have something to keep hidden?"

He grinned. "Just my midget porn fetish. Don't tell anyone."

"You and I are on the same page," I said. "We'll let Larison think
what he wants, because the more scared Horton is, the better for us. But
we're not going to let him hurt anyone. If it comes to that, we'll stop

him."

He nodded. "Thank you for that. I figured as much. Just wanted to make sure."

We pulled our own clothes out of the pile of clean stuff and ate some of the provisions Dox had brought in. Then he napped while I watched the door, the Supergrade in hand. I watched the angle of the sun on the window curtains get increasingly sharp, and still no sign of Larison or Treven. Dox woke up and it was my turn to sleep while he stood sentry.

At a little past six, I was awakened instantly from a light sleep by three sharp knocks. I took a position on one side of the door, the Supergrade up and ready, while Dox opened it. It was Larison.

"Treven's on the way," he said. "Good news. I'll wait until he's here and then brief you. Is that grub? I'm starving."

He grabbed a wrap and started devouring it. Treven showed fifteen minutes later. While he tucked in, too, Larison briefed us.

"We went online," Larison said. "And found only four summer classes at the school. And only one on screenwriting, which is her thing. So we staked out the building where the class is held."

"You see anyone?" I asked. "Anyone who looked like they were looking for us?"

"Hell yes," Treven said. "We saw them—two of them—hanging out exactly where we would have been hanging out if we were trying to get to us."

Larison said, "So we made sure not to be where we would have been if we'd known no one was looking for us."

"The weird thing is, I understood all that," Dox said.

"We picked up a couple of radios at a Radio Shack," Larison said. "Not much range, but good enough for our purposes. We hung way back. Decided to take a chance, and it paid off."

I didn't like the sound of that. "What kind of chance?"

"We don't know how she gets to school," Treven said. "Could be a car, could be a bus, could be a bicycle for all we know. We made Hort's guys monitoring her building, so we couldn't do the same. Which meant we had to take a guess. Car, bus, or bicycle. We guessed bus. We guessed right. Followed her onto an L.A. Metro bus."

I still didn't like it. "How'd you manage it without getting seen?"

"I staked out Hilgard and Charing Cross," Larison said. "The stop right by the school."

"And I waited at the next stop," Treven said. "Hilgard and Sunset."

"Totally lucky that it turns out she rides the bus," Larison said. "But hey, sometimes you catch a break. When I saw her come out and wait at the Charing Cross stop, I radioed Treven. He got on at the next stop, right after her."

"What about Horton's guys?" I asked.

"One of them got on with her at Charing Cross," Larison said. "The other stayed behind."

I nodded. "So she's definitely unwitting."

"Right," Larison said. "If she were witting, they'd both be staying close. Plus, she was wearing earbuds, listening to music, shit no bodyguard in the world would ever tolerate. As it was, the guy who got on with her was doing everything he could to keep away from her, and otherwise be unobtrusive. As we expected, they're not trying to directly protect her, they're trying to anticipate, and eliminate, the threat."

I agreed with his assessment. "What else did you learn?"

Treven cracked a Red Bull. "I saw her get off at Sunset and Gordon. Hort's guy got off with her. I waited and jumped out at the next one—Sunset and Bronson, otherwise Hort's guy would have made me. But as the bus pulled away, I saw Kei walking north on a street called La Baig Avenue. If you look at La Baig—and we did, at an Internet place— you'll see it leads to only two streets, Harold Way and Selma Avenue. The whole neighborhood looks super quiet, nothing but single family houses. No pedestrian traffic. No way to follow her, even if I'd gotten off at her stop, even if Hort's guy hadn't been there. So no way to get her exact address. But—"

"We don't need her exact address," I said. "Assuming she was going home on the bus, and not somewhere else, now we know her stop."

Treven took a long pull of Red Bull. "Not just her stop, but her walking route to the stop. When you look at the map, you'll see she must live on one of those three streets—La Baig, Harold, or Selma. Otherwise, she would have gotten out at an earlier stop—Sunset and Gower."

Larison grinned. "But it's even better. We did get her address."

Treven grinned, too, looking like a kid who'd just pulled a brilliant prank. Larison gestured to him and said, "You tell them."

"So I radioed Larison," Treven said, still smiling, "and as I'm waiting for him, frustrated at getting so close and not being able to really close the deal, a mail truck went by. And I thought, shit, they're just delivering the mail now. Which gave me an idea."

"Pizza flyers," Larison said, apparently unable to resist interrupting. "There was a guy out on Sunset distributing flyers for some pizza place. I gave him twenty bucks for his stack of flyers, then Treven caught up to the mailman."

"Told him I was trying to reach people in the neighborhood," Treven said. "Gave him two hundred bucks for letting me put the flyers into his mail bundles. He told me he could do it himself, but I told him hey, how do I know you won't just throw them out? Let me put them in the bundles, it'll only take a minute."

"The pizza guy, and the mailman, they saw you?" I asked. "Could they remember you? Describe you?"

Treven shook his head. "We were wearing shades. Anyway, what if they could? The mailman would have to cop to taking bribes, and the pizza guy would have to admit he sold his flyers rather than giving them out. Even if someone made the connection between the flyers and Kei's temporary disappearance, those two wouldn't want to get involved."

"Besides," Larison said, "no one but Hort is even going to know Kei's gone missing. The police won't be involved. Even if they do get involved, we didn't give them anything to go on. And anyway, right now, potential police, even FBI, is pretty much the least of our problems."

He was right. "Well? What's her address?"

"A nice little bungalow on Selma Avenue," Treven said. "Again, we might not even need it because I think we'll have a better shot at her by the bus stop than we would by the house. But it was good to confirm she was heading home anyway, and not to, say, a friend's house or whatever. We'll show it all to you on Google Maps. Looks like she's renting a room from the family that lives there. But whatever. The main thing is, we know what time the first class is tomorrow morning, we know her bus stop, and she's got an approximate six-minute walk along a nice quiet street to get there. Wearing her earbuds, if we're really lucky."

We were quiet for a moment. Dox said, "Well, I have successfully procured us food and phones, and Mister Rain has kindly laundered our gamey garments. But I believe the day's glory goes to you."

"Couldn't have done it without clean clothes and food to look forward to," Treven said, and we all laughed.

"It looks promising," I said. "But there a few things to consider. And a few we need."

They looked at me.

"Potential opposition aside," I said, "the first class at UCLA begins at what, ten o'clock? So how early will we need to be in position?"

"No later than eight," Treven said. "And probably earlier."

"Right," I said. "And if we're thinking that, then Horton's guys are thinking the same. That's what they'll be looking for."

"Sunup," Larison said. "Earlier, in fact."

"Agreed," I said. "The key will be to get there earlier than we would reasonably need to for Kei—because Horton's guys expect us to be hunting Kei, when in fact, we'll be hunting them."

"Works out well anyway," Dox said. "I mean, we really don't know very much about her patterns. Does she like to go in early for a workout? Or to meet a friend for breakfast on campus, or to study in the library? We've been watching her for barely twenty-four hours, it could be anything. So we can't afford to time things so precisely regardless. The earlier we get in position, the better, assuming we can find good concealment."

Spoken like a true sniper, I thought. Waiting out a target was second nature for Dox. I think part of him even enjoyed it.

"All right," I said, "we need to be in position before it gets light. Which means we have a lot to do and not a lot of time to do it. To start with, I want to get a firsthand look at her neighborhood. Discreetly. Maybe on a bicycle. I mean, who ever looks suspicious on a bicycle?"

Larison said, "What else?"

"A vehicle. Overall, the U-Haul truck is great cover. But if anyone witnesses the snatch, a U-Haul truck is going to be remembered, and looked for, like a giant neon sign. Even if we swap in some stolen plates, the truck itself will be radioactive."

"That's a good point," Treven said. "Well, a panel truck would work. Could borrow one from a long-term parking lot. I doubt it would be missed until after it didn't matter."

"I'm thinking the same thing," I said. "We park the truck somewhere nice and quiet, use the stolen panel truck for the snatch, and break the circuit by transferring Kei from one to the other. Let's start walking this thing through."

Dox popped a Red Bull and smiled. "Maybe I should have bought a few more of these."

chapter
twenty

It was a long but productive night. One stolen GMC panel van; one
stolen Ford Fusion; assorted items from a hardware store, a sporting
goods place, a supermarket. Mapping out Kei's neighborhood. Identifying the ideal spot for the snatch, and for the switch. Planning the op; positioning the vehicles. We'd slept for a few hours, gotten up while it was
still dark, dispersed, and then regrouped near Kei's house before sunup.

One problem from our perspective was that Selma Avenue, and La
Baig, which led into it, permitted no parking on the street—not even any
stopping, according to the signs. So if we parked the van anywhere near
her house, we ran the risk of an annoyed neighbor coming out to talk
to us or even calling the police. The good news was, there was a motel
on the corner, a long, pink and blue, two-storied affair that stretched
along the west side of La Baig for about two hundred feet starting at the
corner of Sunset. We had parked the van there, on the side of the lot
closest to Kei's house, front end in, rear end facing La Baig. If Larison's
and Treven's intel was sound, and Kei stuck to what we preliminarily assumed was her routine, we would be good to go. And if Horton's guys
were trying to identify trouble before it reached Kei, the first spot they'd
check would be exactly where we'd parked the van.

Which is why three of us were watching it now: Larison, from between two parked cars in the driveway of a small apartment building
across the street; Treven, from the dark stairwell in the center of the
motel; and I, from a prone position on the balcony of the motel directly
above the van. Dox was waiting in the stolen Fusion a few miles away.
The chances of someone stumbling upon any of us at this hour were

slim, but if it happened, Treven and Larison were dressed in the latest Nikes and Under Armour, just another couple of early morning L.A. fitness fanatics. I was less sportily attired, in jeans and a sweatshirt, and would have to be a drunk sleeping it off. Thin cover for action, but reasonable under the circumstances, and in all events better than nothing.

At just before sunup, as the first gray light crept into the sky, a dark Chevy Suburban pulled into the far end of the motel parking lot. I watched it from my perch and felt a warm surge of adrenaline spread through my torso. It was unusually early for anyone to be arriving at, or returning to, a motel. Nothing else at the motel, or in the surrounding neighborhood, had yet stirred.

The doors opened, but no interior light came on. Two big, clean-cut Caucasian men got out, both dressed casually in what looked in the dim light like jeans and bulky fleece jackets. They paused and looked around, then moved out, letting the doors click quietly closed behind them.

The earliness of the hour, the lack of an interior light, the quietly closed doors, the watchfulness... if these weren't Horton's men, they could only have been here to rob the motel. But thieves who moved as stealthily and professionally as these two typically have better uses for their talents than budget motels. They had to be here for us.

They moved silently along the row of parked cars, their heads swiveling, shining penlights into the interiors of the vehicles they passed. They swept their lights along the balcony of the motel's second floor, too, but I saw the light coming my way and simply flattened myself against the ground beyond the angle of their vision.

They came to Treven's position and checked the stairs, but I knew he would have melted away at their approach. I also knew he'd be back as soon as they had passed.

When they came to the van, they stopped. I knew what they were thinking. *A panel van. Perfect for a snatch. And parked exactly where we would have parked it ourselves.*

They shone their lights through the front windows and then tried the side doors, which we had locked.

Try the back door, I thought. *You never know.*

One of them stepped back, scanned, and took a notepad from one of the fleece pockets. He shone his light on the license plate and jotted down the number. Then he slipped the notepad back into his pocket and they circled to the rear of the van.

I was hoping they would give the door their simultaneous attention, but they were too good for that. One tried the door while the other one scanned behind them. I couldn't see him, but I knew Larison would have moved out from concealment, up to the edge of the apartment building wall directly across the street. Either he or Treven could have shot them left-handed from this close, but we didn't have suppressors, and couldn't risk waking up the neighborhood with the sound of gunshots. Because of that, and because we had to assume they were armed, too, we had to be practically on top of them before they knew we were there if we were going to pull this off quietly.

One of them started to open the rear van door. The other was still watching behind them. Larison and Treven only needed a second, but they weren't going to get it.

So I improvised. In ersatz sexual ecstasy, I moaned, "Oh, God, yes, don't stop, don't stop, fuck, yes, that's so good, don't stop…"

They both immediately oriented on the sudden disturbance. I knew the incongruity would cost them precious nanoseconds of processing time: they'd been attuned to a range of possible problems, including sounds of stealth and ambush. And now they were hearing sounds, but not ones they could quickly fit into the threat matrix through which they were approaching their current environment.

"Oh my God, yes!" I said. "Yes!"

For an instant, they were what-the-fuck paralyzed. Then they both reached inside their jackets.

Too late. Larison and Treven had already rushed up behind them, grabbed their gun arms, and jammed the muzzles of their own guns against the backs of their heads. I heard Larison say, "Freeze, or I'll blow your brains through your face." His voice had the kind of command authority that could stand down an attack dog.

I swung down off the balcony to the parking lot and circled around to the rear of the van. Before Horton's men could overcome their surprise and make a tactical decision, I reached inside each of their jackets and extracted a suppressed Glock from a shoulder harness. Quiet enough, yes, but unfortunately for Horton's men, a hell of a long draw.

I shoved one of the guns into my waistband and checked the load on the other. A round in the chamber, as expected, but it doesn't hurt to be sure.

"Lean forward," I told them. "Legs apart, knees straight, faces down, palms against the van. Or we'll find out just how quiet these suppressers are."

The threat was deliberate. I didn't want them to count even a little on any hesitation we might have about the sound of gunshots.

They complied. I handed Larison the other suppressed pistol. He secured his own gun in his waistband and we covered the two of them while Treven searched for weapons. He came away with two folding knives, two mini-lights, two cell phones, two wallets, two notepads, and a set of car keys. He pocketed all of it, secured their wrists behind their backs with heavy plastic flex ties, opened the van doors, and got inside. The flex ties could be defeated by someone who knew what he was doing, but for now all we needed was to inhibit them and slow them down. Larison and I shoved them in, got in ourselves, pushed them face down onto the floor, and closed the doors behind us. Larison kept them covered while Treven moved to the driver's seat. We'd punched peepholes in the van's sides and back. I removed the duct tape covering them and looked through. Between Treven in front and the peepholes in back, we had three-hundred-sixty-degree coverage of the area around the van. So far, it seemed our brief interaction outside had attracted no attention.

One of Horton's men said, "What are you going to do with us?"

Larison said, "The next one of you who talks without being asked a question first, I'm going to pistol whip."

No one said anything after that. We watched the street for five minutes. It was getting lighter outside. Everything was quiet.

Treven stayed up front at the wheel, going through the items he'd taken from Horton's men. I put the duct tape back in place over the peepholes and turned on the rear dome light. Larison and I sat Horton's men up and pushed them back against the passenger-side wall, their legs splayed in front of them. I was going to ask them a few questions myself, but something about Larison's body language—the confidence, and also the menace—made me realize he was going to handle it. And likely handle it well.

"Here's how it's going to work," he said, placing the muzzle of the suppressed Glock first against one of their foreheads, and then against the other. "I'm going to ask you some questions. The first one who gives me useful, accurate information that tracks with what I already know, gets to live. Whoever loses the race to talk first gets an instant bullet in the head. That's the game and there's only one winner. You ready?"

The two men looked at him, then at each other. Sweat broke out on their foreheads. The inside of the van suddenly reeked of fear.

Larison pointed the ominously long suppressed barrel of the Glock at one, then the other. "Who sent you? Why? Where is he? How do we get to him? What else do you know? That's it. Ready, set, go."

Their eyes were bulging now and they were beginning to pant. They looked at Larison. They looked at each other. The one on the right shook his head, as though pleading or in disbelief. Suddenly, the one on the left turned his head and shouted, "Colonel Horton! To protect his daughter!"

The other guy screamed, "Shut the fuck up!" Larison instantly swung the pistol over. There was a crack about the loudness of someone snapping his fingers and the guy's head smacked into the wall behind him. Then he lay suddenly slumped and still, a neat hole just above his left eye.

"Congratulations," Larison said to the remaining guy. "You won the first round. But you have to keep going."

"Jesus!" the guy spluttered. "Jesus Christ!"

"Maybe you didn't hear me," Larison said. "I said, you have to keep going."

The guy was starting to hyperventilate. "You're just going to kill me, too!"

Larison shrugged. "Maybe not. Make me like you. Make me feel grateful to you. I'm as human as the next guy."

"Oh, my God!" the guy wailed.

"Calm down," Larison said. "I know it's stressful. This is the most important moment of your life, and you don't have much time. Because, and I think you know this now, I'm not very patient."

"Horton… Horton sent us. What else do you want to know?"

"Who else did he send?"

"I don't know of anyone else!"

"You sure?"

"Yes!"

"His name is Raymond Trent ," Treven called from the front. "North Carolina driver's license. The dead guy was Carl Ryan. Virginia."

"All right, Ray," Larison said. "What's your connection to Horton?"

Ray swallowed. "We freelance for him."

"What does that mean?"

"We do... contract work."

"You're contractors?"

"Yes. No. I mean, we freelance. Sometimes Horton asks us to do things on the side. You know, moonlighting. Off the books."

"What else has he had you do?"

"I don't know, all kinds of stuff."

Larison didn't answer, and after a moment, Ray hurriedly went on. "Black bag work. Eavesdropping. Surveillance. Sometimes a hit."

So far, Larison hadn't elicited anything we hadn't already assumed. But I was thinking about the four guys we'd dropped at the Capital Hilton. That was an important op for Horton, and we were no easy target, so I knew he would have cared enough to send only the very best. My sense was that Ray and Carl were backup, a B team. If they were pinch-hitting for the four dead guys here, where else would they have to step in? What else would Horton have in mind for them?

"What do you think?" I said to Larison. "Are you liking this guy? Feeling grateful for what he's telling us?"

Larison kept his eyes on the guy and shook his head. "No."

Ray said, "Look, I don't want to die here, okay? This is just a job for me. I'm not trying to protect anyone. Just tell me what you want, I'll tell you everything I know."

"How long are you supposed to watch Kei?" I said.

"Horton told us probably a few days," Ray said. "Until further notice. He paid for a week."

"How long have you been out here?" I said.

"Horton called us four days ago. We flew in the next morning."

That tracked with when we took out the team at the Hilton. Horton must have gotten paranoid—though obviously not without reason—and called on these guys just in case one of us learned about his daughter and decided to make a run at her.

"Did he mention any other travel?" I said. "Any other assignments?"

"No. He just asked us to keep our schedules open—to let him know if anything was going to tie us up in the next couple weeks so he could have first dibs."

If that was true, it meant Horton was planning something else, or was at least planning for a contingency. But that was neither surprising, nor particularly useful.

"Nothing else?" I said.

"No."

I decided to try for a long shot. "Nothing about schools?"

He looked genuinely puzzled by that. "Schools?"

I was disappointed, though not surprised. After all, it wasn't likely Horton would have shared anything operational with these two beyond what was immediately necessary. But Kanezaki had said there was chatter about possible school attacks. And Treven and I had been speculating about the same thing.

Larison said, "Tell me how to get to Hort."

"Get to him? I couldn't get to him myself. But wait… wait. Maybe I can help you think of something. I mean, he lives in the Washington area, I think. I could call him, on a pretext, tell him—"

He was just blathering now. Scheherazade, without even a story to tell.

"—that I need to meet with him in person, something like that. Flush him out for you."

"I don't think he knows anything," I said to Larison. "There's no real reason to think he would."

Larison nodded. "I agree."

Ray said, "Look, I'm really trying to help you. I really am."

Larison said, "I believe you," and shot him in the forehead. Ray's head snapped back, then his body sagged and he slumped over against his partner.

"Maybe we'll get something from the phones," Treven said from up front.

"I doubt it," I said.

Larison took Ray's body by the collar and dragged it forward, away from the rear and side sliding doors. "If we grab Kei, it'll all be academic," he said. "But it's nice that Hort keeps losing guys like this. At some point, he's going to get short on volunteers."

I hauled the other one forward and we covered them with a tarp. We could reveal them to Kei as circumstances warranted, but I wanted to have the option. No sense freaking her out without a reason.

I didn't mind that the two of them were dead. If Larison hadn't been so quick to do it, I would have taken care of it myself. They were certainly here to do the same to us. Besides, as Larison had observed, it was two fewer pieces on the opposition side of the board.

But I'd have to watch him with Kei. Dox had been right. It wasn't just that he was professional to the point of ruthlessness. There was something beyond that, something that made me wonder if he took not just pride in his work, but also a little too much pleasure.

chapter
twenty-one

I watched La Baig, in full daylight now, from the passenger-side peep-hole in the van. Larison had headed out around the corner to a small commercial parking lot on Harold Way, where he'd do some light stretch-es and calisthenics like someone warming up for a run or doing one of the WODs he and Dox seemed enamored of. I estimated we'd have at least a full minute from when Kei first appeared at the corner of Selma and La Baig to when she reached our position—enough time to alert Larison and for him to react. Treven was still at the wheel of the van, waiting for word from me. We had energy bars, canned coffee, and big mouth water bottles to piss in. The only thing left was to wait.

At a little past eight, I spotted someone heading toward us on the east side of the street. There had been several false alarms already—a jogger, a dog walker, two young women probably on their way to the bus and then to work—and I tried not to get excited. But as this one came closer and the sun slanted in on her face, I saw it was her. My heart kicked up a notch. "Here she comes," I said, without taking my eye from the peephole.

"Got it," Treven said. "Calling Larison now." A moment later, I heard him say, "She's on her way."

Treven fired up the engine. I kept watching Kei. Her hair was tied back and she was wearing cut-off shorts and a white tee shirt under a navy fleece zip-up. A leather mailbag was slung over her left shoulder. A beautiful kid, even better in person than in the photos I'd seen. Leggy, curvy, with a long, confident stride. Someone who knew where she was going and how she would get there, and who wasn't going to let anyone get in the way.

Well, she hadn't counted on us. But with a little luck, we'd be no more than a bump in the road for her, immediately felt and quickly forgotten.

I watched her pass Harold Way. There was Larison, jogging down Harold, emerging right behind her.

"Go," I said to Treven.

He put the van in reverse, cut the wheel right, and backed up all the way to the sidewalk on the other side of the street—essentially the middle part of a K-turn. Not too fast, not too sudden, just someone turning in reverse out of the motel parking lot to head south on La Baig. He stopped just as Larison reached Kei. Maybe she heard him coming; maybe some vestigial portion of her brain sensed the danger he radiated. Maybe both. Whatever it was, she started to turn. Too late.

Larison smacked her smartly on the side of the neck with the palm of his hand. Sometimes known as the "brachial stun," the blow is intended to disrupt the brachial plexus network of nerve fibers, or, depending on the location of impact, the carotid sinus. Either way, the result can be temporary loss of coordination, unconsciousness, or even, if the blow is sufficiently severe and well placed, death.

The van stopped. Kei staggered and Larison clasped an arm around her. I moved from the peephole, threw open the rear doors, and caught Kei as Larison pushed her into me. We hauled her into the van and had the doors closed behind us two seconds after. Treven accelerated smoothly south and made a right on Sunset, so calm and courteous he even remembered to use the turning signal.

Kei hadn't lost full consciousness, she was just dazed. We pulled the mailbag off her, secured her wrists behind her back with flex ties, and sat her up against the passenger-side wall. I knelt in front of her and quickly patted her down. Nothing. Whatever she was carrying, it must have been in the mailbag. Larison started going through it. He would disable her phone and confirm there were no tracking devices. Not likely there were, but it was possible Horton had implemented backup measures, hoping to protect her just in case.

I looked into her eyes. I could see she was coming back to herself. We didn't need to do anything to resuscitate her.

After a moment, she blinked hard. She looked around the van, and then at me. "What the fuck?" she said. "Who are you? What is this?"

"It's a kidnapping," I said, using a word she would clearly understand and that would provide some immediate context amid her current confusion. "This isn't a joke. It's about your father. Colonel Horton. You understand?"

"My father... what did he do? What the fuck?"

"It doesn't matter what he did. All you need to know is that he owes us something and we're using you to get it. Do you understand?"

She looked from my face to Larison's and back, and I could see how scared she suddenly was. She didn't answer. I realized there was no need to let her see the bodies of the men her father had sent. She was frightened enough as it was.

"We're going to take your picture now," I said. "To show to your father."

Larison handed me a copy of that day's Los Angeles Times, which we'd scooped up from a driveway on the way to the motel that morning. I propped it on her lap. Larison moved in close and snapped a few shots with her phone. We'd send Horton the proof from his daughter's own phone. That would increase his sense of how thoroughly we controlled her, and keep our phones clean.

I took the newspaper off her and tossed it aside. "We're going to try to make this go smoothly. But there are two ways you could get hurt. One is, if your father doesn't do what we want. Two is, if *you* don't do what we want."

She was breathing hard now and I knew she was fighting panic. Fighting it well. I respected her for it. And with the respect came a sudden and surprising dose of self-loathing.

I suppressed the feeling. I'd deal with the emotional fallout later. Like I always had before.

I looked in her eyes. "You're worried that we're letting you see our faces, is that it?"

She nodded. She was smart—smart enough to know that if a kidnapper lets you see his face, it means he's not worried about you being a witness later. Meaning, probably, he's not planning on letting you be alive later.

"It doesn't matter if you see us," I told her. "Your father is going to know exactly who we are. And he'll explain to you when this is done why you can't go to the police. So we're not worried about you seeing our faces. Does that make sense?"

She nodded again.

"All right," I said. "I get the feeling you're smart. So you probably know about secondary crime scenes, and how you should never let someone take you to one, because once you're at the secondary crime scene, the criminal can do anything he wants to you. And that's true. But the thing is, you're already at the secondary crime scene. We're alone in this van, we have total control of the environment, and total control of you. If we wanted to hurt you, we'd be hurting you right now. But we're not. And we want to keep it that way. Are you with me so far?"

"Yes," she said, and I was glad she felt in control enough to trust herself to speak.

"In a little while," I said, "we're going to transfer you. First to another car, then to a hotel room. We're going to keep your wrists tied and before the transfer we're going to blindfold you, but we don't want to make you any more uncomfortable than that. We don't want to gag you, for example. I don't know if you've ever been gagged, but I can tell you, it's a horrible way to spend a few days. Much worse than you'd guess. Mimi, are we going to have to gag you?"

She shook her head. "No."

"Are you going to try to run away? Or fight us? Or in any way not do what we tell you to do?"

"No."

"Look, for me, this is mostly just business." I tipped my head toward Larison. "But for my associate here, it's extremely personal. You don't want to give him a reason, okay? Trust me, he's looking for one."

She looked past me at Larison, and I could tell from her expression that she believed. Believed utterly.

I let another moment go by, then said, "But I'm sure you're going to be fine. Now, do you have any questions?"

She nodded. "Where are you taking me?"

"I can't tell you that, other than to say it's someplace where we can manage you, and where no one's going to be able to find you until we let you go. Anything else?"

"What did my father do?"

"You're going to have to ask him that. Anything else?"

"Yeah. Why do you keep asking me if I want to ask you anything, when you know you're not going to answer?"

I smiled sadly, admiring how quickly she'd mastered herself, and liking the moxie she'd accessed even in the midst of shock and distress.

"You ask good questions," I said. "I'm sorry I can't answer them all. I can tell you this, though. We're going to change cars a couple times. You and I are going to ride in the trunk in one of them. And it's going to be at least a few hours before we're someplace comfortable, someplace with a bathroom. If you need to go before then, we're going to need to put you in an adult diaper. Can you make it?"

"You can't be serious."

"I'm trying to make this as easy on you as I can, Mimi. But yeah, you better believe that I'm serious."

Kei declined the diaper, and I was relieved. Maybe it wasn't worth much under the circumstances, but I really didn't want to subject her to the indignity. This was going to be hard enough as it was.

We spent the next two hours driving under virtually every overpass on the 101, the 110, and the 10, and going in and out of various underground parking garages, too. I took the passenger seat; Larison stayed in back with Kei. When I was satisfied, I called Dox. "You ready?"

"Ready, partner."

"All right. We're on our way."

We made a left off Venice Boulevard onto South Redondo. As we came to the stop sign on Bangor Street, I saw the Fusion, waiting to make a right—Dox. He pulled out ahead of us, and we followed him south toward the 10. As soon as we were under the overpass, Dox cut right and swerved to a stop on the sidewalk. The trunk popped open. Treven hit the hazard lights, cut right onto the sidewalk and then back onto the street, skidding to a stop so that the passenger side of the van was right alongside the open trunk of the Fusion. I jumped into the back and slid open the side door. Larison was already standing there with Kei, still wrist-tied and now blindfolded. The two of us lifted her easily into the trunk and I squirmed in beside her. Larison slammed the trunk shut and Dox peeled out back onto the road, accelerating to the end of the tunnel, then rapidly decelerating and emerging at a normal speed. Treven would be right behind him in the van, same timing, same formation as when we entered.

What we were doing was creating a kind of shell game using the overpasses and the garages. We still didn't know how Horton had tracked us to the Capital Hilton, and our working assumption was that he had used spy satellites. We had to assume he had access to the resources of the National Reconnaissance Office and the National Geospatial-Intelligence Agency. If so, and if he had a fixed point for a target—such as, say, Dulles Airport, or outside his daughter's house—it was possible he could track that target from the fixed point to wherever the target went, virtually indefinitely. If our working assumption was right, we'd been lucky in Washington, maybe in the hotel parking garage, maybe elsewhere between D.C. and Los Angeles. But we didn't want to rely on luck again. Every time we drove the van under an overpass, or in and out of a garage, we created the possibility that we'd switched Kei into one of the dozens of vehicles that emerged from under the overpass at around the same time we did, or from the garage afterward. Multiply this dynamic by dozens of overpasses and garages times dozens of cars, many of which would themselves continue under other overpasses and into other garages, and we could create a dataset too big for Horton to act on, at least in the time we would permit him.

The plan now was for Treven and Larison to continue the shell game for the next couple hours, then to ditch the van, bleach it out, and get back to the hotel using buses and the Metro system. By the time they were done, Horton would be facing thousands of possibilities, each of which would have to be manually tracked, assuming it could be tracked at all. As for Dox and me, we did one more switch, into the U-Haul truck, which we had left in a giant underground garage in a mall in Westwood. Dox stayed at the wheel and I stayed in the cargo area with Kei.

At a little past noon, I felt a series of short turns that told me were back at the motel. "How are you holding up?" I asked Kei.

"I need a bathroom. Badly. Please don't put me in a diaper."

I checked my watch. "Can you hold on for three more minutes?"

She glared at me. "Barely."

The truck stopped. "Face the front of the truck," I told her. She complied. A moment later, the cargo doors opened and Dox climbed in. He was carrying an extra-large cargo carrier, 59 by 24 by 24 inches. Just roomy enough for someone of Kei's dimensions. He pulled the doors shut behind him.

"All right, Mimi," I said. "One more transfer."

Dox, looking distinctly reluctant, set down the cargo bag and held it open. Kei grimaced, then stepped into it and curled up on her side. "I'm not going to gag you," I told her. "Remember our deal."

I was betting I'd be able to spot when she was planning an insurrection, and that I'd be able to preempt it. In the meantime, she would bide her time, believing she was lulling me. That was fine. The net effect was that she would be unconsciously inhibited by what she thought was hope. Meaning she would be comfortable. And, more importantly, more cooperative.

We zipped her in and opened the door. Dox picked up the bag as though it was filled with nothing but Styrofoam peanuts, slung it over a shoulder, and carried her into the motel. I shut the truck doors and followed him in.

We set her down in the room, unzipped the bag, and helped her to her feet. I opened the folding knife I was carrying and let her see it. Dox was holding the Wilson—not because he wanted to, but because I'd told him to. I wanted to give her every possible psychological excuse not to resist, including the obvious facts of our numbers, our size—or Dox's size, anyway—and our weapons.

"I'm going to untie your wrists," I said. "Take your time in the bathroom. We won't watch you, but the door stays open. If you do anything we don't like, we'll have to diaper you, hogtie you, gag you, and put a hood on you, and leave you like that for what could be days. It's up to you."

I stepped behind her and quickly patted her down. Larison already had, and even if he hadn't, it wasn't likely she was carrying, but this was Horton's daughter, after all, and it would be foolish to assume any woman couldn't be equipped with pepper spray or an FS Hideaway knife. Better to double check. But Kei had no weapons, nor even anything that could be used for one. I took hold of her wrists and cut the flex ties.

She hurried into the bathroom. It was tiny and windowless, and with the door open there was nowhere she could go for concealment. And I'd already checked it for anything that could remotely be used as an improvised weapon. About the only thing she might have done was to wrap her fist in a towel, smash the mirror, and pick up a long shard using the towel as a kind of handle. I judged such a move at this point extremely unlikely. If I was wrong, though, I would have plenty of time to get an upraised desk chair between us, while Dox approached her from behind.

I turned away while Dox dragged a dresser in front of the door. A small thing, but enough to dissuade her from thinking she could get away with a mad dash for the exit. I heard her urinating for a long time. When the sound stopped, I glanced over just to be cautious, but everything was fine—she had already stood and had quickly pulled up her jeans.

She came out of the bathroom and said, "I'm hungry."

I nodded. "We'll give you some food in a minute. First, I want you to lie facedown on the floor."

"Why?"

"Because it'll slow you down and keep you from being tempted to do something that might get you hurt. The alternative is, we tie you up again. I need a bathroom break myself, and I don't want fewer than two people watching you when you're free to move about."

She hesitated, then did as I told her. I used the bathroom, then Dox followed suit. When he was done, I told Kei she could sit on one of the beds. She did so.

Dox sat across from her and said, "I apologize for inconveniencing you, Ms. Kei. We're in a tight spot, and it was your dad who put us here. We need to give him a little incentive to do the right thing. Which I believe he will. Despite the late unpleasantness, he's always struck me as the kind of man who responds to incentives."

"That's what you call this?" she said. "Inconveniencing me?"

"Well," Dox said, "in the end, I don't know that it matters so much what we call it. But I do apologize regardless. Now, you said you're hungry. We've got some pretty good chow from a fancy supermarket, if you like. You look like a salad girl to me, am I right?"

"If by salad you mean cheeseburger, then yeah."

"A cheeseburger's a tall order at the moment," Dox said. "But maybe later. In the meantime, we've got a few sandwiches in a cooler, left over from yesterday. Not as fresh as you might like, but I expect they'll taste fine if you're hungry enough. What would you like? Roast beef, I'm guessing now? With a tasty smoothie to wash it down?"

"Whatever. Yes."

I sat in the desk chair, watching Dox feeding her and doing what he could to make her comfortable under the circumstances. Women were his weakness, I knew, the lady's man bluster mostly a cover for the bottom line fact that he really just adored them. And his southern code of chivalry was no bullshit, either. He wasn't happy about what we were doing, and I realized I'd have to watch him with Kei for the opposite reason I'd have to watch Larison. Where Larison was likely to let his evident hatred of Horton cause him to harm Kei, Dox might get too attached and grow to feel too guilty, and therefore become too susceptible to manipulation.

"Why don't you tell me what my dad did to you?" Kei asked him at one point. "What difference would it make if you did?"

Dox took a sip of the smoothie he was drinking. I was aware that he'd broken bread with her, and felt uneasy about it.

"Wouldn't make any difference to us," he said. "But I don't want to mix you up in this anymore than we already have. I mean, you're close with your daddy, right?"

I saw her weigh the pros and cons of possible responses before settling on the truth. "Yes," she said. "We're close. Which is why I want to know what he could have done to wrong you. I really can't imagine it."

Dox smiled. "I can tell he's lucky to have you for a daughter. And all I can tell you is, part of the burden of being a man, and the nature of the defect that defines us, is that we sometimes have to do things we can't tell our loved ones about."

"Why can't you?"

"Because sometimes things need to be done in the world, and telling you would make you complicit. By keeping you innocent, we save you from having to join us in hell. It might not sound like much, but it is a comfort when you're faced with hard choices."

"But that's ridiculous. You make women sound like children. You think we can't decide for ourselves? That's completely demeaning."

"Demeaning? Hell, I wish someone would do it for me."

"No, you don't. You like keeping it all to yourself because doing so makes you feel powerful."

Dox looked perplexed. "I don't think so."

"I do. You say my dad did something to you, something so horrible that now in your mind it justifies kidnapping and threatening his daughter? You're willing to do all that, but not even to tell me what this is all about?"

Nicely played, I thought. I waited to see how Dox would respond.

"We did some work for your dad," Dox said. "Not the kind of work I'm going to discuss with you. And then, to hide the fact that we did the work, he hired some people to do the same kind of work on us. You follow? You really want to know more?"

"Yes," she said. "I do. And you don't have to be afraid to tell me."

"Well, it's not—"

"It's not a matter of fear," I said. "Like Dox said, the less you know, the better for you. And for your father."

She looked at him. "Your name is Dox?"

"I told you," I said, "your father already knows who we are. We're not trying to keep our identities secret from you."

"Then what's your name?" she said.

She really was smart. She was doing what she could to glean information that at some point might be operationally useful. And she was also establishing rapport, making herself seem human and making her captors feel human, which in itself might create tactical opportunities for her, or, at a minimum, make it more emotionally difficult for us to harm her.

"You can call me Rain," I said. "But enough questions for now, okay? We're tired. We'll have plenty of time to talk more later, if you want."

I had a feeling Dox might have liked to protest, but he must have thought better of it.

I was a little concerned about Kei. She had a natural interrogator's personality—smart, likeable, unthreatening, and inquisitive under the guise of sincere interest. Dox was obviously being careful in response to her inquiries, but I wondered how he might comport himself in my absence. He obviously wanted her to like him. Partly to make her comfortable, partly to assuage his guilt, and partly because, after all, she was gorgeous, and he just couldn't help himself.

We flex-tied one of Kei's wrists to a bedpost and passed a couple hours silently, Dox watching her while I catnapped on the floor. I was awakened by a knock.

Dox and I took out our guns and approached the door. "Yes?" I said.

"It's us," I heard Larison say.

I had previously placed a strip of duct tape over the peephole to prevent anyone on the other side of the door from knowing by the blockage of light that someone was looking through it. I put my face up close and removed the duct tape. Larison and Treven, as advertised.

I moved the dresser, then let them in and bolted the door behind them. "Any trouble?" I said.

Treven shook his head. "No. Ditched those guys, ditched the van, no problems."

If Kei wondered whom he was referring to by "those guys," she didn't ask.

"All right then," I said. "If everything's good to go, it's time to call Horton."

Larison looked at Kei and smiled. "Yes, it is."

chapter
twenty-two

It was a long time before Larison was ready to call Hort. He didn't
know how they'd been tracked in D.C.—satellite, surveillance cameras,
drone aircraft, whatever—and he needed to be certain it wasn't going to
happen again. So he ramped up his already stringent procedures, spend-
ing hours in buses, taxis, malls, and on the subway, making sure he wasn't
just flushing out possible foot and vehicular surveillance, but also that he
was obscuring his movements against more remote potential watchers,
as well.

He was glad he'd managed to persuade the others that their only
move was to take Kei hostage. It had the benefit of being true, of course,
but he had his own, additional reasons for wanting Kei as leverage against
Hort: he recognized that the value of his threat to release the torture
tapes was diminishing.

Larison had long understood that America's political elites insisted
on counter-terror policies like disappearances, torture, drone strikes, and
invasions because the elites perversely benefited from the increased terror the policies inevitably produced. He understood the policies weren't
a response to the threat, but were rather the cause of the threat, and that
this was by design. A frightened populace was a controllable populace.
Endless war and metastasizing security procedures meant enormous
profits for the corporations the politicians served. In this sense, the possible publication of graphic videos of American servicemen torturing
screaming Muslim prisoners had always been, from the perspective of
America's elites, as much a promise as a threat.

Still, in ordinary times, people would have reacted to videos of gruesome torture with disgust and horror. In the most emotionally irrefutable way, the tapes would implicate various establishment players, and the reputations of the men who had ordered the barbarism in the videos would have been sullied; their careers, derailed. And that highly personal threat had outweighed the government's institutional interest in finding ways to increase the danger of terrorism—at least enough for the government to agree to cough up a hundred million dollars worth of uncut diamonds.

But everything had changed now. America was under attack, and who would object to what was on the tapes now? Object, hell—they'd clamor for more. The people who had ordered what was shown on the tapes wouldn't be censured. They'd be heroes.

And that, in essence, was the problem. Circumstances were now eroding the value of the cards he held, so much so that he wondered whether neutralizing the extortion value of the tapes was the purpose of the attacks. Well, even if it wasn't the primary purpose, it must have occurred to somebody. And regardless, the effect was the same. The value of his assets was declining, and he knew he needed new ones. Hort's daughter was one. The daughter, and what she would lead to.

Eventually, he made his way to the graffitied roll-down storefronts and cracked cinderblock walls and peeling real estate lease signs of the blighted industrial district. For a while, he wandered among the jobless, solitary men who gravitated to the area, casualties of a hollowed-out economy. He liked the cover they gave him, liked that no one knew them or cared about them or could tell one from the other, liked knowing that as he made himself complicit among them, the world's callousness and indifference would envelop him, as well.

He paused with his back to the brick façade of a recycling center and looked around. The skyscrapers of the downtown jutted up into a faded blue sky a mile or so behind him. Absent those distant monoliths, he might have been almost anywhere. An old mill town, a dying burg in the rust belt. There was no panic buying here. There was nothing to buy, and no money to use to buy it. It was the last place politicians would ever care about, the last place security forces would ever be sent to protect. He felt anonymous. He felt secure.

He took out Kei's phone, popped in the battery, and fired it up. He had a number for Hort, but he assumed Hort would have a separate, clean phone exclusively for personal use. He checked Kei's speed dial entries and immediately saw one called "Dad." The number wasn't the one he had, so yes, a separate, personal phone.

He brought up the photos he had taken in the van and keyed the entry for "Dad," enjoying the feeling of invading Hort's privacy this way. He waited while the photos uploaded, then called Hort.

One ring, then, "Hey sweet girl, I was just about to open those photos you sent me. How are you?"

"Your sweet girl's fine," Larison said. "For now."

There was a long pause. Larison relished the silence. Could there have been a more pristine way for Hort to convey his sudden shock, and violation, and helplessness? His confusion and impotent rage and, soon enough, his despair?

"I swear to almighty God—"

Larison cut him off. "Look at the photos. She's alive. For now. The guys you sent to protect her, not so much."

There was another pause during which Larison assumed Hort was checking the photos. Then Hort said, "Let her go. Just let her go. She didn't do anything to you—"

"You did something to me."

"Yes. And this is between you and me, and no one else."

"It must be killing you, Hort. To know, right now, that you're the one who taught me to identify the target's most vulnerable area. And to attack him there. And you showed me how, remember? You got to me through Nico."

"That's right, I did. You know what'll happen to him if anything happens to my daughter?"

Larison laughed. "You've already pointed a gun at him, Hort. Now you're threatening to point another? What are you going to do, have his nieces raped and his nephews killed and the other shit you threatened before, twice over?"

"It doesn't matter. If anything happens to her, I will never, ever stop until I've found you. And yes, I will start with your man Nico, and every goddamned member of his extended family, one at a time and saving Nico for last so he can know what happened and who was the cause of the deaths of everyone he loved and the ruination of his entire life. I'll see to it all personally."

"You're missing something really important, Hort. You know what it is? I. Don't. Care. So go ahead. Hang up. Go after Nico right now. Try me."

Silence. Then: "Tell me what you want."

"I want my diamonds."

"What else?"

"A guarantee that the dogs you've sicced on us are called off."

"And you'll let my daughter go?"

"Yes."

"Unharmed?"

"Yes."

"All right, then."

"How?"

"I'll bring you the diamonds myself. And I'll make an announcement tomorrow that I believe will set your mind at ease on the other thing."

"What announcement?"

"I can't tell you now. But you'll be able to watch it on television. I'll make the announcement and immediately fly to L.A. I can meet you tomorrow night, if you like."

Despite everything, Larison couldn't help being touched by the man's devotion. He must have known he would be coming here to die.

But then he wondered if he was giving Hort's humanity too much credit. Hort was a clever bastard, and had outplayed Larison before. He'd have to be careful. Consider every angle. Look at the whole thing from Hort's perspective, and see if he could detect any weaknesses in his own position.

"You might be able to track us," Larison said. "We've been careful, but you got to us at the Hilton, so maybe you'll find a way again. The difference is, this time, I'll be with Mimi. You breach that door, you better be sure you can put a bullet in my brain in less than one second. Because that's how long it'll take me to put one in hers."

"Nobody's going to be breaching any doors," Hort said. "I just want her safe. I don't care about the rest, you were right. You can have whatever you want, as long as you let her go."

Larison considered. It was hard to imagine Hort was going to risk his daughter over the diamonds. The question was, would he call off the dogs. And how would Larison know, one way or the other?

But as he thought about it, he realized it might not even matter. Once he had the diamonds, and Hort was dead, and Rain, Treven, and Dox were all dead, too, let the government try to track him. They'd be wasting their time. Because they'd be looking for a ghost.

chapter
twenty-three

The next morning, the five of us clustered around the television in the motel room. The president was making an announcement from the Rose Garden, and we assumed Horton would have something to do with it.

We'd dragged in the futons and done the night in shifts. Kei slept on one bed; the rest of us used the futons and sleeping bags and the remaining bed, with at least one of us awake at all times. Larison seemed not to sleep much, and when he did, he moaned occasionally and once had cried out. I had my own difficult nights, and therefore my own sense of what horrors might haunt him in his dreams.

Kei had been cooperative. In the presence of all four of us, she had been less talkative, recognizing, perhaps, that we might be easier to manipulate in ones and twos than we would be en masse. I was glad for the respite. I didn't want her to get to Dox.

At nine o'clock our time, noon in Washington, two men strode out of the White House—the president, in the usual dark suit; and Horton, purposeful in his Army Service Uniform, the full fruit salad resplendent on his chest. They walked toward the assembled press corps, then Horton stood back while the president took the lectern.

"Good afternoon," the president said. "I have two brief announcements.

"First, given the recent series of unprecedented attacks on the American homeland and an ongoing state of emergency, I have, as Commander in Chief, ordered National Guard units to key positions in American cities. These Guard units will liaise with and reinforce local law enforcement to ensure we have the maximum possible on-the-ground ability to detect, defuse, and defend against further attacks. And, should the worst happen, to assist in providing critical care to first responders.

"Second, I'm pleased to announce that the position of the head of the National Counterterrorism Center, opened by the tragic death of Tim Shorrock, has been filled. For security reasons, the name of Tim's replacement will be classified."

I wondered about that. Shorrock's name hadn't been classified. Maybe it was just a reaction to current events. Or the usual governmental reflex toward more secrecy. Or both.

"However," the president continued, "my new counterterrorism advisor is right here beside me. I'm grateful to have the advice and assistance of Colonel Scott Horton as my administration combats the continued terrorist threat. Colonel Horton has a long and distinguished career in serving and protecting our nation, and his considerable national security experience will be an invaluable asset as he joins my cabinet. Please direct any questions you have to Colonel Horton."

The president stepped back. A few reporters shouted questions, but the president ignored them. Horton stepped forward and took the lectern.

"Ladies and gentleman," he said, surveying the crowd. "I will be brief."

Maybe it was the solemnity of Horton's expression—itself, I suspected, the product of the heavy knowledge of his daughter's predicament. Maybe it was his erect military bearing, or his baritone, or that cultured southern accent. Whatever it was, even through the television, I could sense the collective attention of the press corps focusing, cohering, anticipating.

"As the president just told us," Horton said, "even as we speak, National Guard units have been deployed to major American cities. The president also spoke of a state of emergency. And while I believe he is correct to use this term, I also believe his application was mistaken. You see, the emergency we currently face is far less from any terrorist threat than it is from our government's overreaction to that threat."

I thought, *What the fuck?* And couldn't process anything beyond that.

There was silence among the reporters. They were staring at Horton, their bodies seemingly frozen. No one was taking notes. I looked at the president, who was standing a few paces behind Horton and to the side. His face was a mask of poorly concealed shock and rage.

"After all," Horton went on, "in America, what is a federal government-declared 'state of emergency'? There is no constitutional basis for such a concept. What does it consist of? When does it end? And while these questions would be problematical enough were they merely rhetorical, they do have answers. I can tell you that today, in the corridors of power in this country, men are seriously contemplating and even planning for the suspension of the Constitution and the imposition of martial law. Our so-called 'state of emergency' is intended to act as a bridge to that suspension and that imposition."

The onlookers in the Rose Garden were still completely silent. On our end, even Dox was apparently at a loss for words.

"Today," Horton went on, "I would like to ask of all Americans a simple question. If the terrorists told us they would go on with these attacks until we tore up the Constitution and surrendered our liberties, what would we say? I submit to you that we would rightly tell them they could go to hell. And yet, we're willing to do these very things as long as we believe it's of our own volition. In the end, though, what's the difference? Either way, the Constitution is destroyed. Either way, our cherished liberties, which our forefathers have fought and died for, which I and members of my family all the way back to the Civil War have fought and died for, are cashed in and gone for good."

Still total silence, bordering on shock, coming through the television.

"I have therefore wrestled with the president's invitation to serve his administration. I ask myself, what should I do? Anyone who tells you that proximity to power, especially during a crisis, is not tempting, is a liar. So the temptation, naturally, is to serve. And why not? After all, I have served my country my entire adult life. The problem, I have come to realize, is that today, I cannot serve our nation by serving the president. Today, service to one would be antithetical to the other. The service the president requires of me could and doubtless will be capably fulfilled by someone else. What's needed instead, and needed urgently, is an example, and I hope others will follow mine."

He paused. No one moved. The attention of everyone, there and in our motel room, was riveted on Horton.

"Therefore," he said, "I must resign my position in this administration and my commission in the United States Army, effective immediately. And I encourage all service personnel who are asked to destroy the Constitution in the diabolical guise of saving it to follow my example. I encourage all Americans, of every stripe, to resist the government's current attempt to pervert and subvert the constitutional guarantee that our government can only be of, by, and for the people. And I encourage all people who cherish their safety more than their liberty to move to North Korea, where they can live in a society more closely aligned to their preferences than the one we have created here in the United States of America."

He paused, then said, "It may be that none will heed my call. I am at peace with that. Because I'll be damned—I will be damned—if I allow any group of cave-dwelling, hate-filled, fanatical losers who have nothing more to offer the world than cowardly attacks on innocent civilians, to coerce me into surrendering the liberties I cherish, that I love, and that I am determined to bequeath to my children just as my parents bequeathed them to me."

He looked out at the faces of the people assembled before him, then pivoted and walked toward the White House, his head high, his posture erect. There was another moment of stunned silence, then the reporters leaped to their feet and began shouting a cacophony of questions. For a single second, the president looked utterly flustered. Then he, too, turned and strode back toward the White House.

We all stared at the television. Finally, Dox broke the silence.

"What the fucking fuck?" he said.

I got up and turned off the television, having no desire to listen to the inevitable feeble-minded cable news commentary. I turned and looked at Larison, Treven, and Dox. "What the hell was that?"

Dox nodded. "Is it just me, or did that sound to anyone else like a man running for high office?"

"It did," I said. "But what office? If they get what they want, I don't think these guys are planning on holding an election any time soon. And, by any time soon, I mean 'ever.'"

No one spoke. I said, "I mean, did that sound like a guy who's trying to launch a coup? Who had the president's counterterrorism advisor killed so he could take the dead man's position?"

"You think we could have been wrong?" Dox said. "About what Horton was really up to? About who sent those unfortunates after us in D.C.?"

"But who else could have known we were there?" I said. "Unless Horton had told someone, someone who… I don't know, had his own reasons for wanting us taken out."

"No," Treven said. "Hort would never have breached operational security unless he wanted us removed."

Larison inclined his head toward Kei, who was sitting on one of the beds, one wrist flex-tied to a bedpost. "And besides," he said, "what about the two men who were trying to protect her?"

"Could someone else have sent them to make it look like Horton had?" I said, thinking aloud.

Larison shook his head. "That's getting a little far-fetched, I think. Parsimony suggests we're right about Hort's goals. But I agree, his tactics are… surprising. On the other hand, Hort never does what you're expecting him to do. He always has an angle. The question is, what's his angle here? You think he thinks this will save her?"

Dox glanced at Kei. "She's not going to actually need saving, all right? We just need her father to think she will."

It was a stupid thing to say in front of Kei. Yes, it was true, but we were counting on her fear that we might harm her to make her more cooperative. But he'd said it, and she'd heard it. Arguing with him wouldn't change that.

Larison looked at Dox. "It doesn't matter what we might or might not do to his daughter. It's Hort's perspective that matters. And I promise you, he doesn't doubt me."

There was a slight emphasis on the last word. To defuse another confrontation, I said, "We've demanded two things. The diamonds, and that he call off the dogs. The question is, how does his stunt pertain to any of that?"

"It doesn't," Treven said. "It has no impact on the first, and prevents him from doing the second. So my guess? The stunt was already in the works. It has nothing to do with his daughter. It's about something else."

That sounded right. "Okay," I said. "But what?"

No one said anything. Dox turned to Kei. "Darlin', if you have any insights into what that was all about just now on the TV, this would be a great time to share them."

She didn't respond at first, and I realized that seeing her father, whether because of what he had done, or just because of her circumstances, had affected her. She was trying to master her emotions.

"Maybe you're just missing something incredibly obvious," she said, after a moment. "My father's an honorable man."

Dox smiled sadly. "Well, respectfully, you don't know him the way we do."

"No," she said. "You don't know him the way I do."

We were all quiet again. I checked the secure site. There was a message from Horton.

"He's coming," I said. "Tonight, with the diamonds. Expects to arrive at LAX around eight o'clock on a private jet. Says he can't risk commercial because of the diamonds. The TSA is going apeshit, everything's being hand-searched. Says he'll meet us anywhere we want."

"He gave you his itinerary?" Treven said.

I nodded. No one had to point out the significance. Either Horton was trying, pretty obviously, to lure us into a trap. Or he was telling us we could kill him without resistance, if we'd just let his daughter go.

But it had to be the second one. He knew we wouldn't expose ourselves more than necessary. Only one of us would show up for the diamonds. The rest would be somewhere else, holding a decidedly non-metaphorical gun to his daughter's head.

"He told me his announcement would set our minds at ease," Larison said. "What are we missing? I don't see it."

No one responded. I didn't think we were going to figure it out. We'd just have to ask Horton. And then I realized.

"We're not supposed to see it," I said. "He wants a chance to talk to us. Whoever goes to pick up the diamonds, Horton wants it to involve a conversation, not just an exchange of a bag."

"What does that get him?" Dox said.

I looked at Kei. "I don't know. But we need to decide who's going to meet him."

Dox stood. "Hell, I'll do it."

I wondered if it was a bluff. I knew he felt protective of Kei, and was worried about Larison.

"No," I said. "I want Horton to feel that special tingling sensation you can only fully appreciate when you wonder whether a former Marine sniper is watching you through a scope right that very second."

"I can't," Larison said. "Much as I'd like to. Of the four of us, the one Hort fears most is me. Because he knows, with me, it's personal. If you want to ensure compliance, you want him to picture his daughter, alone and helpless with me."

I didn't particularly care for the thought of Larison alone with Kei, but I couldn't disagree with his assessment.

Treven said, "I'll go."

The truth was, I would have preferred to handle it myself. I didn't trust Treven. He'd been exceptionally quiet on the subway in L.A. when we'd first discussed going after Horton, and he'd been right at the Capital Hilton, when he'd accused me of suspecting he had a hand in our being set up about the cyanide. But I had no way of knowing, and besides, I didn't want another confrontation. Whatever the relationship between the four of us, it plainly hadn't yet evolved to the point where disagreements could be settled without the possibility of a firefight.

Strangely enough, I wasn't unduly concerned that Treven might abscond with the diamonds. A hundred million dollars is a lot of money, true. But you wouldn't live long to spend it if Larison, Dox, and I were after you. Better to settle for an already galactic twenty-five million and live to enjoy it, too. I imagined Larison had performed the same calculus and had arrived at the same conclusion.

"You'll have to do a hell of an SDR," I said. "We don't know—"

He held up a hand. "How he tracked us in Washington. I know. Satellites, drones, surveillance cameras, etc. I'll be careful."

I nodded again, recognizing I was micromanaging, unable, it seemed, not to.

"He'll want to know when his daughter will be released," Larison said. "Tell him only after we've had the diamonds certified by an expert. If he thinks he's going to hand off another bag full of plastic, I'm going to make him pay."

"The diamonds are only half of it," Dox said. "How's he going to call off the heat now that he's just a civilian? And how would we even know, one way or the other?"

I realized Larison didn't care about heat. He only wanted the diamonds. That wasn't an entirely new development, but still, it made me uneasy. I sensed I was going to have to do something about him, something extreme. But I didn't know what. Or maybe I just didn't want to face it.

I looked at Treven. "Horton's going to give you assurances regarding the heat. We just don't know what form those assurances will take. Let's assume for the moment they'll be worth something, because if they weren't, he'd be putting his daughter at greater risk. So whatever he says, you just tell him you'll pass the information along to the rest of us, and we'll get back to him."

"He's not going to like that," Treven said.

Larison smiled. "He's going to hate it. But he'll have no choice. He's not going to risk sending you back to us empty-handed."

Then he looked at Dox and said, "Not as long as I'm here, anyway."

chapter
twenty-four

Treven sat in a corner of the vast, ornate waiting room of Los Angeles' Union Station, waiting for Hort. The Glock was concealed in an unzipped black hip pouch on the large, mahogany-and-leather chair next to him, but he wasn't expecting any immediate trouble. Even if Hort hadn't just left the government and resigned his commission, his options were fairly limited. Bring in a team for a snatch? They'd have to drag Treven out through the station, assuming they survived the preceding firefight. A straight-up hit? That would get Hort nothing, except maybe a dead daughter. No, the most likely scenario—next to Hort trying nothing at all, given the way they had him by the balls—was that Hort would have forces hanging back and hoping to follow Treven to wherever Kei was being held. Which is why they'd told Hort via the secure site the meeting would be at Union Station. With its multiple levels and points of ingress and egress; its numerous train, subway, and bus lines; and its proximity to three highways and countless surface roads, it would take an army to properly cover the place.

He'd been a little surprised when Rain had agreed to let him be the one to meet Hort. The man had good instincts, and had zeroed in on Treven at the Capital Hilton. But he never had anything firm to go with, and probably had decided he would just have to keep his suspicions in reserve. For the time being, anyway.

He watched all manner of people coming and going along the tiled floors and through the huge archways, the sounds of their cell phone conversations swallowed up amid the high, beamed ceiling and art deco chandeliers, and periodically drowned out by announcements about the importance of being watchful and immediately reporting any suspicious activity. There was a tension in the air that reminded him of the immediate aftermath of 9/11: people hurrying more than normal, as though passage through a train station had become the equivalent of a lethal game of musical chairs; expressions pinched and suspicious and fearful; eyes darting, trying to read faces to which their owners previously had always been happily oblivious. There were cops positioned everywhere, and a half dozen soldiers patrolling in Army Combat Uniforms, their M-16s held ready. Not Hort's men, though. These were reservists, and to an operator like Treven, the difference between a part-timer and a JSOC black ops vet was the difference between a kid playing touch football and an NFL pro. Hort's guys were invisible right up until the moment they were pulling a bag over your head or putting a bullet in your brain. These guys were nothing more than security theater. Their purpose was to look butch, and reassure a jittery public that Something Was Being Done, and Treven supposed they were ably carrying out the role.

Hort showed up at a little past nine o'clock. He was dressed in civilian clothes—khaki pants, a green polo shirt—and carrying a blue nylon gym bag. His face was uncharacteristically drawn, borderline exhausted. He looked like a man who'd lost big, and was now terrified of losing everything else on top of it.

He walked slowly through the waiting area, his head tracking left and right, and then saw Treven. As he walked over, Treven wrapped his fingers around the grip of the Glock and kept his thumb on the exterior of the hip pouch. He could fire right through the thing, if necessary, and the gun would remain concealed until he did. He scanned the room and saw no one suspicious coming in behind Hort, or from elsewhere.

Hort stopped a few feet away. He didn't sit and Treven didn't stand.

"I'm glad it's you," Hort said.

Treven scanned the room again. "You shouldn't be."

"Why not?"

"Because that hotel thing was the second time you've tried to have me killed. I was an idiot to tell you what Larison was planning. He was right. I should have just helped take you out."

"Those men weren't there for you. You're the one who told me where I could find you, remember? I know you're the only one I can

trust. You know what that means to me, after all that's happened between us? Do you have any idea how grateful I am that you would give
me a second chance?"

It was more or less what he'd been expecting. Which made the fact
that he was tempted to believe it doubly irritating. "You have what we
asked for?" he said.

Hort tossed the gym bag onto the chair next to Treven. "It's all in
there. Just a nylon bag, too, no room for tracking devices, though I expect you'll want to check anyway."

"We'll check the contents, too. With an expert."

"That's understandable. Still, I assure you, the contents are what you
have asked for. And now, I'm going to offer one more thing, and ask for
one more favor."

"What?"

"If you want to take me to one of the canyon drives, or the national
forest, or to some other quiet place, I will kneel and look off into the
distance and you can put a bullet in the back of my head. All you have
to do is say the word."

"Is that the offer, or the favor?"

Hort smiled tightly. "That's the offer. The favor is, hear me out first.
And, no matter what you decide, please. Let my little girl go."

His voice cracked on the last word. Treven couldn't believe it. He'd
never seen Hort other than confident, competent, always in control. It
felt like what they'd done had broken him, and despite everything, Trev-
en was suddenly ashamed.

But he couldn't afford to indulge that feeling, much less to show it.
"That's two favors," he said.

"I don't care how you count them. And I don't care what you do to
me. I have never begged anyone for anything in my life, and I am begging
you. Just let her go."

Treven gestured with his head. "Let me see your ankles. And turn
around."

Hort complied. He wasn't carrying a firearm.

Treven looked around the room. Still no problems. "All right," he
said. "Let's go."

"Where?"

"Maybe to one of those quiet places you mentioned. You can say whatever you want me to hear on the way."

They walked through the station and down to the Red Line subway. Treven kept them on the platform while a train roared in and then squealed out. When its departing passengers had moved off, and the two of them were alone for a moment, Treven switched on a bug detector Rain had given him. No response.

"You carrying a mobile phone?" he asked.

Hort nodded. "Yes, but I've removed the battery. I thought you might ask."

All right, then. Either Hort was clean, or he was carrying a device he would switch on later. To counter that possibility, Treven would turn the detector on again when they were alone.

Another train came and went, leaving the platform momentarily empty again, and this time Treven was sure no one was following them, at least through visual contact. They waited again and then got on the next train. It was about half full, everyone looking like a civilian, albeit a tense one. Treven had Hort sit a few seats forward and facing the same direction so he could go through the gym bag without having to worry about Hort trying to disarm him while he was distracted. Not that disarming him would do any good, but it was best to deny an enemy both motive and opportunity.

As the car sped along, swaying in the close confines of the tunnel, he unzipped the bag. Thousands of small, pale stones, some yellowish, some light gray, most of them translucent white. He dug his hand in and moved it around carefully. Nothing other than the stones. He felt thoroughly along the handles of the bag and its seams. No telltale bulges or wires. No transmitters. It was a just a bag. Okay.

At the Vermont/Beverly stop, he had them step out and wait on the platform again. No question, unless Hort had enough people with him to blanket every train on the Red Line, they were clean. They got back on the next train. They rode it to North Hollywood, the end of the line, got off, and walked to Chandler Boulevard, where earlier Treven had parked another stolen car. This one was a dark blue Honda Accord sedan, one of the bestselling and therefore most common cars in America, which a harried housewife had been foolish enough to leave with the key in the ignition while she ran for just a minute into a Culver City dry cleaner carrying a load of shirts.

He gave Hort the key. "You drive," he said.

"Where are we going?"

"I'll tell you on the way."

It was hard to imagine Hort still had access to the kind of domestic surveillance apparatus he might have been able to call into play before his resignation. Besides, unlike the others, Treven knew Hort hadn't used that apparatus in fixing them at the Capital Hilton—he had simple human intelligence from Treven to thank for that. Also, it was night, meaning the birds would have a harder time tracking them. Even so, he had Hort drive an extensive surveillance detection run that incorporated the kinds of overpass and garage maneuvers they'd used to obscure their movements after snatching Kei. Rain's bug detector remained silent as they drove.

They finished on Lake Hollywood Drive, a lonely, serpentine section of the Hollywood Hills overlooking the Hollywood Reservoir. When they came to a curve partly concealed by scrub bushes and some dried-out trees, Treven told Hort to pull off the road and park. Ordinarily, Treven wouldn't have liked the spot for a meeting like this because there was always the chance of a cop driving by. But doubtless Los Angeles law enforcement was more focused on protecting critical infrastructure just now than they were on rousting horny kids parked in the Hills.

Hort cut the lights and the ignition and looked out through the driver-side window. "Not a bad spot to dump a body," he said. "I do hope you'll hear me out first."

"I'm listening."

"You mind if I have a cigar?"

Treven squeezed the grip of the Glock, reassured by its familiar heft. "Whatever you like."

Hort thumbed the switch for the driver-side window, then eased a canister and a cigar guillotine from his front pants pocket. He unscrewed the canister, slid out a cigar, and expertly clipped one end with the guillotine. He tossed the clipped end through the open window, put the cut end in his mouth, slid a wooden match out of the canister, popped it with a thumbnail, waited a moment, then slowly lit the end of the cigar, rotating it methodically to get it going evenly. When he was satisfied, he waved the match out and held it until it was cold before tossing it, too, out the window.

"Cuban Montecristo," he said, settling back in the car seat. "Forgive me, I only have the one."

Treven kept the Glock on him. "Enjoy it."

The implication was clear and there was no need to say it. *It's probably your last.*

Hort blew out a cloud of the sweet-smelling smoke. "I know what you're thinking. You're thinking I'm behind these false flag attacks. That I'm part of it."

"You're going to tell me you're not?"

"Not in the way you think."

Treven's eyes were adjusting to the dark. A gibbous moon was rising, its pale light glowing down on the road surface and reflecting on the reservoir below them. "Explain, then."

"Did Rain brief you on what I told him this coup is supposed to be all about?"

"Yes."

"What did he tell you?"

"The system is broken. The plotters wanted a pretext for seizing power so they could fix everything and then give it back. You thought the whole thing was insane, and wanted us to take out key personnel to stop it."

"I'd call that an accurate summary."

"But then we found out the personnel you had us take out weren't part of the coup. They were opposed to it."

"That is also accurate."

"Then what the hell are you doing, Hort? Whose side are you on?"

Hort sighed. "The plotters are correct in believing the system is broken. They are also correct in believing that without immediate and radical surgery, the patient will surely die. But they are incorrect in believing a coup is what's required. A coup would kill the patient in the name of saving her. What is required is something slightly different."

"What?"

Hort looked at him. "An attempted coup."

Treven didn't respond. He tried to take what he already understood and sort it through the new framework Hort had just suggested. "You're saying... you wanted the coup to start?"

Hort nodded. "And then to stop. And to be exposed for what it really was."

"Why? What does that accomplish?"

"Maybe nothing. In which case, the republic shrivels and dies more or less on schedule, just as it was going to anyway. But maybe, maybe... people wake up."

"To what?"

"To how close they were to losing everything they ought to cherish but have in fact come to take for granted. Did you watch my little speech at the White House?"

"Yeah."

"When I talked about how we would never surrender our liberties if terrorists were explicitly demanding we do so? That's the truth. You know that, right?"

"I guess so."

"Well, I was giving the country a little preview there. Shaping the battlefield."

"I don't follow."

Hort drew on the cigar, held the smoke in his mouth, then slowly blew it out through the window. "The republic is being bled dry by a national security complex so grotesque and metastasized even Dwight Eisenhower wouldn't have recognized it in his worst nightmares and most dire predictions. People are okay with this state of affairs because they don't sense something is being taken from them. But if this country's oligarchy is exposed for what it really is, and for what it's really doing, there's a chance people would fight back. A chance. You understand?"

Treven thought. "You're saying even if someone would willingly give something up, he'll fight to preserve it if he thinks someone is trying to steal it."

"Precisely."

"Then why did you resign?"

"Because, when this thing is snuffed out, the disgusted and disillusioned masses will need a hero. Someone of unimpeachable character and battle-hardened judgment. Someone who has demonstrated by his actions and his sacrifices that he is a selfless servant of the nation who cannot be seduced by power or anything else."

Not for the first time, Treven realized Hort was accustomed to operating at levels of manipulation, deceit, and strategy that Treven found alien. He didn't know whether to feel envious, or relieved.

"That speech," he said. "Dox said it sounded like you were running for office."

"In a sense, I was."

"What office?"

"If things go well, a blue ribbon commission will be formed to investigate the causes of the attempted coup, identify the plotters, and recommend changes to ensure such a thing can never happen again. I will be the head of that commission. And I will ensure that its work is in the best interests of the nation."

Treven squeezed the grip of the Glock as though reminding himself it was still there. "But... you said you wanted the coup to be exposed for what it really was."

Hort chuckled grimly. "Well... for what it almost really was."

"What does that mean?"

"Following the recent string of attacks, it's important the citizenry believes an insatiably greedy oligarchy was to blame. Even though the truth is, most of the oligarchy is pleased with the status quo and wouldn't want to change it. The main thing is that people understand how close they came to losing everything. And that they never know I was involved in steering the course of events."

"Because then you wouldn't be able to steer anymore."

"That's right. And if I couldn't, then this whole thing might go haywire. The coup could become permanent. At a minimum, the innocent could be punished along with the guilty."

"But you are guilty."

"Yes, I am. I have the blood of countless Americans on my hands now. I slaughtered them, men, women, and children, no matter that it was for a larger purpose, and if there is a hell, I will rightly burn there forever."

He drew on the cigar and held the smoke for a moment as though trying to calm himself. Then he blew it forcefully out through the window.

"But while I am alive, I am determined to ensure their sacrifice was not in vain. And for that, I need your help. Because you have put me in an untenable position."

"What are you talking about?"

"I wasn't planning on resigning my position and making my speech quite so soon. I needed that position in order to continue to steer things in their proper direction. But then you people went and kidnapped my daughter and forced my hand."

"I still don't know what you're talking about."

"What I'm talking about is, Dan Gillmor, the new head of the National Counterterrorism Center, who has been running the jihadist groups behind the attacks, is not yet satisfied that the country has been driven sufficiently insane for it to accept a suspension of the Constitution and the imposition of martial law. He has one more attack in mind. Which he believes will provide him with the blank check he craves."

Treven felt the blood drain from his face. "A school."

Hort looked at him. "Yes, that's right. A mass casualty attack on an elementary school. With that, the president will be able to do anything he wants, and the rest of the government and the people will encourage him to do so. The coup will become a fait accompli. I will no longer be able to stop it."

Treven was so angry he could have shot him. "Goddamn it, Hort, what the fuck were you thinking?"

"It doesn't matter what I was thinking. What matters is where we are."

"Bullshit. Why did you have to resign now?"

"Because I could not have disappeared to Los Angeles on the very day the president made me his counterterrorism advisor if I hadn't. Because I believe there is only a slim chance I will be leaving this meeting alive, and coming out here to die without first having set the example I needed to set would not have been productive."

"So you're risking the lives of, what, dozens of school children? Scores? On top of all the people you've already killed? To save your own daughter?"

There was no response.

"You know what we should do, Hort? We should put a bullet in her head so you can know what it's going to be like for all the parents that you've done the same thing to. The same. Fucking. Thing."

The interior of the car was silent. A lone cricket chirped outside.

"Please don't do that," Hort said quietly.

"The only reason I won't is because I'm not like you."

"I know that, and I'm grateful. But Larison is. Please, don't let him."

"Larison can do what he wants." He wasn't sure whether he meant it, or whether in his anger he was just trying to torment Hort.

"Listen to me. I have given you the diamonds. You can kill me now, if that's what you want. Put me in the trunk and drive me to wherever Larison is so he can piss on my body, I believe he would enjoy that. But if you care about your country, let me live just a little while longer. There's no one else who intends to put things right. And no else in a position to do so."

Treven shook his head in disgust. "You are the most self-serving, lying hypocrite I've ever known."

"I'm aware my request that you let me live long enough to set things right is self-serving. I can only say that if you prefer, you're welcome to shoot me here instead. Either way, please, Ben. I'm asking you. Let my girl go. She didn't do anything to you, or to anybody. You don't even know her. Please. Just let her go."

His voice broke and he stopped. He cleared his throat, blew out a long breath, and wiped the back of his hand savagely across his cheeks, one way, then the other.

For a while, they sat silently, Hort's cigar slowly dying in the darkness.

"The others," Treven said, aware he was conceding something and that Hort would recognize as much. "They don't want just the diamonds. They want you to clear us. Get us off whatever hit lists you've put us on."

"I'm a civilian now, Ben. I can't do anything anymore. I could though, as the head of the commission I mentioned."

Treven stared at him. "You're unbelievable."

"I thought you might find it to be another disgracefully self-serving statement," Hort said. "But it is a fact."

Treven didn't respond. Once again, it was what he expected from Hort. But that didn't necessarily make it a lie, either.

"Look at it this way," Hort said. "You have the diamonds. And I'm a civilian now, you can get to me anytime. Let me finish what I have begun. Help me stop the school attack. And let Mimi go. What's the downside to you? Just let her go."

Treven watched him. He'd never seen Hort look so diminished. He wasn't sure if it was some objective thing that had happened to the man, or if it was the new light in which he was seeing him.

"Why'd you try to take us out at the Capital Hilton?" he said, after a moment.

"I didn't try to have you taken out. I told you, I was after the others."

"I'm not buying it. You would have told me."

"How? You had no cell phone, at least not one you were ever using. And you didn't check in with me."

It might have been true. Impossible to know for sure. But he hated that he wanted to believe it.

"Whatever. Why'd you try to have the others taken out, then?"

"You know why. They know too much. About my involvement. About everything."

"So do I."

"I told you, you're the only one I trust."

"Even if I believed you, and I don't, the others? As far as they're concerned, you're as motivated to kill them now as you were before. Maybe more so."

"It may be that I still have the motivation. But I no longer have the means. You have to get it through your head, I'm just a civilian now. You have the diamonds, you can go anywhere you want. And as I said, you can always come after me later. You could even come after my daughter if I do anything to cross you. I don't see what I could reasonably do to stop you."

Treven thought. They'd all agreed that if he had the opportunity as expected, he should kill Hort. Maybe they'd discover afterward that the "diamonds" he'd given them were fake, like the ones he'd given to Larison. Maybe they'd still be hunted by a national security state on steroids. But if having his own daughter in jeopardy wasn't enough to get Hort to play ball this time, the working assumption was that nothing ever would. This way, they'd at least have the satisfaction of knowing he'd died before they did.

The problem was, a lot of what Hort had told him made sense, if sense was the right word for it. The situation wasn't what they'd been assuming it to be. Hort alive might be more useful to them than he would be dead. He might be able to stop the coup and set things right, as he'd put it. Without him, this fucking thing he'd set in motion would probably take on an unstoppable life of its own, if it hadn't already.

And there was that school to think about. How was he going to feel, if he knew about something like that and let it happen anyway? He'd done a lot of dark things in the course of his job, he knew, a lot of ambiguous things. Some of them kept him awake at night. Some made him wonder about punishment and reckonings and even hell. But he could honestly say everything he'd ever done was intended to keep Americans safe. Sometimes he felt like that knowledge was all that kept him sane in the face of what the task sometimes required. So what was he supposed to do now? How would he live with himself if some people blew up a school—a school, for Christ's sake—and he could have stopped it, but didn't? Compared to that, the possibility of someone blackmailing him with some bullshit video suddenly seemed unimportant.

He wasn't sure. He didn't trust his own motivations much more than he trusted Hort's. And he didn't know what the others were going to say. They'd made an agreement, and these weren't the kind of people who took you to court for a breach of contract.

"Shall I finish this cigar?" Hort said. "Is it my last?"

Treven hoped he wasn't being played. If he was, he supposed he was a three-time loser. He would deserve whatever he got.

"Just tell me about the goddamn school," he said.

chapter twenty-five

Waiting for Treven made for a stressful night. Dox brought in pizza; we ate; and then, to pass the time, we watched the news, which was nothing but breathless so-called "terrorism experts" fantasizing about the latest existential threat and how it could best be combated, along with blow-dried talking heads obsessing over the semiotics of Horton's stunning departure from the Rose Garden earlier that day.

As the evening went on, Larison had gotten paranoid, becoming convinced that Hort had brought a team that had snatched Treven and tortured our location out of him. He'd pointed his Glock at Kei and had sworn if anyone breached the door, she was going to be the first to die. To which Dox had said, with uncharacteristic menace, "Put your gun away. You're scaring her."

"She should be scared," Larison had answered.

"Well, congratulations then, because she is. Now, like I said, put your gun away and stop talking like that. There's no need for it."

Larison looked at him. "Don't tell me what to do."

Dox pulled his Wilson Combat. "Son, this time I'm not doing Cleavon Little for you. You get in a mess with me, you're going to have to find your own way out."

"Both of you, shut the fuck up," I said, deliberately playing the alpha. If it worked, and they accepted my dominant position, it would give them a reason to listen and a means of saving face. If they didn't accept my position, things were about to get a whole lot worse.

There was a long and tense silence. Then, reluctantly, Larison slid his Glock back in his waistband. Dox, watching Larison unblinkingly, slowly did the same.

I motioned Larison over to the bathroom. "Give us a minute," I said to Dox.

We went inside and I closed the door behind us. "Look," I said quietly. "He's got a soft spot for girls, and when you scare her like that, it presses his buttons."

"That's his problem."

"All right. But you're a professional. What's the upside for you? What are you getting out of it?"

He didn't answer.

"My point is, it's not like you. We've spent a decent amount of time together at this point—two hits, a cross-country drive, a snatch—and you're always in control. What's got you running so hot now?"

He looked away. "I don't know."

"You want to talk?"

He laughed. "You trying to be my shrink?"

"I'm trying to be your friend."

"Well, don't."

I looked at him. "How many people do you know who would understand the shit you've done? And how it weighs on you?"

Again, he didn't answer.

"Look," I said, "do what you want. But you have to stop running so hot. It's making Dox jumpy, and it's starting to make me jumpy. If I can help, let me help, but either way, we all need you cool. I need you cool. Like you usually are. Okay?"

After a long moment, he nodded. "Okay."

We went out and returned to waiting. No one waved any more guns. I was going to have to do something about Larison, and I didn't know what. Shake him? Shoot him? How could I get through to him? I thought, *if I ever work with a team again, just kill me,* and then had to stifle a crazy laugh because, with this team, that was exactly the problem.

At nearly one in the morning, there was a soft knock at the door. All of us stood, save Kei, who still had one wrist flex-tied to a bedpost. All the guns came out again. Larison was looking at Kei; Dox was looking at Larison. I checked the peephole. It was Treven.

"Easy," I said to Larison and Dox. "It's him."

I opened the door and Treven came in. He was holding a gym bag. That was encouraging. I locked the door behind him.

"You get the diamonds?" Larison said.

"Wait a minute," I said. "Don't brief us yet." I gestured to Kei. "Dox, could you put the headphones on her?"

We'd picked up a pair of over-the-ear headphones and a radio so we could talk in her presence without being overheard. Dox put the headphones on himself, adjusted the radio volume to his satisfaction, and then slipped the headphones onto Kei's head and over her ears. She bore it well, her expression neutral but not blank; her posture, resigned but not beaten.

"Right here," Treven said, holding up the bag.

Larison nodded. I didn't like how eager he looked. "Did you do him?" he said.

There was a pause. Treven said, "No."

Larison's mouth dropped open. "What?"

"I'm not going to lie to you," Treven said. "I could have. But based on what he told me, I think it would have been a mistake to do it right now."

"Goddamn it," Larison said, "Hort always has a line of shit. Always. When the hell are you going to figure that out?"

Treven looked at him. "You know," he said, "I'm getting a little tired of you."

I thought, *Christ, here we go again.*

"Listen," I said, in my best command voice. "We're all a little strung out. You're professionals, you know the signs and you know the causes. We've been going balls-out for a week now, Las Vegas to Vienna, back to the East Coast, gun fights, three days non-stop driving in a portable sauna all the way to California, worrying about satellites and drones and however the hell Horton tracked us in D.C.... no privacy, no breaks, and barely any sleep. It's amazing we haven't killed each other yet. But let's not kill each other now, okay? We need to dial it down. Or we're all going to die."

No one spoke. Either the moment had passed, or Dox was going to have to do another movie impression. Or we were all going to shoot each other. One of the three, anyway.

Finally, Larison said, "What did he say?"

Treven looked at me and said, "You were right about the schools."

We all listened quietly while he briefed us. When he was done, Larison said, "You can't really believe him. Don't you see what he's doing?"

I looked at Treven. "He told you where and when the school attack is supposed to go down?"

Treven nodded. "Lincoln, Nebraska. Smack in the middle of the country. Three days from now, on the first day back from summer vacation. Some kind of back-to-school assembly that morning in the auditorium, apparently. This guy Gillmor is running a team of four guys. Hort says they're going to show up with machine pistols and just hose the room down. Nothing fancy, not a lot of logistics, just pure horror and destruction tailor-made for cable news."

"Exactly," Larison said. "It's another setup. We're supposed to show up with our hair on fire exactly when and where Hort tells us to. This time, he'll have snipers positioned in vehicles all around the school. He fixes us, finishes us, goes home and has a beer."

"There's one more thing," Treven said. "They're going to hit the building with drone-fired Hellfire missiles while the shooters are inside."

"What's the point?" Dox said. "Kill the shooters?"

"Yes," Treven said. "Just like Hort was trying to kill us after we did Shorrock and Finch. And also increase the destruction. But don't you see? If we try to stop this, we won't all be fixable in the same place at the same time. Some of us would have to take out the shooters. Someone else would have to take out the drone, or find the ground team operating it."

"So Hort fixes us in two places instead of one," Larison said. "It's the same bullshit, and you're falling for it. Again."

"What if you're wrong?" Dox said to Larison. "What if Horton's telling the truth? A bunch of children are going to be slaughtered, and we'll be part of it."

Larison looked incredulous. "Part of it how?"

"We took out Shorrock and Finch," Dox said. "We helped set this in motion."

"Not our fault," Larison said. "We thought we were stopping it, remember?"

"You didn't care if we stopped it, started it, or fucked it in the ass," Dox said. "You just wanted your damn diamonds."

For just an instant, Larison's expression twisted. I read it as, *What did you mean by that?* I sensed him fight to not glance at Treven, who shook his head the tiniest fraction, as if to say, *I didn't tell them.*

Hort's words flashed in my mind:

He's a man who has too much to keep hidden. A man in turmoil.

I wasn't sure how I knew. It was all preconscious, nothing I could articulate. But I knew. Larison was gay. Treven knew, and Larison knew Treven knew, his secret.

It was over in an instant. I didn't think Dox had spotted it, and I suspected Treven and Larison would have been confident neither Dox nor I had noticed anything, either. I didn't even know what it meant, exactly. Was this what was stressing Larison out? Why would Dox or I even care?

But Larison cared. That was clear. It was a secret, and he wanted to keep it that way.

"It doesn't matter what I wanted," Larison said, fully in control again. "What matters is that whatever these people might or might not be planning at a school or anywhere else, it has nothing to do with us. Even beyond the fact that you can bet it's an ambush. And even if we survived it, you want to do something that would help put Hort back in power? We're lucky he's defanged for the moment. You want him coming after us again? Because he would. His motives haven't changed, only his means."

"You can all do what you want," Treven said. "I've already made up my mind. I'm not going to stand by and let this thing happen. I've done a lot of fucked-up things in my life, but I'm not going to do that."

"Fine," Larison said. "We'll have the diamonds confirmed tomorrow. If they check out, we split them a quarter apiece and go our separate ways."

There was no disputing his logic, but still I didn't like his point. What would he do if he thought we knew his secret? Would we be at risk? But Treven knew, and Larison seemed to tolerate that. But what about the diamonds? Was he really going to walk away from three-quarters of what had originally been his own?

Dox looked at me. "I'm not going to stand by and let this happen, either. Even if the diamonds check out, how could we enjoy the money if it came at the cost of the lives of a bunch of schoolchildren?"

"What the hell does one have to do with the other?" Larison said.

Dox ignored him. "Can you contact your Asiatic friend and see what he can do? Either to head it off himself, or, if he can't, to help us out with a little intel and the necessary hardware."

I nodded. But inside, I was struggling. I wondered whether among the four of us, Larison was the only one without a conscience. Or whether he was the only one with a brain.

My mind flashed to that breakfast meeting with Horton, and the conviction I'd heard in his little speech about having to meet your maker. He hadn't been thinking about what he'd done. He'd been thinking about what he was about to do. And I was an idiot to have missed it.

"I'll see what he can do," I said. "And tomorrow, Larison and I will take a sampling of the diamonds to a jeweler. If they check out, we're all free agents again."

No one pushed back about the division of labor. Everyone understood that no one was going to be left alone with the diamonds, and no one was going to be the sole conduit for an expert's certification.

Things had gotten hellishly fraught. Being part of this detachment reminded me about the old maxim for war: Easy to get into. Hard to get out of.

"One thing you might not be considering," I said to Larison.

He looked at me. "What's that?"

"My contact. He told me if we could get him proof, he could get us a pass. Get us off the president's hit list or whatever it is we've landed on."

Larison shook his head disgustedly. "You don't think it's a coincidence that Hort says he wants the same thing? Proof that these attacks have been false flag?"

"I don't follow."

"Hort has an uncanny ability to frame whatever he wants so that it sounds like exactly what you want."

"But we want the proof either way."

"Then go get it. I told you, I'm done."

There was nothing more to say. We bunked down in shifts again, but I barely slept at all. I was putting myself in Larison's shoes, seeing us the way I imagined he did. And the image was keeping me wide awake.

chapter twenty-six

Early the next morning, Larison and I went out with our share of the diamonds to have them tested. It was a little awkward to be walking around with a fanny pack that, if the diamonds were real, contained something in the neighborhood of twenty-five million dollars, but the safest thing to do at this point was for each of us to be responsible for his own share. Certainly Larison wasn't going to take his eyes off his portion—he'd been screwed by a switch before, and he wasn't going to let it happen again.

We did a thorough surveillance detection run, finishing up at the Beverly Wilshire, where Horton and I had shared breakfast an impossibly long time before. The previous night, I'd uploaded to the secure site a thorough briefing on the contents of Treven's conversation with Horton. I used a lobby payphone to call Kanezaki now.

"You find anything?" I said, when he'd picked up.

"Yes. And it tracks with what Horton told you."

"How so?"

"Two things. First, during one of his revolving-door stints outside of government, Gillmor headed up a DARPA-funded company called Novel Air Capability. Usually called NAC."

"Okay."

"What I'm telling you is top secret SCI—"

"Give me a break."

"Sorry. I guess it's a habit. Anyway, NAC has created a prototype drone. They call it the Viper."

"That's a scary name."

"Well, they needed to come up with something good to match the Predator and the Reaper. Anyway, this is an extremely versatile aircraft. Component parts, thirty minutes assembly time. It's small—with the wings folded, it'll go in a truck about the size of the one I got you. Vertical takeoff and landing; stealth configuration; twenty-four hours loiter time; capable of carrying and firing two Hellfire missiles."

"Shit."

"It gets worse. The ground control system is radically simplified and mobile. They call it the Viper Eye."

"Why am I not surprised?"

"You ever see someone flying a radio-controlled plane?"

"Yeah."

"That's pretty much what we're talking about. The only real difference is that this one is operated by video rather than line-of-sight. That's because of the distances the Viper can travel, and so that the operator gets a bird's-eye view of whatever he's targeting. But the control system itself just looks like a ruggedized laptop with a couple of joysticks attached. You don't need the kind of training a traditional Predator or Reaper ground station operator gets. You really only need a few runs to acquire fundamental competence with the system. They're marketing it to domestic law enforcement."

"Without the Hellfires, I hope."

"Yeah, as a domestic spy drone. But the point is, it's designed for ease of transport, ease of training, ease of use."

"Let me guess. One of them has gone missing."

"That's right."

"You think that's what they're going to use on this school."

"This school, and if that doesn't do the trick, on others."

I didn't answer. I was remembering my conversation with Treven in the truck, when I'd told him I thought schools were going to be the next thing. I realized I hadn't fully believed it at the time. Hadn't accepted, deep down, that anybody would go that far. But of course, that was naïve. The triumph of hope over experience.

"You there?" he said.

"I'm here."

"Anyway, I think the plan is for Gillmor's unwitting false flag team to get into the school auditorium and shoot it up with automatic pistols. If Horton is right, and it's only a four-man team, some people will get out. Four's not enough to lock down the whole school, just enough to do major damage once the team is inside. So there will be some witnesses. And while the team is in the building, Gillmor's going to level the place with two Hellfire missile strikes. The survivors will talk about a bunch of crazed Islamic terrorists screaming *Allahu Akbar*, and the working assumption will be they used pre-positioned high explosives to go out like martyrs."

I considered. "Are you sure of your information?"

"Why do you ask?"

"Because if that's the plan, there are a lot of problems. First, you're going to have witnesses describing a strange airplane. Maybe with rockets flying off the wings."

"You think that's a problem? It's barely relevant. First of all, Iran has publicly announced the development of its own drones. So even if there's a sighting, a senior White House official calls up a pet reporter and 'leaks' that the government thinks it was Iran. The public is already prepped to hate Iran like some kind of nation state version of Emmanuel Goldstein, so when the pet reporter reports the anonymous government 'leak,' it slots perfectly into an existing narrative, and the public swallows it as fact."

"If I didn't know better," I said, suppressing a smile despite everything else, "I'd think you had your own roster of pet reporters."

"Hey, in this town, it's more important than an entourage. Anyway, forget about Iran. The bottom line is, anytime there's a major event, you get a certain number of witnesses describing strange pre- and post-incident occurrences. The corporate media's been trained to ignore it unless they're told otherwise."

"What if someone shoots video with a cell phone?"

"People have shot video of UFOs. Of the Loch Ness Monster. It's always explainable."

"Are you telling me the Loch Ness Monster is real?"

"I can neither confirm nor deny."

"What about the debris? The FBI will pick through the place. Forensics teams will be able to tell what caused the explosion."

"Look what the FBI did on the anthrax investigation. They'll be instructed to tell the public what the public needs to hear, and to close the case. And outside of a few blogs the establishment media will be instructed to marginalize, that'll be the end of it."

"But we're talking about physical evidence. On the scene."

"John, listen. You don't get it. The country is traumatized. People want to believe in their leaders, so they will. They won't be able to believe the truth. Look, it doesn't matter whether the CIA killed Kennedy. It doesn't matter whether nine-eleven was an inside job. Even if you could prove such things, the proof would be ignored, because as a matter of almost religious faith, the country can't accept such notions. Especially at a time like this."

"But Horton's whole plan is to expose this thing for what it was. More or less."

"That's different. Or at least, I hope it is. Horton isn't a nobody with a cell phone camera and a conspiracy theory. He's an insider, with a reputation he's carefully stage-managed. That reputation he's created— his brand—is essentially a counternarrative. He's undermining 'I can't believe Americans would do such things' with 'I'm an American, and a hero, too, and you know I'm honest.' Horton is one communications-savvy bastard, I'm telling you."

I couldn't help smiling a little. "I guess it takes one to know one."

"You're right, it does."

"Okay. Let's assume your information is good. Can you stop this thing?"

"Maybe. With your help."

"How did I know you were going to say that?"

"Because it's true."

"Why can't you just call the Lincoln police?"

"And tell them what? I heard someone's going to bomb a school?"

"Yeah, that."

"Assuming they would even take me seriously, and assuming I didn't get disappeared to a black site for doing it, the plotters would just divert to a secondary target. Remember, this is just four guys with machine pistols and a monstrously portable drone. There's no pre-positioning and there's almost no planning. The whole thing is nothing but a fire-and-forget exercise—if they want, they can just choose another school. And, absent the shooters—who they won't need after the first one because the *Allahu Akbar* witnesses will already have been created and will already have insured the proper narrative structure—they can repeat as necessary. We have to stop them in the act."

"Well, then send some people in."

"Who? I don't have that kind of juice with the paramilitary branch. Besides, who's going to gear up and parachute into Lincoln, Nebraska, on my say-so?

"Goddamn it, stop manipulating me."

"I may be manipulating you, but I'm telling you the truth."

Christ, he sounded just like his mentor, my late friend Tatsu. For a moment, it made me sad. Tatsu would have been proud of his protégé.

"What's your plan," I said, hating that I was conceding.

"Some element of you and your guys can drop the shooters before they get inside. They're not well trained, they're not expecting any opposition. A school is about as much as they can handle."

"What about the Viper?"

"If I can locate the operator, you drop him, too."

"That's a big if. And, forgive me, I prefer not to loiter around ground targets that have been selected for double Hellfire missile strikes."

"I have a few ideas, and a few leads I'm chasing down. I don't expect the operator will be far from the school. The less distance the Viper has to fly, the less chances for sightings. Likewise, they'll want to launch the missiles close on to the target. Less opportunity for people to see two plumes of fire tracking in from miles away."

"But you said—"

"Yes, in the end, it's all explainable. But no sense having to explain more than necessary."

"It doesn't sound like you have much to go on."

"I don't, yet. But one more thing. If you're the operator, given the parameters I just described, what else do you need?"

I thought. "Someplace... quiet. Private, removed. So I can park, assemble the drone, and get it airborne without anyone seeing. And then operate it without interruption."

"Bingo. And how many places like that do you think there are in the vicinity of Lincoln?"

"Probably a lot."

"Yeah, that's the problem. But I'm looking into it. Plus there's one more thing that could be a game-changer."

"What's that?"

"I have a friend in one of the phone companies."

"A friend."

"Whatever you want to call him. He's been monitoring Gillmor's mobile phone for me."

I smiled. There was something satisfying about the tools of the national security state being turned against their owners.

"You think Gillmor's the operator?"

"He's had the training. He has the access. Plus, did you catch at the president's announcement that Gillmor wasn't named? For security reasons?"

"Yeah, I wondered about that at the time."

"I don't think they want that much publicly known about this guy before the attacks. They want him to have the freedom to move about as he needs depending on how many schools need to be hit. The good news, if you want to call it that, is that my read of the country's mood is that they're not going to need to hit too many. We're close to a tipping point already."

"Yeah, I get that feeling, too."

"Also," he said, "if you were committed enough to blow up a school, or multiple schools, how many people could you outsource it to? How many people could you count on to not lose their nerve at the last minute? Yeah, I think it's going to be Gillmor. And if it is, we should be able to track his phone all the way to Nebraska."

I thought for a minute. On the one hand, I didn't want to do this. It was too dangerous; there were too many possibilities for setups; there were too many unknowns and too many hidden agendas.

But on the other hand...

What I had told Horton that first morning was true: I've taken more lives than I'll ever be able to remember. When I was younger, I had ways of shielding myself from thinking about all the mothers, fathers, wives, siblings, children. I ignored whatever elements in a target's file might

have caused me discomfort. I assured myself that if the target had enemies, he must be in the life. My subconscious mantra was that if I didn't
do it, someone else would. Rationalization was my narcotic. And, as with
all drugs, over time, I habituated to mine. I needed more and more to
accomplish less and less. Eventually, there was no dose at all that could
confer the comfort I craved.

Now, with too many yesterdays and fewer and fewer tomorrows, I
find I'm increasingly troubled by knowledge I was once adroit in avoiding.
The knowledge that following my brief encounters with every stranger
I agreed to eliminate, I left nothing but tears and trauma, a wreckage of
interwoven lives forever riven and malformed. The knowledge that there
would never be a way to account for the amount of pain I have brought
into the world. The knowledge that the world would have been margin-
ally better off if I had never been born to begin with.

There was no way to resurrect the lives I'd taken or rectify the damage I'd done. That side of the balance sheet was immutable. The only
thing, maybe, was to offset it. To do something to save more lives than
I'd cost, prevent more pain than I'd inflicted.

It wasn't much. But what else did I have to hope for?

Hating the feeling of being manipulated, and of being a fool, I said,
"We'll need some hardware."

"Of course."

"And a private plane to get us to Lincoln. Even if we had time to
drive, we're all too strung out at this point. I think we'd kill each other
before we got there."

"I'll get you there."

"I need to talk to the others. I'll call you back later today."

I hung up and checked my watch. Almost ten o'clock. Stores were
opening soon.

"Come on," I said to Larison. "I'll brief you on the way."

We walked to Harry Winston on Rodeo Drive, the store we'd agreed
on after looking on the Internet that morning. We wanted someone reputable, and we figured Harry Winston was about as reputable as it got.
Neither of us had been happy to leave our hardware at the motel, but
we couldn't very well walk into a jewelry store carrying, either. Larison's
danger vibe was enough of a problem. If an alert security guard then saw

a bulge in our waistbands or around our ankles, we would have a little too much explaining to do.

En route, I briefed him on Kanezaki's intel. Unsurprisingly, he wanted no part of it. I wanted to bring up that weird moment from the night before, when Dox had employed, innocently, I was sure, a sodomy reference. But I didn't know how to do it. *Don't worry, I don't give a damn?* Or, *don't worry, I won't tell anyone?* What if I was wrong? And what good would it do anyway? But the thought that Larison had a secret, and might suspect that Dox and I had stumbled upon it, concerned me. This was a guy who was more than capable of killing to keep his private matters private.

We got to the store at just after ten o'clock. A gemologist named Walt LaFeber helped us. He seated us in front of a glass table in the corner of the store while he went around to the other side. On the table were a microscope and a number of other instruments.

I took out an envelope in which we had placed twenty stones of varying sizes, and emptied it carefully on the table. LaFeber picked up one of the larger stones and touched it with what looked like a current detector.

"What's that?" I asked.

"Believe it or not," he said, "it's just called a diamond tester. Diamonds are very good conductors of heat, and the instrument measures thermal conductivity. Yours looks good so far."

He examined the stone with various other devices, which, he explained as he worked, identified color, hardness, specific gravity, and various internal characteristics.

After about ten minutes, he said, "Congratulations, this is quite a fine stone."

"It's real?" Larison said. "A real diamond?"

"Oh, yes. Quite."

"How much would you say it's worth?" Larison asked.

"Based on its size—nearly five carats—and its structure, shape, and color, I'd say you're looking at somewhere in the neighborhood of twenty thousand dollars. Possibly more. A very fine stone."

"That's a nice neighborhood," I said, and even Larison smiled.

LaFeber checked the rest of the stones. They weren't all as impressive as the first one, but he estimated the least of them at over five thousand dollars. It looked like Horton had delivered.

There was no charge for the service. It was strange. We'd shown him stones worth in the neighborhood of a quarter million dollars, and didn't even have to pay anything. I supposed it was one way the rich got richer.

We thanked LaFeber and walked out into the sunlight of Rodeo Drive, oblivious consumers flowing past us. Shopping, it seemed, would be the last thing to go, even in the face of rolling terror attacks.

We headed east on Wilshire Boulevard. I considered that I was suddenly worth something like twenty-five million dollars. But the thought felt unreal. Not just because of the amount. But because I still had to live to spend it. And because, at the moment, I couldn't say the prospects for that looked particularly promising.

Larison and Rain boarded a bus on Wilshire and rode it toward Koreatown, where they would change to a Metro train. The wrong direction from the hotel in Santa Monica, but they were taking zero chances and weren't going to follow a direct route to anywhere, especially now that they had the diamonds. Not today; maybe not ever again. Which was fine by Larison. He'd been living in a state of low-grade paranoia for years now. He accepted it. He was accustomed to it. He had no more problem with the necessity of watching his back to protect his life than he had with the necessity of brushing to preserve his teeth. It was just the way things were.

Rain was good cover. Larison made people nervous, but when civilian eyes lighted on Rain's Asian features, they were reassured and kept right on going. Larison could almost see the unconscious calculation appear for an instant in their expressions: *not Muslim-looking. Peaceful Japanese. No problem.*

He almost couldn't believe he had the diamonds. This is what he'd worked for, what he'd planned for, what he'd taken on the entire U.S. government for. True, Hort wasn't dead—that punk Treven had fallen for yet another line of trademarked Hort bullshit—but Larison supposed he could accept that, at least for the moment. The original plan was to use Rain, Dox, and Treven to take out Hort, and then to close up shop by doing them, too. But Hort was a civilian now, he could be gotten to, so maybe it didn't really matter if the order of operations had been reversed. In the scheme of combat plans being changed by a collision with battlefield reality, this was a pretty minor alteration. And, in the end, an irrelevant one.

He'd act at his first opportunity, probably as soon as they got back to the motel and he was armed again. There were really only two considerations. First was the noise of the gunshots. But they still had the suppressed weapons they'd taken from the dead guys outside Kei's apartment. If he could access one of those without alerting anyone to what he was up to, the noise part would be taken care of.

Second was the reaction of whoever didn't get shot first. Action always beat reaction, and he was fairly sure he could drop all three of them before the last to go had a meaningful chance to react. But fairly sure wasn't entirely comforting under the circumstances, given the penalty he would incur for a miscalculation. Treven, Rain, and Dox were all formidable men, and Larison had to expect an exceptionally fast reaction when the shooting began. He decided he would drop Treven first, because Treven was the best combat shooter. Then Rain, because Rain had the sharpest instincts. And Dox last, because he was the biggest target and therefore the hardest to miss.

Dox. He hadn't much cared for the big sniper initially, but his respect for him had grown. That stunt at the Hilton in D.C. was one for the record books, and Larison had to acknowledge that without it, they almost certainly all would have shot each other a second later. And when they'd almost gotten into it the night before, he couldn't help but be impressed by how easily Dox had shed his good ol' boy persona and suddenly presented himself as lethally calm and quiet. It was a rare man who could maintain that kind of dangerous poise in Larison's presence. He wondered if maybe he ought to revise the order of operations and take out Dox first.

The problem was, some part of him didn't want to take out any of them. Not even Treven, who had been dumb enough to let Hort walk away when he so easily could have left his body facedown in a remote canyon pass in the Hollywood Hills.

They were competent. Reliable. And they worked well as a team. Yes,

Treven was annoyingly earnest, and Dox was a ham, and Rain reminded Larison too much of himself for Larison ever to fully trust him. But... fuck, every time he ran through a scenario of dropping them, he found that unlike his usual dispassionate appraisal of angles and distances and odds, he felt something heavy and unpleasant and ominous, instead. As though some part of his mind was imagining what it was going to be like to live with the knowledge, and the images, that would dog him afterward, and was asking him, warning him, not to take on that weight. The cost, as Rain had put it. He was carrying too much already.

He tried to shut that shit down, but he couldn't. He reminded himself he had no choice, that it was a simple matter of operational security. He wasn't persuaded. He told himself they would do the same to him. He didn't believe it. He reasoned that it was better to make a mistake in one direction and live than to make one in the other direction and die. The words rang hollow.

The worst part had been when Rain had pulled him aside and tried to talk to him. What had he said? *I'm trying to be your friend.* And the hell of it was, Larison thought it was true.

But he'd also felt himself slip for an instant when that clown Dox had said the thing about ass-fucking. How many times had that sort of thing happened a million years ago in the barracks? Every time it had, some part of Larison's mind started to panic that he'd been busted, that someone knew, or suspected, and was taunting him. But it was never the case. It was just how people talked. And he'd learned to suppress the reflex. So why had he slipped the night before? He thought Rain had spotted it, but he couldn't be sure. The man didn't show much.

But what if he had? First Treven, then Hort, now Rain and Dox... the number of people who knew, knew what he was, was growing. It was getting out of control, and if he didn't shut it down now, he would lose the ability outright.

He understood on some level that it shouldn't matter. Attitudes were changing, even DADT was dead... but the thought of people knowing, of looking at him differently, treating him differently... he hated it. It would be like revealing a terrible, exploitable weakness.

And that wasn't all, either. There were also the people who knew he was alive and relevant, rather than presumed dead and therefore forgotten. That number was growing, too. It was possible Hort would have told others besides Treven, Dox, and Rain, and if he had, then the genie was already out of the bottle. But Larison guessed Hort hadn't. Hort liked to keep his cards close to the vest. And if he had told others, so what? Then the damage was done. Regardless, the thing to do now was to shut it all down while shutting it down was still as least theoretically possible.

He looked out the window at the passing urban landscape, and felt more trapped than he ever had in his life. What the hell was wrong with him? His mind was telling him one thing. His gut wouldn't go along for the ride.

He didn't know what to do. He didn't want to die. He didn't want to be outed. But he so wanted to be able to sleep again, to lie down on a bed without dreading what he would see when he closed his eyes and he was left alone and defenseless with his dreams.

He was afraid of being weak. And he was afraid that failing to do the tactically sound thing here was the weakest move of all.

The trick would be to not think about it. Get back to the motel, get the Glock, wait for the moment, see the opportunity, act to exploit it. Yes, like that. No thinking. Just pattern recognition, and reflex, and done.

And not just Treven, Rain, and Dox. Kei, too. No one left who knew anything about him, or who could tie him to anything, or had any way to track him.

Except Hort, of course. But Larison would clip that loose end in short order, too. And then he'd be done. Free of all these entanglements. Free.

He didn't have to like it. He just had to do it.

chapter
twenty-seven

Treven and Dox waited at the motel with Kei. Kei was sitting on one bed; Dox, on the other; Treven, increasingly antsy because Rain and Larison had been gone so long, pacing in what little space the room afforded.

Treven hated waiting. When he was alone, he could wait patiently for days, even for weeks. But this was different. The whole operation was shot through with problems. Larison was acting increasingly unstable. There had been several near blow-ups among them, any one of which, had it gone critical, would have been fatal. And then there was Hort, suddenly scrambling all the pieces on the board with his stunt at the White House.

He hoped he'd done the right thing in letting the man live. He told himself it was logical, but part of him wasn't buying that, part of him knew it was emotional. Treven looked at Larison and Rain and Dox and didn't want to be like them. He needed some line he wouldn't cross, some sense of command authority and unit loyalty. Something that would represent the difference between a soldier with a conscience and a killer under contract. Wherever that thin line was, he knew he was dancing right along the edge of it now. Killing his commander would push him over forever.

But his decision gnawed at him anyway. Hort was dangerous. He might have been tracking them right at that very moment through means none of them fully appreciated. Sure, the others assumed Hort had found them in Washington via satellites and surveillance cameras and all the rest because they didn't know Treven had simply tipped the man off, but that didn't mean the satellites and surveillance cameras didn't exist. And sure, Hort had made his big speech and stepped down, and so presumably had lost his official access. But he still had friends in high places, and low ones, too. It was Hort himself who had schooled Treven in Sun Tsu: *When strong, feign weakness. When weak, feign strength.* Hort had certainly acted weak in the car last night, and the more Treven thought about it, the more nervous it made him.

Dox was making him nervous now, too. The big sniper was sitting with his back against the headboard and his legs stretched out on the bed. His eyes were closed and he held his Wilson Combat in his lap, as serene as a sleeping toddler and the gun a favorite stuffed animal. The man had at least as much patience as Treven, it was obvious from the stillness with which he sat while they waited. It made sense—it would be a piss-poor sniper who couldn't wait out a target—and, ordinarily, Treven would have admired and even been reassured by the trait. But now, it was making him feel like the source of Dox's apparent serenity was some secret knowledge Treven himself lacked.

Dox, his eyes still closed, said, "What's on your mind, son?"

Christ, did the guy read minds, too? "What do you mean?"

Dox opened his eyes. "Well, either you're trying to wear out the carpet in our luxury suite here, or something's making you antsy."

"It's nothing. I just don't like waiting."

"I thought you ISA studs could outwait a rock. You trying to disabuse me?"

Treven chuckled. "It's nothing."

"It's all right. I'm feeling antsy myself."

Treven looked at him. Propped serenely on the bed, he looked about as antsy as a statue.

"That's how you act when you're antsy?"

Dox grinned. "Oh, yeah. My blood pressure's way up at the moment. When I'm feeling relaxed, I'm practically invisible."

Treven couldn't tell if he was serious or joking. "Well, what's bugging you?"

"Your friend, to be honest."

"Larison?"

Dox nodded and turned to Kei, who, though she hadn't said or done anything different since they started talking, somehow seemed to be following their conversation with interest.

"Darlin'," he said, "would you mind wearing the headphones for a few minutes? Nothing special, just the dreaded OpSec, which is what we badasses call operational security."

"I don't mind listening," Kei said.

Dox smiled a little sadly. "I know you don't. Would you trust me, though?"

Amazingly, Kei nodded as though she indeed did trust him. Dox, Treven decided, just had a way with people. Those kids in the minivan at the Capital Hilton had practically fallen in love with him inside five minutes. And now, he'd somehow gotten a woman who he'd helped kidnap to apparently believe he had her best interests at heart. Treven wished he knew the trick. He would have liked to be able to do it himself.

Dox got up and put the headphones on Kei, then walked over to Treven. "Let me ask you something," he said quietly. "How well do you know that hombre?"

Treven wondered where he was going with this. "Not that well. I tracked him down in Costa Rica for Hort, and then we wound up working together on this fucked-up op."

"Then you don't really know him."

"Why are you asking?"

"I'm just trying to get a handle on him. I'm usually good at reading people, but when I try to read Larison, it's like the pages are blank. That, or it's too dark to see them."

"Yeah, I know what you mean."

"What do you think he's thinking right now?"

"How do you mean?"

"I mean, if you were him, and you just found out the diamonds are real, and Horton is now a civilian, and you don't give a shit about schoolchildren being murdered, what do you do?"

Treven didn't answer. He'd been half-consciously grappling with the same question.

Dox waited, then said, "Do you just take your cut of the diamonds and walk away?"

"I don't know."

"Cause that's a lot of loose ends you're leaving behind."

"That's one way of looking at it."

"And that's just the cold-hearted calculus of the cold-hearted opera-tor I'm trying to imagine. It could be even worse."

"How?"

"You think Larison has any... secrets?"

Treven was suddenly and profoundly aware that, this whole time, he'd been wrongly assuming Dox was a little bit dull. And, equally suddenly and profoundly, that he'd been completely, dangerously wrong about that. He wondered how many people had come to the same real-ization in the moment before Dox put out their lights forever. He supposed he should count himself lucky, for having learned the lesson so cheaply.

"Secrets?" he said, hoping his expression hadn't betrayed anything.

Dox looked at him, the hillbilly gone, the expression more akin to that of a human polygraph. "Secrets," Dox said again. "Because, if he had any, and he had reason to believe that we might know or even suspect those secrets, I'm a little concerned about what conclusions he might draw."

Treven didn't answer. He thought Dox was right, but wasn't sure about the implications of acknowledging it.

"I think you know what I'm talking about," Dox said. "And that's why you're not answering. You think I'm wrong?"

Treven shook his head. "No."

"Well, we can handle Larison. One way or the other. But one thing I cannot abide is what he might do to this girl here. If those diamonds are legit, we don't need her anymore. And we've put her through enough. I say we let her go. What do you say to that?"

"Just let her go?"

Dox nodded. "Right now. Before the angel of death gets back here and starts trying to implement whatever conclusions he might have ar-rived at during this morning's absence."

Treven thought. He didn't want to be a party to the girl's death any-more than Dox did. But it was also dangerous to do this kind of thing without even an attempt at consensus.

"Look," he said, "even if I agreed with you, and I'm not saying I don't, we can't just let her walk out of here right now. Rain and Larison aren't back yet, and we have to assume she'd go straight to the police."

"She doesn't even know where she is," Dox said. "I could take her out blindfolded, drop her off wherever, and drive away, and that would be that."

"Are you that sure she couldn't find her way back here? There are sounds, smells… some identifying thing we missed in this room. Or a sense of the turns you make and the distances you go. She's smart. I can see that, and so can you."

"All right then, what would you say if I drove her someplace and waited for you all to call me? I could let her go then, with plenty of time for all of us to vamoose."

"What if the diamonds aren't real? We don't know yet."

"What if they're not? Look at her. You going to put a bullet in her head? Or watch while Larison does?"

Treven didn't answer.

"Of course you're not," Dox said. "And you should be proud and relieved that you couldn't—that your parents didn't raise someone who could. Now, this has gone on long enough. If Horton has called our bluff, I say so be it. We've got other things to do, like stopping a group of ruthless zealots from massacring a bunch of schoolchildren in the name of the greater good."

The reference to his parents, both long gone, hit home. For a moment, Treven wondered whether Dox had deliberately seemed to suggest the impractical idea that they let Kei go immediately because he knew it would get Treven to object on practical, and therefore persuadable, grounds. He realized Dox must have been waiting for the right moment to initiate this whole conversation. He'd probably been hoping Treven would give him an opening, and, when he sensed they were likely running out of time, he'd found one himself. Treven felt like an idiot for having thought the man was dull. If there was a dull one in the room, it was himself.

"Christ," he said. "Larison's going to get back here and go postal. And Rain might, too."

"Rain'll be just fine. I know him. As for Larison, well, he's unarmed for the moment. I recommend we keep him that way, until we're sure he's had time to properly adjust to our new circumstances."

Treven thought for a moment. "If the diamonds are real," he said, "I think Larison will get over this. I think."

Dox nodded as though already knowing where Treven was going. And approving of it.

"But if they're not real," Treven said, "and he feels like Hort fucked him again, and we were complicit, we're going to have to kill him. Because if we don't, he'll kill us."

Dox nodded again, and again Treven had the uncomfortable sense that he'd been guided along to his conclusions by exceptionally deft hands.

But that didn't change the essential accuracy of the conclusions themselves. "All right," he said. "Get her out of here. You better hurry. They could be back soon."

Dox looked at him, then held out his hand. "Ben Treven, I'm glad to know you're one of the good guys."

Treven shook his hand. "I wouldn't go that far. Now go."

Rain and Larison got back about an hour after Dox had left with Kei. Treven unlocked the door and let them in with his left hand. In his right, he held the Glock.

They came in and he locked the door behind them. They glanced around the room and at the open bathroom door. Treven braced himself.

"Where's the girl?" Larison said.

"With Dox," Treven said.

"Oh, shit," Rain said, putting his fingers to his temples like a man struggling with a migraine. "I knew this was going to happen."

"Knew what was going to happen?" Larison said. He turned to Treven. "Where are they?"

Rain said, "He took her, didn't he?"

Treven nodded.

Larison's face darkened. "Took her? What the fuck is going on?"

Treven looked at Larison. "I'll tell you the truth. He thought you were going to come back here and kill her. And you know what? I agreed with him."

"What if I was?" Larison said. "Hort was supposed to call off the dogs. Instead, he neutered himself. He broke the deal. That means he pays the price."

"Are the diamonds real?" Treven said.

Rain nodded. "They're real."

"Good," Treven said, still looking at Larison. "That's more than enough. We're not going to kill some innocent girl because of your grudge against her father. I don't care what you call it. That's what it is."

Rain said, "All right, let's be practical for a minute. We can all kill each other afterward, if we still want to. What did you work out with Dox?"

"I'm supposed to call him when you two are back," Treven said. "And then the four of us are supposed to meet at some café you like in Beverly Hills."

"Shit," Rain said, "we just came from Beverly Hills. What café? Urth?"

"That's the one. The guy is pretty particular about his food."

"He has one of the cell phones?"

"Yes."

"All right, call him. But best to use a payphone. No sense blowing more than one of the phones."

"You want me to change the location?"

"No, I don't want to say anything about where we're meeting on an open line. Urth is fine. We paid up for the room?"

"We're paid up."

"What's Dox driving?"

"The Honda I boosted."

"Then the truck's still here?"

Treven nodded his head toward the bed stand. "Keys are right there."

"All right. There's a payphone on the northwest corner of Lincoln and Pico. Call Dox, tell him we'll meet him as planned as soon as we can."

"Where's my gun?" Larison said.

"Top dresser drawer," Treven said. "Yours and his." He waited a moment, but Larison didn't move for the dresser. That was good. If he had, Treven was going to shoot him right then and there. He wondered if Larison understood that.

"We'll pull the truck around in about fifteen minutes," Rain said. He seemed to know exactly what was going on, and Treven wondered what he had planned. Talk to Larison? Kill him? He couldn't read Rain much better than he could read Larison.

Whichever it was, he hoped Rain knew what he was doing. He nodded and went out.

chapter
twenty-eight

Larison wanted to go to the dresser and get the Glock. He wasn't even sure what he was going to do with it, but he felt so outplayed and so boxed in that he just needed to be holding a weapon. It was like this sometimes when he woke from one of the dreams, arms shaking and heart hammering and torso slicked with sweat, and the only thing that could bring him down was the feel of a weapon in one hand and solid objects, totems of the waking world, under the other. But Rain was standing between him and the dresser, and he didn't know what Rain would do if he made a move. Would Rain try to stop him? Larison had sixty pounds on the man, maybe more, but he'd watched Rain take out those contractors in Tokyo and they were even bigger than Larison. Anyway, even if he could beat Rain hand-to-hand, there wouldn't be much value to reaching the gun if he got to it with a broken arm, or worse. He decided the safer course was to stand down, for now.

Rain was watching him, and Larison had the sense the man knew exactly what he was thinking.

"Well?" Rain said. "What are we going to do?"

"What do you mean?" he said, telling himself he was playing for time.

"What would you say if I told you about a four-man team, three of whom independently came to the same conclusion about the fourth member?"

Larison didn't answer.

"In case I'm not being clear," Rain went on, "the conclusion I'm referring to is that you were going to come back here and punch that girl's ticket."

"So what?"

"Were we right?"

"What difference does it make?"

"In a way, none. Because when you have three people out of four thinking the worst of you, there's a problem even if the three people are mistaken. And that problem is you."

Larison didn't answer. Christ, if he only had that gun. Just the feel of it in his hand. To hold all this shit at bay.

Rain watched him. "You want to know what Treven didn't say?"

Again, Larison didn't answer. The dresser was eight feet away. Could Rain really stop him?

"He didn't say the other thing we were all thinking. Which is that you weren't just going to punch Kei's ticket. You were going to try to punch everyone's."

Larison gritted his teeth. He'd never felt so exposed. They knew too much about him. They'd seen through him. Somehow he'd faltered. It was all out in the open now. All of it.

"Were we wrong?" Rain asked.

Larison looked at him. "Stop fucking around. You want to finish this, let's finish it."

"What do you think I'm trying to do?"

"You're trying to fuck with my head, and I don't like it."

Rain walked over to the dresser.

Larison, distracted by his own inner turmoil, was slow to react. He said, "Don't!" But in the time it took him to get the word out, Rain had already opened the drawer. Rain glanced back at him, then reached in and came out with the Glock.

Larison watched, fascinated. A weird placidity settled over him. He tried to think of something to say. Nothing came out. There was a moment of weakness in his knees, but he thought that was relief more than fear. Yes, relief.

Rain checked the load in the Glock. He held the gun and looked at Larison. His expression was grimly purposeful.

Larison smiled. It seemed important to let Rain know he wasn't afraid. That, on some level, he was even complicit.

Rain tossed him the gun. Larison was so astonished he almost couldn't react. At the last instant, he got his hands up and caught it. He stood staring at it for a moment in shock.

"What a waste," Rain said. "Overall, we've been a pretty solid detachment. We've survived two ambushes and a hunt by the national security state; we've scored a hundred million dollars; our biggest enemy just neutered himself, as you put it... and we're going to cash all that in because we just can't help killing each other. Does that make sense to you?"

Larison blinked. Was Rain fucking with him? He could tell by the Glock's weight the magazine was full. Still, he racked the slide to be sure. A bullet ejected. Larison caught it in the air and looked at it. Standard nine-millimeter round. The gun was loaded.

"What are you doing?" Larison said. He was holding the gun, but he felt suddenly terrified.

"I'm doing for you what Dox once did for me. The thing I told you about in Vienna—Kwai Chung."

"You told me he saved your life."

"That was the obvious part. He also proved to me I could trust somebody. Of the two, I think the second had the more lasting effect."

Larison tried to think of something to say and couldn't access the words.

"How do you think Horton wants it?" Rain said. "You think he wants you killing everyone who might know your secrets? Or trusting people to watch your back?"

Larison looked at him. He wanted to ask what Rain meant by "secrets." But to ask would be to reveal. And besides, he could sense, on some deep, unexplainable level, that Rain... already knew. The same way he could sense that he also didn't care.

"What about the others?" he heard himself say. Christ, it sounded so weak. So pleading.

"Dox expects people to act honorably," Rain said. "If you let him down in that regard, he also believes the honorable thing is to track you down and shoot you. But he does like to give people the benefit of the doubt."

"I can't figure him out."

"He grows on you. Anyway, you think Dox or Treven cares about you as anything other than a friend or a foe? Each of us just pocketed more money than we can ever spend. The trick now is to live to enjoy it. And we have a better chance of doing that watching each other's backs than we do trying to preemptively kill each other. Isn't that what you told me in Vienna you wished you had? Someone who really had your back? Well, how are you going to get that if you reflexively kill people because you're terrified of trusting them?"

Larison blew out a long breath. Then another. He felt like he was going to jump out of his skin and told himself to Calm. The Fuck. Down.

Rain looked at him. "You mind if I take my gun out of the dresser?"

Larison shook his head. A minute ago, he would have killed Rain to stop him. Now… it didn't matter.

Rain took out the Wilson Combat, checked the load, and eased it into his waistband.

"What's the plan?" Larison said, unable to let go of his own gun, though he had no intention of using it.

"Well, it might be selfish," Rain said, "but I'm pretty sure the three of us are going to Nebraska to try to stop a massacre."

"Why is that selfish?"

"Because you could argue we're not doing it to save the lives of others. You could argue we're doing it so we can live with ourselves."

Larison didn't answer. He knew Rain was deliberately echoing what Larison had told him in Vienna, about the nightmares. It had been weak of him to tell Rain that, and he wasn't sure why he had. But… the idea that there was something he could do, that there was a way to beat back those awful dreams… he wanted to believe it.

"I didn't know it when I agreed to this op," Rain said. "At least, I didn't know it consciously. But I need to take all the shit I've done and the horror I've inflicted and do something good with it. And yes, Horton used that notion to manipulate me, and even though it turns out I was wrong about what the op was really about, it also turns out that maybe I'm going to get my chance anyway. And I don't want to blow it."

"Why are you telling me all this?"

"Because if we make the wrong choice here, I don't think there's a way back. I've come close before, very close, right up to the edge of the abyss. I don't want to fall into it. And right now, I'm teetering."

Larison swallowed. He thought he'd never been so confused. Or so suddenly exhausted.

"I need... a little time," he said.

Rain nodded sympathetically. "Yeah, I remember the shock of trusting someone. It fucked me up, too. You get used to it, after a while."

Larison shoved the Glock in his waistband. He felt like he'd been punched in the gut. "What the hell did you just talk me into?"

"I didn't tell you anything you didn't already know. You were just trying not to hear it."

Rain held out his hand. After a moment, warily, Larison shook it.

chapter
twenty-nine

Dox drove the Honda Treven had stolen east, toward Union Station. From there, Kei could catch a Red Line train and be home in no time.

He'd hated having to zip her back into the cargo bag to get her to the car, but Treven was right, no sense taking chances about her figuring out where they'd held her. The truth was, he was less worried about her being able to run to the police than he was that she'd feel bad if she didn't. Better to just deny her the ability, and therefore save her the guilt.

The worst part of it was how willingly she'd let him do it. He'd taken the headphones off her and said, "Darlin', I'm not comfortable waiting around for the bogeyman to get back here. He's just too unpredictable for my tastes. So, with your permission, I'd like to take you home now."

She'd looked into his eyes, smart enough to search for a lie, trusting enough to want to believe none was there, insightful enough to see that none was. Then she'd nodded and said, "Okay." And that was that. He carried her out in the bag, unzipped it inside the trunk, closed her inside, and drove off, taking care to use an indirect route with plenty of bridges and underground parking garages along the way.

He'd been driving for nearly an hour when his mobile phone rang. He picked up. "Yeah."

Treven's voice: "All right, they're back. The stones are real."

"Well, that's good news. What's going on with our friend?"

"I don't know. Your friend is alone with him right now. Trying to talk him down, I think."

Dox didn't like the sound of that. "Talk him down?"

"I don't know what to tell you. He asked me to step out and call you from a payphone. And to tell you we'd meet as planned as soon as the three of us can get there."

Dox hoped there would be three left. If whatever talk Rain was trying didn't work out, there would likely be only two. Or one.

"All right, thanks for letting me know. I'll see you in a little while."

He clicked off and finished the route on Ducommun Street, an empty cul-de-sac a few blocks from Union Station, where he parked in front of the busted chain-link fence in front of an abandoned warehouse. He got out with Kei's mailbag and looked around, squinting against the sun and the heat. Someone had spray-painted *No Parking, Tow-Away* in now-faded red on the boarded-up doors of the building, but amid the weeds growing through the cracks in the pavement and the garbage collecting at the bottom of the teetering loading dock, he didn't think he was likely to encounter any objections.

He walked around to the trunk and opened it. Kei shut her eyes and lifted a hand to shield her sweaty face from the sudden invasion of light.

She squinted up at him fearfully. "You're really going to let me go?"

He wondered if he could feel more low. He was never doing something like this again, no matter what the stakes. Never.

He held out his hand. "I promise you, I am. And I'm sorry, that was a long drive. I can see where you might have started to doubt me. Plus, it must have been god-awful hot in there."

She paused for a moment, then took his hand and sat up. She looked around.

"We're a few blocks from Union Station," he said, "but, as you can see, not in the most upstanding of neighborhoods. If you don't mind, I'll just follow you in the car while you walk the few blocks to make sure you make it all right."

She put some weight on his hand and stepped out of the trunk. She looked around again. "Okay."

She was still holding his hand. He squeezed hers briefly and then let go.

"I know it's pretty lame under the circumstances," he said, "but I apologize for what we did to you. I shouldn't have let myself get caught up in it. It was wrong, and I'm truly sorry."

She said, "Thank you."

He shook his head, ashamed. "You don't have one single thing to thank me for. I did a terrible thing to you."

She looked at him. "I knew you wouldn't hurt me. You were the reason I wasn't scared."

That only made it worse. "I don't think that's worth very much, actually."

"It was to me."

"Darlin'," he said gently, "are you familiar with a thing called the Stockholm Syndrome?"

"I know what it is. And I don't have it. If the police had kicked in the door to that room, I wouldn't have shielded you with my body, I can tell you that."

He smiled. Ordinarily, he might have taken an opportunity like that to comment on the possible upside of her throwing her body over his. Instead, he said, "Well, now you've gone and burst my bubble."

She laughed, just a little. "It could have been a lot worse for me. You made it better. I kept looking at that scary guy, Larison, and thinking, 'Dox wouldn't let him.'"

He wondered if she was playing him. "You really thought that?"

She nodded. "I did."

He looked down at the ground. "If I did something to make this a little less worse of an ordeal for you, I'm glad. But it was still an ordeal, and I was still a part of it. Trust me, I know you're bursting with relief and gratitude right now, but later? It's all going to settle in. You'll realize what you've been through. Being held like we held you is no joke."

"You sound like you know."

He wondered whether he should say more, and then did anyway. "Not so long ago, some men held me. I'm not going to tell you what they did, other than that it involved electric shocks, repeated drownings, and threats to Nessie. So yes, I'm not unacquainted with what you're going to be dealing with in the coming days and weeks. I wish there were something I could do about it, but I can't, other than to say again I'm sorry."

She raised an eyebrow. "Nessie?"

He shook his head, knowing he shouldn't have joked like that, determined not to follow up. "Never mind."

He handed her the mailbag. She took it.

"What did my father do to you?" she said.

He shook his head again. "I don't want to talk about it. It never should have had anything to do with you. I want you to tell me something else, instead."

"What?"

He looked around at the cracked road, the barbed wire, everything baking under the unblinking Los Angeles sun.

"What are your plans? I mean, for the future. Film school… you want to make movies?"

She smiled. "That's what I want. Pretty far afield from my dad, huh?"

"I'd say. But I'm glad. I like movies. When am I going to get to see yours?"

"I don't know. I wrote a script I think is great. But financing is hard these days. We'll see."

"Financing, huh?"

She shook her head slightly as though not understanding what he was getting at.

"When you get home," he said, "check the bottom of your mailbag. There are a bunch of little stones in there. They don't look like much, but they're diamonds. I don't know what movies cost, and probably what I put in there wouldn't be enough for Harry Potter, but I think they'll get you started."

She looked at him, then said, "Are you serious?"

He gave her a mock-stern look. "In the short time you've known me, have I ever not been?"

She looked at him for a moment longer, then stepped in wordlessly and hugged him. He hugged her back, but tentatively. He was ashamed to receive her gratitude, and he also didn't like how good she felt in his arms. The Wilson Combat was in his front waistband, coming between them, and he supposed that worked as a metaphor.

After a moment, he broke the embrace. "All right, you." he said. "Now git. I'll follow you to make sure you reach the station all right. And I'll keep an eye out for your movie."

She hesitated. "Am I ever going to see you again?"

He shook his head. "That's Stockholm Syndrome talking."

"The hell it is."

He smiled, and tried not to show how crappy he felt. "Well, I know your cell phone number. Who knows?"

"Will you call me someday? Not right away. Just… after this has started to seem unreal."

He kept the smile in place. "I'd like that." The way he'd phrased it, it wasn't even a lie.

He followed her to the station as planned. When he was satisfied she was in a safe area, he pulled out alongside her. She turned and looked at him, and he thought she was going to come to the car. So he gritted his teeth and held up a hand in goodbye, and pulled out into traffic. He checked the rearview as he drove and the sight of her standing on the sidewalk, alone and watching him leave, made him feel sadder than he'd felt in a long time.

chapter
thirty

The next morning, the four of us stood on the tarmac at sleepy Santa Monica Airport. Kanezaki had flown commercial to LAX that morning, where he was changing to a chartered jet that would pick us up here. We could have met him at LAX, but security at major airports was extreme at the moment and we didn't want to risk it—even if we'd been willing to leave the firearms behind, which we weren't. So I'd dropped the others off at Santa Monica Airport and then driven the truck to a nearby U-Haul place, hoping Kanezaki would only be hit with a penalty for accidentally returning the truck on the wrong side of the country, rather than the cost of replacing a truck he'd failed to return entirely.

We'd spent the night at another downmarket L.A. motel. Kei was gone, and it was a relief—even, I thought, for Larison. Larison and Dox had spoken, but they'd been out of earshot and I couldn't hear what was said. At the end of it, though, Dox had pulled the obviously stunned Larison in for one of his big hugs. Larison seemed as surprised and discomfited as I'd been when it had first happened to me. I wanted to tell him he'd get used to—Dox would say enjoy—it after a while, but I supposed he'd work that out on his own. In the meantime, it was good he was figuring out that while there might not be a worse enemy than Dox, there was also no better friend.

I hoped I'd done the right thing in tossing Larison that Glock. When I looked back on it, I felt like I wasn't entirely sure of my own motivations. It was either the noblest, or the stupidest thing I'd ever done. And the problem was, it was still too early to tell.

I'd checked the secure site that morning. There was a single message from Horton:

Call me. This thing has got to be stopped.

And thank you. I won't forget it.

The last part must have been about letting Kei go, and maybe specifically for saving her from Larison. Probably, in the overwhelming relief that must have washed over him after several nights of the worst fears he'd ever grappled with, he'd meant it. But I doubted his gratitude would last. I decided not to call. Larison had been right. Horton was an inveterate manipulator, and I didn't want to give him another chance to lay out a line of bullshit.

There wasn't much traffic at the tiny airport, and I had no trouble recognizing the plane Kanezaki had told me to watch for: an oddly bulbous private turboprop with a set of stubby wings under its nose and the main wings set way back. A Piaggio P180 Avanti. It came in from the northwest, taxied, turned, and stopped. The door opened and Kanezaki walked out onto the tarmac. He saw us and waved.

We all climbed on. I paused to shake Kanezaki's hand; Dox, naturally, suffocated him with a hug. Kanezaki closed the door behind us, and five minutes later, we were airborne, the pilot on course for Lincoln.

"Damn," Dox said, reclining in one of the plush, leather-clad seats. "I might have to get me one of these."

The strange thing was, he could. But I didn't think he really meant it. The money still didn't feel real. We had too much heat on us, for one thing. And we were too focused on stopping this horror we'd inadvertently helped start, for another.

"I was right about Gillmor," Kanezaki said. "He's in Lincoln now."

"Your friend is tracking his cell phone?" I asked.

He nodded. "Which means we need to divide the labor. We're expecting four shooters on-site, and a ground team—presumably one man—operating the drone from somewhere else. You guys need to decide how to take it all down."

"Depends partly on what toys you brought us," Dox said.

Kanezaki got up and went to the back of the plane, then came back with a couple of long canvas bags. He set one on the floor and handed the other to Dox.

Dox unzipped the bag and grinned like it was Christmas morning.

"Well, goddamn," he said, extracting and hefting a long black carbine. "Knight's Armament SR-25, integral suppressor, twenty-round magazine, and oooh, the Leupold Mark 4 HAMR. Haven't played with one of these before. Gonna be somewhere I can zero it?"

"We'll find a place," Kanezaki said. "Lots of open fields where we're going."

He knelt and unzipped the other bag. "Here's your commo," he said. "INVISIO Digital Ears X5 Headset and X50 Multi-Comm. Hands-free, in the ear, boom mic. All encrypted and we'll all be able to talk to each other."

"Other weapons?" Larison asked.

Kanezaki reached into the bag and took out a pistol I was quite familiar with. "HK MK23 SOCOM, Knights Armament suppressor. One each."

He handed it to Larison, who reflexively checked the load. Treven said, "Great gun, but with the suppressor it's the size of a rifle. What do we carry it in?"

Kanezaki went to the back again and came back with a large black attaché case. He opened it. An HK with attached suppressor was held in place with foam inside. "I know there's no good way to conceal one of these on your body in an urban environment," he said. "But you can access it inside the bag in less than a second. By the time it's out, it won't matter who sees it. And if the attachés aren't the right cover, I have gym bags, too."

Treven nodded, satisfied.

I said, "Body armor, I hope? You know, just in case."

"Dragon Skin vests," Kanezaki said. "Capable of stopping multiple 7.62 rounds."

He pulled out a folder and opened it. "This is a satellite and street view of the school and environs," he said. "Some of it is Google; some is military. It should at least give you some ideas. I have a van waiting on the other end. After we land, we'll do a drive-by."

We looked at the maps. The school was a square brick building outside the downtown, two stories, surrounded mostly by dirt and grass fields. It had one main entrance, but secondary points of ingress and egress on the other three sides.

"If all four shooters plan on using the front entrance," I said, "then we're good to go. But if they split up, we'll need a man on each side of the building. Which leaves us one short to engage the drone operator."

Kanezaki looked up. "You're not counting me."

"That's right," I said, "I'm not. Tom, we've been through this before. You're a great intel guy but you're not a door-kicker. Pick the wrong entrance to cover, and you might wind up in a one-on-four. It doesn't make sense."

Dox said, "I think there's a better way."

We all looked at him. He said, "Look at these buildings around the school. What do we have here... a church, a video store, car dealer, and a Holiday Inn, it looks like. Nothing but flat fields in between, and from any one of those vantage points, I have full coverage of two sides of the school. With a spotter on the ground for target confirmation, and my new friend the SR-25 here, and with the distances being so short, I could drop four targets in four seconds. If Tom here does the spotting for me, I say that would free up Treven and Larison to cover the other two sides of the building. And free up Rain to engage the drone operator, wherever he's set up shop."

I didn't know whether he really needed Kanezaki to do the spotting, or if he was just giving him something to do to placate him. I said, "Either the spotting for you, or the driving for me. Depends on where and when we locate Gillmor, and what the terrain is like."

No one objected. I thought it was a sensible approach. Treven and Dox were the two best combat shooters, Dox was the only sniper, and that left me for the guy operating the drone, who would likely be alone and, even if armed, distracted by the task at hand.

"What's security like at this school?" Treven asked.

"In ordinary times," Kanezaki said, "nonexistent. But with all the speculation about attacks on schools, a lot of towns are putting police in place at the entrances. I think we'll see some of that."

Treven nodded. "Security theater."

"Exactly," Larison said. "One or at most two bored cops at the entrance with their .38s holstered? Speed, surprise, and violence of action, and they'll be dead before they even realize there's a problem."

"The area looks like eighty percent farmland and fields," I said. "Lots of room for privacy. If your friend can't give us a fix on Gillmor's cell phone, we're going to have a hell of a time finding him."

"I'm working on it," Kanezaki said grimly. "In the meantime, let's see if can figure out from these maps where we would set up if we were Gillmor."

We spent the rest of the flight refining our plan and getting some much needed sleep. When we landed, it was evening, and though residual heat still radiated from the tarmac as we got off the plane, the day was getting cooler. We pulled on baseball caps and sunglasses just in case anyone was looking for us all the way out in Lincoln. "Only way to travel," Dox said, the SR-25 bag slung over his shoulder as we headed to the car rental to get Kanezaki's promised van.

We picked up food, then drove out to the school. The sun was getting low in a blue, cloudless sky that went on forever, and even in the van, the air smelled of cut grass.

The school was on the edge of town, an area that was mostly single family houses, with a few farms and a single mixed office and retail center. I thought the plotters might have chosen the school for its relative remoteness: fewer potential witnesses to describe aspects of the carnage the plotters didn't want seen.

A little farther out, we passed a construction site. Dox said, "Hang on, I like the look of this."

We circled around and drove back through the plume of dust we'd kicked up on the road behind us. "Doesn't look like much is happening here," Dox said.

He was right. There was no equipment and no material, just a four-story I-beam and cinderblock skeleton without even a chain-link fence around it. No windows in place, no roof, no doors.

"I believe what we're looking at," Dox said, "is an abandoned building site, popularly known as a victim of America's ongoing recession. Also known as an ideal urban sniper hide. Look at that—line-of-sight to the front of the school, two-hundred yards. Easy pickings. I'd like to go in when it's dark and confirm, but I believe we just found my place. What time are our terrorists due to arrive?"

"The assembly's at eight forty-five," Kanezaki said. "So probably just after that."

"Well then, I propose we insert me at zero three hundred, the still of the night. I'll zero the rifle at first light. Won't be many people around, and the suppressor will reduce the sound some. You didn't bring a sleeping bag, did you?"

"Shit, no," Kanezaki said. "I didn't think of it."

"That's all right, I'm sure there's a Wal-Mart around here. I'll pick up some thermal hunting gear and a foam pad to prone out on. Watch the sunrise, it'll be nice."

We got Dox his gear, and went back to the building site after dark. Dox went in, and reported that he liked what he found. Then he and Treven, who looked the most at home in the area, checked us into an anonymous highway motel, two adjoining rooms on the second of two floors. We ate and checked the gear and went over our plans. Kanezaki used a satellite phone to call his telephone company friend. Apparently, Gillmor had his phone on the day before in Lincoln, but it was off now.

"If we can't locate him," I said, "the op's blown."

Kanezaki nodded. "I'll have to call in a bomb threat. Get them to evacuate the school. But all that does is divert the attack. And next time, we might not know what school."

We were all quiet. I knew we all felt like we had to stop this. And we knew if we couldn't stop it here, we probably couldn't stop it at all.

Kanezaki said, "What about Horton?"

"What about him?" I said.

"I know he stepped down, but he's still got contacts. Maybe he knows something, or could find out. Can you call him?"

"He might not be well inclined to us just now," Larison said.

I thought about the secure site message. "No, I think you're wrong about that. But I've reached the point where I wouldn't trust anything he tells me."

Larison smiled. "Better late than never."

"What can it hurt?" Kanezaki said. "Use my sat phone. No way to triangulate on its location."

I thought for a moment. He was right—it was hard to see the harm. But Horton had lied to me and set us up. I felt like I had nothing to say to him. I didn't even plan on letting him live when this was all over.

But that was stupid. Tactics first. "All right, give me the phone," I said.

Horton picked up so fast, he might have been waiting for the call. "Horton."

"You wanted me to call you."

"Thank God you did. I was getting ready to call the Lincoln police with a bomb threat. But that wouldn't stop the attack, it would—"

"Only divert it, I know."

"Please tell me you're there. And you're going to stop this thing."

"The last time you figured out where I was going to be, you sent four shooters."

"That was, bar none, the biggest mistake of my life."

I imagined the sentiment was heartfelt. Not that it mattered. "How did you track us there?" I said, thinking about Treven.

"National technical means."

Maybe it was true. I had no way of knowing. I wasn't even sure why I'd bothered asking. It just felt like a loose end, and it bothered me.

"If you're in Lincoln," he said, "I want to help. Anyway I can."

"We're here," I said, hating that I was giving him the satisfaction.

"Good."

"So is Gillmor."

"Yes, I know."

"I need to know where. His cell phone is turned off. Do you have any way of tracking him?"

There was a pause, then, "Let me make some calls. How can I reach you?"

"I'll call you."

"Thank you," he said, and I clicked off.

Nobody slept. At three in the morning, Kanezaki drove Dox out to the building site. I called Horton. He still hadn't found anything. Kanezaki's phone company friend told him Gillmor's phone was still dark. I started to feel very bleak. It wasn't just that we weren't going to be able to stop the attack. It was that I was going to feel responsible for setting it all in motion.

I resolved that, no matter how this turned out and no matter how long I had to wait, Horton was going to die. It was thin, and I supposed in the end it wouldn't really matter, but the thought was distracting, at least, and mildly comforting. It helped me drift off for a while.

chapter
thirty-one

W hen it started getting light outside, I called Horton again, expecting the worst.

"Good news," he said.

I tried not to get my hopes up. "What?"

"That drone. The Viper. When it's powered up, it navigates by GPS. It has to uplink to the satellite. So—"

"We'll know where it took off from."

"Correct. I have a friend in the NRO who is watching for that signal and that signal alone. As soon as we have the coordinates, I will get them to you."

"We might not have much time. We don't even know for sure that he's going to be in the Lincoln area."

"I know. But we should be all right. The Viper can loiter for a whole day. I doubt Gillmor wants to run it for that long, but he doesn't have to wait until the very last minute, either. My guess is, he'll have it up at least an hour before the shooters go in. That'll allow him some wiggle room in case he has any mechanical or other problems. But I need to be able to reach you."

I gave him Kanezaki's sat phone number, glad I didn't have to give him a cell. "I'll be in a car," I said. "Call me as soon as you know."

I told the others, then used the commo to raise Dox. "Hey," I said. "I'm not waking you, am I?"

He chuckled. "I like when you tease me. What's going on?"

I told him.

"Well, that's good," he said, sounding mildly pleased—mildly pleased,

I knew from experience, being his only affect when he was in his sniping zone, no matter what the news he was reacting to.

"How's the view?" I said.

"Pretty in this light. I can see everything."

"You're on the roof?"

"One floor down. Doubt anyone could see me from overhead, but why take chances?"

"All right, good hunting."

"You, too, partner. If you don't take out that drone, my good work will be wasted. And I don't think Treven and Larison will be happy, either."

What he meant is that Treven and Larison, on the ground at the school, would be well within the Hellfire blast radius, and therefore incinerated. Along with God knew how many children.

"Yeah, I've thought about that."

"Okay. No pressure or anything."

"Right. I'll talk to you as soon as we know more."

We pulled on the Dragon Skin vests, and set out at a little before eight. We would have liked to get in position earlier, but outside Dox's sniper hide, concealment and blending opportunities were scarce. Strange men loitering outside a school tend to draw attention. The good news was, the shooters faced the same problem.

While Kanezaki drove, we all checked the gear one last time. Good to go. We dropped off Treven and Larison a few blocks from the school. They were wearing jeans and tee shirts and baseball caps. With the gym bags in which they were carrying the HKs, they easily could have been a couple of locals on their way to a job in a hardware store or at a construction site. We wished each other good luck, and no one said what was really on our minds: if I didn't hear from Horton soon, we were going to have to come up with a hell of a Plan B.

But we did hear from him, ten minutes later. "We got him," he said, with uncharacteristic excitement. "Not in Lincoln, but close by. Tiny town called Palmyra. Spelled Palm, Yankee, Romeo, Alpha. Nothing but farmland. You have a navigation system?"

"Yes. Give me the coordinates."

He did. I input the information. "Twenty-five miles," I said to Kanezaki. "Keep going on Route 2. I'll tell you when to turn."

He punched it. "Watch your speed," I said. "Can't afford to get pulled over."

"If we get chased, we get chased," he said, and I supposed at this point it was true.

"What else can you tell me?" I said to Hort.

"It's obvious Gillmor chose the spot for proximity to the school but also for privacy. Most of the area is flat, and not well suited for the clandestine launch of a drone, but he's at the end of a dirt road. Looks like an abandoned granary or something, in a depression by a pond and surrounded by trees. He could put the drone up there, get it up high, and I doubt anyone would ever see it. It'll reach the school without ever passing over anything but fields and farmland."

"How long is the dirt road?"

"A little under a quarter mile."

I wasn't going to approach using the obvious route, let alone one as likely as a road. "Other points of ingress?"

"None. But the fields look perfectly crossable."

"You're looking at the satellite photos. What's my best point of access?"

"Drive east of the road and go in by foot. That'll put you on the other side of the granary, and should give you some cover and concealment. I imagine Gillmor is armed."

"All right, I'll let the rest of the team know. Call me if there's a change."

"Roger that."

"Oh, and Horton?"

"Yes?"

"If this is another setup, you better kill every last one of us. Because if there's even one left, he will find you."

There was a pause. "I don't expect to live long in any event, but yes, understood. And good luck."

I clicked off. Kanezaki had the van up to nearly a hundred. I was glad the road was flat and straight, but I thought the van might tear itself apart en route regardless.

"Okay," I said, using the commo, "that was Horton. We've got a fix on Gillmor. Kanezaki and I are on the way, ETA fifteen minutes. Assuming we don't crash first."

"I'm in position," Treven said. "Teachers are arriving. And some kids. Cop at the front entrance."

"In position," Larison said. "Dox, you there?"

"Not only am I here," Dox said, in his serene sniper voice, "but I'm looking at you at this very moment right through my little reticled scope. I'm glad we worked out all our animosity earlier, aren't you?"

There was no answer. Dox said, "Hey, man, I'm just kidding."

"Goddamn it, don't kid like that!" I said, fearing another eruption, hoping my intervention would placate Larison.

We hit a pothole and the van almost went into orbit. "Jesus!" I said, pulling my seatbelt tighter.

Kanezaki, serene as Dox, said, "Sorry."

He kept it pinned until we turned off the two-lane, and by the time we came to the dirt road to the granary, he had it under the speed limit. We kept going for another quarter mile, and then he pulled over to the side in a dip in the road. "I'm not waiting in the van," he said. "And we don't have time to argue about it."

He was probably right. "Okay," I said. "Stay to my left as we approach. When we get to the granary, you circle left, I'll circle right. Let me engage Gillmor first, okay?"

"Why?"

"It's not about the glory. If the drone's still on the ground, we can just shoot him, or you can, it doesn't matter to me. But if the drone's up, we have to try to make him bring it back, right?"

"That's a good point."

"Yeah, I try to think of things like that."

"Okay, you engage him first."

"Good idea. Also, let's not assume he's alone. Keep your eyes open. If Gillmor's at the controls and you see someone else, then by all means, shoot the other guy, he'll just be security, and that'll be one less thing we have to worry about."

"Got it."

He looked scared. It wasn't confidence-inspiring.

I glanced at the HK he was holding. "You know how to use that, right?"

"I've had the training, yeah."

Which was another way of saying, *but not the experience.*

"Okay," I said. "Remember. Aggressive stance, gorilla grip, front site on the target, press the trigger."

He gave me a tight grin. "Dox always said you micromanage."

Damn it, he was right. He was either going to perform or not. Whatever I said to him at this point wasn't going to make the difference.

"All right," I said. "Let's go." For the benefit of the others, I said, "Kanezaki and I are moving in on the granary now. Should be on target in five minutes."

We headed north a quarter mile across flat grassland, then west, keeping low and moving quickly. There was a stand of trees between us and our objective, but, other than that, no cover or concealment anywhere. I tried not to think about snipers and what we would look like if one were watching us from that granary. When we reached the trees, we paused. I could see the granary. It was circular, about twenty feet high, but it was crumbling and offered no sniper hides, at least nothing that looked in our direction. Thank God. I couldn't see around it. There was a truck partly visible next to a pond to the right, which might have been good news, but no sign of people. We were going to be in a hell of a jam if Hort's intel was wrong, and there was nobody here.

"Children going in the front entrance," I heard Dox say in the earpiece. "Lots of 'em. Walking in from the neighborhood and some getting dropped off by their parents. No sign of our shooters."

"My side's clear, too," Larison said.

"Same," Treven said.

"John, I hope you're in position," Dox said. "Our timeline's getting kind of tight."

I didn't want to speak, but I tapped the boom twice with a finger.

"Roger that," Dox said.

I looked at Kanezaki. He was pale. I hoped he was going to be okay. I inclined my head toward the granary. He nodded once and we moved in, our guns up now. I didn't know who'd trained him, but I had to admit they'd done a good job. Despite his obvious fear, he had his HK out at high-ready, his head was swiveling to increase his range of vision, and he propelled himself with a nice, smooth shuffle.

We reached the wall of the granary. It smelled of earth and hay and I had the urge to cling to it you always get just before you move out from your last position of decent cover. Still no sign of anyone at the truck.

I signaled left to Kanezaki. He nodded and moved off. I headed right.

At the limit of the structure's circumference, I crouched and darted my head around and then back. In the instant I'd been exposed I'd seen Gillmor, a tall, wiry Caucasian in hunting fatigues and with a graying high-and-tight. He was standing, facing the road, working the keyboard of what looked like a large laptop suspended at waist level from a strap around his neck.

I stepped around, the HK on him. I checked my flanks quickly, then said in a loud, command voice, "Gillmor. Do not move."

He started and glanced over at me. But his hands stayed at the controls.

"Get your hands up!" I shouted.

I heard Dox in my ear: "Shooters have arrived. Running at the front entrance. Larison, you win the prescience prize. Engaging them now."

I heard a soft crack. Another. Then two more.

"Thank you for playing," Dox said. "Next contestants."

"Your four shooters are done!" I said, swiveling left and right to check my flanks. "They didn't even make it inside. Now hands up, or you're dead right there!"

He raised his hands and turned to look at me.

"Circle him!" I called out to Kanezaki. "Watch the truck, I don't know if there's anyone inside it."

Kanezaki moved out, past Gillmor, his HK up.

Gillmor glanced at him, then back to me. "Who sent you? Was it Horton?"

"Call it back," I said. "The drone."

"No."

"Call it back," I said, my voice flat-lining. "I won't ask again. I will shoot you in the head."

"It doesn't matter whether I die," he said, nodding. "The mission will still succeed."

Okay, I thought, and shot him in the head. The HK kicked, there was a crack about as loud as the thump of a sewing machine, and a hole appeared in his forehead. His body shuddered, his knees buckled, and he folded to the ground on his back.

"Jesus Christ!" Kanezaki shouted. "How are we going to stop the drone now?"

"Check the truck!" I said. "And stay alert."

I heard Dox chuckle. "Cop's freakin' out. He's wondering, 'Who were these four guys who were charging me, and why did their heads all suddenly uncork?'"

I rushed to Gillmor's body and examined the laptop. Two joy sticks, telemetry readouts, a video feed that looked like it was coming from a camera in the drone. I recognized the terrain from the maps we'd been reviewing. The east/west rural highway we'd driven in on from Lincoln. The river just south of it.

Oh shit, he's programmed it to go straight for—

Gunshots to my right. I spun. Kanezaki was down. I saw movement at the far end of the truck.

I charged for the granary.

No time to think about Kanezaki. I hoped he'd taken the hits in the Dragon Skin, but I didn't know. "Dox," I said into the commo boom as I got to cover, "Gillmor's down, but he's programmed the drone to go straight to the school. I think he set the Hellfires to go at the last minute and then for the drone to follow them in, or maybe for them to detonate on impact with the drone. It's coming at you from due east. ETA three, maybe four minutes. Can you take it down?"

"I don't know. Where are its avionics?"

I darted my head around and back. Three gunshots rang out from the far side of the truck and rounds struck the granary wall. Chunks of dislodged concrete hit me.

"I don't know, I didn't design the fucking thing! The nose, I guess."

"Guess you can't ask Gillmor?"

Another gunshot, another spray of concrete. I was distantly aware that if the shooter was firing even when I didn't show myself, he couldn't be that good.

"Gillmor's dead!" I said.

"Well, under the circumstances and assuming we don't have any other drone architecture experts on hand, I'd have to call that a fail."

Unless, I thought, the shooter was covering for someone coming in from my left. I moved out to the other side of the granary, the HK up. "Treven, Larison, you need to clear out of there now."

"I'm going in," Treven said. "They have to evacuate."

"You don't have time!"

"Gotta try."

There was a pause.

"Goddamn it," Larison said. "I knew this was going to happen. I'm going in, too."

"Use the sides," Dox said calmly. "If you come around to the front, you will have to engage a very upset police officer."

"Roger that," Treven said.

"Going in," Larison said. "Goddamn it."

The other side of the granary was clear. It was just the one guy, then. And he wasn't that good. I wondered if I could charge the truck from here.

"Dox," I said. "Do you see it?"

"Not yet, but I'm looking."

I heard Treven and Larison shouting, "There is a bomb in the school! This is not a joke and it is not a drill! Everyone needs to evacuate now and scatter to at least one hundred yards! Move! Move!"

"Come on, baby," I heard Dox say. "Where are you? Come to Dox."

I sucked in a deep breath and blew it out, readying myself to charge the truck. I counted one, two—

I heard three soft cracks, then a gunshot. I tore around the side of the granary and straight for the truck.

There was no need. Kanezaki was on his feet, to the left of the truck, the HK up at chin level and angled to the ground, smoke drifting up from the muzzle of the suppressor. I dropped down and looked under the chassis of the truck. There was a prone body on the other side.

"Is he dead?" I called out.

"I think so." He sounded like he was in shock.

"Well, fucking make sure!"

I heard another soft crack. Then, "He's dead."

Dox, in my ear: "Goddamn it, I am taking fire."

He said it so calmly it took me a minute to understand what it meant. "Someone's shooting at you?"

Treven and Larison were still shouting. Sounded like pandemonium inside the school.

"Yeah," Dox said, "it's that cop. He must have seen me. Good eyes. He'd need a hell of a lucky shot to hit me from there, but still I'd be grateful if someone could knock him down or something. I'd prefer not to shoot a police officer. Treven, Larison?"

"I'm on it," Larison said.

"Thank you," Dox said. "Still no sign of the drone. Kids are all running out of the school, though. Nice work there."

A few seconds went by. I heard a sound—half thud, half crunch—and Dox said, "Thank you, Mister Larison! Ooh, that had to hurt."

"What happened?" I said.

"Clubbed the cop," Larison said. "Took his gun."

I heard him say, "Here, I'm sorry about that, sir. We're from the government, we're not here to hurt anyone. The school's under attack and you need to run away from it before the bomb blows up, do you understand? Just run with the kids, they need you."

"I see it," Dox said. "Going pretty fast. Gonna have to lead it some."

Kanezaki and I ran to the drone controls. "You all right?" I said.

"He hit me in the vest. Knocked me down. I'm okay."

Gillmor, on his back, his legs folded under him, his eyes staring and sightless, was still holding the controls. We looked at the screen. I could see the school through the drone's camera. The drone was heading right for it.

I heard a soft crack. The image on the screen shuddered, then stabilized. "Hit it, but not on the nose," Dox said. I heard a series of additional cracks. The screen image shuddered violently, but stabilized again.

"The hell's that thing made of?" Dox said. "I just put sixteen rounds in it. All right, switching magazines."

"Larison, Treven, get the fuck out of there," I said. "You've done all you can. There's no more time. Go!"

The school was at the center of the screen and rapidly expanding. I thought the drone couldn't be more than a few seconds from impact.

"All right, sweetheart," I heard Dox say. "Come here. Come take what I've got for you."

There was a methodical drumbeat of cracks. The image of the school shuddered. It shook. It stabilized, filling the whole screen—

And then the camera veered and began to spin wildly.

"All right!" Dox said, jubilation creeping into his normally super-calm sniper tone. "Score one for the home team."

The sky flashed past on the screen, then the ground, then everything was moving so fast I couldn't make out any features at all. A moment later, the screen went dark.

"Where did it go down?" I said.

"Not the school," Dox said. "The parking lot, though. Hot damn, that was close. Nobody hurt, I don't think."

"Did the warheads detonate?"

"No, sir. Gillmor must have had them set to blow on nose-first impact."

"Treven, Larison, you all right?"

"Fine," Larison said. "Walking away southeast."

I heard sirens in the background. "Same," Treven said. "Could use a pickup. Feeling a little conspicuous at the moment."

"Go to the bug-out," I said. "Dox, you especially. That cop is going to report sniper fire coming from your position. We'll rendezvous in twenty minutes. Or less, the way Kanezaki drives."

I expected Treven and Larison would be able to ghost away just fine in the tumult outside the school. But it wouldn't be long before coherent witnesses came forward and described them to arriving police. And Dox needed to get far from his hide.

Kanezaki pulled out an iPhone and took photographs of Gillmor's body and the controls on top of it.

"What are you doing?" I said.

"This is our proof." He started moving the phone in a small circle, talking as he did so. I realized he must have switched to video mode.

"We need to go," I said.

He held up a finger. "The man on the ground is the new head of the National Counterterrorism Center, Dan Gillmor, who was controlling the drone that attacked a school in Lincoln today. This is Palmyra,

Nebraska, about twenty-five miles away."

He walked over to the guy he'd shot and took his picture, too, then filmed the truck and its license plates, talking the whole time, dates and coordinates and identifying details. Then we ran back to the van, which he proceeded to drive as though the trip out were just a warm-up. We reached the bug-out point, a church a mile from the school, in under fifteen minutes. Kanezaki cut his speed and pulled into the parking lot.

"It's us," I said into the commo, and Dox, Larison, and Treven melted out from behind a dumpster. They got in the van and we drove off at a normal speed.

I climbed in back. Everybody shook hands. I said to Dox, "Good shooting."

"Hell," Dox said, "if it had been good, I would have dropped it on the first shot."

"Hey," Treven said, "you put it down. That's all that counts."

"Well," Dox said, looking at me, "I don't want to blame anyone else for how long it took me, but I don't think the avionics in that particular model of drone are in the nose, unless they're severely hardened. I finally just shot the shit out of the thing, and hoped I'd hit something vital. Which apparently I did."

We all laughed. "Tom," Dox said. "Are you all right? Did I hear you say you were hit?"

"In the vest," he said. "I'm okay."

"You're going to be sore later," I said. "But the hell with that. Nice shooting."

"You shot Gillmor?" Dox said. "I thought that was Rain."

"No, his security," Kanezaki said.

"Who had me pinned down," I added.

"Oo-rah!" Dox said. "Somebody give me that man a cigar. Was that your first kill?"

"I guess it was," Kanezaki said.

"You guess," Dox said. "That's funny. Well, you know what they say. You never forget your first. Glad he was shooting back at you. That'll make it a little easier later."

I looked at Larison. "Thanks for listening to me."

He paused, then said, "I was having my doubts on the way into that school a minute ahead of a couple of Hellfire missiles. But... yeah."

He turned to Dox and said, "Don't ever fuck with me again about being in your sights. Ever. You understand?"

I thought, Christ, here we go again. But Dox just grinned and said, "All right, all right, I was just trying to relieve the tension. Message received and I will not do it again."

He held out his hand and, after a moment, Larison shook it.

"Where are we heading?" I said. "The airport's the other way."

"I want to get the hell out of Nebraska," Kanezaki said. "Let's just keep driving and we'll figure it out as we go."

"My God, not another road trip," Dox said. "I'm still recovering from the last one."

We all laughed at that. I realized I didn't even care where we were going.

chapter
thirty-two

We only made it as far as Des Moines. The parasympathetic back-
lash against a combat adrenaline surge is ferocious, and we were
all exhausted already. As soon as we knew we were safely outside Lincoln, we started to flag. We pulled over at a highway motel, and checked
into two adjoining rooms. We watched the news for a while, but it was all
extremely confused. Overall, it was being presented as a failed terror attack, which on one level, of course, it was. As things stood, it seemed like
it was going to help the plotters' aims, albeit not as much as a successful
attack would have. But people were still panicking about the ostensibly
new threat, and how they couldn't send their children to school anymore, and how the government had to do more to protect them. Maybe
with the emergence of evidence of what happened, including Kanezaki's photographs and video, the narrative might change. And, of course,
maybe Horton would do something to steer things in the direction he
said he wanted them to go in. But overall, the whole thing was dispiriting.
We watched until we couldn't take it anymore. Then we all passed out.

When we woke, we turned on the television again, and it seemed
the narrative had indeed changed. Now there was talk about a group of
secret commandos who had killed the jihadists and foiled the plot and
evacuated the children. I wondered what was next.

Kanezaki uploaded his material to Wikileaks. Without more, it
might get dismissed as fringe conspiracy theory stuff. Some anonymous
spokesman would explain how Gillmor had been operating the drone to
take out the terrorists; that the terrorists had learned of his position and
gunned him down in cold blood, causing the drone to crash; but that his

resourceful men had still managed to eliminate the terrorist threat, even as their brave leader lay dying.

I found I didn't care all that much. We'd done what we could. And we'd done it well. Now all I had to do was find a way to slip out of the country and enjoy my twenty-five million.

Kanezaki's sat phone buzzed. It was Horton. Kanezaki handed the phone to me.

"Thank you," he said. "I do not deserve to be the beneficiary of your acts, but I am."

"How so?"

"I'm certain that very soon, I will be sent to hell, one way or the other. But in the meantime, you have given me the tools I need to redirect this thing as I always hoped, and to turn it into a force for good."

"All the people who were killed in those attacks," I said. "I'm glad it'll have been for the greater good."

I felt vaguely hypocritical saying it. On the other hand, I'd never bombed a bunch of innocents.

"It would have been worse if it had been for nothing," he said. "Or for less than nothing."

"Well, then, you got what you wanted." I thought, but didn't say, *you're still going to die*. But I supposed he knew that. He'd already acknowledged as much.

"There are two things I want you to know," he said.

"All right."

"First, I have introduced into proper channels the notion that you four men were inadvertently placed on the president's kill list. That your presence there was due to an intelligence failure that itself was the result of your intrepid penetration of the organization sponsoring these attacks. That in fact it was you, all of you, who ignored the danger of a mistaken nationwide manhunt to continue your mission and save the children at that school. You will face no further hostilities from any American military, intelligence, or law enforcement personnel, or otherwise."

I wished I could believe him. "I thought you said you didn't have that kind of juice since you resigned."

"Given my background and since my speech, I am not without influence. And my influence is set to grow."

"You knew that at the time. When we had your daughter. But you didn't say anything."

"You wouldn't have believed me. And besides, you needed to give me something to work with. Which you have. The wreckage of that drone is currently in the custody of local Lincoln law enforcement. The federal government will have a hard time taking it away from them and disappearing it, given the magnitude of what just happened in their community."

"There's more evidence on the way," I said.

"Such as?"

"Photos and videos of Gillmor. All uploaded to Wikileaks. You couldn't stop it now if you wanted to."

"Stop it? I welcome it. In fact, I have uploaded my own judicious trove of information to the good people of Wikileaks, who will see to its proper dissemination more faithfully than the New York Times or Washington Post ever would."

"What information?"

"Hard evidence of who was really behind this coup. Along with some unrelated but probably even more damning evidence of the sexual and financial improprieties of the individuals identified. With more such evidence to come."

I thought back to what he had told me about Finch, about how he was an information broker. Had Horton somehow acquired...?

And then it hit me. "You," I said. "You're the information broker. Not Finch."

"That is correct."

I wasn't connecting the dots. "Explain."

"The best way to tell a lie is to conceal it in a lot of truth. Which is why throughout this thing, nearly everything I told you has been true."

"Then why did you have us kill Shorrock and Finch?"

"Because they were trying to stop the coup, of course."

I thought for a moment. "And they thought you were, too."

"That's right. But we wanted to stop it in different ways. And at different times. And besides, they were the only ones with knowledge of my direct involvement. If I hadn't had them removed, then when I became America's hero by declining the president's offer as I did, they would have been in a position to contradict me. As it stands, I can make clear that they were in fact killed by the plotters because they were trying to stop the coup."

"But they were killed by the plotters. By you."

"I recognize there's some irony at work here."

"So the reason you needed them to die of what looked like natural causes—"

"Was twofold. First, I didn't want Finch to conclude from Shorrock's death that he might be targeted for opposing the coup, too."

"Because that would have made him harder to get to."

"Yes. And second, because when the president named me his new counterterrorism advisor, I couldn't have any questions about whether I might have had something to do with Finch's death."

"You knew the president was going to appoint you."

"Of course."

"Because you had information that would ensure the right people made it happen."

"Correct."

"But you leaked that cyanide was involved." I still saw no advantage in mentioning to him that we hadn't even used it.

"'Leak' wouldn't be quite the right word. That information was disseminated very selectively."

"To make us suspects. So we would be removed."

"Yes, although in retrospect I'm not displeased my attempts failed."

"And this was because, how did you put it? We could contradict you."

"Also correct."

"But we could contradict you now."

"I'm hoping you won't. But even if you try, I don't think it'll go well for you. I have assets now, and as I said they are set to grow dramatically. I don't think you would want to pit your public word against mine. And even if you could damage me that way, and I don't believe you could at this point, it would draw attention to all of you, and I think you've had enough of that. If I were you, I would just quietly enjoy my newfound wealth."

If it was a threat, it was a subtle one. I said, "Why do you keep saying your assets are increasing? What does that mean?"

"Yes, that was the second thing I wanted to mention. In the coming days, as news of the false flag, oligarchy-inspired nature of recent events leaks out into the establishment media, you will read a variety of very flattering pieces about me. About my courage and insight and integrity. Did Treven brief you on our conversation about a blue ribbon commission?"

"Yes."

"Well, the commission is already in motion. With the brand I have begun to establish and am having the media help further, and as head of the commission, I will be a very powerful force for good in this country."

I didn't answer. I was thinking, *you can still be gotten to.*

He laughed. "I know what you're thinking. And you're right. So let me just ask you this. Give me a year. I expect it'll take me that long to make sure things are running smoothly. If you don't like what I'm doing, you can always come after me sooner. But if you do approve of my purpose and my performance, and you do want to extract some measure of good from the recent horrific events of which, whether you like it or not, you have been a part, then you will let me finish my work. After that, I plan to retire. I have a place in Virginia. Very quiet and secluded. I like to sit alone out there on the porch in the evening, enjoying a whisky and sometimes a cigar. I imagine I will live there quietly, alone with the agony of my hellish culpability. Until someone decides to relieve my agony with a bullet."

"Yes," I said, after a moment. "Until then."

chapter
thirty-three

We all split up after that, saying our farewells under an indifferent blue sky outside the Des Moines Greyhound station. But for the sounds of traffic from the nearby highway, the area was quiet, even somnolent. No one was around to notice us amid the cracked pavement and boarded-up brick buildings, the weeds creeping up over the curbstones, the trees swaying in the slight breeze, their leaves on the verge of autumn.

Kanezaki had a lot of explaining to do at headquarters, but I imagined he would not only survive it, but turn it to his advantage. He was becoming increasingly formidable, and I couldn't help feeling some pride in his development. He'd acquitted himself well at the granary, and, for all I knew, his determination had saved my life. Certainly it had saved me the unpleasant task of rushing the guy behind the truck. I told him how well he'd done, and asked him how he was feeling.

"A little bit... shocked," he said. "Numb. I wasn't really thinking. I didn't know what happened at first. I got knocked down, and then I got up, and I just... shot him."

I smiled. "They say you can't keep a good man down."

He looked a little sheepish. "I don't know how to feel about it."

"Different people feel different ways. In a few days, you might find yourself upset. You might not feel anything at all, other than satisfaction and relief that you put him away before he did you. Either way, if you want to talk to someone who knows a little about these things, get in touch, okay?"

He nodded. "Thanks for that."

"And pass along my thanks to your sister for getting us out of the hotel in D.C. She was really something."

"I will," he said. "She asked after you, by the way. She's settled down since we were kids, and I think she's happy, but I guess deep inside, she's still got a thing for bad boys."

I laughed. "What's her story, anyway?"

He blew out a breath. "That's a long one. I'll tell you another time."

The way he said goodbye, making sure everyone knew how to contact him, I knew what he was thinking. He had himself a clandestine collection of ice cold killers. With that, plus his intelligence reach, who knew how much he could accomplish?

I thought about disabusing him. But then I thought about how many ops he'd dragged me into over the years, and decided it was foolish to tempt fate.

Dox went to his place in Bali. Said he wanted to kick back for a while and enjoy his ill-gotten loot.

"You're not going to call Kei, are you?" I asked him as we said goodbye.

I thought he was going to deny even considering it, or maybe deflect me with a joke. Instead, he said, "There was something special about her, partner. There really was. But no, I'm not going to call her. It would be wrong."

"Yeah," I said, respecting his regret and his resignation. "It would be."

"What about you? You fixing to go to Virginia and pay your last respects to Horton?"

"Maybe," I said.

"Because he tried to set us up?"

"Yes."

"Well, ordinarily in a situation like this, I'd say hell yes, let's take care of business. But this time…"

"You're thinking about his daughter?"

He nodded. "Yeah, I think we made her suffer enough. I really hate the idea of taking her daddy away from her. But also… I don't know. I just feel like, what's the point? We got a good outcome. Plus, what if he really is trying to set things right in the corridors of power and such?"

"That's exactly what he wants us to wonder."

"What if it's true?"

I was still ambivalent. "Larison might have ideas of his own, you know."

"I'll let Larison worry about Larison. I only worry about you. Besides, I think he's going to leave old Horton alone."

I wondered about that. "Why?"

"Just a feeling. He got his diamonds back, didn't he? I don't think revenge is going to be a huge priority for him, even if he'd never admit that, even to himself."

"I guess we'll find out."

"I guess we will. You did a nice job, Mister Rain, as head of our little band of brothers. I wasn't sure you had it in you."

I laughed. "I don't know about that. How many times did we almost blow each other's brains out? Which we would have at least once, if it hadn't been for you."

"Well, I won't deny doing a hell of a Cleavon Little impersonation just when it was called for. But think of it this way. With someone else in charge of this crew, we wouldn't have almost blown each other's brains out. We would have done it."

I thought he was giving me too much credit, but I didn't say anything one way or the other.

"Okay, Mister Modest," he said, "time to go. Try not to miss me too much, okay?"

"I'll try."

"Hell, come on out to Bali. Now that you're single again, you can enjoy my island properly. I know all the best spots and the prettiest ladies. Unless you think you're going to crawl back to Delilah."

I laughed to cover my confusion and told him I'd see him in Bali. That much, at least, I was sure of.

It was a little awkward with Treven. He was still active-duty military, and he didn't say where he was going. I had the feeling the life wasn't for him, but that neither was retirement, not even with a tax-free twenty-five million. I thought maybe he was just someone who needed a structure, and a direction, like a train needs a set of tracks.

I still wondered for reasons I couldn't quite articulate whether he might have been working both sides of the op at one point. Maybe it was that he didn't kill Horton when he could have. At the time, I couldn't fault his reasoning, but I also suspected reason wasn't the real basis for his reluctance. I sensed the presence of some kind of attachment there, something between him and Horton. Or maybe what I sensed was just Treven trying to cling to that structure I thought he needed, a structure that had always given him purpose but that events were peeling away from him. Maybe the fear of losing that structure had caused him to reach out to Horton at some point, to try to play both sides against the middle. But I supposed it didn't matter anymore. I didn't want to admit it to myself, but a part of me was glad I would probably never know. I didn't want to have to do something about it. It was easier to let it go.

Larison was also sketchy about his next moves, and I assumed he was going to his lover. I hoped it would work out for him. My own attempt at romance with a civilian had resulted in the civilian in question trying to have me killed. And she was the mother of my child. Of course, I said nothing to him, neither about his personal life nor about Horton.

He thanked me when we said goodbye, and I wasn't sure for what— for keeping his secret; for keeping him from walking away from us in a way he would have regretted; for taking the chance I had taken in trusting him.

"Don't mention it," I said. "It was all just self-preservation."

"Bullshit," he said. "I owe you."

"Owe me what? You brought me in on an op that made me twenty-five million."

He didn't answer right away, and I realized he was thinking his original plan hadn't involved my keeping the diamonds. And that his recollection of whatever he'd originally planned must have been producing uncharacteristic stirrings of conscience. I thought I'd been lucky things had worked out as they had. It could easily have gone another way.

"I don't know where I'll be, exactly," he said. "But if you need me, I'll have your back."

Coming from Larison, an offer like that would be as rare as it was meaningful. I appreciated it, and I told him so. I had a feeling I'd see him again, and I told him that, too.

And so our detachment dissolved. For a time, anyway.

I went back to Tokyo, of course, as I always seem to, like a salmon swimming upriver to the spot where it was born. I settled in, and enjoyed the feeling of a lull in my life. The city continued to recover steadily from the trauma of the earthquake and tsunami, and I gave an impossibly large and appropriately anonymous amount to relief efforts in the north. Revelations about the corruption that led to the Fukushima reactor meltdown were astonishing, even for a cynic like me. Still, nothing seemed to come of it. Japan, it seemed, at least in terms of apathy, was not so different from America.

Because there, too, the news was astonishing. Revelations, indictments, charges of treason. Most of it true, as Horton had foretold, the lies woven so carefully into the fabric that no one who didn't understand the entire tapestry would ever spot them. Horton, again as he foretold, developed an enormous following. There were calls for him to run for president. To his credit, I supposed, he demurred, and I imagined that what people believed was his noble resistance to the allure of power would one day burnish his legend.

But despite all the revelations and arrests and the outrage, I didn't really see all that much change. The wars kept grinding along. There were no populist revolts, no peasants with pitchforks storming the Capitol or burning the barons of Wall Street, even in effigy. There was talk of a third party—a second party would have been the more accurate way to put it, I thought—but nothing meaningful came of it. Though Wikileaks was the conduit for everything that was coming out, the New York Times and all the others were getting the credit, as though they would have touched any of it if Wikileaks hadn't forced them, exactly as Kanezaki had said. Overall, people seemed to want to understand perfidy as a problem with personalities rather than as something insidious in their institutions.

Horton kept at it, working the levers of his popularity and power, but I had the sense the commission, far from being a vehicle he could steer as he wanted, was more a vessel that was gradually coming to control and contain his ambitions. I wondered how disappointed he was, and whether, in the dark, quiet hours of the very early morning, he ever lay in the sleepless grip of something like despair, the souls of all the lives he'd cut short pressing in close upon him.

I wasn't worried about his coming after any of us. I thought he'd been telling the truth when he'd said he didn't think we could do him much damage. And killing one of us without killing us all would have been dangerous. If any of us decided he was a threat again, Horton would have a real problem to contend with. And then there was his daughter, of course. Maybe she'd told him Dox was a softie. But Horton wouldn't know about the rest of us. Would he really risk reprisals? I doubted it.

Watching his faraway machinations from my haven in Tokyo, as remote as the Marvel Comics Watcher on the moon, I wondered whether Horton had misread his own country. Maybe democracies, maybe all cultures, had life cycles, the same as the humans who comprised them. And maybe there were things cultures could do to extend their lives—the equivalent of exercise and eating right, or, to analogize to what Horton had done, the equivalent of radical surgery—but those things would, in the end, matter only at the margins. Maybe, regardless of the efforts of the exceptional few, the genes hidden and inherent in a culture's own DNA would dictate a length of years, and make inevitable the onset of sclerosis, and senility, and death, as ineluctably as the Fates cutting the thread of an individual life.

I didn't know what I wanted. I trained at the Kodokan and reflected at quiet shrines and enjoyed my jazz clubs and coffee houses and whisky bars. I took long, nocturnal walks through the damascene city, and considered what I'd been part of, and what I'd almost caused. I wondered about my son and I missed Delilah. I thought about Horton. I made no decisions.

I was sleeping better than I had in a while. I hoped it would last.

author's note

Although the D.C. Capital Hilton was in fact the home of the 10th Annual Convention of the American Constitution Society, there is no garage level in the hotel. Other than this detail, all locations in this book are described as I have found them. Photos and more on my website: www.barryeisler.com.

acknowledgments

My thanks to:

Lara Perkins, for being an amazing editor and handling all the business stuff so well, too.

Stephen Blower, Kodokan Fourth Dan, for his devastatingly elegant judo—and his generosity in describing (and demonstrating) what it's like to play at Rain's level.

Mike Kleindl of Tokyo Food Life, for introducing Rain to L'Ambre and so many other fine Tokyo establishments.

Dave Camarillo, author of Guerilla Jiu-Jitsu, for helping me choreograph the Tokyo sequence where Rain takes out the contractors, and for being a great teacher and friend, too.

Ken Rosenberg, for helping with financial aspects of the backstory.

Novelist Victoria Dahl, for Dox's very wrong phrase, "straining the gravy."

Dr. Peter Zimetbaum, for the usual invaluable help on cardiology issues.

Elke Sisco, for assistance with the German dialogue.

Daniel Velez, for assistance with the Spanish dialogue. Albóndigas.

Koichiro Fukasawa and Yukie Kito, for assistance with the Japanese.

Novelist J.A. Konrath, because without his encouragement this novel might have been published by a legacy publisher, meaning you would have had to wait until next year to read it.

Novelist Lee Goldberg, for Los Angeles culinary, cultural, and transportation advice.

Ron Winston, for sharing his peerless expertise on diamonds.

Clint Overland, a good man who's done some bad things, for his insights into the attraction of using terrible skills for a noble end.

The extraordinarily eclectic group of "foodies with a violence problem" who hang out at Marc "Animal" MacYoung's and Dianna Gordon's www.nononsenseselfdefense.com, for good humor, good fellowship, and a ton of insights, particularly regarding the real costs of violence.

Jeroen Ten Berge of JeroenTenBerge.com and Rob Siders of 52Novels.com, for terrific cover design and formatting services.

Tracy Mercer and the Four Seasons Palo Alto, for generous hospitality, endless jasmine tea, and perfect feng shui.

Naomi Andrews, Alan Eisler, Judith Eisler, Montie Guthrie, Tom Hayes, Mike Killman, novelist J.A. Konrath, Lori Kupfer, Dan Levin, Doug Patteson, and Ted Schlein, for helpful comments on the manuscript and many valuable suggestions and insights along the way.

Most of all, my wife Laura, a very patient woman and an awesome editor, too. Thanks, babe, for everything.

sources

Much of the backstory and the technology, and many of the incidents, described in this book are real. Here's a partial bibliography.

The media-lobbying complex.
http://www.thenation.com/doc/20100301/jones/print

The president's assassination list, including American citizens.
http://www.salon.com/news/opinion/glenn_greenwald/2010/01/27/yemen/index.html

http://www.washingtonpost.com/wp-dyn/content/article/2010/01/26/AR2010012604239.html

The president's claimed power to indefinitely imprison American citizens without charge, trial, or conviction.
http://www.salon.com/news/opinion/glenn_greenwald/2009/05/22/preventive_detention

Coup plots in Turkey.
http://www.economist.com/world/europe/displaystory

http://www.guardian.co.uk/world/2011/jan/18/wikileaks-cables-turkey-military-arrests

A BBC documentary on Operation Gladio.
http://www.informationliberation.com/?id=16921

And a book on Gladio.
http://sandiego.indymedia.org/media/2006/10/119640.pdf

Behind TV Analysts, the Pentagon's Hidden Hand.
http://www.nytimes.com/2008/04/20/us/20generals.html

News Corp press properties as the extortion arm of a global conglomerate.
http://www.alternet.org/story/151713/the_big_lie_at_the_heart_of_
rupert_murdoch%27s_media_empire/

Corporatism as the American Way: Booz Allen, the NSA, the Pentagon.
http://www.salon.com/news/feature/2007/01/08/mcconnell

The metastasis of Top Secret America.
http://projects.washingtonpost.com/top-secret-america/articles/a-
hidden-world-growing-beyond-control/

Golden parachutes for top military brass becoming defense contractors.
http://www.boston.com/news/nation/washington/
articles/2010/12/26/defense_firms_lure_retired_generals

Anti-Islamic Center fervor produces a radical Islam PR bonanza.
http://www.nytimes.com/2010/08/21/world/21muslim.html

How many secret wars is America really fighting?
http://www.washingtonpost.com/wp-dyn/content/
article/2010/06/03/AR2010060304965.html

http://www.alternet.org/story/151904/our_commando_war_in_120_
countries:_uncovering_the_military's_secret_operations_in_the_
obama_era/

Russian False Flag Attacks and Aftermath.
http://trueslant.com/barrettbrown/2010/03/23/vladimir-putin/

Excellent run-down of Israel's botched Dubai hit.
http://www.gq.com/news-politics/big-issues/201101/the-dubai-job-mossad-assassination-hamas

Domestic use of drones equipped with night vision, infrared, and thermal imaging.
http://tpmmuckraker.talkingpointsmemo.com/2011/01/are_unmanned_drones_coming_to_a_police_dept_near_y.php

Drone aircraft used for domestic surveillance.
http://www.usatoday.com/tech/news/surveillance/2011-01-13-drones_N.htm

The August 6, 2001 President's Daily Brief warning "Bin Laden Determined To Strike in U.S."
http://news.findlaw.com/hdocs/docs/terrorism/80601pdb.html

The growing public/private domestic surveillance partnership.
http://www.privacylives.com/washington-examiner-d-c-expanding-public-surveillance-camera-net/2011/01/24/

A huge proportion of government Internet censorship is devoted to blogs.
http://yuxiyou.net/open/

JSOC, The Knights of Malta, and crusader challenge coins.
http://whowhatwhy.com/2011/02/23/pulitzer-prize-winner-seymour-hersh-and-the-men-who-want-him-committed/

Attempted coup against Franklin Roosevelt, and Congressional Committee to investigate.
http://en.wikipedia.org/wiki/Business_Plot

TSA doing searches at trains, buses, etc. Even cars.
http://motherjones.com/mojo/2011/06/tsa-swarms-8000-bus-stations-public-transit-systems-yearly

The New York Times spikes stories when the government asks it to.
http://news.firedoglake.com/2010/12/01/the-war-on-wikileaks-and-the-radical-theory-of-breaking-conspiracies/

http://www.democracynow.org/2008/4/1/exclusivebushs_law_eric_lichtblau_on_exposing

http://consortiumnews.com/2011/06/30/the-nyts-favor-and-fear/

Precedent for a commission composed of officials who have demonstrated their integrity—here, by resisting calls to torture.
http://www.pen.org/viewmedia.php/prmMID/6067/prmID/172

The Salt Pit.
http://harpers.org/archive/2010/03/hbc-90006791

Camp No.
http://www.harpers.org/archive/2010/01/hbc-90006368

The Beslan school hostage crisis.
http://en.wikipedia.org/wiki/Beslan_school_hostage_crisis

The government's astonishingly weak and shoddy case against the anthrax suspects.
http://www.salon.com/news/opinion/glenn_greenwald/2011/07/19/anthrax/index.html

How easy it is in Washington to corrupt a wannabe player—this one, Harold Koh.
http://www.salon.com/news/opinion/glenn_greenwald/2011/06/29/ko

George Carlin's more-relevant-than-ever take on who owns America and what they want.
http://www.youtube.com/watch?v=acLW1vFO-2Q

Two videos of the brachial stun in action.
http://www.youtube.com/watch?v=00je-NmU4Tg

http://www.youtube.com/watch?v=DcaOr1TBA1w

Why is John Rain so paranoid about mobile phone tracking?
http://www.wired.com/dangerroom/2011/07/global-phone-tracking/all/1

Horton's speech in the Rose Garden draws on certain rhetorical techniques described in more detail in *The Ass Is A Poor Receptacle For The Head.*
http://www.amazon.com/dp/B0050O7VLW

And for a real life equivalent in Norway.
http://www.washingtonpost.com/world/europe/head-of-norways-delta-force-says-finding-boat-to-island-retreat-caused-no-real-delays/2011/07/27/gIQAqtkOcI_story.html

Novel Air Capability, the inspiration for the drone in the book.
http://www.technewsdaily.com/7-next-generation-uavs-0855/1

A real world example of the way narrative is used to shape public perceptions of terrorism.
http://electronicintifada.net/blog/benjamin-doherty/how-clueless-terrorism-expert-set-media-suspicion-muslims-after-oslo-horror

Dox's Knight's Armament SR-25 sniper rifle in action.
http://www.youtube.com/watch?v=-Yv1uC3qZkk

also by
barry eisler

Fiction

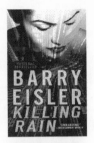

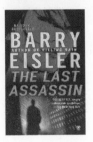

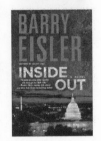

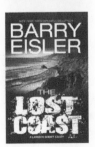

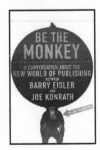

Non-Fiction

recommended reading

AFTERSHOCKS

If you're fond of Japan, as I am, I hope you'll consider buying a copy of *2:46: Aftershocks: Stories From The Japan Earthquake*, with a foreword I was humbled to be asked to contribute. One hundred percent of the purchase price goes to relief efforts in Japan.

Or download the Kindle edition for free and consider a donation to the Japanese Red Cross through QuakeBook.org. Thanks.

STIRRED
by Blake Crouch and J.A. Konrath

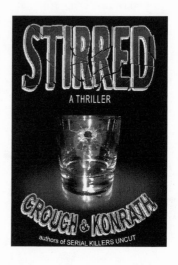

In her twenty-five-year career with the Chicago police department, Lt. Jacqueline "Jack" Daniels has seen the worst of humanity. She's lost loved ones and narrowly escaped death on countless occasions—and she has the nightmares to prove it. Jack is the best the Chicago PD has to offer, and she has brought some of the city's most notorious criminals to their knees. All, that is, but one…

Luther Kite is evil incarnate. Depraved and inhumane, he takes life for the sheer pleasure of watching his terrified victims die. He is a monster among monsters, taunting and frustrating law enforcement every bloody step of the way. But when the kills become too easy, he sets his sight on the one victim who can offer him a true challenge, the only woman who is a match for his extraordinary skill: Jack Daniels. And when it comes to killing Daniels, only Kite's very best work will do.

Fast-paced, suspenseful, and darkly comic, *Stirred* brings together J.A. Konrath's Jack Daniels and Blake Crouch's Luther Kite for a final heart-stopping showdown that will leave readers reeling!

http://www.amazon.com/Stirred-Jacqueline-Daniels-Mysteries-ebook/dp/B0050KIRDC

RUN
by Blake Crouch

For fans of Stephen King, Dean Koontz, and Thomas Harris, picture this: a landscape of American genocide...

5 DAYS AGO
A rash of bizarre murders swept the country...
Senseless. Brutal. Seemingly unconnected.

4 DAYS AGO
The murders increased ten-fold...

3 DAYS AGO
The President addressed the nation and begged for calm and peace...

2 DAYS AGO
The killers began to mobilize...

YESTERDAY
All the power went out...

TONIGHT
They're reading the names of those to be killed on the Emergency Broadcast System. You are listening over the battery-powered radio on your kitchen table, and they've just read yours.

Your name is Jack Colclough. You have a wife, a daughter, and a young son. You live in Albuquerque, New Mexico. People are coming to your house to kill you and your family. You don't know why, but you don't have time to think about that any more.

You only have time to....

RUN

http://www.amazon.com/Run-ebook/dp/B004PGNF0W

THE DELILAH COMPLEX
by M.J. Rose

As one of New York's top sex thera-
pists, Dr. Morgan Snow sees everything
from the abused to the depraved. The
Butterfield Institute is the sanctuary
where she tries to heal these battered
souls.

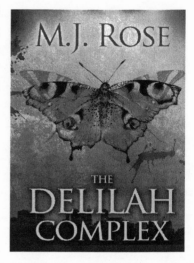

The Scarlet Society is a secret club of
twelve powerful and sexually adventur-
ous women. But when a photograph
of the body of one of the men they're
recruited to dominate—strapped to a
gurney, the number 1 inked on the sole
of his foot—is sent to the New York
Times, they are shocked and frightened. Unable to cope with the trag-
edy, the women turn to Dr. Morgan Snow. But what starts out as grief
counseling quickly becomes a murder investigation, with any one of the
twelve women a potential suspect.

The case leads Detective Noah Jordan—a man with whom Morgan has
shared a brief, intense connection—to her office. He fears the number
on the man's foot hints that the killings have just begun. With her hands
tied by her professional duty, Morgan is dangerously close to the demons
in her own mind—and the flesh-and-blood killer.

". . . M.J. Rose is a bold, unflinching writer and her resolute honesty puts
her in a class by herself."

—Laura Lippman

"Utterly fascinating! . . . This is one book that will keep you glued to your
seat."

—New York Times bestselling author Lisa Gardner

http://www.amazon.com/Delilah-Complex-MIRA-M-Rose/
dp/0778322157

About the Author

Barry Eisler spent three years in a covert position with the CIA's Directorate of Operations, then worked as a technology lawyer and startup executive in Silicon Valley and Japan, earning his black belt at the Kodokan International Judo Center along the way. Eisler's bestselling thrillers have won the Barry Award and the Gumshoe Award for Best Thriller of the Year, have been included in numerous "Best Of" lists, and have been translated into nearly twenty languages. Eisler lives in the San Francisco Bay Area and, when he's not writing novels, blogs about torture, civil liberties, and the rule of law. For more information please go to www.barryeisler.com.

9308228R0

Made in the USA
Charleston, SC
31 August 2011